Bowling Green Bay

The Navy Cadets

C.R. Cummings

Also By
CHRISTOPHER CUMMINGS

The Green Idol of Kanaka Creek

Ross River Fever

Train to Kuranda

The Mudskipper Cup

Davey Jones's Locker

Below Bartle Frere

*Bowling Green Bay

Airship Over Atherton

The Cadet Corporal

Stannary Hills

Coasts of Cape York

Kylie and the Kelly Gang

Beyond the Barrier Reef

Behind Mt. Baldy

The Cadet Sergeant Major

Cooktown Christmas

Secret in the Clouds

The Word of God

The Cadet Under-Officer

Through the Devil's Eye

The Smiley People

Barbara at her Best

Bowling Green Bay

The Navy Cadets

C.R. Cummings

DoctorZed
Publishing
www.doctorzed.com

Published 2019 by DoctorZed Publishing

DoctorZed Publishing books may be ordered through booksellers or by contacting:

DoctorZed Publishing
10 Vista Ave
Skye, South Australia 5072
www.doctorzed.com

ISBN: 978-0-6484096-6-3 (hc)
ISBN: 978-0-6484096-5-6 (sc)
ISBN: 978-0-6484096-4-9 (ebk)

National Library of Australia Cataloguing-in-Publication entry

   Author: Cummings, C. R., author.

   Title: Bowling Green Bay/ Christopher Cummings.

   ISBN: 9780648409663(hardcover)

   Series: Cummings, C. R. The navy cadets.

   Target Audience: For young adults.

   Subjects: Adventure stories, Australian.

   Military cadets--Queensland--Fiction.

Cover image © ID 140071544 © Jarn Verdonk | Dreamstime.com
Cover design © Scott Zarcinas

Printed in Australia, UK & USA

DoctorZed Publishing rev. date: 10/04/2019

Bowling Green Bay

The Navy Cadets

C.R. Cummings

DoctorZed
Publishing
www.doctorzed.com

Published 2019 by DoctorZed Publishing

DoctorZed Publishing books may be ordered through booksellers or by contacting:

DoctorZed Publishing
10 Vista Ave
Skye, South Australia 5072
www.doctorzed.com

ISBN: 978-0-6484096-6-3 (hc)
ISBN: 978-0-6484096-5-6 (sc)
ISBN: 978-0-6484096-4-9 (ebk)

National Library of Australia Cataloguing-in-Publication entry

Author: Cummings, C. R., author.

Title: Bowling Green Bay/ Christopher Cummings.

ISBN: 9780648409663(hardcover)

Series: Cummings, C. R. The navy cadets.

Target Audience: For young adults.

Subjects: Adventure stories, Australian.

Military cadets--Queensland--Fiction.

Cover image © ID 140071544 © Jarn Verdonk | Dreamstime.com
Cover design © Scott Zarcinas

Printed in Australia, UK & USA

DoctorZed Publishing rev. date: 10/04/2019

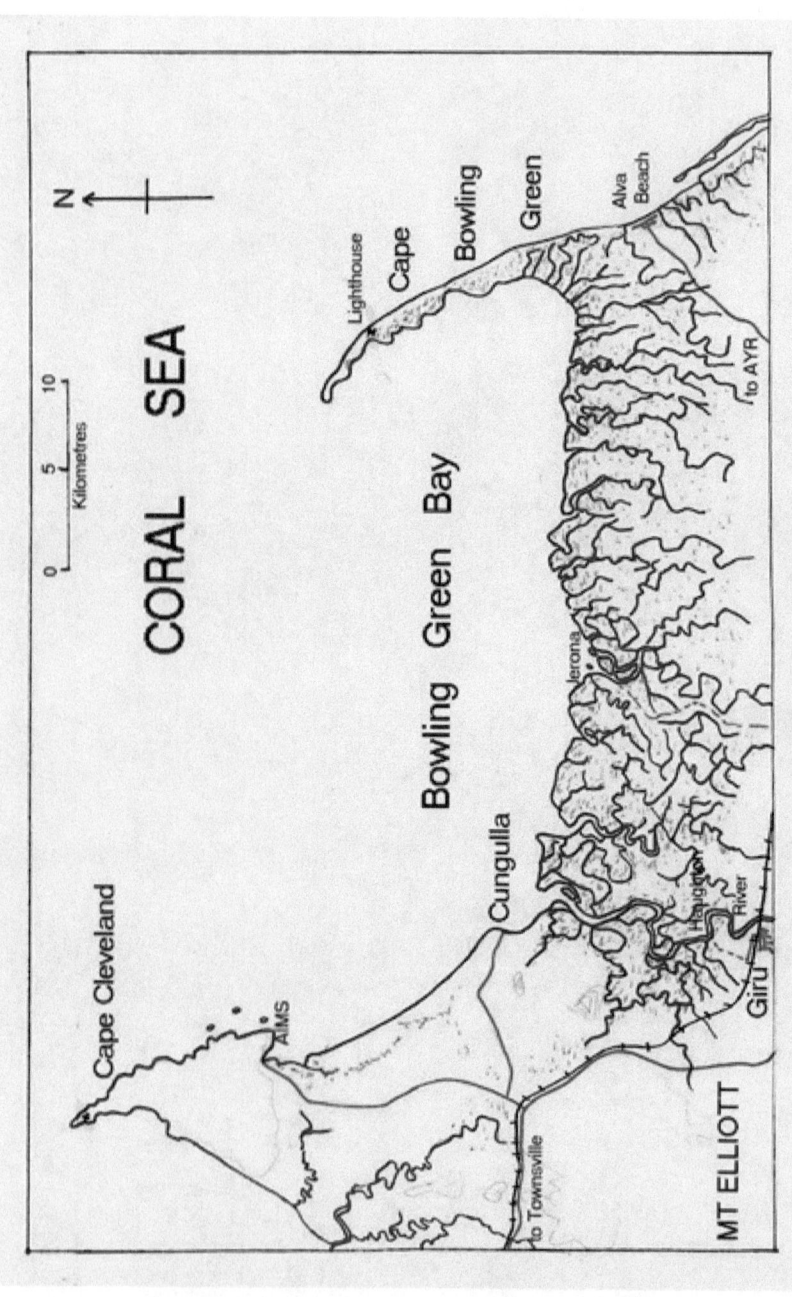

Chapter 1

FISHING

Four teenagers dressed in hats, long sleeve shirts, long trousers and joggers sat in a 5-metre aluminium dinghy. The boat nudged the metre high bank of the mangrove creek while the four talked to another teenager who stood on the bank. In the boat was Martin Schipholl, 14 and a part-time Navy Cadet who was about to start Year 10 at High School.

Martin looked up at his big sister Letitia and shook his head. *There is too much tension in the group,* he thought. From the moment the fishing trip had been proposed he had doubted if the grouping would be comfortable, particularly after the events on Endeavour Island earlier in the year. *Having Letitia here is embarrassing for me and is causing some angst with Carmen and Anne.*

Then Martin glanced at his friend Andrew Collins and gave a wry smile. *Even if Andrew is smitten by her!*

Letitia was 16 years' old and would be starting Year 12 in a few weeks' time, and while she was a very friendly and outgoing person, she was also quite uninhibited. To Martin's shame and occasional intense embarrassment, Letitia was a nudist who liked nothing more than to flaunt herself. The fact that she was a very busty blonde just added to the sexual tension and jealousies that had already split the group.

And she had a reputation around their school. Other students usually did not say anything openly to Martin. But he overheard comments a few times that had left him feeling deeply hurt. Speaking to his sister about her behaviour had been hard and only resulted in her getting sulky and truculent.

The most recent time, just before school broke up for the Christmas holidays, overhearing the Year 11 boys saying she was 'easy' had really stung.

I wish she would change and not risk getting hurt, he thought.

It was Letitia's presence on the fishing trip that had resulted in Martin's particular friend Mark not being there. Mark was another Navy Cadet and his girlfriend Jill had a strong dislike of Letitia.

Jealousy really, Martin had rationalized, although Jill was a very attractive girl. When she had heard that Letitia was going on the trip she had refused to come, and Mark had sensibly stayed home with her.

But three others, also all Navy Cadets, had come. Anne Maudsley was a Townsville girl, but Andrew and his big sister Carmen came from Cairns, 350 kilometres to the north. They were in Townsville for the January school holidays and were staying with their Aunty Bev and Uncle Mel. They had first done this the previous year which was when Martin had met them. Andrew had saved Martin from drowning after a group of bullies had thrown him off the Nathan Street Bridge into Ross River. A friendship had grown during a series of adventures in the following weeks[1].

Andrew and Carmen had travelled to Townsville after Christmas and the friends had teamed up. Anne, a very pleasant and shapely girl with mousy fair hair, nice blue eyes and a smattering of freckles, had also joined in. She went to Heatley, the same school as Mark and Jill. She sat there now, smiling but looking a little anxious under her streak of light green 'Red Indian' war paint of zinc sun cream across her nose and cheeks. Like the others Anne wore long pants and a long sleeve shirt and a hat, in her case a wide-brimmed straw hat. Sunglasses completed her ensemble.

Now, after ten days of the usual holiday activities of canoeing, sailing, shopping, ten pin bowling and sightseeing the friends had come to a bit of a loose end. Being a keen angler Martin had suggested a fishing expedition and this idea had been enthusiastically accept by most of the group.

After some discussion it had been decided to spend a day on the Haughton River, approximately 40 kilometres east of the city. Martin's father had agreed to take a day off work (He was a self-employed civil engineer) and had driven them there and provided the boats and other essentials. He and Mrs Schipholl had come along to be the supervising adults.

Travelling in two vehicles towing two boats, the group had driven that morning to the small sugar mill town of Giru and then on through farmland and salt marshes to Cromarty Landing, a concrete boat ramp on the banks of the mangrove lined Cromarty Creek. The boat ramp was

---

[1] Read *Ross River Fever* by C. R. Cummings.

apparently in the middle of nowhere with not a building to be seen, just a muddy vehicle track and parking area. Being a Friday and a working day there was only one other vehicle and boat trailer parked there, but Martin knew that on most weekends there were dozens.

The two boats had been launched from their trailers and the vehicles parked while the group made their preparations. They had then motored downstream into the main channel of the Haughton River. This was a multi-channel stream which formed a maze of waterways amid a vast mangrove swamp. The swamps extended east-west for over 50 kilometres and were 10 kilometres deep. Much of the area was part of the Bowling Green Bay National Park but there were pockets of private property. The area was so large that they only passed one other boat with two middle-aged fishermen in it anchored in midstream.

The friends had started fishing, with limited success. The morning had slid by and cut lunches had been consumed. Then all the teenagers had transferred to one boat.

Legally one of the adults should have been in their boat but Mr Schipholl had asked Mrs Schipholl to join him in his.

"We are going back up the creek a bit to try to get some good wildlife photos and we don't want any noise to disturb the birds and so on," he explained, adding: "You kids will all want to talk and won't enjoy being quiet."

"But none of us has a power boat licence," Martin objected.

His father had shrugged. "So you just stay tied up here for an hour or so. You have been in small boats all your life. Besides you are all navy cadets and know boats," he had said by way of explanation. "Anyway, you aren't likely to bump into any water police or 'Boating and Fisheries' patrols on a work day."

The parents had motored off. Letitia had then asked to be put ashore. "I want to see if I can spot a crocodile," she said. "I heard there are lots in these creeks. I will just be over there near those trees," she said, pointing across the grassy flat to where a clump of large mangroves showed.

"Don't you sit near the water," Martin warned. "There are some big crocs in this river."

Andrew nodded. "My word yes! Don't you be anywhere near the edge of the water where one can just lunge up and drag you in," he added.

At that thought Martin shuddered. He had only ever seen the monster saurians a few times, mainly at the 'Billabong Sanctuary' zoo but he had a healthy respect for them. "Watch out you aren't near one that is nesting either," he commented. He knew that crocodiles liked to construct their nests among long grass on the river banks.

Letitia nodded. "This is OK. There are no nests here," she replied, indicating the grassy flat she was standing on.

From his seat in the boat Martin could just see up over the bank and he had to agree. The open area was about 50 metres across, but the grass was mostly short, wiry tufts of saltwater grass and half the area was just bare mud flat from which the sun's rays shimmered. On the other side appeared to be another channel of the river with more mangroves beyond.

It was a blistering hot day- mid-summer in North Queensland- with the temperature hovering in the high thirties. The air was still and because of that mosquitoes and sandflies continually bothered them, despite liberal coatings of insect repellent. Looking around Martin was struck by how everything seemed to be either green or grey. The water was deep and a dark green with patches of black. It lapped at grey, greasy looking mud from which sprouted mangroves with dark green leaves. Only when he focused did Martin note that there were browns and yellows- mostly dead leaves either on the mangrove trees or lying on the mud or water as leaf litter.

And the whole place had its own peculiar scents- stank as Andrew put it- of saltwater and indefinable rotting vegetation odours. Continual sucking and popping noises came from the mud among the trees as crabs and other small creatures lived their lives. And it was really hot.

What on earth possessed us to come here on a day like this? Martin wondered, wiping perspiration from his face with his cloth hat before using it to fan himself.

Anne now spoke for the first time. "And don't get sunburnt Letitia. You put plenty of sunscreen on."

Letitia hadn't said she was going sunbathing but the knowledge that everyone assumed that caused Martin to burn with shame again. *I wish I had a normal sister,* he thought- for the thousandth time.

Andrew ogled Letitia- for even in shirt and jeans she was very curvy- and said, "We can't stay too much longer. The tide will start to ebb soon."

"Don't forget there is a Cyclone Watch too," Carmen added.

Andrew snorted at that. "Oh piffle Sis! It is only a Category One and it is over five hundred kilometres away."

Martin agreed with Andrew but did not say so. The tropical cyclone had formed out in the Coral Sea the previous night but even though the gigantic revolving storms were usually hundreds of kilometres across this one was reported to be 500kilometres east of Cape Flattery. Because of the way the North Queensland coastline curved this put both Cairns and Townsville about the same distance from it.

The cyclone doesn't matter. It is days away and we are only here for a few more hours, Martin told himself. But having been on the edge of a few cyclones over the years he was still a bit anxious at the thought of one. *There is no predicting which way they will go,* he thought.

Letitia walked off and Martin lowered himself back to his seat at the stern. "Push off Andrew," he instructed. Andrew, who had been watching Letitia, did so and the boat slid out into the deeper water. Even though all of the others were senior to him in the Navy Cadets they accepted that he was captain on this trip as his parents had paid for the boats. Carmen was a 3rd Year cadet with the rank of Leading Seaman and both Andrew and Anne were 2nd Years ranking as Able Seamen. Although he was almost the same age Martin had joined later and was still only an Ordinary Seaman, having only recently been promoted from Recruit.

The boat was moved a few metres downstream and then tied to a mangrove root so that the combination of a gentle breeze and a slight current held it out in deep water. Martin noted that the current was still moving sluggishly downstream, the direction of movement indicated by the way a few floating leaves and a slick of muddy scum were going.

The tide must be on the ebb, Martin decided. A glance at his watch showed him it was 1320hrs. *Only another hour and we must start back,* he thought. Their agreed time to be home was 1630hrs.

Anne looked up said, "Is the tide going in or out?"

"Out," Martin answered.

"When was high tide?" Anne asked.

That stumped Martin. He had glanced at the Tide Tables the day before but had not memorized them.

To his chagrin Andrew answered. "High Water was at 1127," he said.

Martin bit his lip. Secretly he envied Andrew his nautical knowledge and skill and was determined to prove he could be just as good a sailor.

Thinking thus he carefully swung his fishing rod back and then cast the hook half way across the river. Then he picked up the copy of the Tide Tables and began to memorize them for the next few days.

Silence settled, broken only by the occasional plop of a fish jumping or of a bird cawing. The friends sat and quietly fished, content to be together.

Five minutes ticked slowly by. Anne wound her line in and made another cast. The distant cackling of fruit bats- flying foxes as North Queenslanders called them- came from a colony roosting further upriver. From the mangroves came occasional sucking, popping or snapping sounds.

Then Anne shrieked with delight. "I've got one! I've got one!" she cried.

Martin turned and saw that Anne's line was being pulled taut. "Lucky you!" he called.

There were a few moments of excitement and then Anne reeled the fish in. Martin instantly recognized it as a Sooty Grunter. He said so but Carmen shook her head. "It's a Mangrove Jack isn't it?" she queried.

That led to a short debate which was ended by Anne pulling a reference book out of her bag. "Neither. It's an Estuary Cod," she said. Snapping the book shut she looked at them. "But is it legal size?"

None of them knew. Andrew shrugged and looked along the river. "Who cares? You aren't likely to bump into any Fisheries people here," he said.

That attitude bothered Martin. It was the second time that day the suggestion had been made to risk breaking the regulations. The first time had been over what to do if they caught a barramundi. They did not know if it was the 'open' season or if it was 'closed'.

Martin now said, "We had better find out. There are pretty stiff penalties for taking undersize fish."

To his relief Andrew nodded and pulled out a chart which he unfolded and studied. "If it's an estuary cod then the minimum legal size is thirty-five centimetres," he said.

Carmen produced a ruler and Anne did the measuring. The fish was just judged to be just legal so it was added to the small cooler where two whiting caught by Mrs Schipholl already rested.

They resumed fishing, slapping at mosquitos and sandflies and chatting. Both girls rubbed on more sun cream and Martin had a big drink from his drink bottle. Another glance at his watch told him they only had about twenty minutes before they must start back up the river.

But now he needed badly to do a pee. Glancing around he decided to go ashore at the downstream end of the grassy flat where they had dropped Letitia. It was only a few metres to the shore, so he hauled the boat into the mangroves by the painter and then looked for a spot to step ashore that wasn't muddy.

But that wasn't easy to find. There was no beach of any sort. As is usual in mangrove streams the banks were steep, in places almost vertical, and the exposed mud was a grey slick. Wrinkling his nose with distaste Martin edged past Andrew and steadied himself then jumped. Luckily he had judged it well and he got a foothold on some relatively dry tufts of saltwater grass.

A few seconds later he was up on top of the flat. "I won't be long," he said. "I will just go over there for a moment and then go and get Letitia."

Nobody made any comment to that, but Martin noted a 'look' on Anne's face which caused him to blush. Once again, he was annoyed at his sister's uninhibited proclivities and he silently cursed. He had no desire to see her with no clothes on- although he did almost every single day at home. Not that he didn't like seeing other girls without their clothes on- that was something he ardently desired to do- and one in particular, the blonde named Chloe who had been in Sheena's Gang along Ross River the previous year.

Now she is a real nature's child, he thought. But why his family?

Musing over the nature of the world and the variety of people in it he made his way across the flat, skirting along the edge of the mangroves growing there. He kept glancing to his right to check whether Letitia was liable to see him for he had no desire to expose himself to her. It was an attitude he felt was somewhat silly as they had both gone nude at home until he reached puberty and then the embarrassment had caused him to make sure he was always clad.

There was no sign of Letitia but when he glanced back Martin saw that the others could still see him. Not wanting to cause Anne or Carmen any embarrassment he continued on until he had several mangrove trees between him and them. Another glance to the right revealed a bit of coloured cloth about 50 metres away.

Sis will just have to lump it then, Martin thought.

By this time he was almost right across the island and he could see the next channel. *This will do,* he decided. Stopping among the mangroves on the bank he unzipped his shorts and began to pee.

A sudden sound made him start with anxiety and he glanced to his left. To his surprise he saw two men in a 'tinnie' with an outboard motor. The motor was not going which was why Martin had not noticed them until one spoke. Their boat was close to the bank, only 10 metres away, and both men were concentrating on hauling something up from over the side.

Crab pot? Martin thought as he quickly zipped up his shorts.

Luckily, they had not seen him and he hoped they wouldn't as they looked a villainous pair. One was thin and wiry and wore only dirty grey shorts. His skin was deeply tanned and he had long, greasy hair gathered in a pony tail. The other was a bear of a man in a blue singlet and baggy blue shorts. He had a round face with the stubble of a beard, the hair mostly white from middle age.

The bear said, "Take it slowly. We don't want to lose it."

The thin man grunted and replied, "Stop fussing Joel. I've got it. Hey, what's that?"

Andrew heard it too and looked downstream through the thin screen of leaves. It was a powerful motor and approaching fast. Both of the men looked at each other and the one named Joel turned to the other with a look of alarm on his face. "Drop them back overboard Corey, quick!"

Corey, the thin one, swore and let go of the rope and then tossed a float over the side. Then he bent to pick up another rope and float that was already on board. As he did the approaching boat swept into view and Martin stared.

It was a big, bright yellow motor launch with two men in light blue uniform shirts. On the side was painted FISHERIES PATROL.

Both of the men near Martin stopped struggling with the rope and crab pot and looked at each other in obvious dismay. Martin noted this and thought, *These guys are up to no good and they've been caught red-handed!*

The two Fisheries Patrol officers obviously thought so too as their boat at once changed course and swept around in a curve to come alongside. As it did one of the patrol officers, a handsome young man in his twenties, stood up and grinned. "What's the go this time Joel?" he called.

Joel gave a shrug and opened his mouth to answer but before he could speak there was a sharp bang and a bright red splotch appeared on the front of the handsome fisheries patrol officer's shirt. The officer's eyes opened in pain and surprise and he looked down in shocked disbelief and then clutched at his front before crumpling into the boat.

The other patrol officer stared in horror and then looked across at the tinnie. Martin saw his eyes open wide and his mouth sag agape and then he ducked and twisted the throttle. The motor roared and the Fisheries boat began to move.

Bang!

This time Martin actually saw the smoke of a discharging firearm spurt out from a weapon that was held in Corey's hands. At that range it was hard to miss, and Corey didn't. The patrol officer gave a convulsive jerk and blood sprayed from the back of his shirt, neck and head. His cap flew off and landed in the water. The motor immediately slowed to idle.

Shotgun! thought Martin as his stunned mind tried to grapple with what he was seeing. It was so shocking and so unreal that he had trouble accepting it.

But the second patrol officer was now down, also sprawled in the bottom of his boat which began to drift downstream.

Joel was obviously also taken by surprise. "Bloody hell Corey, what you do that for?" he shouted.

Corey swore, spat and snarled, "Because I ain't gunna spend another three years inside just for havin' a few bloody undersized crabs in me boat."

"Bloody hell! What we gunna do now?" Joel cried, waving his arms in dismay.

Corey clutched the double barrel shotgun tightly, his fingers clenching and unclenching on the barrels. "Sink their boat and feed them to the crocs. Get this tub moving so we can stop it drifting off around the corner. There might be more people there and we don't want any witnesses," he replied.

Only then did it start to dawn on Martin that he might now be in some danger himself. *I am a witness. They could shoot me too,* he thought.

That sent a chill or real fear through him and he stayed standing still, wishing he had more than a few leaves between him and the men.

Then, as Joel sat to start the outboard, Letitia's voice sounded clearly from along to Martins' right.

"Martin, what's that shooting?" she called.

Martin saw both men's head jerk round and they stared upstream. *Bugger!* he thought. He glanced to his right and to his horror saw Letitia sitting up in the knee-high grass near the bank of the river. Worse still she was looking at him and was obviously going to call out again

For a split-second Martin silently cursed and the shameful notion of staying hidden so that the men didn't notice him flitted across his mind. Then he shook his head.

I can't just leave Sis. These mongrels will just kill her, he thought. Acting on that he spun on his heels and started running towards her.

Chapter 2

RUN!

A s he ran Martin glanced back over his shoulder. To his dismay his eyes met those of Corey. Corey's eyes widened and he snarled and then swore. Terror flooded through Martin, spurring him on. He ran.

Killer's eyes, he thought, his whole being seeming to dissolve in terror. Fear made his feet fly. The tufts of wiry grass snagged at his ankles, almost bringing him down. For a moment he stumbled, then regained his balance and ran on.

Martin's mind raced even faster than his feet. *He's got a gun. He can just shoot both of us,* he thought.

Glancing back, he saw that his fears were well founded. Through a gap in the foliage he got a glimpse of Corey with the shotgun. It was broken open and Corey was tugging at the expended cartridges. Even as Martin watched Corey extracted one and tossed it into the river.

He will reload and be after us in a few seconds, Martin thought, more spasm of fear flooding through him.

By then he was fast approaching his sister. Letitia was kneeling on her towel, dressed only in a bikini, her face a picture of anxious confusion.

"Martin?" she cried. "What's going on?"

There were times, and this was one of them, when Letitia so annoyed, even exasperated Martin that he disliked her intensely, almost hated her. "Get up! Run!" he shouted.

"What? Wha?"

She never got any further. Martin grabbed her left wrist and wrenched to her to her feet. "Aaargh! Martin!" she wailed angrily.

"Shut up and run!" Martin snapped, dragging her after him as he turned to head back across the island.

"But my towel! My clothes! My bag!" Letitia cried, pulling back and reaching down. She picked up the towel and then bent over again. Her grasping fingers managed to close on the handle of a small carry bag.

Martin bared his teeth and snarled. "Those men just murdered two fisheries officers. Now they will kill us. Run!"

"M... m... murder?" Letitia gasped, glancing over her shoulder to where the heads of the two men could just be seen.

Martin also glanced that way and noted that the yellow Fisheries boat with its crumpled corpses was just visible. "That boat. The man with the shotgun just killed the two officers in it. Now they are going to kill us because we saw them. Now for Christ sakes run!" he snapped.

Letitia went pale and gasped, then finally fear flooded across her face as she 'got it'. She stopped pulling back and began to run. As she did her large breasts began bouncing wildly, held in by the very brief and loosely tied bikini top. Martin barely noticed. Her body was a sight he was all too familiar with. To him she seemed to be all curves and bulges and quivering flesh and the fact that the sight aroused him rankled.

Still clutching her towel and bag Letitia began running as fast as she could. But then she tripped. Martin stopped and hauled her to her feet, swearing in his exasperation.

"Run or we are dead!" he gasped. He pushed her and then followed.

Letitia hurried on, stumbling frequently on the tufts of wiry grass and then slipping and stumbling on a slick patch of mud. As he ran behind her Martin noted her wobbling buttocks and her large breasts swinging and bouncing. To counteract this, she had to clutch them with both arms and that also hindered her running.

Martin caught up and passed her, alternately looking ahead for the first view of their boat and backwards for the first sign of pursuit. He was sure Corey would not give up.

Ahead of him Martin saw three heads poking up over the bank. The others were now watching, and their eyes had gone round and their mouths sagged open at the sight of Letitia running towards them.

Martin glanced back and got a glimpse of movement back in the mangroves. A stab of fear so intense it made his chest tighten so hard he could barely breathe cut through him. "Andrew, cast off! Get the motor going! Run! We have to get out of here!" he shouted.

Still the others stared in stunned disbelief. Martin yelled again and this time Andrew nodded, tearing his wide-eyed gaze from Leittia and bending to the motor. Martin glanced back and experienced another chilling stab of terror. Corey was up on the island and now running across the grassy flat!

"Oh help!" Martin whimpered, almost voiding his bowels in fear.

And there just below him was the boat. Letitia began to pick her way carefully down, but Martin took one look at Corey and pushed her.

"Jump you stupid bitch!" he shouted.

The others looked shocked at his language and Letitia turned to snap back at him, then slipped and fell on her bum and slid down into the water. Shrieking in fright she splashed in the muddy shallows. Her bag, which she had looped around her wrist, flailed back and forth spraying water and mud as it did, causing the others to cringe back.

Carmen made a grab and caught Letitia's bag and held on. By then Martin was at the last dry clump of grass on the side of the bank and he did jump. He landed hard on the seat between Anne and Carmen and then fell heavily on the seats and fishing gear. Driven by sheer terror he scrambled to his feet, heedless of the bumps, bruises and scratches and shook his fist at Andrew.

"I have just seen two Fishery Patrol officers murdered. The man who did it is that man there with the shotgun. He will kill us if he can, now get this boat going!"

Andrew glanced across the top of the grassy flat and blanched then bent to the motor which was now running.

"Grab Letitia," he cried.

Carmen and Anne both had. "We've got her. Get going Andrew," Carmen called.

She and Anne were both leaning over the side and had Letitia by one arm and her hair. Letitia floundered in the muddy, murky water, splashing and crying for help. Martin grabbed at the end of her now very soggy towel and pulled but it just slid off her and came away in his hands. Cursing he threw it down into the bottom of the boat and moved to help the girls.

Andrew dithered for another couple of seconds but then began to open the throttle. Martin turned to him. "Go Andrew, go!" he shouted. "We've got her. You just get us away from here and we will get her aboard."

Andrew nodded and set his jaw then opened the throttle. The boat began moving. Immediately Anne let out a cry of alarm.

"The drag is too much! Stop! We can't hold on."

Andrew eased the throttle and the boat slowed until it was barely stemming the tide. Martin cast a glance in Corey's direction and noted that the man was half way across the flat and moving fast. Driven by desperation he pushed in between Anne and Carmen and then felt the boat heel over so much he feared they might capsize. "Pull!" he cried.

Grabbing Letitia by an arm he obeyed his own command. Both Anne and Carmen did likewise and Letitia came sliding up over the bulwarks. With her came cascading muddy water and flailing legs. Crying with pain she slid into the bottom of the boat, limbs working and mouth agape. Landing on her back she squirmed and struggled to get up.

"Go!" Martin cried.

Andrew did. He tore his gaze from Letitia and glanced over the top of the bank then suddenly ducked and twisted the throttle fully open. As the boat gathered speed, he pushed the control column to starboard so that the boat turned back towards the bank.

Carmen looked up from where she was struggling to help a muddy, writhing Letitia and cried: "Wrong way!"

Martin glanced around and then his racing mind agreed with Andrew's plan. "No, it's not. Keep close to the bank Andrew," he shouted.

As he did, he glanced back over his shoulder and got a glimpse of Corey. The man was only about 25 metres from the bank and was swearing and raising the shotgun. But then he went out of sight as the mangroves along the upper part of the island blotted out the view.

Martin glanced at the bank and for the first time began to hope. "He will never be able to run through those mangroves as fast as we can motor along," he said.

Carmen nodded. "You are right. Good work Andrew," she said.

Anne had fallen on her bum in the front of the boat, and as she struggled back onto the seat she became smeared in mud.

"What happened? What's going on?" she cried.

As the boat roared on upstream against the current, Martin quickly related what he had seen. The others were all horrified but did not doubt his story. If nothing else Letitia's mud smeared form and obvious fear convinced them. Carmen dragged the mud-soaked towel from under Martin's feet and draped it over Letitia's shoulders.

Anne looked fearfully back. "What will we do now?" she asked.

Martin pointed upstream. "Find my mum and dad and get out of here. We need to get to civilisation or we are dead. Then we can tell the police," he replied. He had no doubts about that.

We need to be where there are so many people Corey won't dare shoot us with so many potential witnesses, he thought.

Andrew bit his lip and also glanced back. "What if they follow us in their boat?" he queried.

That was a terrifying thought, but Martin knew it was highly likely. "They probably will. They need to catch us before we reach safety," he replied.

"Well here's the end of the island," Carmen observed.

And it was. They went churning upstream past the last of the mangroves. As they did Andrew turned away towards the river bank to their right but they all looked back down the eastern channel to try to get a glimpse of the crook's boat.

It was not in sight but at that moment Martin thought he heard the roar of another outboard motor. "Just ease up for a moment Andrew. I want to listen," he said.

Andrew did so and instantly they all stiffened and looked scared as the unmistakable sound of another outboard motor at full throttle reached them. It was more of a thrumming vibration than an actual sound but it chilled Martin to the core.

"Oh, here they come! Oh! Oh!" Anne wailed.

"Go Andrew!" Martin commanded.

Andrew opened the throttle and turned the boat to starboard. This sent the boat curving over to the bank on their right. This was actually the left or western bank of the river. As they roared along, they kept glancing back, fear obviously gripping them. Martin looked anxiously around for any sign of help and as he did the image of just how big the swamps were caused him more shudders of fear.

We are a long way from help, he thought.

Suddenly the river divided. Before Martin could speak Andrew turned the boat to starboard and they went racing up the right-hand channel.

As they did Carmen looked around, a worried frown on her face. "Are you sure this is the right channel Little Brother?" she asked.

Andrew looked around and then bit his lip. "I hope so," he replied.

Martin felt a squirm of unease in his stomach and also studied the banks. But they were just mangroves and there was no obvious landmark he could identify. A terrible feeling of apprehension gripped him and doubt grew to certainty. "I think we have gone up the wrong channel," he said.

Andrew looked sick and bit his lip again. "Sorry," he muttered. "What do you want me to do?"

Martin's mind raced as he tried to picture the map in his mind. "Go a bit further. As soon as we get around a sharp bend slow down and turn us around, then stop us close to the bank and facing back the way we came," he said.

In his mind was the concept of catching the murderers by surprise and either tipping their boat over or making a getaway before they could turn around. But in his heart he knew it was a desperately slim hope and he felt sick to his very core.

Andrew did as he was instructed, and the boat was brought to a burbling stop right in close to the mangroves. These were less than a metre to starboard and Martin was able to reach out and grab one of the large aerial roots that stuck out into the deeper water.

As he did Anne let out a little gasp and pointed. "Oh! What's that thing?" she cried.

Martin looked and almost laughed aloud. "A mudskipper. They are quite harmless, at least to humans," he replied. He glanced at Carmen and they both smiled. In June and July the previous year they had taken part in a series of sailing races against some friends in Cairns and the group of boys they were competing against, army cadets mostly, had used an old home-made catamaran which they named *Mudskipper*.

This mudskipper was about 15 centimetres long and as he watched it slither and skip across the slimy black ooze away from them Martin could not help smiling again.

So did Carmen. "They look so cute with those big bug eyes," she commented.

Martin agreed. "That's a big one," he explained, pointing to several smaller ones which were also hopping away.

There were more mudskippers, several quite small but the sudden roar of a racing outboard quite close to them chased thoughts of wildlife out of Martin's head and replaced them instantly with almost gibbering terror. The friends all looked at each other in alarm.

"Oh, here they come!" whimpered Anne, clutching at her lifejacket and biting her lip.

Martin braced, ready to let go and to signal to Andrew to open the throttle. But then the roaring sound faded quite noticeably. Almost hyperventilating with fear, he crouched and tried to peer through the forest of mangrove roots to the next stretch of creek. But there was no sign of the crook's boat and the sound faded even more.

Letitia, who was hunched in a muddy ball near his feet, looked up. "Have they turned back?" she asked.

Martin shook his head. "Ssh! Listen," he instructed. A faint ray of hope eased his breathing.

Andrew turned his head from side to side then pointed off to starboard into the mangroves. "They are over there, in the main channel of the river," he said.

After listening for a few seconds Martin had to agree. The motor noises were growing louder again but were definitely coming through the forest on his right.

The river has a bit of a loop in it there, he thought.

"You are right. They didn't follow us up this creek," he said.

Carmen looked around and bit her lip. "Could we keep going on up this creek to somewhere safe?" she asked.

Martin did not think so but wanted to be sure. "Pass me the chart," he said.

Andrew did so and they all crowded to look at it. Martin pointed to where he thought they were. "This is the creek but it just splits up into a lot of smaller creeks and they all end in the middle of this huge swamp. If we go up it we will have to walk through the mangroves for a few kilometres."

"What other choice do we have?" Andrew asked.

Martin pointed to the mouth of the river. "There is a town here, a place called Cungulla. There are lots of people there. Maybe we should try to reach it?"

"Is there a police station?" Carmen asked.

Martin shook his head. He had been there fishing a couple of times but did not think there was.

Letitia looked up. "No. I went to party there one night and it got pretty wild and the police had to come from Townsville."

Carmen bent over the map. "How far is it?" she asked.

"About five kilometres," Martin estimated.

"So about the same distance as back upstream to that Cromarty Landing?" Andrew said.

Martin nodded. As he did he glanced back over his right shoulder. The sound of the outboard motor was now definitely behind him. But what to do? He really wanted to get back to his parents who were somewhere upstream, but the murderers were now between him and them. Torn by the enormity of the possible consequences of a wrong decision he hesitated.

At that moment a fish went plop behind him. So highly strung were his nerves that he swung round to look. He was just in time to see the swirl made by a large fish as it cut through the spreading ripples made by the one that had jumped.

Big fish chasing little fish, Martin thought. Then his mind translated that into their own situation. *If it gets caught it is dead—and if we get caught, so are we!*

He looked up the winding creek behind the boat and experienced a sense of dread. A chill crept through him making him shiver despite the sweltering heat. Suddenly the place took on a sinister appearance. The water was dark green or black; the mud was dark grey or black; the leaves of the mangroves were mostly dark green. Martin experienced a sudden intense desire to be out of that environment. But which way, upstream or down?

Anne now took out her mobile phone. "I will ring the police," she said.

"And then my parents," Martin added.

But then Anne shook her head. "I'm not getting service," she muttered.

"Are you sure?" Martin asked. "We are only a few kilometres from town."

Anne tried again and then lifted unhappy, anxious eyes to meet his. "My provider is NinjaPhone. I think it only works in the cities. Try yours Carmen."

Carmen shook her head. "I left it in the car. I didn't want it to get wet or muddy, so I left it in my bag. I didn't expect anyone to ring me."

"I'll try mine," Letitia said. With difficulty she loosened the draw string of her bag and reached inside. But the bag was sopping and even before Letitia at last extracted the mobile phone Martin had concerns that it might not work.

It didn't. The screen was blank and remained that way despite attempts to turn the phone on. "It must have got wet!" Letitia wailed.

"It did," Martin confirmed. "The water has probably shorted the electrics. It might work again when it dries out."

Carmen looked at Martin. "Have you got a phone Martin?"

Martin shook his head. "I do, but I left it at home."

Carmen turned to Andrew. "And I suppose yours is in the car too?"

Andrew nodded. Carmen bit her lip and looked anxiously around. Martin felt guilty but there was no help for it. He rarely used his mobile phone. His mind raced. *What should we do?* he wondered.

Anne then added to his worries. "What if those men meet those two old guys who were fishing back up the river? They might ask them if they have seen us and when they say no they will know we didn't go that way," she said.

That was an appalling thought. *Then they will come back downstream looking for us and this is a pretty obvious creek to check,* he thought. For a few seconds he again considered continuing up it and taking their chances in the mangroves. Then he shook his head. *Those men will be familiar with this environment and they will be able to track us in the mud,* he thought. *Then there will be no witnesses.*

He clenched his fists as the tension and fear built. It was very hot and sweat trickled down his face. He wiped it away and slapped at a mosquito then unclenched his jaw. "We go downstream, and we need to get going now," he said.

"What if that motor we can hear isn't the murderers?" Carmen said.

That was another awful thought. But Martin was sure it was. "It may not be, but we can't just stay here and wait to get caught," he said. "We must go."

Suiting his actions to his words he shoved the boat away from the mangroves. "Open the throttle Andrew," he instructed.

At that Letitia let out a sob and looked up, her muddy face all streaked with tears. "But what about mum and dad? Those men might meet up with them."

That caused Martin another bout of sickening apprehension and doubt, but he shook his head. "They might, but they won't associate them with us and even if they ask mum and dad will not know where we are. Come on Andrew, move us," he replied.

Andrew did so. The tinnie set off back down the winding mangrove creek, slowing as they approached each bend so that they could listen for motor noise and to check that the men weren't just waiting in ambush.

After a few minutes they came to a bend to the left and as they rounded it Martin saw the wider channel of the main river opening out ahead. The sight caused his chest to tighten up and his heart to beat faster. Once they went out into it they were committed.

There will be no turning back, he thought.

He gestured to Andrew. "Stop for a moment so we can listen," he said.

Andrew did. They all listened. The sound of an outboard could be heard in the still air but it sounded a long way off and Martin could not determine whether it was coming towards them or going away.

"Let's get going," he said.

Andrew eased the throttle open and the boat surged out into the main stream. Here he turned to port and headed downstream. Martin looked back but saw no sign of the crooks. Turning to look ahead he saw the island he had so recently been on. "Go to port," he said. He did not want the girls seeing the dead men in the patrol launch.

But this desire to protect them failed. As they sped northwards past the downstream end of the island the patrol launch appeared close to starboard. Martin silently swore and bit his lip as the others all gasped and then stared in horror.

The men didn't have time to sink it and the tide has carried it down, he reasoned.

The patrol launch was down by the bows and much lower in the water. *They must have holed it,* Martin thought.

His eyes took in the awful scene, the two crumpled bodies with dark stains on their shirts and the outflung arm with clutching hand. Worse was the sudden sight of the younger patrol officer's face. His eyes were still wide open and staring and his mouth was open in surprise. Flies were already beginning to swarm.

Letitia blanched and then retched over the side. Carmen shook her head. "This is awful," she muttered. Andrew just looked grim and very pale under his sunburn.

"Keep going Andrew. There's nothing we can do for them," Martin said.

Then he had to grip the gunwale tightly as he began to shake. Fear and reaction both made him shiver. Apprehension clutched his stomach into a nauseous ball and he looked back at the drifting patrol launch, wondering what death might be really like.

Then his eyes caught movement on the river beyond the slowly sinking patrol launch and his heart skipped a beat.

It was the murderers!

Their boat was racing downstream with a white bow wave creaming out on both sides. "There they are!" Martin cried, pointing. As he did a wave of fear so intense it virtually paralysed him engulfed his body.

The others looked back and most let out cries of dismay or fear. Andrew looked over his shoulder and Martin saw him grit his teeth as he bent to open the throttle to its fullest.

Anne looked anxiously at Martin then turned to Andrew. "Oh go!" she cried.

Martin gripped the sides and tried to calm his wildly beating heart. *Oh my God! They have found us. Can we get away?*

Chapter 3

BOWLING GREEN BAY

To his own shame Martin experienced a spasm of terror so acute he almost voided his bowels. In his mind's eye he saw the shotgun blast striking the young patrol officer's shirt and the sudden shock of surprise even as death overcame him.

Turning to Andrew, he cried, "Go Andrew, go!"

Andrew did. After casting another glance over his shoulder at the other boat he crouched and held the throttle wide open. The tinnie went racing down the river, its engine roaring on full throttle.

As they roared along Martin looked back, intently studying the boat behind them. Its bows were canted up and it was throwing out an impressive spray of white foam from the bows. The heads of the two men were just visible.

Andrew also looked back then called, "Is it catching up Martin?"

"Not sure. Yes. Yes it is, but slowly," Martin replied, dread catching at his stomach as he spoke.

Carmen also looked back. "They should catch us fairly easily," she commented.

Andrew took a look then nodded. "They should but it looks like they haven't got a very good trim. They are too much down by the stern."

Carmen bit her lip and studied the other boat. "You are right. That is causing a lot of drag. If they put her on more of an even keel she would go faster."

"That's what we should do," Andrew said. "Trim the boat so she is at her best angle for planing."

Carmen looked around the boat and nodded. "You are right. Let's use a bit of seamanship and get this vessel trimmed." She began moving objects and directed Letitia to move her legs forward of the front thwart. Anne was told to sit beside her and then Carmen began picking up objects. "We need to jettison any extra weight," she added.

Martin understood what she meant. *A lighter boat will go faster for the same horsepower,* he reasoned. From his reading and his own experience, he could see that even small changes could be important. *Those murderers appear to have a similar boat to ours and an engine of about the same power so they should catch us up,* he thought.

After a couple of minutes of watching the water flow around the hull, of adjusting people's positions and of moving things Carmen declared her self-satisfied. "That's about as good as we can do," she said.

"We can chuck more stuff out," Andrew replied.

"Not yet. Our gear doesn't weigh much," Carmen replied.

Martin suspected that every little bit mattered, but he held his tongue and resumed watching their pursuers. Their own boat at least was slipping easily across the surface of the flat, smooth water.

The girls sat or crouched, Carmen with a grim but determined face, Anne with one of shock and anxiety and Letitia's with an expression of open fear. Letitia huddled in the bottom clutching the muddy wet towel around her shoulders, her knees and lower legs sticking out.

The river curved slightly to the right and Andrew aimed to cut across the curve to take the straightest possible course. Martin stared anxiously ahead, then called over his shoulder, "Be careful Andrew. Don't cut the corners too close on the bends. The shallow water is on the inside of the bends."

Andrew nodded and glanced back. Then he nodded with apparent satisfaction. "They aren't catching up," he commented.

That was what Martin had been afraid of but he saw that Andrew was right. The murderer's boat appeared to be no closer.

Two hundred metres, he estimated.

The desperate race went on, the river curving slightly back to the left. Carmen picked up the now sodden and mud smeared map and studied it. Martin looked over her shoulder and tried to work out where they were.

"Here I think," Carmen said.

Martin nodded agreement. "That is a big island. Once we are around this we are in the estuary. Then it is only a couple of kilometres to the town."

Carmen pointed to a narrow channel marked on the map. "Could we take a short cut through there?"

Martin bit his lip and then shook his head. "I've never been along it. It looks fairly narrow and winding. We could find ourselves stuck. The tide is going out fast."

That was obviously true. A glance at the banks showed that it had dropped at least half a metre in the last hour. Once again Martin looked hard at both banks, searching for a way of escape. But both banks, as far as he could see, were lined with a thick jungle of mangroves.

As the river curved back to the right, he noted that it was becoming wider. From about 100 metres it was now at least 200. And it was also becoming shallower and small sand bars and mud banks were becoming visible right across the channel. Andrew kept the boat in the deepest channel he could see which was hard over on the left side of the river and close to the wall of mangroves.

The opening of the side channel they had been discussing appeared but to Martin it seemed to just go off at an angle and then end at a wall of mangroves. Worse it looked shallow. Steep banks of wet mud sloped down to where a very narrow waterway, only about 5 metres wide, showed.

Martin again shook his head, and when he looked back at Andrew to speak he met his eyes. Andrew also shook his head. "Could be a death trap," he said.

So they ignored the opening and raced past it. They went on following the deep channel around to the right. As they roared along Martin kept looking ahead and then astern. It was obvious that the other boat was not catching them up.

Barring an engine failure or running out of fuel we should just make it to safety, he thought.

Then he looked back and let out a little involuntary cry of alarm. The others all looked at him and then astern. Carmen spoke first. "The murderers have taken that side channel," she said in a flat tone that half concealed her concern.

"They obviously know the river better than us," Martin answered.

"But we can still get away, can't we?" Anne asked, her voice quavering with fear.

"I think so," Martin answered.

Then he glanced ahead and felt another stab of anxiety. The river was curving back to the left around the big island and as it did it was opening out even more into an estuary hundreds of metres wide, and right across its whole width it was studded with sandbanks through which snaked half a dozen channels.

"If we don't run aground," he added.

As they roared around the wide, sweeping curve to the left Martin studied the area ahead of him. Reflected glare off the water made him squint and he shielded his eyes.

That is the open sea, he thought, noting a flat line in the distance.

He was struck by how the whole scene seemed to be flooded with bright light. The glare and brightness washed out much of the colour and also made it hard to see where sea and sky met. Only a shimmering black dot right in the distance indicated the presence of a boat or ship.

Then the glint of sunlight on corrugated iron roofs caught his eye. This came from his left front beyond the end of the big mangrove island. The roofs still looked a long way away, at least 3 or 4 kilometres, he estimated, but the sight at least gave him hope.

"That must be Cungulla," he said, pointing.

The others looked. Carmen said, "Keep over to port Andrew."

Even as she did, they reached the northern end of the big island and Martin looked to port to see if there was any sign of the murderer's boat.

And there it was!

For a moment he could not believe his eyes—did not want to believe them. But he had to. There was the murderer's boat racing along parallel to them and about half a kilometre away. Even as he saw it Martin noted the faces of the men turn in their direction and an arm go up to point.

They've seen us! he thought.

Then his heart began to hammer and his mouth went dry. "There they are," he said bitterly.

They all looked and exclamations of dismay and fear broke from most of the others. Carmen shook her head in dismay and said, "It was a lot shorter through that narrow channel."

Anne gasped and pressed her hand to her breast. "Oh! They are level with us now aren't they?" she cried.

"They are," Carmen answered.

Martin shook his head and looked around for some way of escape. As he did, he saw that they were racing straight towards a snag, a muddy tree which had been washed down by a flood and was now lying embedded in the mud with its twisted, leafless branches poking up.

"Andrew! Watch that snag!" he cried.

Andrew, who had been watching the murderers, leaned over to

look and his face went pale. Instinctively he pulled the tiller to avoid the obstacle and the boat skidded to starboard. For a moment Martin was sure they would slam into the tree trunk broadside on but at the last minute the boat's hull bit into the water and the pressure shot it away from the snag. The boat bumped lightly against the snag but then skidded across into deeper water.

"Missed!" Anne cried.

"And now we are in the wrong channel," Letitia added.

They were. Martin looked around and bit his lip. The river had now opened out into a dozen channels, some large but mostly small and all looking quite shallow. The channels criss-crossed the ever-widening estuary and hundreds of sand islands now lay exposed between them. The deepest channel now appeared to be over to their left but there was a chance that others would also be deep enough.

We have to get across to port to get to the town, Martin thought.

"Brace me. I need some height to try to pick the deepest channel," he said to Carmen as he moved to stand on the forward thwart. Carmen and Anne both held his legs and he steadied himself and shielded his eyes against the glare to study the channels ahead.

Anne looked anxiously up. "We have to beat those men to the town, don't we?" she asked.

"Yes, we do," Martin replied. He didn't want to say it but he now estimated that the murderers were closer to the town than they were.

Letitia looked across, and said, "They will get there before we do."

Martin felt a surge of anger at his sister for stating the obvious and frightening the others, but he said nothing, concentrating on directing Andrew as to which channel to take. And that became ever harder. As the river widened out the channels became shallower until the boat was stirring up a long train of mud and sand in its wake and the propeller and even the keel began to scrape on the shallower parts of the bed.

If we run ourselves aground, we are done for! Martin thought.

The responsibility of making sure they didn't by picking the right route suddenly felt like a crushing burden and Martin began to sweat and tremble. But he managed to maintain focus and got Andrew to steer into a deeper channel that veered back towards the town. But then it curved away to the right from it and then they had to dodge another log sticking up out of the sand.

The tide was obviously draining quickly away and that knowledge added to the stress. Already Martin could see areas of mud and sand that were so dry that the crabs were emerging to forage.

This is getting bloody tricky! he thought, clenching his fists and biting his lip with anxiety.

And it was now obvious that the main river channel was way over to port and was the one the murderers were in. *They are almost at the town now,* Martin noted grimly.

For a few minutes he toyed with just heading for the town anyway and risking the men taking action.

Anne obviously thought the same. "Surely those men won't do anything to us if we go over to the town? Then there will be too many witnesses."

But there was nobody in sight on the mudflats or on the beach. Nor were there any boats visible other than the two larger ones out to sea. Martin squinted against the glare and tried to study the details of the town, but it was at least a kilometre away and mostly hidden by a line of trees and the shimmer of a heat mirage. Suddenly it didn't seem such a sanctuary after all.

By this time, they were down level with the start of the town but so were the murderers. Even as Martin turned to check their location, he noted the bow wave on their boat die down.

"They have slowed down," he said.

Andrew nodded. "They have us cut off," he said.

"So what do we do now?" Anne asked, a hint of hysteria.

Carmen pointed out to sea. "See if we can reach that right-hand boat out there," she suggested.

Martin looked and the vessel sprang into clear focus, shimmering as a black silhouette above the heat mirage on a glassy sea.

"That's a trawler," he said. He thought the second one was too but it was much further away and its details were obscured.

"It will have to do," Carmen said with finality.

Andrew nodded. "We don't have many other choices," he said.

He studied the channels and began to steer a course for the open sea, now only a few hundred metres away. Martin could only agree, his moral qualms about endangering other people now swept aside by the self-preservation instinct.

But it wasn't as easy as that. The trawler looked to be at least 2 or 3 nautical miles out to sea and the estuary proved to be much shallower than Martin expected. Even when they reached what looked like open water they kept scraping the bottom as they hit small sandbars in the muddy soup of water.

Suddenly the boat slithered to a stop, the engine racing and the propeller pushed up out of the water. Martin was aghast.

"We've run aground!" he cried, looking at the ripples flowing across a very shallow sand bank.

"Push!" Carmen cried, letting go of Martin and swinging her legs over the side.

Martin instantly saw they had no other choice. He moved to the side and clambered over into ankle deep water. Luckily the bottom was sand, not mud so his feet didn't sink in and he could get firm traction. Anne joined them but Leitita sat hunched under her towel.

Carmen shook her head in annoyance. "Letitia, get out! Help us push. Andrew, lift that motor up so it doesn't drag, and keep it going," she yelled.

Letitia looked anxiously around so Carmen shouted at her again. "Oh, for heaven's sake! Letitia we can't push with you in the boat. Get out and help push."

Letitia now stood up and let the wet towel slip off. She moved to step over the side, and then slipped. As she fell hard on her bum on the thwart she made such a spectacle that Andrew and Anne both goggled. Martin flamed with embarrassment as she did not look very sexy or attractive, just floppy and ungainly.

After struggling to her feet Letitia mumbled 'sorry!' and slid over the side. Then she turned and leaned on the boat to push. As she did her breasts hung down and bobbled. Andrew gaped and then looked away, obviously embarrassed.

They began to push, skittering through the water. Andrew stayed in, holding the motor up and keeping the propeller turning. As he ran Martin glanced across the estuary and noted that the murderers were now off the middle of the town.

I don't think they have worked out what we are going to try to do yet, he thought hopefully.

Then he glanced ahead and noted dry sand and called on them to detour around it through the shallows. As they pushed, he noted Anne staring in amazement at Letitia's bouncing bosom.

Bloody hell! Martin thought. *I wish she wasn't such a bloody show off!*

Then the boat slid out into knee deep water and Letitia stumbled. She fell with a splash and then struggled to her feet to run after them, her whole body quivering and bouncing so that even Martin had to goggle.

But they were afloat. Carmen held the boat and yelled, "Get in! Get in!" Martin sprang aboard then helped Anne to get in. Carmen also sprang in and shouted at Andrew. "Go Andrew, go!"

The motor was lowered and the boat began to move. But Letitia had only just caught up and was holding on while splashing along beside them. Then she tried to jump aboard, misjudged and fell in, sliding in between the thwarts so that she landed on her back.

Carmen grabbed Letitia's hand and pulled her up. Anne also helped so Martin, flaming with shame, turned away and stared ahead to look for more sandbars and shallows. When he next glanced aft Martin saw that Letitia was again crouched beneath an even more sodden towel. She looked thoroughly miserable and frightened.

Once again Martin looked to check on the murderers and to his dismay saw that they were again moving at top speed, a white bow wave creaming up.

They are after us again, he thought.

He turned and looked out to sea, hoping that the still distant trawler was their salvation.

Then they slid to a standstill again on another sandbar. "Out!" Carmen yelled.

Within seconds they were all over the side except Andrew. Even Letitia was quick and they started pushing. This time the water was deeper and very quickly they ran into water that was almost waist deep. Carmen was able to jump aboard in time and Martin managed this as well but Letitia floundered, let go and tripped. She vanished in a huge splash of brown muddy water. Anne clung on and was hauled in by Carmen.

Letitia stood up and came floundering after them. Andrew had to ease the throttle until she reached them but that was in water so deep that Letitia had trouble hoisting herself over the gunwale.

It was left to Martin and Carmen to pull Letitia aboard. She slid onto the midships thwart and looked sick and embarrassed. Then she groped for her towel as Andrew opened the throttle. Carmen looked down at the water which was now swilling around in the bottom of the boat.

"Letitia, where's your mobile phone?" she asked.

"In my bag... oh!" Letitia replied. Forgetting the towel, she bent down and picked up the bag. It was soaked and water poured from it. A look of shame mottled Letitia's face as she groped in the bag to extract the phone. After pushing at several buttons, she swallowed and then shook her head.

"It's dead! Oh, I'm sorry!"

That was bad news. Martin asked Anne to try hers again and then again set himself to help guide Andrew out into the deeper water of the bay.

Bowling Green Bay is a huge oval shaped feature about 40 kilometres across and mostly quite shallow, not reaching more than about 10 metres. The northern side is open to the Coral Sea and it was towards this that they were fleeing. To the northeast and just visible were a few tiny black dots. These were the tops of trees showing over the curve of the earth and they showed where the 15 kilometres long sand spit named Cape Bowling Green juts into the sea.

From the base of Cape Bowling Green, on the eastern and southern sides of the bay, the shore of the bay is kilometre after kilometre of sandy beaches backed by swamps and mud flats or dense mangrove forests. Along the western side from Cungulla is a long sandy, scrub-covered peninsula which merges into mangroves and then ends in a 20 kilometres long range of rugged mountains. Mt Cleveland is the highest and the top of the range is Cape Cleveland. On the other side are Cleveland Bay and the port of Townsville.

Over there, where the mountains began, was the Australian Institute of Marine Science, a dozen large buildings. Only the most fleeting glimpses of white flecks in the heat shimmer indicated their position but Martin knew they were 20 or 30 kilometres away.

No chance of reaching them, he thought.

The murderer's boat was closer and would easily cut them off. He turned and saw that it was even then negotiating the last few bends of the main channel before the open water.

Bloody hell! Talk about between the Devil and the Deep Blue Sea!

he thought. *Well, not so blue,* he added, noting that the water had a muddy brown look. Turning he looked at the nearest trawler. It was still at least 2 nautical miles away.

But we have a chance, he thought, noting as he did that the water was almost flat calm with just a few small ripples spreading across its surface. There was no breeze so there were no wind waves and the heat was still sweltering, eased only by the wind of their own motion. The second trawler looked to be 5 of 6 nautical miles away and was almost hidden by the heat mirage.

Well, we are out in the bay now, but can we get to the trawler first? Martin wondered.

Chapter 4

THE DEVIL ON THE DEEP BLUE SEA

Martin wiped sweat from his face and looked around. *I hope the engine doesn't give out,* he thought.

It had been racing hard for half an hour now, and it was the shimmering thin plume of blueish smoke emanating from it that bothered him after a couple of splutters attracting his attention. He shielded his eyes against the glare and squinted back at the murderers. They were now out in the open water and definitely chasing them.

But we have gained a bit, he thought.

Andrew looked back too and then said, "How far behind do you reckon they are?"

"About a kilometre," Martin replied.

Then he turned to look ahead. The trawler still looked to be more than twice that but was now emerging from the heat shimmer so that details were becoming visible.

Definitely a trawler, he told himself as he noted the booms and nets hanging out on each side. It looked to be moving slowly across a sea as flat as glass.

Carmen also studied it. "Did that fishing boat just turn and start heading this way?" she queried.

Martin had been aware of some change but he was still so overwhelmed by all the sights and smells of the recent past that he was not sure.

Anne had also been watching and she now nodded. "I think it did," she agreed.

"Then we will get to them all the quicker," Andrew commented.

"Yes, but can they save us?" Martin muttered under his breath. Through his mind ran several grim scenarios and also the moral dilemma resurfaced.

We are placing those fishermen at risk. They could get shot too, he thought. He wasn't sure what the crew of a small trawler was but decided it was probably only four or five.

Should we? he wondered.

Then he looked at his sister sitting pale and trembling, the wet towel again draped over her.

Poor old Letitia is having trouble handling this, he thought. Then another ghastly notion came to him: the murderers might not kill the girls immediately. *They might rape them first,* he thought. The thought of such appalling things happening to his sister and to the other girls made him feel physically ill. *I must save them if I can,* he decided.

Within 2 minutes it was obvious that the trawler was in fact heading towards them and Martin noted that the nets were being reeled in and hoisted up.

They must have finished fishing for the day, he decided.

He estimated that the trawler was now less than a kilometre away and colours were becoming clear—a blue hull, white deckhouse and brown booms and mast.

A glance behind showed that the murderers were still chasing but that they had not really closed the distance.

We might make it yet, Martin thought, wiping more sweat from his eyes.

He bent and picked up a water bottle from the mess in the bottom of the boat and had a drink, ignoring the slightly salty taste. As he screwed the top closed, he studied the now rapidly approaching trawler. With the combined speed of both vessels the distance was closing rapidly. With every second he became both more anxious and more relieved. The trawler was a small flush deck vessel with a wheelhouse and deckhouse. There was a white radar scanner revolving on top of the wheelhouse. The hull number became visible, black letters and figures edged in white: K 3496.

A glance at his companions revealed they were all tense and leaning forward expectantly, anxiety and hope mingled on their drawn faces.

"Won't be long now," Anne muttered.

The last few hundred metres seemed to just slip by in moments. Martin discovered that he was so tense he was holding his breath. Steadying himself against the side and against Carmen's back he took several deep breaths and then shifted his attention back to the murderers. To his surprise their boat was still racing after them.

They must see that we have reached some sort of safety? Martin thought. That was followed by a feeling of apprehension so strong it gripped his stomach and made him nauseous. *Surely they won't follow us onto the trawler and kill everyone?* he worried.

Men were now visible on the deck of the trawler, two of them. A big, bearded gorilla of a man wearing a dark blue singlet and dark blue shorts stood near the bows and a shirtless, thin man with scruffy hair and straggly beard stood beside him. There was another man in the wheelhouse, but Martin could not make him out. Then, to his surprise, two females in their twenties or thirties appeared, clad only in very short shorts and loose, grubby singlets.

Carmen and Anne began waving and Martin joined in. The big bearded man waved back. The bow wave of the trawler died away and it began to lose way.

"They are stopping," Anne commented.

"Oh thank God! We are saved!" Letitia cried. Tears began to trickle down her cheeks.

Martin looked back at the murderers and then at the now stationary trawler. "Port side to," he said.

That will put the trawler between us and the murderers, he reasoned. As he did he saw the man in the wheelhouse reach up and pull down a radio handset. *Good, we can radio for help as soon as we are board.*

Carmen shielded eyes against the glare and stared back at the murderers. "We will need to be quick getting aboard when we get there. Those men are still chasing us," she said.

Andrew steered the boat in a wide curve to bring it around the stern and alongside the now stationary trawler. As he did the big gorilla yelled and gestured to come in on the starboard side, but he ignored that. As the boat passed under the stern the gorilla and the two women crossed the fish deck to meet them and the thin man went forward to the wheelhouse.

As they slid past the stern Martin took a quick look back at the murderers. They were now only a couple of hundred metres away and he noted that one was holding something up to the side of his head.

Radio? Martin wondered.

Even as he thought this he glanced at the trawler and saw the man in the wheelhouse stop talking on his radio and hang the handset up. A little niggle of puzzled concern wormed its way into Martin's brain where it was overwhelmed by the surge of relief.

Safe! he thought.

His thoughts shifted to seamanship. As they closed alongside, he said, "Grab that anchor there Carmen. We might need to use it to tie on."

Carmen bent and groped to untangle the boat anchor from the shirts, towels, bags and fishing equipment in the bows. As she did Andrew throttled back and Martin leaned out ready to grab the trawler's rail. Looking up he met the gorilla's eyes and the man gave a wide grin and Martin noted that he had tiny black eyes that seemed to twinkle and glitter. The two women were leaning over the rail and close up they did not look as attractive. Both were very tanned and their skin had a dried-up, leathery look.

As the boat came to a stop another man stepped out of the wheelhouse and came to lean over the rail. Martin idly noted that this man had a black eye patch and long fair hair that was tied back in a pigtail.

The man gestured and said, "Give us your hand."

Martin shook his head. "Girls first," he said. "Anne, you get aboard."

Anne stood and he steadied her as she reached up for the man's hand. As she took it, Martin heard Carmen gasp and cry out: "Long John Silver!"

Andrew echoed this. "Long John Silver! Anne, let go! He's a pirate!"

Martin was puzzled and then flustered. He saw a look of fury cross the man named Silver's face and his remaining eye flicked from Carmen to Andrew.

"You! You little bastards!" he snarled.

Silver at once tightened his grip on Anne's wrist and began to drag her up over the bulwark. Martin stared in shocked disbelief but had enough presence of mind to reach out to grab at Anne's shirt.

Then his surprise turned to stunned shock as Carmen suddenly stood up and whacked at Silver's face and head with the boat anchor.

"Let her go you mongrel!" she screamed.

Silver did, springing back and crying out. His hands went up to his face as blood suddenly showed. Still Martin stood in a state of uncertainty, quite shocked by Carmen's savage attack. But then Carmen lost her balance and grabbed at Martin's shirt. He managed to clutch at her arm but they both fell forward. That banged his right knee very hard on the thwart and then he had to let go of her to break his fall as he landed on the boat's gunwale.

"What the? Bloody hell!" he cried.

Then Anne pitched forward between the boat and the trawler, her head and arms splashing into the water. Only a sudden grab by Andrew which caught the waistband of her jeans stopped her sliding right overboard.

"Grab her Martin! Get her aboard!" Andrew called. Then he shouted again. "Letitia! Wake up! Help!"

Martin's mind was now racing even as he landed heavily and then tried to push himself back up to a kneeling position.

Silver, Long John Silver, he thought, memories of their adventure on Endeavour Island the previous April flooding his mind.

He had only met Long John Silver briefly when they were trying to escape on the pirate's yacht but both Carmen and Andrew had been chased by the man. He was one of a gang of murderous smugglers who had tried to catch them to get a box of drugs they had accidentally stumbled on. Martin had taken the box and run into the jungle and later handed it back in exchange for his friend's freedom.

Silver lost an eye in the gunfight with the rival gang, he remembered. Now he looked up and saw that Silver was still reeling back, blood streaming down his face and from his mouth. It looked as though Carmen's savage blow had done some real damage. *Broken a cheekbone or knocked out some teeth?* he thought.

But there was no time for speculation. The gorilla was shouting angrily and lunging down to grab at them and Anne was splashing and screaming and still half over the side.

Martin's mind kept racing. *These people are friends of the murderers. They have been talking to each other on the radio,* he thought, the little images clicking into place. The thought of those murderers sent a spasm of pure terror through him and galvanized him into action. *They must be nearly here now. We must get away!* he thought.

Ignoring the searing pain in his right knee Martin leaned out and shoved hard against the hull of the trawler, fending off the gorilla's grasping hand as he did. That sent the boat sliding sideways away from the trawler. But in the process he lost his balance and teetered. Then the gorilla grabbed his hair.

Driven by desperation Martin jerked back but the gorilla hung on. Pain burned across Martin's scalp. Then Carmen was on her feet again and striking at the gorilla with the anchor. He took a vicious blow across the wrist and let go but the violent motion so upset the boat that it tipped suddenly and water slopped aboard.

"Letitia!" Andrew screamed. "Lean the other way! The other way!"

Martin fell forward beside Anne. His face hit the water but he managed to hold on and heave himself backwards. More water flowed over the side. Carmen fell heavily on top of him as she pushed at the trawler and that tipped the boat even more. Martin was sure they would capsize and a sense of sickening failure swirled in his guts.

But Andrew had acted. He had grabbed Letitia and thrown her and himself the other way. The boat righted itself but rocked alarmingly. Martin blinked the stinging salt water from his eyes and squirmed desperately to get up. But he couldn't. Only when Carmen's weight was removed from his back could he do so.

With a gasp he slid back into the centre of the boat, noting that Anne and Carmen were still half-overboard. He grabbed at Anne and hauled so that she was dragged back aboard. Martin was dimly aware that in the process her shirt was being snagged but the situation was so desperate that he had no time for any concern over a few bumps and bruises.

"Go Andrew. Get us out of here," he shouted.

Andrew nodded and opened the throttle while Martin grabbed at Carmen and hauled with all his might. She came slithering back aboard, all spluttering and dripping. In the process she let go of the anchor. But she was back aboard.

Martin looked up as the boat began to move. He noted that they were just out of arms reach of the men on the trawler. But then he saw an enraged Silver, blood streaming down his face and his mouth open as he shrieked curses and obscenities. To Martin's dismay he saw Silver lift a gaff hook, a sharp pointed pole with a curved hook near the end for snagging game fish and hauling them aboard.

Silver's lone eye blazed hate and fury as he raised the gaff hook. Martin stared at it in horror and terror flooded through him. In an instinctive attempt to save himself he raised his hands to try to fend off the coming blow. Silver threw the gaff hook with all his strength and Martin doubted if he was quick enough. But his arms were just far enough up because the boat also suddenly shot forward.

The weapon missed. Its shaft struck Martin's forearm and the hook then grazed his leg before it buried its head in the bottom of the aluminium boat with an audible *thunk!*.

Missed! Martin thought as he stared at the gaff hook in almost stunned horror. *He tried to kill me!* he thought, his mind still trying to come to grips with the stunning reality of the situation.

His eyes met Silver's lone eye and again the hate in it caused him to feel sick with apprehension. Then Silver shook his fist and screamed: "Bastards! I'll get youse!" With that he turned and ran back into the wheelhouse.

Still half paralysed with fear and disbelief Martin watched him go. *They will be after us now,* Martin thought.

By now Andrew had the throttle wide open and the boat was moving fast. It shot past the bow of the stationary trawler and as it did Martin looked to his right to check where the murderers were. To his horror they were just there, heading to cross close under the trawler's stern.

He saw the murderers look at them and as he did Corey pointed at them and bent down to pick up his shotgun. But they were too close to the trawler and vanished behind it before they could turn or before he could get the gun.

Martin looked frantically around seeking salvation. *Where can we go?* he wondered.

Chapter 5

WHERE?

For a few heartbeats panic blinded Martin and fuddled his brain. *We must run! But where to?*

Then the adrenalin pumped again and he blinked and wiped sweat from his face and looked around. All around most of the horizon was nothing but open sea. The other direction was the flat line of the land but it looked a long way away. Even so Andrew turned towards it. Martin agreed.

No point in heading out into empty sea, he thought.

Away from the trawler and the murderers was the first obvious answer. A glance showed Andrew looking grimly back, his left hand gripping the throttle at full. At that moment the boat was racing almost directly away from the trawler.

Martin's mind now shifted into top gear and he did instant calculations of angles and distances. "A bit more to the right… I mean to starboard Andrew," he called.

That will keep us hidden from the murderers for a few more seconds, he thought. And every second looked like it would count!

Then the murderer's boat shot into view around the starboard side of the trawler. As it rounded the stern it turned and set off after them. Martin felt his bowels go queasy and a spasm of terror coursed through him. Even as he looked back he saw that the killer Corey was lifting up his shotgun to aim it at them.

Can he hit us at that range? Martin wondered, estimating the distance at about a hundred metres.

To his eyes the barrels of the shotgun were aimed directly at him. The urge to duck, to thrown himself flat in the bottom of the boat, was added to the physical reaction of trembling and on liquid bowels.

"Get down! Duck!" he shouted.

But he did not move himself. Nor did Andrew, who just hunched a bit lower. Carmen, Anne and Letitia all bent lower and as they did Martin saw a puff of smoke billow from the shotgun. Martin felt his body tense and he cringed in anticipation. But apart from one *ting!* somewhere near the back of the boat and a sudden flurry of small splashes twenty metres back none of the shot reached him.

A second puff of smoke followed and again there was a burst of spray and disturbed water.

Out of range, Martin thought. Then he watched in a mixture of relief and dismay as Corey began reloading the gun. *How long can we keep this up?* he wondered.

At that moment a vicious *crack!* close to his head made him really flinch. *What was that?* he wondered. Then his eyes focused on the front of the trawler and he saw a man there with his right elbow poking out almost at right angles and his head hunched down and realized he was looking at a person aiming a rifle.

Long John Silver… and he's got a rifle! he thought.

With that the fear flooded back in. Martin had done just enough training and shooting as a navy cadet to know that rifles were much more accurate than shotguns and that they had a much longer range.

A kilometre of more, depending on the type, he thought.

Wondering how far they were from the trawler he studied it for a second and then literally jumped as another bullet snapped by close to his head with a vicious crack.

"Oh shit!" he cried as fear washed through him. Now he sat down and hunched in a trembling ball, his flesh crawling in anticipation of the bullet strike.

We are only about 300 metres away, he decided, normal shooting range at the rifle range, and the trawler was also following them.

A third shot followed. This time it struck the water behind them and then whacked into the transom. Andrew cried out in fright. Martin looked at him and yelled, "Are you alright?"

Andrew nodded but looked very pale, his freckles standing out clearly. "A .225 of something like that," he commented.

Martin nodded. He did not know enough about guns to comment and as Andrew had qualified as a Quartermaster Gunner he accepted his opinion. He crouched, shivering in fear and waiting for the next shot.

Andrew suddenly slewed the boat to port and his judgement was impeccable. Just as he did a bullet struck the water right where they would have been and a spurt of spray shot up.

Good! Martin thought. But in his heart he doubted that they could keep dodging for long. *Not long enough to save us all,* he thought.

Andrew at once swung the boat the other way and then instantly pushed the tiller hard back over and turned them to port. The double bluff worked and another bullet went skittering harmlessly over the oily flat surface of the sea until it plunged in.

Martin looked back and saw that the rifle shooting had caused them at least one small advantage. The murderer's boat had been forced to also swerve out of the line of fire. For a moment Martin gave a mirthless grin as he noted Corey waving his fist and shouting back at the trawler.

Suddenly the murderer's boat swung around and headed back towards the trawler. Hope surged in Martin.

Have they given up? he wondered.

But he did not dare voice the thought. It was short lived anyway as he watched the boat close the trawler, then swing round to run parallel and close alongside. There was a shouted conversation and then Silver passed the rifle down to Corey.

Andrew, who had been watching this, turned to them. "Oh bloody hell, they mean business now," he croaked. "That mongrel has a rifle now, as well as a shotgun."

Martin saw a small black object thrown down into the murderer's boat and then it sheered clear of the trawler and resumed the pursuit.

But we have gained another two hundred metres at least, Martin thought, judging by the size of the trawler. Through eyes that were blurry from hyperventilating he watched Corey raise the rifle and aim it.

Andrew was watching as well and he swung the boat to starboard but just a fraction to late. Another bullet whacked into the stern and this time penetrated. It thudded into the bottom and then into Anne's bag. It struck so hard the bag hit her leg and she cried out in fright and began to whimper.

"Are you alright Anne?" Martin asked.

Anne looked at her trouser leg and rubbed it and then nodded. "Yes. Just a bump," she replied, her voice quavering with fear.

Martin shook his head. *This can't go on,* he thought. *There are too many of us crowded into this boat. We make too compact a target.*

Again, Andrew looked back. Then he turned to Martin. "Are we getting away?" he asked.

"Not sure," Martin answered, shaking his head.

"That's not very nautical!" Andrew replied, managing a grin.

"I don't feel very nautical!" Martin snapped, fear giving his voice an edge.

Andrew held up one hand with the index finger vertical. "Use your finger or a pencil, measure the height to the trawler's mast," he instructed.

Martin knew what he meant. He had read it in stories about the old sailing ships. *If I hold the finger the same distance from my eyes each time the trawler will look higher or lower against it, depending on whether they are catching up or not.* So he held out his hand and lined his finger up, squinting with his right eye to measure the height of the trawler's mast against it.

"Getting away, from the trawler anyway," Martin said. He had no doubt. The trawler looked smaller with every minute. But not so the pursuing small boat. It appeared to be slowly catching up.

Another bullet snapped past fearfully close and Martin trembled but held his pose. *They probably think I am giving them the finger,* he thought. That at least caused him a sardonic grin, until another bullet cracked past so close his facial expression instantly changed to shock.

"Bloody hell!" he croaked.

Anne cringed, looking terrified. "Where are we going?" she cried.

Andrew answered. "Away from them."

"Where's that?" she asked, looking wildly around the horizon.

At that Andrew pointed directly ahead. "Wherever that is. We can't deviate much of they will catch us by cutting across the chord," he explained.

"Cord?" Letitia asked looking bewildered. "What cord?"

"The chord of the circle; a line from one edge to the other that doesn't go through the centre," Andrew replied, shaking his head as he did.

"What do you mean?" Letitia asked.

"If we turn to the right or left they will do the same but for them the distance will be shorter," Andrew explained.

"Will it?" Letitia asked, frowning and making Martin feel embarrassed.

He shook his head. "Yes it is. Now shut up and keep down!" he snapped, disgusted by the sight of his sister's mud-smeared semi-nude form. To avoid her angry look he turned and studied the view ahead. To port he could just make out a tiny white object jutting above the horizon.

Cape Bowling Green lighthouse, he decided.

The long, narrow sand spit that was the actual cape was out of sight over the curve of the earth but a few trees stuck up to mark a line of hazy dots amid the heat shimmer.

The distant trees extended off to his left front to where they were lost in the haze. Beyond them loomed the shape of a distant mountain, blue and almost lost in the haze as well. It looked like a cardboard cut-out.

Cape Upstart, Martin told himself. He knew it was at least 50 or 60 kilometres away on the other side of the Burdekin River delta and Upstart Bay.

Ahead a few lumps and dots in the shimmer indicated trees on the shoreline of Bowling Green Bay as it curved around to the west. In the far distance a few hills and mountains looked in the haze but Martin was quite unable to name them.

But he could name the big range of mountains that stood up from the plain to his right. *That is Mt Elliott,* he told himself. It was a very obvious range, standing up abruptly from the coastal plain and isolated from any other high ground.

The swamps they had fled from were just visible between Mt Elliott and the sea and then there was a long, low, tree-covered strip of land that ended in the rugged Cape Cleveland Range to his right rear.

No chance of going back that way, he decided.

But what was ahead of them? Martin screwed his face up as he concentrated on trying to bring the chart to mind. But all he could remember was that the whole southern shore of Bowling Green Bay was many kilometres of sand bars, mudflats, mangrove swamp and lots of creeks and inlets. It was not very promising. There were a couple of small fishing hamlets but he did not know their names or which creek they might be on.

This is not looking very hopeful, he thought, biting his lip with anxiety as he did.

He glanced back to check on their pursuers and was surprised to see that the trawler was now quite distant, several kilometres away in fact. It was still following them but was obviously much slower. And the murderer's boat had not closed the distance. That was something.

As long as we don't run out fuel we might make it to shore, he thought. But what then?

Martin looked around and then down, again curling his lip in disgust at the sight of his sister. Then he spied the chart amid the swill and mud in the bottom of the boat. The chart was in a plastic bag but this had come open at the top during the struggle and the chart was now soaked but it was still legible. Bending quickly Martin grabbed it.

As he did there was a vicious *crack!* just above him and he felt a wash of hot and cold fear. *A bullet! That would have hit me if I'd been standing,* he thought.

For a few seconds sheer terror held him still, shaking and his senses swirling in a sour bile of fear. Then he shook his head and bent to study the chart.

Anne interrupted him by calling anxiously, "There's a lot of water in the boat!"

There was too. Martin looked at it and felt another swirl of anxiety. His eyes focused on where the gaff hook was embedded in the bottom. Water was bubbling in and as the gaff hook moved it even spouted up like a small fountain.

Letitia reached out and grasped the gaff hook but Carmen grabbed her arm. "Don't pull it out! It is plugging the hole. Start looking for something to bale with."

As the girls bent to do this Andrew called, "And look for any bullet holes that might be letting water in and plug them."

Martin swept his gaze around the bottom and sides of the boat but there was so much muddy water and so many floating objects that no bullet hole was visible to him.

But we've taken on a lot of water, he thought. He raised his eyes to look ahead as the ghastly concept of the boat sinking entered his consciousness.

Bloody hell! We are still several kilometres from land, he thought.

But then his eyes noted more trees springing into view on the horizon. They were tiny dark blobs half lost in the heat haze but they indicated land. *And there are some sand dunes,* Martin noted with relief. They indicated a beach rather than mangroves.

Another glance behind showed that the murderer's boat was still following but had not managed to close the distance. Martin now focused on the chart, trying to orientate it by the main features.

We need to reach civilization, he thought.

His gaze noted several small settlements or 'localities'. The nearest was named Mud Crab Landing and there was also a place called Jerona further to the west.

Probably just fishermen's huts but there should be people there on the weekend, he decided hopefully.

Carmen looked up from bailing with her hands. "Where are we going?" she asked, indicating the chart.

Martin shrugged and spread his hands, the chart still gripped in his left. "Not sure. If I had a compass…"

Carmen nodded her understanding and so did Andrew. He added, "You could take bearings on things and work out exactly where we are."

"How would that help?" Anne asked, wiping strands of wet hair from her face.

Martin answered. "If we know where we are we can work out a compass bearing to steer to get to where we want to go," he explained.

"After taking any magnetic variation into account," Andrew said.

"And magnetic deviation," Carmen added.

"Deviation?" Anne said in an uncertain tone.

Carmen saw the look on her face and managed a smile. "Deviation is the amount a magnetic compass is pulled of line by any metal objects in a ship. You have to know what it is to compensate. If you… Aaah!"

The last was wrung from her as a bullet snapped past. To Martin's horror he saw Carmen suddenly clutch at her left upper arm and then drop down.

"Carmen! Are you alright?" he shouted.

"Hit… Hit in the arm!" she replied through clenched teeth.

Andrew swore but did not leave the tiller. Instead he set the boat weaving slightly.

"Anne, see if she is alright!" he called.

Martin and Anne both dropped down and grabbed hold of Carmen. To Martin's dismay he saw bright red blood ooze between Carmen's fingers and then trickle down her upper arm. Firmly but gently he prised her fingers away from the wound and stared at it. The bullet had struck the outside of the muscle. It had sliced across, half cauterizing and half tearing its way through the flesh.

"Could have been worse," he said between gritted teeth, his emotions made worse by seeing the blood well up to flood the cavity. "Hold her arm tightly just here Anne," he instructed. Anne, looking very pale but determined, did as she was told, taking a firm grip around the arm just above the wound.

Martin did not hesitate. He scooped up some seawater and drenched the wound. The blood instantly diluted and was washed away, to almost as quickly be replaced. But it was long enough to give Martin another look at the injury.

Nothing too serious, he thought with relief.

"No major blood vessel torn and the bone isn't broken," he called, mostly for Andrew's benefit.

"First Aid kit," Anne yelled to Letitia. But she had seen the need and was already opening the small locker under the bow to extract it.

Anne then said, "I will do the bandaging. You hold her arm Martin."

Martin didn't argue and took a firm grip, giving a shaking Carmen a comforting smile as he did. Anne quickly extracted some antiseptic and wiped it in the wound, causing Carmen to cry out as the liquid stung the exposed nerve ends. Then Anne quickly added a pad before deftly bandaging the arm.

"There, good as new," she said, as she patted Carmen's shoulder.

Martin let go and helped Carmen to sit with her back against the thwart. As he knelt to do this he was reminded of the water now sloshing around the bottom of the boat.

"Get on with bailing you... aargh!"

Suddenly he was flung on his back, his shirt and shorts being instantly soaked. Even as he struggled to get up Martin knew what had happened. Andrew's yell confirmed it.

"We've run aground! Quick, out of the boat and push!" he shouted.

With a convulsive heave fuelled by extreme fear Martin hurled himself over the side to splash in knee deep water. The bottom was sand and he was able to quickly scrabble to his feet. By then the others were out of the boat, even Carmen. They grabbed it and started running, casting fearful glances back as they did.

Crack! Crack!

Two more bullets snapped past, just missing Martin and actually passing between him and Anne. *He means to kill us alright,* Martin told himself, his whole being now quivering with terror. And the murderer's boat was catching up with horrifying speed!

They ran into deeper water and leapt aboard. "Lie down!" Martin ordered, pushing Anne flat as she scrambled in. It was lucky he did as another bullet cracked past and he was sure it would have hit her if he hadn't.

Andrew opened the throttle and the boat surged into motion again. An anxious glance astern showed Martin that the murderer's boat had halved the distance.

Bloody hell, they are close now! he thought.

The distance had narrowed so much that Martin could make out the facial expressions on the men. He saw Corey grin as he reloaded the rifle. That done Corey raised it and aimed directly at Martin. The distance was now so close, no more than 100 metres, that Martin was sure the game was up.

I am dead this time, Martin thought.

A feeling of being paralysed or mesmerized seemed to grip him but he shook his head violently and hunched lower.

The rifle muzzle did not appear to waver. It was still aimed directly at him. Martin swallowed and felt his flesh cringe in anticipation of the blow.

Then Martin stared in astonishment. Corey was rolling head over heels on the bows of the boat, his arms and legs flying out. Martin distinctly saw the rifle go flying in the air. Corey vanished into the sea ahead of his boat, a splash marking his fall.

"They've run aground! They've run aground too!" Andrew cried, his voice a hoarse croak.

We have a chance! Martin thought.

But again he did not voice it. Instead he looked ahead and tried to decide which way to go. The distant trees still looked a long way off and the sea in between was littered with sand banks.

Chapter 6

UP THE CREEK!

Martin shielded his eyes from the glare and squinted to try to see better. But most of the low-lying coast ahead was still hidden by the shimmer of the heat haze and the reflection of the afternoon sun did not help. He licked dry lips and knew he was very dehydrated.

And sunburnt, he added.

That thought caused him to glance at Letitia. She was kneeling in the slush and bailing with her hands. Her body was streaked with mud and at every scoop her breasts wobbled and jiggled so much that Martin bushed and looked away.

Once more he pushed unkind names out of his consciousness and turned to look back. The murderer's boat looked to be 200 metres behind and the men were splashing about in the water. It looked as though one was pushing the boat while the other was bending over groping for the rifle.

I hope they can't find it, Martin thought.

But even as he did he saw Corey straighten up, the rifle in his right hand. *Oh shit! That's bad news,* Martin thought.

Corey tossed the rifle into the boat and moved to help his crony shove the boat across the shallows. Faster than Martin feared possible he saw the two men scramble into the boat and then the white creamy curves of a bow wave sprang up.

"Here they come again," he said as he bent to help with the bailing.

Andrew nodded and kept glancing back but then said, "Don't you bail Martin. Stand up and try to pick the best course. If we run on another mud bank it will be the end of us."

Martin agreed to so he stood up and braced himself. Then he shielded his eyes with his hand from the fierce glare of the afternoon sun and tried to detect the shallow water amid the ripples and small waves that were springing up.

"The tide is still going out isn't it?" he asked.

Andrew nodded. "Yes. Low water is about 1830 this evening."

A glance at his watch and a quick mental calculation caused Martin to groan inwardly. *That is nearly three hours away.* It seemed an awful long time. *And it will be even longer until it gets dark.* That wouldn't be until about 1930hrs at this time of year.

Can we keep ahead of the men for that long?' he wondered.

There was nothing for it but to try. For the next ten minutes, the boats roared across the sea without the slightest deviation of course. As they did, Martin noted that Corey appeared to be cleaning the rifle.

He will start shooting at us again soon, he deduced.

The only good thing was that they had gained at least 200 metres when the men ran aground. But they looked to be slowly clawing that lead back.

Then a pattern of small ripples drew Martin's attention and he realized it was caused by the gentle swell breaking on submerged sand bars. Just in time he directed Andrew to starboard. As it was, they scraped the bottom but were able to drag clear and continue on.

But from then on it got worse. Every minute or so they had to make another detour, weaving around the sand bars. For the pursuers it was easier. They could follow and even take short cuts and Martin's hopes began to sink as he saw the following boat creep slowly closer.

They are catching up, he fretted.

That made him look ahead. The whole of the coastline had now emerged from the heat shimmer and it just looked to be one long line of grey-blue trees interspersed with short patches of white that he knew were sand dunes at the back of small beaches. He preferred landing on sand but the nearest beach was some distance to port.

That is no good. If we turn, they will cut the corner and close the distance, he thought unhappily. The murderer's boat already looked to be well within rifle range again.

Exposed patches of muddy black sand began to appear and Martin noted that the whole of the sea between him and the shore looked to be a maze of such sandbanks.

And they are getting bigger by the minute as the tide goes out, he thought gloomily.

But that also made the deeper channels more obvious and Martin directed Andrew to steer the boat into one that looked as though it led all the way to the now fast approaching wall of mangroves. With the decreasing distance the foliage had now changed colour and was more nearly its real dull, dark green.

Looks like we have to take to the mangroves, he thought.

Once again Martin looked in all directions in the hope of seeing another boat or something. But all he noted was that the Cape Bowling Green lighthouse had sunk below the horizon and that the mountains of Cape Cleveland were now a misty blue from distance.

The other things that caught his attention, though briefly, were the state of the sea and sky. The sea still had a millpond look as there wasn't a breath of wind. The sky was still clear and brassy, and the glare made him squint and look away.

Then the immediate peril of the murderers returned to claim his attention when a sharp *snap!* near his ear made him flinch.

Then a sound like a sharp handclap told him what it was. *Corey is shooting again,* he thought as the fear welled up to almost paralyse him.

Once again, he turned to look at the mangroves. *Will we make it time?* he wondered.

Then he shuddered. He had been pushing to one side the concern about what they would do when they reached land, but now he forced himself to consider it.

Those men will follow us for sure. They can't possibly let us escape now, he thought. It was a sickening prospect and he felt physically ill but he made himself think ahead. *Do we split up and hope some of us escape or do we stay together?* he wondered.

A glance at his sister made him twist his lips. She was still bailing but was shivering and sobbing as she did.

I can't leave her, he thought. So how to escape?

And the decision was close upon him as the boat scraped across another sand bar. Andrew steered it into another deep channel which led straight to a tiny gap in the wall of mangroves. These were close now, less than a kilometre, and Martin scanned the trees to try to detect the best spot.

This became quickly obvious. It was where the deep channel came from. The channel wound its way through dozens of large dry sand bars. To try another route would obviously be folly. To run aground out in the open would be the end.

Crack!

"That was close!" Martin cried, flinching and ducking.

Andrew slewed the boat as much as he dared in the channel, but now he had sand bars close on either side so there was little room to manoeuvre.

"Which way?' he called.

A gap in the wall of mangroves was now opening up ahead of them and Martin pointed to it. "Up that creek," he replied.

Letitia looked up and wiped mud and water from her tear-stained face. "Where are we going?" she croaked.

"In there," Martin replied, grimacing at the sight of his sister's bobbling breasts. The sight was so disturbing he snapped at her. "Keep bailing! The water makes the boat heavy and slows it down."

Letitia nodded and bent to continue bailing. Martin glanced back and bit his lip. It was going to be very close! The murderers were now less than 300 metres behind.

By this time the boat was closing the land fast. They had to detour to starboard to get around the end of a large sand bank and then the channel swung sharply that way. That was bad news because it meant that the murderer's course would be only a hundred metres away on the other side of the sandbar, and it wasn't high enough to shelter them from view!

Andrew studied the problem and eyed the rapidly approaching murderers. Their faces were now plainly visible again and Martin saw Corey grin just before he raised the rifle again.

"Down!" he warned.

They were just in time. The bullet snapped past close between Martin and Letitia. By then they were so close that he heard Corey swear in annoyance. A second shot followed. It struck the water right beside the boat's starboard side and Martin distinctly heard a *ting!* as it ricocheted and then struck the hull. For a moment his terrified gaze darted to and fro seeking the place where the bullet had struck but nothing was visible.

Then they were past. The murderer's shouted angrily as they went by on the opposite course, but Corey did not fire again. Martin turned to look ahead.

The deep channel ran straight for several hundred metres, passing between two walls of mangroves and then vanishing from sight at a left-hand bend.

We have to get around that bend, he thought, desperation gnawing at his stomach like hungry rats. A glance showed that the mangroves here were still half awash, their feet in the muddy water.

Then they were racing along in calm, deep green water between two walls of mangroves. These offered no breaks and Martin saw that the channel was slowly but definitely getting narrower. A glance behind showed that the murderers were just rounding the end of the last sand bank. He had hoped to get out of sight but now could only chew his lip and pray.

Looking at the mangroves depressed him as well. True it was land, of a sort, and true they offered cover. *But it will be hard, slow going getting through all those exposed roots that are sticking up,* he thought. *And the mud will slow us down and we will leave tracks that even an idiot could follow.*

But there seemed to be no choice, so they kept on, the creek slowly growing narrower as it curved gently to the left. Martin glanced back and felt a twinge of hope. The murderers were out of sight around the bend!

Suddenly the mangroves ended on the right and he felt a real surge of hope. But this died even as he looked at the open country coming into view. The outside of the bend was a steep, muddy bank nearly a metre and a half high but that wasn't what caused his hopes to plummet. They could climb the bank easily enough but beyond it was a vast, flat saltpan. Dry salt crystals on its surface glittered in the sun and reflected a glare so bright he had to squint.

Andrew called to him even as he kept steering the boat to port, parallel with the bank and only 10 metres from it. "What about here?"

Martin realized that he was the only one who could see over the bank as all the others were crouched or sitting while he was standing. Shaking his head, he replied: "No good! It is a mudflat for a kilometre or so. We will just be sitting ducks if we try to run across it. There is no cover at all."

Andrew nodded. "Keep going then," he replied, turning his attention to the curving stream ahead.

Letitia looked up and began to wail. "Oh, I can't do this anymore! I can't!"

"You must," Martin replied. "Those men will murder us for sure and they will do horrible things to you before they do."

Martin felt sure that Corey was that sort of man. He saw Anne blanch while Carmen bit her lip and nodded agreement. They all resumed bailing, their breath coming in gasps.

The creek continued to curve to the left until they were heading back in almost the opposite direction to what they had come in on. The mud flat on the right ended and became mangroves again.

I hope we aren't just heading back out to another mouth of this creek, Martin thought anxiously.

Then he let out a gasp of horror. This was joined by squeals of dismay and terror from Carmen and Letitia. Only 50 metres ahead a large crocodile, at least 4 metres in length, was slithering down the bank. As the boat swept towards it the reptile launched itself into the water, its tail swishing to and fro and its legs going at what looked like incredible speed.

There was a splash and the croc vanished from sight, directly in their path!

Andrew swore and swung the tiller, but they were so close and it had happened so fast that they could not avoid the spot. Heart in mouth Martin braced, his eyes scanning the water for a sign of the creature. But then they were in the disturbed water and a moment later they were through and roaring on along the deep, calm creek.

Gasping for breath with fright Martin shook his head and looked back. There was still no sign of the croc. Andrew glanced back as well and then shook his head. "I think we just scared him," he commented.

"I think he just scared us!" Andrew replied. Martin gave a sickly grin and then he focused his gaze ahead.

Anne leaned out to look back. "I hope it attacks those horrible men," she said.

It was a nice thought, but Martin did not count on it. *It will be deep now and wondering what is going on,* he reasoned.

Then another squeal of terror from Letitia caused him to jerk his head round. Ahead of them, 50 metres to port, another crocodile was slithering down off the bank into the water. This one was only 2 or 3 metres long but it was still a saurian, *crocodilius porosis*, the genuine man-eating salt water croc. Martin's heart hammered with anxiety again.

But once more the croc vanished under water and the boat swept past the spot and on. Andrew shook his head. "Bloody hell! As if it wasn't dangerous enough," he commented.

"We are up the creek alright," Andrew added grimly.

The creek had straightened out again and ran for about half a kilometre northeast. That was not what Martin had hoped for, but he did try to locate it on the chart. As he moved his finger across the wet plastic cover he muttered and found his hands were shaking.

Is it this one? he wondered.

There was a large creek marked about 5 kilometres west of the locality named Mud Crab Landing and to his dismay it looked to be part of a real maze of creeks amid a huge area of mangroves and mud flats.

Then Carmen gasped and said, "Here they come."

Martin looked back and felt his chest tighten up again. The murderer's boat had swept into view around the bend and was now only about 200 metres behind.

They are catching up fast, he thought, the apprehension gripping his already nauseous stomach.

Both banks of the creek were nothing but mangroves, some areas dry but others still half submerged. A few tiny creeks led into the dark wilderness, but none was large enough to offer any hope of a hiding place, so Andrew kept the boat heading along the main stream.

Tension now really gripped Martin. He could see Corey watching them, the rifle half raised, and he sensed that the end, when it came would be sudden. Desperately he cast about for some plan that might give them a chance of survival.

"When we get ashore, we need to split up into two groups," he said. "That way at least some of us might get away."

Andrew and Carmen both agreed. It wasn't discussed but Martin understood that the brother and sister pairs would stay together and that Anne would go with one or the other. Letitia gave Martin a scared but thankful look.

They were near the end of the straight reach by then and the creek curved sharply to the right. As Andrew steered them around it the boat suddenly slewed and listed to port. To everyone's dismay a large quantity of water swilled across and splashed about on that side.

Bloody hell! We've taken on a lot more water, Martin thought.

Andrew called out. "Bail you lot! We are sinking."

They did, even Martin using his hands. He knelt and scooped for all he was worth, flinging the cold muddy water over the port side. A glance astern showed that they had gone out of sight of the murderers again. Hopefully he cast a glance at both banks.

No change, nothing but a wall of half flooded mangroves. And the creek had straightened out into a 200-metre straight reach and was even narrower. Now it was only about 25 metres wide.

Another croc, a small one, slid into the water and vanished in a swirl of ripples. But seeing it caused barely a palpitation. The real threat from the murderers was now too close and Martin was feeling very stressed and desperate. His mind cast about for anything he could use as a weapon or of some way to hide and catch Corey by surprise. But there was nothing of any real use.

But we can lighten the boat, Martin thought. That might help.' "Throw everything out," he ordered.

They did. Bags, fishing lines and tackle boxes were all cast into the water. Letitia even picked up the sodden towel and looked questioningly at him. "Yes, and that," Martin agreed. Her modesty was now totally irrelevant.

Letitia tossed the muddy towel overboard and then picked up a plastic water bottle. "Not that! Drink the water first," Martin cried.

Letitia did so. Martin grabbed another bottle. It was only half full and he drained it in one guzzling gulp. The others copied his example and more bottles were cast over the side to bob on the surface. Out of the corner of his eye Martin noted another big crocodile splash into the water.

The murderer's boat roared into view around the bend. To Martin's dismay he saw that it was obviously catching them up.

This is going to be close! he thought grimly. Then he saw Corey kneel and brace himself to aim the rifle. The distance was now only 150 metres.

"Get ready to duck," he called.

At that moment he saw Corey's head turn to look back and the murderers' boat slewed sideways. Its engine noise suddenly sounded ragged and then it cut out.

"What happened?" Anne asked as they all looked back.

Hope surged in Martin's chest. "Their engine has broken down," he suggested.

But then he saw the other man, Joel, heave the motor up so that the propeller was clear of the water. The distance was rapidly opening out again, but Martin distinctly noted a dark blob at the end of their propeller shaft. Joel turned and reached back at it.

Carmen let out a little whoop. "Yippee! They have something wrapped around their propeller."

Andrew looked and nodded. "Letitia's towel maybe?" he suggested.

Martin also nodded. "Or a shirt or something," he added, remembering the fishing lines and other odd items they had just cast over the side.

Within ten seconds they gained another hundred metres. *Maybe we have a chance,* Martin thought.

But even as he did, he saw Joel tug the item free and fling it away. The motor was lowered back into the water and he started it again. The sound of that motor starting dashed Martin's hopes again and he bit his lip.

Letitia wailed. "Oh, here they come!"

As they rounded another bend to the right Martin had a glimpse of a white bow wave spring up at the bows of the murderer's boat.

At least we gained a couple of hundred metres, he thought.

But the wash of warm seawater over his ankles made him look down and he saw that their own boat was now dragging very sluggishly along.

And the boat was sinking! Despite all of them bailing as hard as they could the water level was rising!

This can't go on much longer, Martin thought grimly.

Andrew obviously thought the same as he called, "We can't stay in the boat or she will sink in mid-stream. I am going to put us ashore at the next likely spot out of sight of the men."

Carmen looked back and nodded. "Do that," she agreed.

And they were at the next bend.

The moment of truth! Martin thought.

Chapter 7

BAD TO WORSE

"We are going to beach as soon as we are out of sight so get ready," Andrew ordered.

The boat swept around the bend and the murderer's boat vanished from view. Martin continued to bale, flinging the handfuls of water out in a desperate attempt to keep them going. The others also continued to fling out some of the muddy water that was now ankle deep. It was sloshing around the bottom of the boat and affecting its trim.

This can't last! Martin thought.

"Get ready!" Andrew called.

Martin turned to look and saw that a narrow muddy creek went off to the left. It was only 5 metres wide but looked deep.

"What about that?" he asked.

Andrew shook his head. "Wrong way and too narrow," he replied. Martin knew that he was right.

That creek looks like it heads back towards the sea, he thought.

Then the motor suddenly coughed. They all stared at it in horror and it coughed again and began to splutter. Martin glanced astern and noted that the murderers were still out of sight. He opened his mouth to tell Andrew to put them ashore but saw that he was already acting to do that. Even as the motor spluttered into silence the tiller was swung slightly to turn the boat to port and it slid up onto a sloping shelf of blue grey mud.

"A beach would have been better!" Letitia cried as she stared with distaste at the soft mud.

Martin agreed but there wasn't one. His sister's attitude at that moment just irritated him "Just get out and run!" he snapped. But she didn't. She just crouched there. "Go! Get out! Run!" he shouted.

Letitia stood and then hesitated, so Martin shoved her. She pitched forward over the side and landed face first in the mud with an enormous splat. By then Anne had jumped and she let out such a cry of dismay that Martin jerked his head around to look. To his horror he saw that she had sunk nearly to her waist in soft mud.

Uh oh! Bad mistake! he thought.

Knowing that the murderers were only seconds away he looked wildly around and then acted. The aerial roots of the mangroves were only a few metres away from the front of the boat.

If I dive flat, I should reach them, he thought. So he dived onto the mud in a slithering belly flop.

It didn't hurt but he knew at once it was going to be hard work. The mud was so soft it seemed to envelope him, even as he slid forward half buried in the quivering mass. The nearest root was nearly a metre away and seemed to fill his whole vision. Driven by desperation he scooped at the mud with his hands and elbows. It was just enough to maintain his forward momentum and he slid forward and was able to reach out and grasp a root. It was slippery and little too thick to grab securely but he managed to get a grip.

Wiping gobbets of mud from his face he looked back. "Letitia, grab my leg and climb up," he called.

Letitia was kneeling and scooping thick dollops of slick mud from her face. But she nodded and flung herself forward, reaching out as she did. She didn't quite make it but Anne was next to her, squirming desperately and she stopped for a moment to grabbed her arm. That didn't work as the mud was so slippery but Anne at once grabbed Letitia's hair and hauled her forward. Letitia screamed in pain, but her scrabbling hands caught Martin's feet and she latched on. Luckily his socks and gym boots gave enough grip and she began to claw her way up his leg, snatching desperately at his shorts. Martin at once reached down to help, also grabbing her hair.

Heaving with all his might he slid Letitia up past him until she could grab the mangrove roots. As soon as she had a grip on one Martin turned and reached back for Anne. She was easier. Not only was she lighter but she had more clothes he could grab, and he heaved her right up past him in one desperate movement.

Then he looked around to see how Andrew and Carmen were faring. To his relief both had followed his example and had dived so as to slide up the mud bank. They had already reached the mangroves and were scrabbling and slithering to get to their feet on the firmer mud among the tree roots.

Andrew grabbed Anne and pulled her in among the roots and then he reached for Letitia. Carmen scrambled over and reached down to help Martin as he hauled himself up among the roots. As he clawed his way to his feet, slipping at every movement Martin glanced back. As their own motor had now stopped the sound of the murderer's motor was plain to hear and growing rapidly louder.

"Quick! Into the forest! Here they come," he gasped. The terror surged in him so that everything became a frantic, heart-pumping blur.

Frantically they scrambled and slithered in among the mangroves. As they did Martin looked back to his left and saw the murderer's boat sweep into view and his heart leapt with fear.

"Go! Go!" he croaked.

But it was like a nightmare come true. Their feet sank to their ankles or knees in the soft mud and the thousands of aerial roots of the mangroves blocked and snagged and tripped at every step. But terror drove them and they crawled and stumbled frantically to get away.

And there was Corey, only 25 metres behind and already raising the rifle butt to his shoulder, his face a mask of savage satisfaction. The friends were only ten metres into the forest by then and still quite clearly visible.

"Get down! Crawl!" Martin shrieked, his voice breaking with fear. And down he went, his whole being quivering with anticipatory terror.

Now the roots were almost impenetrable, but fear fuelled them and they clawed and dragged themselves under and between them. As they did, Martin noted that no shots had been fired and through eyes, now stinging from salt and mud, he snatched a glance back over his shoulder.

We are out of sight! he noted. The mangroves were just high enough above the water level for the murderer's boat to be out of sight. *Dead ground the army cadets call it,* Martin thought as he continued to claw his way forward, hauling himself by his arms.

"Don't try to walk. Slide!" he called.

The others were all desperately struggling to make progress and through eyes that were streaming with tears as the mud stung them he saw that both Anne and Letitia were wide eyed with apparent panic. But at least they were still trying to get away.

Behind him Martin heard Corey call angrily; "Oh shit! Bloody hell!" That made him give a sardonic grin.

He has jumped into the mud, he thought.

A tiny flicker of hope grew. Another glance behind showed no sign of Corey or his crony Joel. And the mud was becoming firmer. Martin grabbed a tree trunk and hauled himself to his feet to look back. Sure enough, Corey was struggling in knee deep mud, squirming and trying to keep his balance as he did. Several times he slipped and he had to use the butt of the rifle to keep himself from falling right over. Then he did slip and pitched face forward into the mud, the rifle going splat as well.

If he had had any breath to spare, Martin would have cheered aloud but instead he blinked to clear his streaming, blurry eyes and looked to see what the other man was doing as Corey struggled to get to his feet.

The other man, Joel, was busy securing his boat to their boat and even as Martin watched he saw him reach down for the shotgun.

Oh no! Both of them, he thought, the fear flooding anew.

"Get up. It's firm enough. Get up and run!" Martin gasped.

The others did so and they began to scramble and clamber through the mangroves in a gasping, terrified group. All were sucking in great gups of air and Martin saw that they could not keep it up much longer. But there was no choice.

Staying alive depends on getting away, he thought, desperation lending him strength.

The mud had become darker, almost black and it was firmer. The types of mangroves also changed to a larger tree with buttress roots. As he scrambled over them Martin had a vague awareness of scuttling creatures fleeing to either side: crabs, mudskippers and so on.

Just beside Martin was his sister and he was dimly aware that she was presenting an amazing spectacle of mud-smeared bouncing and wobbling as she scrambled over obstacles.

Another glance behind sent a jet of fear through Martin. A flicker of colour indicated that Corey was now up on the edge of the mangroves.

"Stop you bloody kids!" Corey shouted.

"Keep going!" Martin and Carmen both cried simultaneously.

Crack! Thud!

A bullet slammed into a tree nearby but did not hit any of them. Martin heard Corey swear and then heard the crunch and crackle of vegetation being trampled and deadfall being broken as Corey started after them.

Oh bloody hell! He's only about fifty paces behind, Martin thought. *If we come to a clearing we are dead.*

With that in mind Martin blinked and squinted to see what lay ahead. To his dismay the glare of sunlight showed that there probably was a clearing not far ahead of them.

There was, and only another 50 paces. The friends burst out of the mangroves and came to a sobbing, confused standstill on a small mudflat about 10 metres wide and 50 long. The mud was mostly dry and light grey with small tufts of wiry salt water grass growing in clumps. But the real problem was that on the far side of the clearing was another mangrove creek. The water in this was only about 5 metres wide but it looked to be deep and was a turgid, muddy colour as it flowed swiftly by with the outgoing tide. Beyond the creek were a steep, slippery looking mud bank and another thick mangrove forest, the aerial roots forming a dense thicket all along the bank as far as they could see.

Even as Martin came to a gasping standstill his head jerked left and right, his eyes seeking the best escape route. Then he heard squeals from Anne and Carmen and a cry of sheer terror from his sister. Turning to look in the direction they were staring in Martin also let out an involuntary gasp.

Lying on a sloping bank not 10 metres to their left was the biggest crocodile Martin had ever seen. It was enormous, a monster reptile of horrifying proportions. And it had seen them. Even as the sheer size of the monster registered in Martin's mind, he saw it lift its head and start to swing its massive bulk around towards them.

"Run!" he cried, and they all did.

As one they turned and ran to the right, gasping and with the adrenalin spurting into their bloodstreams. Martin felt a stab of terror even worse than the fear of being shot as a glance behind showed the creature now half way round and with its huge jaws open. The sight of those rows of ugly yellow teeth set his legs going even faster.

But their haste was partly their undoing. In her terrified flight Letitia cannoned into Anne and both went tumbling on the mud. Martin swore but skidded to a stop and reached down to grab at his sister's arm. But that didn't work. The mud on her arm was so greasy that he could not get a good grip and he had to grab at her arm pits. She cried out and sobbed but scrambled to her feet, her eyes wide with terror. By then she was almost in a state of gibbering panic.

Carmen and Andrew had hauled Anne to her feet but then Letitia tripped again, on a mangrove root this time. With terror swamping his senses and making his vision blurry Martin grabbed at her again.

Crashing and crackling noises close behind caused Martin to glance over his left shoulder. It was Corey! The terror stabbed again, causing him to sob and hyperventilate.

Too late! Martin thought as he saw Corey dash out of the mangroves only 25 paces away, the rifle in his hand.

A dozen panicky thoughts flitted through Martin's mind: run, or fight? Or dive into the water? Or surrender and hope for mercy? *Run!* his instincts told him but the others were crowding at the far edge of the mangroves to help Anne up again. He saw their horrified gaze focused on the scene behind him and he turned to look, even as he ran.

Corey came to halt and yelled at them to stop then raised the rifle butt to his shoulder. Martin glanced back, noting Corey and behind him the advancing croc.

He hasn't seen the croc! he thought.

For the briefest moment he considered warning the man but then he clamped his mouth shut. As Corey aimed the rifle Martin felt a surge of terrors in his bowels and nearly voided himself.

He is going to kill us! he thought.

But suddenly Corey became aware of his danger. He swung his head away and looked over his left shoulder. Martin's gaze followed, like staring through a misty tunnel. The giant croc had come charging up the slope, jaws agape and Corey had obviously heard it.

The man swore and swung the rifle to aim at the croc. Martin felt his whole chest tighten up with dread.

He should run! he thought.

But Corey didn't. He stood his ground and fired. The shot obviously hit the huge beast as it gave a loud grunt and a violent twitch, its massive tail swinging to and fro. Where the shot hit it, Martin had no idea. He saw no bullet hole or blood, but it was instantly apparent that it had not killed the beast

Enraged, the crocodile came surging forward. Corey worked the bolt of the rifle, ejecting the spent cartridge. Then he tried to push the bolt forward in a desperate attempt to fire again. But the bolt would not close and Corey shouted obscenities and bent over in his struggle to force a new round into the breech.

Mud, Martin thought as he watched in mesmerized horror. At the same moment that the thought occurred to him it must have occurred to Corey. *He has left it too late to run,* he thought.

Corey tried to. He sprang sideways, but then tripped. He fell hard on the mud, his legs and arms jerking in a desperate scrabble to get up.

Too late!

Gripped by absolute horror Martin watched as the huge crocodile lunged forward. Chomp! In a flash its giant jaws had snapped shut on Corey's lower body. The sound of bones crunching was audible even above the man's shrill scream of terror.

Corey half rose but the crocodile just hauled him off his feet and began dragging him backwards towards the creek. In an extremity of pain and desperation Corey hammered at its head with the rifle and with his clenched fist. But the blows had no obvious effect on the armoured hide of the saurian.

Transfixed by the dreadful spectacle the friends stood and gaped. *How can we save him?* Martin wondered. Then, to his own dark doubt the thought crossed his mind that he did not want to.

Then he realized that the peril was far from over as 'Grizzly' Joel burst on the scene, shotgun in hand.

Joel skidded to a stop and also gaped in horror. Corey reached out a bloody, clawing hand for him, gasping.

"Save me! Aaargeee!"

Joel raised the gun then hesitated.

Corey gasped in agony again. "Shoot! Shoot!' he screamed before a convulsive bout of coughing wracked his body. To Martin's horror a froth of bright red blood gushed from Corey's mouth and nostrils. The crocodile now had him around the chest and lower body.

Joel did. He dashed over and aimed at the crocodile's head and fired. *Bang!*

The crocodile gave a great twitch and its jaws flew open. A mangled, blood-soaked Corey flopped out and lay writhing on the edge of the steep bank beside the creek.

The shot had obviously really hurt the crocodile as it gave a great roar of pain and anger, causing them all to take a pace back in fright. The creature swung its head back and forth and then scurried forward with astonishing speed in a direct attack on Joel.

Joel fired again and then flung the shotgun aside and fled. The croc powered after him, moving at a quite terrifying speed. Joel fled back into the mangroves just in time. Then he stumbled and they all gasped in horror. But he was up in an instant and managed to spring aside even as the huge jaws slammed shut.

Only the density of the mangroves at that point saved him from the determined rush of the monster. These baulked the croc in its rush and it had to change to clambering over and between the roots and trunks. Joel darted behind a tree, his face ashen with terror. Then he suddenly sprang upwards and Martin saw his sandshoes vanish among the lower branches and leaves of a large buttress rooted mangrove.

The man was just in time. The crocodile lunged after him among the tree trunks and roots, its great clawed feet scooping up gobbets of mud as it scrabbled for traction. But it was just too late. Joel had climbed up out of sight.

Only then did Martin realize they were wasting time. *We should be getting away from here,* he thought, *not watching this ghastly spectacle.*

But then he saw the crocodile's head swivel in their direction and its yellow eyes seemed to focus right on him. The monster was obviously enraged and half blinded by pain as it let out another fearsome bellow and then changed direction and headed for them.

"Run!" Carmen shouted.

"Climb!" Andrew yelled.

Near them were more of the large mangrove trees with buttress roots. Martin glanced over his shoulder at the rapidly approaching crocodile and again the terror kicked in.

"Up the tree!" he shouted.

But even as he did his mind was thinking: *Can I get up in time?*

Chapter 8

THE GIANT CROC

Anne fled to the right, Carmen and Andrew to the left. Letitia ran to the nearest big tree, a couple of paces ahead of Martin. The giant croc came bellowing after them, its massive tail scything to and fro and its body swaying in a way that would have been comical if it had not been so deadly.

When she reached the tree Letitia let out a wail of despair and began trying to climb the rough, reddish barked trunk. Martin arrived a second later and looked up. To his dismay the nearest branch was nearly another metre above Letitia's reaching hands.

"Jump! Jump!" he shrieked his voice cracking with fear as the croc came crashing and slithering towards them.

"I can't!" Letitia wailed.

But she tried. She gave a galvanic leap upwards and clawed at the rough bark. That put her muddy buttocks at the level of Martin's eyes and he had to consciously overcome his normal reluctance to look at his sister's near nakedness.

Another glance showed the croc only ten metres away and baulked by a few thin roots. The monster began clawing and thrashing at them and Martin saw several snap even in the few moments when he was looking. Letitia had managed to get a grip and was trying to lift herself up using her arms, but she lacked the strength and was merely jerking about.

I must get her up! Martin thought.

Desperation helped. He bent and grabbed at her thighs and tried to heave. But to his dismay she just slid down through his grip, the mud and sweat mingling to give her a greasy coating.

Frantic now to save her Martin knelt against the trunk. "Step up on my shoulders!" he shouted.

It took a moment for Letitia to understand, and even then her feet twice slipped as she tried. But then she got a foot up on his left shoulder and Martin at once forced his leg muscles into action and stood up, heaving her upwards.

It was almost enough. Letitia went upwards, screaming and scrabbling as she did. But then Martin could lift no higher. *I have to change my grip*, he thought, all mechanical advantage now lost and his strength fast failing.

Gasping with effort and fright he grabbed her right shoe and heaved again, changing his stance as he did. Up she went and then suddenly the weight came off.

Martin looked up and saw that she had managed to get a knee up onto the branch and was dragging herself up onto it with all her might, her left leg kicking and flailing as she did.

As she scrambled higher Martin glanced around to check where the croc was. At that moment Letitia's flailing left foot kicked him in the side of the head. His senses spun and he staggered and had to clutch at the tree trunk for support.

And there was the croc!

It was within arm's reach and lunging at him! With a desperate effort Martin jerked back and then felt himself trip and then slip backwards. A sickening sense of defeat swirled through him as he went down on the mud and roots.

Done for! he thought.

Then a terrible pain in his head made him cry out and he blinked as he felt his body being dragged and scratched. But through his stinging, blurred vision he could still see the croc. It was clawing up over the buttress roots near his feet and its jaws were opening and closing rapidly, the huge yellow fangs showing clearly in their long, deadly rows.

Even as his mind tried to work out what was going on— *The croc hasn't got me, what has?*—Martin saw a trouser leg and realized it was one of his friends.

It was Carmen and she had him by the hair. *That's why it hurts so much,* his mind informed him in a detached sort of way.

Everything now seemed to be moving in slow motion as he watched the croc slither over the roots. Its jaws yawned open again. Just in time Martin clambered and slithered to his feet and he was able to jump backwards.

He would have fallen again if Carmen had not kept her tight grip. Then another hand seized Martin by the shirt and he was hauled across more roots just as the croc lunged again. Through eyes now misted with terror and panic he saw the giant jaws snap shut within centimetres of his right foot.

Carmen and Andrew both had him. They half hauled, half pushed and he was shoved over another set of buttress roots to his left. Then he was trampled and knocked flat by both as they scrambled to get away from the croc.

They were just in time. Once again the massive jaws snapped shut with a sickening *chunk!*

Martin squirmed, writhed and scrabbled to get to his feet, oblivious to the mud that was being smeared and plastered all over him. Somehow, he got to his feet and he looked wildly around to try to pick the best way to go.

The croc was almost within arm's reach and it was trying to swing its head to get at him. But a tree trunk and some aerial roots blocked that. Likewise, the roots snagged and entangled the crocs clawed legs and stopped its twitching tail from coming around behind him to knock him of his feet.

The mongrel is jammed between two trees, Martin thought, his eyes taking in the massive bulk of the creature and also the movements and sounds that indicated the relative positions of his sister and friends.

Wanting urgently to re-join them he acted on impulse, dashing forward and taking a running jump. His right foot came down hard on the crocodile's back. As it did, he looked down and was amazed to note the beauty and intricacy of the patterns of scales in its thick hide. In places the mud had flaked off and patches of yellow and brown showed clearly through.

Moving at the speed he was his foot only rested on the croc's back for a moment, which was just as well as the action enraged the creature even more and it gave a massive twitch to try to get at him. But his left foot landed 3 metres beyond the croc and he was not tumbled over. Except that his foot sank into soft mud and he stumbled and felt a sudden sharp pain in his ankle.

The instinct of self-preservation was already working in overdrive and Martin's hands grabbed at trees and roots and he avoided a bad fall. Instead he stumbled and staggered along, aware that he was being scratched and his clothes snagged and torn by the vegetation.

Regaining his balance, he looked around to get his bearings and saw that the croc had jerked itself free and was now turning towards him, hissing and bellowing as it did. Its yellow eyes seemed to glisten and radiate malevolence, or would have except one looked closed.

Martin turned and fled as the giant crocodile again lumbered into scrabbling pursuit. He followed the muddy, frantically hurrying forms of Carmen and Andrew who had circled back past the croc as well. They dashed to a tree, which looked like the tree Letitia had gone up. It was, and there she was, reaching down. Andrew grabbed his sister under the arms and heaved her up, ignoring her protests. Letitia reached down and grabbed Carmen's shirt and hauled.

Carmen was a much more athletic person than her and quickly got a grip and swung herself up onto the branch.

"Come on Andrew! Martin lookout!"

Martin did. His ears and general awareness had kept him informed of the proximity of the giant croc as it thrashed around in the roots, its rage and bellowing making its presence obvious. To escape its next rush, he ran sideways to the next tree and sprang up. His hands both closed on the branch, but it bent under his weight.

Bugger! Made a bad choice then! he thought as the terror flooded through him.

The croc had turned and was clambering over the roots towards him. Desperation gave Martin strength and he swung and flicked himself upwards, getting his chest and then his stomach over the sagging branch. Just in time he jerked his feet upwards.

Snap!

Missed! But only just! The croc was right there, just below him. *Must get higher,* he thought as he wondered how high crocodiles could reach.

Anne was there, eyes wide with fright. She reached out and steadied Martin as he scrambled up, getting first his knees and then his boots on the branch. Then he reached higher and grabbed another branch and, just as the croc sprang up on its hind legs to bite at him, he swung his feet away and up.

The croc's lower jaw just scraped his left foot as he did and that sent such a spasm of icy fear through him that he propelled himself up onto the next branch without even knowing how he did it. Nor did he pause there as he could see the croc slithering around and getting ready to spring again. There were more branches above and Martin grabbed them and dragged himself upwards through the web of small branches, ignoring the scratching and ripping that resulted.

Once again he was just in time, the croc lunging up and getting its forelegs on the trunk so that it was able to brace itself and stand on its hind legs. To Martin's amazement and horror he saw that the monster's open mouth was only a few centimetres from his feet.

If it jumps it's got me, he thought.

Once again he sprang upwards, reaching out as he did to grab overhead branches. Next to him Anne was climbing with frantic jerks, sobbing and crying as she did. They were just in time. The croc did jump. But the branches blocked its spring and the tip of the snout just grazed Martin's ankle before he jerked it up and over another branch.

Even so the croc nearly got him as its massive weight caused the tree to jerk and sway so violently he lost his grip with his left hand and his left boot slid off the branch it was on. Only by a convulsive and desperate jerk did Martin regain a good grip.

The croc hissed and then lunged again. Martin saw it coming and tried to swing even higher. Then, to his absolute dismay, he heard a sharp *snap!* and felt the branch start to sag. He looked at it in horror and saw that it had indeed snapped. Frantically he reached across to another branch. It was no thicker, but he had no choice. As he swung across his body dropped half a metre.

The croc again snapped at him, just missing but its ugly great head was right there next to his feet. The rough leather of its hide scraped down the outside of his right calf sending a shaft of pure terror up through him. The sight of its jaws opening for another attack almost paralysed Martin. In desperation he swung himself, hanging by both arms. A swirl of very primeval emotions now gripped him as the great saurian again lunged upwards.

As it did Martin swung his feet apart and then, seeing an opportunity, slammed both boots back against the underside of the croc's lower jaw. The huge jaw snapped shut with a sort of slobbering crunch and the croc grunted, shook its head and slid back down.

Martin cried out with both fear and triumph before hauling himself higher. A wide-eyed Anne helped him up. "We can't go any higher. We are near the top of the tree," she said as he settled his foot into a fork beside her.

What she said was true. Martin looked around and noted that they were right up among the small branches and the whole tree was bending and swaying from their weight.

This is not good, he thought, looking desperately around as the crocodile slithered around below them. It was still looking up and appeared to be getting ready to spring again.

Then the croc launched itself up the trunk again. It just failed to reach them, but its lunge sent Martin's heart leaping into his mouth yet again, leaving it hammering there for what seemed like a very long time. And the crocodile did not just slide back down again but seemed to be trying either to get a foothold to climb up or to push the tree over.

The mangrove swung wildly and the top level shook so violently under the impact of the croc's weight that it was only by clinging grimly on that Martin and Anne were able to stay safe.

"Bloody hell!" Martin cried as the smaller branches whipped at his face and arms as the tree shook. Fear slithered in his belly as his mind considered how strong the roots might be.

They are only in mud. Can the croc push this tree over? he wondered. *The bloody thing must weigh a ton.*

For a full minute the croc hissed and pushed and its eyes glared at them. The mangrove shuddered and shook and Martin felt sure it was leaning more than it had been. By this time he was so scared he felt nauseous.

Can we get across to the tree the others are in? he wondered. It was only 5 metres away but looked to be a few metres higher and to have bigger branches and a thicker trunk. But the only branches they might use were much lower, down near the bottom, and well within the reach of the croc.

Andrew obviously thought the same as he called across. "Martin, try to get over here."

"We will. Anne, climb down to that branch there and try to step across while I distract this bloody reptile," Martin said.

Anne looked at the branch and then at him with wide, fear-filled eyes. "I can't!" she cried.

Carmen now joined in. "You can Anne. Look, I am here to help you."

She moved to stand on a thick branch that stuck out and crossed just above a horizontal branch a metre down from where they were.

The croc obviously saw the movement as it suddenly shifted the focus of its attacks to the other tree, roaring and shoving and lifting itself right up on its hind feet, its forepaws clawing at the trunk and branches as it tried to reach Carmen. She scuttled back to a higher level but that left them all wondering what to do.

The croc slid back down, snapping off some of the smaller branches lower down as it did. It then lay on the mud at the base of the tree, its eyes staring unwinkingly up at them. From time to time it opened its mouth slightly and let out a hiss.

Martin was able to settle himself more securely and as his hammering heart rate slowed he managed to resume thinking more clearly. He carefully studied the monster croc and now he noted several wounds in its hide and what could only be a trickle of blood coming from its side just behind the left front leg.

It's been hit alright, he thought. But would the wounds be fatal or even enough to make it sick and go away?

It was during that lull he first noticed the mosquitoes. Now he became very aware of them as they began to settle in swarms to bite his exposed flesh. Worse still they settled on his shirt and began stabbing their proboscis through the material into his back. Mostly this was in the area between the shoulder blades where he could not each them.

"Bloody mozzies!" he snapped, writhing and slapping at them. "How do they know to bite us on the back."

Andrew gave a short chuckle. "They probably go to mozzie school and learn human anatomy," he called back.

But they were all being bitten and as Anne scratched at her bare ankles she commented that she was also being bitten by sand flies. These were tiny black midges and while a few landed on Martin they did not seem to bother him. He had noticed this on other occasions and now could only shrug and be thankful.

Suddenly the croc raised its head and swung it to its right. Martin tensed and clung on tighter.

What has it seen? he wondered.

The croc lifted itself up onto its legs, its massive belly coming clear of the soft mud with a sucking, squelching sound. Then it turned and went scurrying off through the mangroves, crashing and crushing its way over the roots.

Where is it going in such a hurry? Martin wondered.

The croc almost vanished from view before the reason became clear. A cry of fear from over in that direction and the rustle of vegetation as someone went clambering hastily up through it told its own story.

Joel has tried to get away but the croc has chased him back up into the tree, Martin thought.

The friends looked at each other and Martin risked moving down a branch to get a better look. The croc was now 50 paces away and was looking up into the tree where Joel had taken refuge.

Is this our chance to get across to the other tree? he wondered.

Carmen thought so as she again edged down and out onto the big branch and gestured to Anne, all the while darting glances over her shoulder at the croc. Anne looked very pale and scared, but she nodded and carefully lowered herself down, half her focus also on the croc. A minute later she stood on the cross branch, her arms above her head holding another branch. Inch by inch she eased herself out along the branch until the one overhead bent so much she was in danger of falling backwards. Carmen moved out and held out her hand and Anne let go of the overhead branch and grasped it and hurried on across.

Despite their care the girls made some noise because the giant croc lifted its head to look in their direction. Martin watched it, his apprehension growing as he nerved himself to make the crossing. After a time, the croc lowered its head again and the monster then lay there on the mud with its mouth slightly open. Twenty metres beyond it lay the mangled remains of Corey. He was not moving and Martin wondered if he was dead.

Why doesn't that stupid croc just go and eat Corey and leave us alone, Martin thought peevishly as the itches, bites, scratches and after effects of fear all combined to irritate him.

Ten minutes went by and the croc made no move. Reluctantly Martin decided this was his chance. Very slowly so as not to rustle any leaves, he eased himself down the tree to the cross branch. Here he paused to study the croc. It had not moved and its eyes appeared to be closed.

Go now! Martin told himself.

Chapter 9

SCALY PET!

With his heart again hammering with fear Martin leaned down to peer through the foliage to get a better view of the croc. What he saw more clearly were the mangled and bloody remains of Corey. The sight was stomach churning and horrifying but Martin just felt glad.

He was the most dangerous, he thought.

The giant crocodile lay on the mud 50 metres away, its head tilted up so that it could look up into the tree Joel was taking refuge in.

It's not looking this way. I will move now, he told himself.

But it took a conscious effort of will to force his muscles to work. Carefully Martin took a grip with both hands on the branch above his head. Then he began edging out along the other branch, sliding one foot at a time. His weight caused both branches to bend a little and that made the leaves rustle slightly.

A glance showed the croc still lying on the mud, so Martin studied the branches. Now he had to transfer his weight to the ends of the branches coming from the other tree and they looked thinner and weaker. Reaching out he grabbed the next branch above his head and then shifted his other hand to also grab it. The branch swung down and back, sending spasms of alarm through Martin's already over-shocked nervous system.

As he swung back Martin used his stomach and thigh muscles to try to swing himself forward. In doing so the branches all shook but he managed to keep his balance and to shift his right hand along the next branch. Now the trickly bit, moving both feet.

Reaching across the gap with his right foot Martin felt for the branch to get a firm footing. As he glanced down to check his footing his boot slipped and he fell downwards and backwards again. A small cry and a gasp escaped him as he teetered and tried to haul himself back upright.

Then, to his horror, the new branch he was holding onto began to bend. Audible groans and crackling sounds came from it. Desperately, Martin tried to regain an upright stance but the branch bent even more and he had no choice but to move his left foot quickly across to the new branch below him. But the movement upset his balance and he fell backwards, clinging to the weakened branch with his hands. Adrenalin pumped, and as the foliage shook and rustled he glanced towards the crocodile. Aghast, he saw that it had turned its head to look in his direction.

Snap!

The branch suddenly gave way with a loud crack. Just in time Martin let got and threw himself sideways, his hands scrabbling for the bottom branch. He hit the branch side on but luckily managed to get his right arm hooked around it and his left leg over the top. Desperately twitching and scrabbling he got his left arm around the branch as well. Shocked and terrified he came to a jerking stop, hanging upside down from the branch like a sloth.

For a few moments all Martin could do was cling on until the wild swinging motion stopped. Out of the corner of his eye he was dimly aware that the mud was now not very far below him and that the branch he was clinging to was muddy and slippery.

The crocodile had never been far from the top of his awareness and Martin now turned his head to check what the monster was doing. To his horror he saw that he was hanging down below the bottom of the foliage and that he had a clear view of the creature. Which meant it had a clear view of him!

Even as he realized this he saw the croc raise itself on its legs. A moment later its huge tail and body switched around and it began charging towards him.

Absolute terror gave Martin strength and he heaved himself up and astride the branch. But his haste was almost his undoing because, just as he was congratulating himself on managing that feat, he became aware that in the process he had landed heavily on his testicles astride the branch.

Waves of nauseating agony lanced through Martin and he gasped in pain and terror. Dizziness and fear were added to the agony and he tried to force himself to get his legs up. Worse still he was having trouble keeping his balance and despite clinging tightly to the branch he felt himself sliding around so that he again hung underneath.

And there was the croc! Martin screamed and gasped then twitched himself away. The croc sprang up, jaws agape.

Done for! Martin thought.

Snap!

The massive jaws clamped shut, scraping his back and the teeth catching in his shirt. Martin found himself starring into the monster's eyes from only centimetres away.

But then the croc fell back down, a tooth snagged in Martin's shirt. This almost dragged him off the branch and he clung on desperately. Then the shirt tore and the tooth came free. As the croc landed on the mud with a huge splat Martin forced his overwrought body to push through the pain barrier. Franticly he reached up and began clawing his way back up onto the top of the branch. As he did the giant croc slithered around to try to get into position for another spring. The sight and sound of the monster inspired Martin to use every last ounce of energy to haul himself up.

Carmen was there, reaching out and shouting. "Get up Martin! Get up!"

"Can't... pain," Martin gasped.

Carmen reached down and grabbed the tattered remnants of his shirt and hauled. Andrew scuttled to the branch over his head and grabbed Martin's hair. Both lifted and heaved. They were just in time. The whole branch lurched upwards as the croc came springing up again. This time the jaws snapped shut right beside Martin's face and he felt the creature's scaly hide slide down his side and leg as it fell back. The branches had just blocked its lunge.

By now the agony was subsiding but Martin was still weak and disoriented. It took all his efforts to reach up and start climbing. By then Carmen was back up at the next level and Anne was grabbing at Martin's shirt. There were more ripping noises, so she shifted her grip and hauled again. Martin ignored the pain in his groin and the pain in his head and reached up to haul himself higher. Once again he was just in time and was just able to avoid another spring by the crocodile.

A few moments later he was higher still, clinging on with his boots only centimetres from the croc as it tried to climb up. Martin felt hot breath and spittle and could only sob and cling on while sitting astride the next branch as the croc shook the tree and then tried to push it over. For several minutes the enraged beast kept roaring and snapping but it was unable to claw its way upwards. The monster stood up on its hind legs and leaned up the trunk.

Then Andrew dropped down and as the croc made another lunge his arm went down very quickly and came up even faster. The croc let out a bellow and slid back down.

Carmen gaped in fright. "Andrew, what did you do" she cried.

"Stabbed him in the nose with my clasp knife," Andrew replied. "Come on Martin, get up. What's the matter?"

Despite his fear and shock Martin was reluctant to say what the problem was in front of the girls, but he also saw that some explanation was needed.

"N... nuts," he gasped. "Crushed me nuts."

Andrew grinned as he slid the claps knife back into his pocket. Martin noted that it was tied around his waist by a lanyard. Reaching out Andrew took his sleeve.

"Reminds me of a joke," he said. "But first let's get you up higher."

With some effort and a lot of scraped skin Martin managed to reach another branch up but then found his upward progress blocked by Letitia. But he was safe, at least for the moment. The croc tried a few more times but could not get higher and the tree was bigger and stronger than the one Martin had left and defied the croc's efforts to uproot it. The croc gave up after a few minutes and slid down to lie at the base. A trickle of blood was visible on its snout and it blinked from its good eye from time to time and hissed.

Slowly Martin's heart rate eased to normal and then he was assailed by waves of trembling. He shivered and shook so much that he had trouble hanging on and had to wedge himself into the fork.

Minutes passed slowly and the mosquitoes and sand flies resumed their attacks. Martin slapped and scratched and was hotly aware that Letitia was also being bitten all over her bare skin. She frequently slapped in underneath her legs and around her bum. It was all a bit much.

Serves her bloody right! Martin thought sourly. *She might wear more clothes in future.*

Carmen glanced up and pursed her lips but then said, "What do we do now?"

"We stay put until Martin's big pet moves on," Andrew answered.

"That might be hours!" Letitia cried.

Carmen nodded. "Could be," she agreed.

Martin shuddered and tried to make himself more comfortable. Partly this was to allow him to use both hands to slap at the mosquitoes and sand flies. These became a real plague and they all slapped and squirmed. Carmen suggested they team up to slap each other's backs so Martin climbed up beside his sister while Andrew, Carmen and Anne took turns hitting the insects on each other.

Letitia began to whimper. "Oh! I hate this!" she cried. "I want to go home!"

"Well you can't!" Martin snapped back.

"But I'm scared!" Letitia replied, tears beginning to course down her cheeks.

"We are all scared!" Martin snapped back. "Anyway, you are the one who wanted to see a crocodile! So enjoy it!"

"Oh Martin!" Letitia began.

Martin just scowled at her. "Sorry Sis. There's nothing we can do but wait," he said.

He was angry with her and all the little embarrassment over her continually flaunting herself and her alleged behaviours added fuel to his emotions.

Carmen spoke next. "Don't fight you two. We have enough problems without that," she said.

Time crept slowly by and so did his thirst and discomfort. Carmen looked at her watch. "Five o'clock. Your mum and dad will be back at the boat ramp now and wondering where we are," she commented.

That thought got Martin all concerned. But there was nothing they could do.

They will be very upset when we don't appear, he thought, picturing the mental distress and wondering what his parents might do next.

Anne nodded. "They will get help, won't they?" she asked.

"When they realize we are in trouble," Carmen answered.

Andrew also nodded. "But they won't have any idea where to look for us. They will search the Haughton River first and then the creeks leading off it. We are miles from there up another creek altogether."

"But..." Anne started.

Andrew shook his head. "Sorry Anne, but I think we are on our own for a while," he said. "Probably for tonight at least."

"Tonight!" Anne cried anxiously.

"It will be dark in a couple of hours, but they won't start looking in this area before then," Andrew commented.

Martin gloomily agreed with this assessment. He said: "It will take most of that time to alert the Emergency Services people."

"But... but haven't they got search helicopters?" Anne said.

"Yes, but they take half an hour or so to get wound up and that is after they have been asked to help," Andrew said.

Anne was visibly upset and both Carmen and Andrew moved to comfort her. "You mean we could be here in the dark?" she asked.

Martin met Letitia's eyes and made a face. "Yes," he replied.

"But... but we can't!" Anne wailed.

Andrew shrugged. "We don't have much choice. I'm not leaving this tree while our scaly friend is lying at the bottom waiting for dinner."

That comment made Martin glance down at the croc. It still lay there, eyes half closed and mouth half open. By moving a bit Martin could also see the clearing and the creek bank and he noted that the mangled body of Corey still lay there.

That will probably attract more crocs, he thought, but he didn't say that as he did not want to scare Anne any more.

The friends relapsed into silence, each wrapped in their own anxious thoughts. Except it wasn't complete silence. Mosquitoes buzzed and crabs and other marine creatures began making their usual noises in the mangroves. These included loud clicks, sharp clapping sounds and odd gurgles and squishing noises. Some were so loud that Martin jumped with fright and looked around to see if they indicated the arrival of another predator.

More time slowly passed. Overhead the sky darkened and the shadows increased. The sun went off the clearing and the creek, giving it a gloomy, sinister appearance. Then flying foxes began to squawk and chatter somewhere off to the north and the first ones went flapping overhead on their way inland. A big fish jumped in the creek, landing with a splash that caught Martin by surprise and made him flinch.

God I'm a bundle of nerves! he thought. More minutes dragged by. *Mum and dad will be beside themselves with worry now.*

The thought upset him, but he could only shake his head and ease his sore bottom into a more comfortable position on the branch. The insects continued their relentless attacks. Letitia slapped and rubbed and to Martin she looked a real sight—all mud streaked, sun burnt and blotched by insect bites.

"I should have smeared more mud on," she said.

"You should have worn more clothes!" Anne snapped. That led to an uncomfortable silence. Martin shook his head.

We can't afford to start fighting among ourselves, he thought.

The sun went off the tops of the trees and the whole forest descended into gloomy shadows. Martin saw that the creek was now almost drained dry and noted that it was very narrow and deep.

No chance of wading that, even now at low water, he thought. *In fact low water is probably the worst time to cross it,* he decided, noting the steep, slippery banks of grey mud that sloped down into it. Images from nature films of crocodiles slithering at high speed across soft mud came to reinforce that idea.

And the croc did not move.

Slowly darkness set in and with it another wave of voracious insects. The mosquitoes seemed to double in number until they were slapping every few seconds. Martin hit at his face and neck so many times the skin went numb. He felt very dry and itched all over.

No chance of rescue now, he thought, eyeing the sky a sit darkened and the first pale star appeared. *This is going to be a long night!* he thought gloomily.

Chapter 10

TERROR IN THE NIGHT

Fully dark now, Martin noted. *Or at least as dark as it is going to get.* And that was pretty dark! He could barely make out the others and only a weak half-moon and a few stars showed through the gaps in the leaves. And with the darkness had come fear, seeping in like a cold fog under a door. And the ears didn't help. To compensate for the loss of sight the hearing became more acute and the numerous noises all played on the imagination. There were loud snapping noises that could have been made by crocodiles breaking sticks or tree roots. There were clicking and shuffling noises that Martin was afraid were made by the crocodile trying to position itself for another lunge.

Or another croc moving into to join it! he worried. *There must be hundreds, no, thousands, of crocs in this swamp.*

Then a loud sucking, squelching noise nearby caused his hair to stand on end and he felt his muscles tighten with an involuntary spasm. Slashing, swishing, buzzing, rustling, the darkness was full of mysterious and unexplained sounds, all of which seemed to be threatening.

After another loud clapping sound Letitia let out a sharp gasp. "What was that?" she whimpered.

Andrew answered. "Probably one of those crabs with the big claws clicking them together," he suggested.

"This is awful. What will we do?" Letitia asked.

"Stay here," was Martin's short answer.

"All night?"

"Yes. Even if we could safely get down there is no way I am going to try walking through this mangrove forest in the dark," Martin retorted.

He was tired, thirsty and had a head ache and that combined with the fear made him quiet short-tempered with his sister.

She can be a really ditzy bitch sometimes! he thought.

Then the crocodile did move. It slithered, shuffled and grunted and Martin tensed and peered down, trying to see the creature. But it was completely invisible in the darkness. Seconds ticked slowly over but no attack came. And weak moonlight did not help. The few beams that penetrated the foliage threw a distorted dapple pattern of shadows and the light reflected on the upper surfaces making it hard see what was below. Despite this Martin slowly relaxed, as far as he could amidst the continual onslaught of the insects.

Letitia and the others kept slapping, scratching and muttering as well. Andrew finally spoke up loudly in an exasperated tone. "Oh bloody hell! I prefer the croc to these bloody mozzies."

"At least the sand flies seem to have gone to bed," Carmen replied.

Andrew snorted and slapped and the croc slithered and bumped the tree, sending them all into another tense period of anxiety. In the distance the fruit bats—flying foxes in local parlance—could be heard taking off and several flapped loudly overhead. A few smaller bats flitted around them, invisible but the beat of their wings plainly audible.

"What was that?" Letitia cried.

"Only a bat!" Martin snapped.

"A bat! What is it doing?"

Again, Martin marvelled at his big sister's ignorance. "Eating insects, I presume," he answered.

"Will they hurt us?"

"No. They are trying to catch mozzies I think," Andrew told her.

For a while they discussed bats. Andrew questioned whether the flying foxes would eat insects. Martin tried to keep the conversation going as much to help pass the time as to take their minds off the horrors of the night.

More minutes dragged by. The air was completely still. "What's that glugging noise?" Letitia asked.

Martin had to concentrate and only then noticed the gurgle of moving water. It had been there all afternoon as a constant background but was now a bit louder.

"The tide going out," he answered.

"Tide? I thought it went out this afternoon," Letitia said.

Andrew answered her. "Low water was at 1835. It should be starting to come in by now."

"So how can it be going out?" Letitia demanded to know.

"Because it keeps draining away until the incoming water backs it up," Andrew explained.

The notion of the tide coming in brought a new and worrying notion to Martin's mind: if the water level rose the crocodile would rise with it.

I wonder if that croc will be able to get us when the tide is right in?

It was a real worry and now he wished they had climbed as high as they could safely do in daylight. But rather than alarm the others he kept the idea to himself while planning what to do if the threat did develop.

Time began to really drag. It was hot and humid despite it being night. And there was more embarrassment. They all had to go to the toilet and the sound of the pee splashing seemed even louder and more embarrassing than in daylight. This also annoyed the croc which several times coughed or moved and that got them all anxious and tense again.

After several hours the insect attacks seemed to ease up but discomfort took their place. Sore muscles and cramped limbs became the dominant concern. Martin found he could only sit in any one position for a few minutes before the pain and discomfort drove him to find another. The others obviously had the same problem as there was constant fidgeting and movement.

Andrew shifted with a grunt and then grumbled. "Bloody bum's getting sore."

Carmen answered him. "Just don't go to sleep little brother. If you do and you slip out of this tree you will be history."

"My oath!" Andrew agreed.

But the notion of spending the whole night awake, clinging to the thin branches was so appalling that Martin did not want to consider it. Instead he started a conversation about their canoe trips. But the others were not in the mood and the discussion fizzled out in the darkness.

Yet again Martin changed position. Then he tried to sit in a fork with his face towards the trunk. He sat astride the branch with his legs dangling down on either side and his arms around the tree. But it was not the discomfort that made him give it up after a few minutes, it was the terrifying notion of his feet dangling down closer to the crocodile. A mental image of the monster reaching up to clamp onto one of his feet sent shivers through him and he just had to draw his legs up and then try to find a position higher up.

That led to grumbles from Letitia and a general reshuffle as they all changed position. Martin pulled himself higher but ended up leaning against his sister. She said nothing and he felt somewhat comforted by her closeness. But his mind would not rest and he sat there brooding over the murders and about death and over what their chances might be.

Mum and dad will be frantic by now but at least they will have the authorities out looking for us, he thought.

But he accepted that there was really no chance of anything happening before daylight so he could only shrug, slap at the mosquitoes and change to a more comfortable position.

More time dragged by. The discomfort increased until his whole body felt like one huge mass of itches and aches.

This is beyond belief, Martin thought as he moved yet again.

Images of his nice warm bed and his home flitted across his mind. Knowing that less than an hour's drive away was a First World city with a population of 200,000 and all the facilities and services of such a place made their current situation seem even more surreal.

Then a faint tremor made him restless. *What was that?* Martin wondered. Then he heard it rather than felt the vibration and that at once filled him with hope. "Helicopter!" he cried.

"Where?" Anne queried.

Martin swung his head from side to side trying to pinpoint the source of the sound. Then he heard it very distinctly and both he and Andrew pointed and said, "There!"

"Where?" Anne asked.

Martin shook his head as their arms were hard to see in the darkness. Moving closer he held up his arm until he was sure she could see it.

"Thanks," she replied.

Then the clattering buzz of helicopter rotors came to them very clearly and hope surged even higher. But the sound died away just as abruptly. Andrew closed down part of the hope by saying, "It must be searching along the Haughton."

"How can they search in the dark?" Anne asked.

"They have powerful searchlights and some helicopters have infra-red or thermal imaging stuff," Andrew replied.

Martin stared hopefully in the direction of the distant sound but after a few minutes his hopes began to sink again.

It is a long way away and they won't come searching in this area tonight, he decided.

Just once he got a glimpse of a distant flashing strobe light and then the flicker of the helicopter's spotlight but then it was gone, hidden by the leaves. The sound died away and he only heard it twice more and each time it was obviously fainter and further away. All he could do was adjust his cramped muscles and ease his numb buttocks and hope they would last the night.

Another source of anxiety was now being generated by the sounds of water. For some time he had been aware of trickling, gurgling noises amid all the clicking, plopping, splashing and sucking that seemed to fill the mangrove forest.

That is the tide coming back in, he told himself. *And as the water level rises that croc will float up with it!*

About twenty minutes later a distinct splashing, swishing sound jerked him from a doze to fearful wakefulness.

Is that the croc? Martin wondered.

So did the others and when the noises got louder and ended right under the tree there was no doubt it was. Letitia then embarrassed Martin even more by saying, "Is that water I can hear?"

"The tide coming in," Andrew answered.

"Is that a problem? It won't reach us here will it?" Letitia asked, alarm clear in her voice.

Martin shook his head with exasperation. "No. Tides in this part of the world rarely get above three metres and we are five or six up."

He hoped it sounded convincing but found he was gripped by apprehension. Images of crocodiles propelling themselves up out of the water to half their body length while striving to get food dangled over the water caused him severe doubts about just how high the monster might reach if the water got deep enough.

What is the tide tonight? he wondered.

He knew that sometimes there were only a high and a low, but with the moon as it was, there were two peaks each day during that time of the month. Anne wondered the same and asked.

Andrew answered: "Only two point two metres," he explained.

"It was a lot higher this afternoon wasn't it?" Anne queried.

"Yes, nearly three metres," Andrew agreed.

"Why is that?" Anne asked.

Andrew answered her. "Because the moon has a stronger gravitational pull then the sun."

"But? But that doesn't make sense," Letitia said.

"Yes, it does. The moon was up during the day, so you had the combined effect of the sun and the moon."

"Oh, you are teasing me!" Letitia cried. "The moon comes up at night."

Once again Martin felt embarrassed by his sister's ignorance. Her comment led to an explanation of the phases of the moon by Carmen and Andrew. This got Letitia asking about how that affected the water. A discussion about gravity and tidal movements took their minds off their predicament for the next twenty minutes. The discussion was ended by a sudden sharp thud at the base of the tree. The tree suddenly shook and Martin's heart went into his mouth with fear.

The croc is trying to climb up, he thought. Anxiously he peered down but he could see no sign of the saurian.

Then the whole tree shook again and both Letitia and Anne let out squeals of fright. Martin clung on and tensed himself ready to try to climb higher. It was the croc. The creature shoved and grunted and then tried to clamber up. They all gibbered and scrambled higher until the branches became so thin they sagged and began to bend and snap.

Below in the darkness was a slithering sound, and then a large splash. Martin thought the croc had slipped back down onto its belly but he could only just make out vague movements in the shadows so wasn't sure.

It is the not being able to see that is the worst, he decided, knowing that his imagination was magnifying their peril. He found he was panting as though he had run a race and that he was perspiring freely.

A few more cracklings and some splashing about indicated that the croc was still at the bottom of the tree. Only slowly did Martin decide that the creature wasn't going to make another lunge. After a while his heart rate slowed down and he relaxed his grip on the trunk and settled more comfortably on the branch he was on.

That was truly terrifying, he thought, swallowing to try to moisten his dry throat.

That made him aware of how thirsty he was and also of how hot and humid the air was. A glance at his watch showed him it was only 2245 but the air felt so hot that he was uncomfortable.

Water is going to become a real problem by tomorrow morning, he thought.

And then he needed to pee again. He held on as long as he could but then had to ask, "Can you guys just move aside so I can climb down a bit lower please?"

"Why?" Letitia asked.

"I need to do a pee," Martin replied gruffly.

Andrew chuckled. "Don't go too far down. Your pet monster is still lurking there."

As Martin climbed down the others began to discuss the crocodile. "It is the biggest I have ever seen," Carmen said.

Andrew agreed. "It is the size of that fibreglass copy at Hartley's Creek Zoo," he added.

"If you sat on its back your feet wouldn't touch the ground," Anne commented.

All of which made Martin reluctant to go any lower, so he stood next to Anne and burned with shame while he relieved himself into the night.

I hope Anne can't see anything and isn't offended, he thought.

As he listened to the pee splattering on water Martin expected to hear the crocodile react but there was nothing. Thankfully he finished and then moved back to where he had been, ending up with Letitia pressing against him.

More minutes dragged past. The forest noises persisted with an increase in the swilling, splashing sounds. The moon became more visible as it slid down the west of the sky. The stars twinkled overhead but below them was all dappled darkness filled with gurgling noises.

Then, to his dismay, Martin realized that he could see water. It looked to be very close below them. To check he broke off some small sticks and tossed them down.

Several times sharp barking, grunting noises sounded off in the forest. "What's that noise?" Letitia asked.

"Barking flat dogs," Andrew answered.

"What?"

"Puk puks. Crocodiles," Andrew explained. "They are males calling for mates or marking their territory or something."

That was another frightening thought—there were more crocs out there in the darkness. Suddenly the one at the base of the tree let out a sharp grunting bark and began coughing and wheezing. It thudded against the tree and there was a crackling and crashing of tree roots and saplings breaking as it thrashed around. Splashing indicated that the water must now be well over the floor of the forest.

Then the giant croc went slithering and splashing off towards the tree Joel was presumably still taking refuge in. Martin sighed with relief as the splashing, crackling sounds receded.

Moved away, he thought.

At that moment a great roaring, slithering, splashing commotion broke out in the clearing on the creek bank. Martin's chest went instantly tight and his heart hammered with fright.

Bloody hell! What's that? he wondered.

Andrew offered an answer by commenting: "Sounds like another croc trying to take that bloke's body."

Whatever it was the commotion lasted for a good ten minutes. Then it receded down the creek and out into the main waterway. Thinking about that got Martin wondering if their boat was still there.

I hope so, he thought.

And then another series of growls and grunts and splashings nearer at hand sent his hair on end with fear again. The friends clung to each other and stared anxiously into the darkness.

"Sounds like a fight," Carmen suggested.

It did and it went on for quite a while. All they could do was hold on and wait. Then the sounds died away and relative silence settled again. Martin checked his watch and saw that it was nearly midnight.

Past the top of this tide, he thought.

After dozing for a while Martin again checked his watch and noted it was only 0135. *It is going to be a long night,* he thought, gloomy depression mixed with foreboding now taking the place of his earlier optimism.

Hours dragged by. Martin began to feel sharp pains in his muscles, some of which began to cramp. That got him worrying about being unable to hold on or run. More mosquitoes arrived.

After a time he became aware that the light had changed, had faded to a less distinct pattern of dark and light. For the hundredth time a sudden noise made Martin start in fright. He stared into the darkness and then up at the sky.

Where is the moon? he wondered. A check showed him the moon now well down to the west.

"What time is moonset?" he asked.

Carmen answered. "About 0300. I think."

Soon after that the moon vanished behind the foliage and with it went the dapple of shadows. It became darker yet perversely easier to see without the sharp contrast.

It had and the darkness was even more intense. All of the fears doubled in strength and Martin had to consciously suppress a feeling of rising panic.

This is awful! he thought.

More time passed. Letitia complained about the heat and the mosquitoes and they all grumbled about being uncomfortable. The gurgle and suck of water among the aerial roots seemed to become louder and a fresh swarm of mosquitoes arrived and began their attacks. Then another series of loud grunts and growls accompanied by loud splashing sounded from the creek. The noise got louder, and Martin went all tense.

That is coming here, whatever it is, he thought, the fear making his scalp tingle as the hair stood on end.

Chapter 11

WHERE IS THE CROC?

Martin clung to the tree and Letitia clung to him, pressing against his arm.

"What is it?" she whispered.

"The croc coming back, or another one," Martin answered. Anxiously he stared down, his eyes straining to see in the darkness. What he did glimpse was the starlight reflected off the water suddenly dance and vanish as ripples disturbed it. And the water didn't look very far below his feet. "Get higher everyone," he croaked, his mouth dry with fear and thirst.

"We can't!" Andrew answered. "We are as high as we can go without the branches bending or breaking."

That was true and all they could do was cling on and peer down to try get a warning glimpse of the creature before it lunged. Martin tensed himself, ready to spring aside or to lash out. He noted Andrew go into a crouch with his pocket knife in his right hand.

A little knife like that won't do much good, he thought.

Carmen obviously through so too. She held Andrew's shirt and said, "Keep away Andrew. That pocket knife won't penetrate that monster's hide."

Andrew grunted. "I am going to try to stick it in an eye," he commented. Then he added, "Besides, I stuck him in the snout earlier and he didn't like that. I read a story once about a man treed by a cro..."

He didn't get any further as the croc had reached the trunk of the tree and it now made a convulsive heave and launched itself upwards. It rose with such shocking speed that it sent Martin's heart straight into his mouth and which caused them all to gasp or cry out in fear.

As it did Andrew leaned across and did a hard downwards jab with his pocket knife. For a second Martin feared that Andrew had miscalculated and that the croc had got his hand but the saurian let out a savage grunt and then fell back with a slithering splash that shook the tree so much Martin almost lost his grip. Then he had to grab at Letitia as she lost her grip and fell. Only by a frantic grab with his left arm did he stop her dropping straight into the water. His arms went under her breasts and he gripped her as tightly as he could, aware that her sweaty, muddy skin was allowing her to slip through his grasp. With a desperate heave he lifted her up so that her feet could find a branch and he held on for dear life.

With a scrabbling effort Letitia grabbed the branches and then scrabbled to try to get her feet back on a bough. Martin hung on grimly, aware that her sweaty, muddy skin was so slick she was still sliding slowly down through his grasp. He tightened his grip even more, squashing the breath out of her.

Carmen had not noticed this, her attention being focused on Andrew. "Did you get him?" she cried.

Andrew straightened up. "I tried for his right eye but only stick him somewhere on the side of the head. I nearly lost my knife," he replied.

"Lookout!" Anne yelled. "Here it comes again!"

The croc made another leap, its tail and body thrashing the water into a foam as it propelled itself upwards. Martin swung back and Letitia jumped upwards, getting her feet out of the way just in time. The croc's jaws snapped shut with a sound like two planks being clapped together. Then the croc snorted with rage and slid down the trunk again.

As it did Andrew darted forward and leant across. His hand stabbed down and the creature gave a huge twitch. Its body slammed against the tree and they all had to cling on. Andrew was left dangling by his left arm, his feet scrabbling for a branch to settle on. Carmen reached across and grabbed his shirt and helped steady him.

Andrew let go of his knife and grabbed at the branch overhead. The knife dropped to the length of its lanyard and hung there.

"Got the bastard that time!" he cried, his breath coming in short, sharp gasps.

"He would have gotten Letitia if that branch hadn't got in his way," Anne added.

That was true and Martin could only shudder and hang on as his sister changed the grip with her hands and then found the branch to stand on. Thankfully he released his hold on her.

Carmen suddenly pointed down. "Watch out! Get ready! It is going to try again," she called.

They all crouched, tense and ready to spring, the huge shape only dimly visible and that mainly by the froth of its movements showing pale in the darkness.

But the croc didn't jump again. It snorted and bellowed and there was a curious lapping noise amid the splashing. Then it bumped the tree trunk a couple of times before noisily swimming off towards the tree Joel was presumably still in.

Relative silence settled, broken by the gurgle and swish of water. Martin lifted his watch to look at it and saw it read 0325.

Only a couple of hours to low water, he thought.

He opened his mouth to make this comment when a very loud roar over near the creek caused him to go rigid with fright. His hair stood on end and he clung on with a cataleptic grip.

Anne cried out,her voice quavering with fear: "What is that?"

Andrew answered. "Sounds like a fight," he suggested.

It did. There were a series of loud roars and grunts and the snapping and clashing of huge jaws all amid almost continual loud splashes and thumping, slapping noises. The noises got louder for a minute or so and then ended abruptly. After that a few wavelets washed in among the tree roots and then a frightening silence settled.

"What happened?" Anne whispered.

Again Andrew answered. "I think two crocs had a fight."

"What, over that man's body?" Anne queried.

Andrew shook his head. "No. I think that another croc was attacking the big one."

"Oh, surely not! It is so big nothing would be game to tackle it," Anne replied.

Andrew answered: "I'm not so sure. The big brute was shot three times and I stabbed it three times. It was bleeding and that blood in the water may have attracted other crocs. I think it was weakening."

"So, you think it is gone?" Anne asked hopefully.

"I didn't say that," Andrew answered. "Stay alert."

They did. But Martin found it increasingly hard to do. As the silence continued and the tension eased out of him he found he was feeling very weak and drowsy.

"Don't doze off," he said, as much to himself as to the others.

Time began to drag again. Martin found he was continually licking his lips and knew he needed water.

And the others must too, he thought.

He became aware that he had developed a headache and his eyes felt hot and gritty. To try to ease them he had to blink and rub at them to get them to water. Mosquitoes resumed their attacks and the air temperature did not seem to drop at all so that he was continually on the edge of perspiring.

After what seemed like forever he noted that it was 0430. "Low water again," he said.

They all peered down but in the darkness it was hard to distinguish mud with pools of water on it from deeper water.

Anne looked around and sniffed the air. "What is that noise?" she asked.

Martin listened and realized there was a regular, rhythmic swilling sound. He opened his mouth to answer but Andrew beat him to it.

"Little waves breaking along the bank of the creek and among the mangrove roots," he said.

For a while the friends discussed the likelihood of rescue by helicopter and then Letitia asked: "What are we going to do when it is daylight?"

Martin had been thinking hard about that. "Get out of here, if the croc will let us."

"How?"

"By boat if we can. If not, we walk," Martin answered.

"Soon be dawn," Andrew commented.

Martin glanced at his watch. 0450. *Yes,* he thought. He strained his eyes to see if he could detect any hint of greyness in the sky.

There was but the light came slowly. By 0510 he was sure he could just make out a vague lightening in the sky to the east, but the mosquitoes were now so aggressive his attention was continually distracted.

"Bloody mozzies!" he snapped as he slapped at them.

"Dawn biters," Andrew replied.

Martin knew that some species of mosquito only bit at daybreak, but the knowledge did little to ease the annoyance. The others suffered likewise and then the sand flies also returned. Suddenly Martin realized he could make out the creek through the gaps in the foliage. The tide had gone out and the mud of the clearing showed grey amid the grey of the leaves and muddy water.

Now, where is that bloody croc? he wondered.

Anxiously he looked in all directions as the light slowly improved. A hint of green appeared on the leaves.

Andrew moved lower down to the next branch and peered under the foliage in all directions. "I reckon we should go now. It is light enough to see," he suggested.

"Where is the croc?" Anne asked.

Andrew shook his head. "Can't see him."

At that moment there was a rustling sound over amongst the leaves where Joel had taken refuge and then there was a distinct slithering noise and a thud. The friends all looked at each other in the half-light. Letitia grabbed Martin.

"What's that?" she gasped.

Realization burst on Martin at the same moment that Carmen cried out. "It is that other man. He has just climbed out of his tree."

"Quick!" Andrew cried. "He will get that gun."

"Or the boat," Martin added.

Andrew began climbing down as quickly as he could. Martin shoved Letitia aside and began following. But Carmen preceded him and Anne blocked the way.

"Look out Anne! Either get down or move aside," he croaked.

As Andrew slithered down the trunk Carmen called to him. "Watch out for that croc," she cried.

"Can't see it," Andrew answered.

For a moment he crouched at the base of the tree, opening the blade on his clasp knife as he did. Then he moved off across the wet mud towards the clearing. Carmen slid down to the mud and Martin was so close behind he almost landed on her head. Now he was gripped by a feverish anxiety to get to the gun or the boats before the man.

As he landed in ankle deep ooze Martin steadied himself against the wet trunk and peered anxiously in all directions through the dripping, damp grey wilderness.

Where is that bloody croc? he thought.

Then he saw Andrew flit across a patch of light and move out into the open. Carmen was close behind him so Martin followed, not waiting for Anne or Letitia.

The mud was firm enough to walk on but the croc had so churned up the area round the base of the tree that it was almost a wallow. There were numerous puddles in the ooze and the whole surface was slick from the tide. Martin floundered along in Carmen's wake, his gaze darting in all directions as he searched for any sign of the croc. He could see all the crushed and broken roots and deadfall where it had been but none of the shadowy shapes he could see looked like a crocodile.

By then Andrew had made his way out into the clearing beside the small creek. "The body's gone," he called.

That didn't surprise Martin. *It might have just washed away on the tide,* he thought. But darker images of crocs dragging it away or tearing it apart also clouded both his mind and his judgement.

Carmen stopped on the edge of the clearing to look around. "That was probably what those crocs were fighting over," she commented.

Martin pushed through the roots and snagging foliage to join her. "Any sign of that croc?" he asked.

Andrew looked into the now almost empty creek beside him and shook his head. Then he bent down and picked up the mud-caked shotgun.

"Here's the shotgun," he said.

At that moment the silence was shattered by the roar of an outboard motor bursting into life. They all jerked their heads around to stare in that direction then set of running.

"Quick!" Carmen cried. "We must get that boat."

Martin glanced behind. Anne was down and she was helping Letitia to get down the last few metres. Satisfied they were alright he broke into a slithering, stumbling run to follow Andrew and Carmen.

As they slipped and slid across the muddy clearing the sound of the outboard changed and Martin felt his chest tighten up as something like despair gripped it.

Too late! he thought. *The mongrel is getting away.*

They plunged back into the mangrove forest, following their own tracks from the previous day. As they pushed and clambered and slipped their way through the muddy tangle the sound of the outboard motor changed again. First it revved and roared and then settled to a loud splutter, obviously receding.

Andrew swore and then, in his haste, slipped over. Cursing he dragged himself back to his feet.

"The bastard is getting away!" he cried.

It was only 50 paces through the belt of mangroves, but Martin fell three times during it, almost poking out his eye on a small stick the second time. He was soon plastered with mud and gasping for breath. But the urgency of the situation drove him on.

Andrew was first to reach the bank of the main creek. As he got there he skidded to a stop and then swore.

"Oh bugger! The mongrel has taken our boat as well."

"There it is there," Carmen cried.

Martin joined her on the edge of the mangroves and his gaze followed her pointing arm. Their boat was there, but it was in mid-stream and only the tip of the bow was showing. It was plainly sinking. The only sign of the other boat was a series of ripples criss-crossing the creek. The sound of its motor was still audible, but it was rapidly getting fainter.

Anne came panting through the trees and joined them. She stared in dismay at their sinking boat, now drifting away from them on the outgoing tide. "Can we get it back somehow?' she asked.

Andrew shook his head. "No chance. You would need to dive in and tie a rope to it, and I'm not diving in that creek for anything," he said with feeling.

Martin could only agree. Just looking at the swirling muddy water made him feel tense.

That big croc might be in there, and even if it isn't there are plenty of others, he told himself, images of the crocs sliding into the water the previous afternoon crowding his mind.

Letitia, once again coated in wet mud, slithered and stumbled through the trees to join them. "Have they gone?" she asked.

"Yes," Martin replied. Then he shook his head in disgust at her appearance.

Letitia frowned and looked around. "So what do we do?"

Martin shook his head in exasperation. "Looks like we walk!" he snapped.

As he said that the bow of their boat slid under, leaving only a few circular ripples on the surface. As these settled Martin noted that amid the gentle swirls of the outgoing tide there was a definite pattern of ripples. The ripples were moving towards them, upstream.

Like corrugated iron, he thought, noting the very regular spacing and rounded profile of the tiny waves.

Then the possible meaning of the regular wave pattern came to him. "Are those ripples storm forerunners?" he asked.

He now remembered that there was possibly a cyclone out in the Coral Sea.

Andrew and Carmen both studied the phenomena. "Looks like it," Andrew agreed.

"What are they?" Anne asked.

"Storm forerunners, waves pushed out ahead of a cyclone," Andrew explained.

Letitia shook her head. "What from?" she asked.

Once again Martin felt embarrassed about his sister's ignorance. "There was a Category One cyclone forming out in the Coral Sea yesterday morning," he answered.

Anne spoke next. "But that was over five hundred nautical miles away. It can't affect this area surely?" she said.

Andrew looked very thoughtful. "If there is a cyclone out there it could be a lot closer than that by now."

"What do you mean?" Anne asked.

"Well, cyclones can travel at between ten and fifteen kilometres per hour. It could now be as much as one hundred and fifty miles closer to us by now," he replied.

Letitia crossed her arms across her front and hugged herself. "I thought cyclones went much faster than that. I thought they went at hundreds of kilometres per hour," she said.

Once again Martin shook his head. "No. That is the wind speed in the cyclone. We are talking about the speed of the whole system as it moves across the ocean."

"What do you mean?" Letitia asked.

Martin cast about for an analogy and luckily his teacher's explanation came to mind. "Think of a child's spinning top," he said. "The top is set spinning and it goes round and round very fast. But the top only wobbles across the floor slowly."

"Oh, I see!" Letitia replied, nodding as comprehension dawned. "But surely it won't bother us."

Martin wasn't so sure, but Andrew shook his head. "No. We will be safe home by the time anything could reach this area. It will take another day or two to travel this far, even if it comes in this direction. It is more likely to go west and cross the coast north of Cairns. Now let's get moving."

"Where are we going?" Anne asked as Andrew turned back towards the mangroves.

Andrew pointed west. "Inland. If we keep going, we will get through the mangroves and come to dry land, to cane farms or something."

"Mango plantations maybe," Carmen added. "There are a lot of mango plantations in this part of the world."

"Through the forest?" Letitia queried.

"You can swim up the creek if you like!" Martin cried, exasperated by her silly comment.

And then she made another spectacle of herself. As she turned she slipped. She landed hard on her bum with a loud *splat!* For a moment she writhed, all bobbling muddy curves. Then she began to slide down the slope toward the water. Anne grabbed her hand, but it just slid free. Martin acted quickly, leaping down into the churned-up mud where they had struggled ashore the previous afternoon. Quick as a flash he snatched at her hair, catching it just as she slithered by on her back. It worked. Letitia was brought to a squirming halt, screaming with fright and pain.

"Oh, shut up!" Martin snapped, disgusted by his sister's behaviour.

She did, but she obviously resented his tone. With a scowl she took his outstretched hand and then was able to roll onto her front. For a few seconds she knelt there while she sank deeper into the ooze.

Martin eyed the grey green water close behind his sister apprehensively. "If I was you I'd get away from that creek before another croc comes sliding out and grabs you," he said.

That got her moving. With a cry of fear Letitia glanced behind her and then began clawing and scrabbling her way up the muddy slope. Martin waited until she was up past them and then moved over to push at her buttocks and then to give her feet something to push against.

The others helped drag Letitia up among the trees and Martin then followed, with some difficulty as he had trouble dragging each foot clear of the suction of the mud. Andrew reached down and gave him a hand up as he got closer.

Thankfully back on relatively dry land Martin found himself being embarrassed again as Carmen said, "Letitia, I think we should give you a mud coating. It will protect you from the sun as well as from the mozzies."

Letitia looked down. "Sorry!" she said. "I don't mean to be such a spectacle." Then she giggled. "I'm pretty well covered as it is," she commented.

She was, but her femaleness was, if anything, emphasized by the coating of grey mud. Andrew stared at her and then looked away, plainly interested but embarrassed. The other girls now got to work and picked up handfuls of mud which they smeared on Letitia's neck, shoulders and back. Letitia herself wiped it all across her already mud-caked front.

Andrew watched and then went red with embarrassment.

"Let's get moving," he said. "Those men might come back."

Chapter 12

TEST OF COURAGE

A nne blanched and looked anxiously back down the creek. "Oh, surely they won't!" she cried.

"We are witnesses to murder and one of the murderers has just left," Andrew answered.

Carmen nodded. "And there is something fishy going on on that trawler too," she added.

Martin clenched his jaw and felt his stomach tighten with apprehension. *They are right,* he thought. *We aren't out of the woods yet.*

Andrew picked up the mud smeared shotgun from where he had rested it while rescuing Letitia and then led the way back into the mangroves. Martin took a last look along the creek and followed. The others made a line behind them.

The friends churned and slithered their way back to the clearing. As they came out into it Martin again looked anxiously in all direction for any sign of the giant croc. There was a sinister looking slide mark in the mud near where the body of Corey had been but there was no sign of any croc.

Andrew went out into the clearing and walked around, head down, obviously searching.

"What are you looking for Andrew?" Carmen asked.

"That rifle. That bloke dropped it somewhere around here," Andrew replied.

Martin agreed with that idea and joined the search. "What about the shotgun?" he asked. "Has it got any ammo?"

Andrew broke the gun open and then shook his head. "No."

"So why carry it?" Letitia queried.

"Because we might be able to bluff those men if we run into them. They won't know we don't have any cartridges," Andrew replied.

"It might make a useful tool too," Carmen added.

Martin agreed so they searched for a few more minutes. Then Martin saw the rifle. It was almost buried in an area of churned up mud. Huge claw marks in the mud indicated that several large crocodiles had been there during the night. Eyeing the muddy green water in the creek he made his way over and grabbed it by the barrel.

As Martin pulled the rifle free of the mud Andrew looked horrified and shook his head. "Martin! Never pick a gun up by its barrel," he cautioned.

Martin realized that the weapon was now pointing directly at his chest and he experienced a wave of hot and cold as the fright surged through him. Quickly he swung the weapon so that he had it by the stock and the wood. Then he tried to open the breech. It wouldn't move. "Jammed," he said.

"Doesn't matter," Andrew replied. "It's got at least one bullet in the magazine. I saw that Corey trying to reload before the croc got him. So bring it and we will wash it."

Anne looked puzzled. "But won't the water wet the gunpowder?"

Andrew shook his head. "No. It's not a musket Anne. The powder, propellent of some sort, is sealed inside the brass cartridge case. It will go off as long as it is in the breech."

Martin scraped off the worst of the mud but did not want to go near that evil looking water in the creek to wash the rifle.

Later, when I find a safer spot, he told himself.

Then he licked dry lips and looked up. He noted that the sky to the east was now flushed pink and that the first rays of sunlight were just reaching the tops of the taller trees.

Soon be full daylight, he thought.

Then another, more worrying idea came to him and he said, "We need to get moving while it is cool. It will be a scorcher of a day when that sun gets up and we don't have any water."

"No, we don't," agreed Carmen. "We need to find water, or we are in trouble."

"I'm really thirsty now," Letitia added.

"We all are. Now let's move," Carmen replied shortly.

She turned and led the way west along the bank of the creek. Andrew followed, then Anne. Martin went behind her and Letitia came last.

A check of his watch showed him it was only 0550. *It might be a long day,* he thought as he struggled through the entangling mangrove roots.

These grew in a thick belt on both banks of the winding, muddy creek. At times they grew in such dense clusters that the friends had to clamber over them. At other times Carmen detoured away from the creek to find an easier path. It was very slow going and also very hard to walk in a straight line. And the whole place stank of rotting vegetation and salt.

Then a cry from Letitia attracted all their eyes. She was jigging up and down, breasts bouncing while she slapped and rubbed at herself.

"Green ants! Green ants!" she shrieked. "Oh, get them off me!"

Oh bloody hell! Martin thought as he moved back to help his sister.

He eyed her mud-caked skin and was very reluctant to touch her anywhere. Luckily Carmen and Anne came to his rescue and set to work removing green ants from her arms and back and even plucking them out of her hair. She plucked them off her front and Andrew stood for a minute and stared with fascinated interest. Then he blushed and moved away.

Martin had a few ants on him but just picked them off and could only shake his head and sneer at the fuss his sister was making.

Then it was on again. 0615 came and went. The sun was fully up by then and its rays set up a sharp dapple of bright and dark that made it difficult to see any distance through the mangrove forest. That made Martin even more anxious lest they blunder into another crocodile that was lurking in the shadows.

After a few hundred metres the type of mangrove tree changed, back to the big buttress root variety that had been their salvation the previous day. This part of the forest was easier to walk through but there were still quite large puddles to avoid or jump and also the usual noises to make them all jump with fright and look anxiously around. And all the varied fetid smells of the mangroves had to be to put up with.

At one of the puddles Martin edge forward, sinking almost to his knees in the soft mud. Letitia stopped and asked what he was doing.

"I'm going to wash this rifle," Martin explained.

So they all stopped while he rinsed and sluiced off as much mud as he could. Then he tried again to open the breech. But it was still jammed. Shaking his head he said, "Still stuck. I'll try again later. Here, take the rifle while I get out of this muck."

"Safety catch on," Andrew said as he moved forward.

Martin found the safety catch and applied it and then passed the weapon to Carmen. She then reached out and helped him keep his balance as he dragged his feet clear of the suction.

Carmen handed him back the rifle and they resumed walking, the sound of their movement added to by the sucking, squelching noises of the area of soft mud they had to traverse.

Then Martin became aware of another noise. "Stop! Listen!" he called.

They did and the sound came to them clearly, a humming vibration that could only be made by a helicopter. Anne cried with joy and Letitia clapped her hands. "They will soon get us to safety," she said.

But Andrew shook his head. "No, they won't. They are searching the Haughton and its tributaries. We are miles to the east of there. It could be quite a while before they widen their search area."

Martin looked up and then added, "And we need to be out in the open, not in under the tree canopy."

"So let's get out to one of those big mudflats," Carmen said.

She set off again, pushing through small trees and bushes and climbing over those aerial roots that she could. The others followed. Martin kept glancing in the direction of the searching helicopter and began to fret that it might fly over and not see them. He was also thirsty and was aware that he was sweating.

What a dilemma! he thought. *If we go fast we perspire and might get heat exhaustion but if we go slow the helicopter might not see us if we are still in the mangroves.*

But there were no clearings and, if anything, the mangrove forest got thicker. Then they blundered into another problem. Carmen suddenly let out a yelp of pain and clapped her hand to the side of her face. Then Andrew also cried out and he slapped at his arm and began moving quickly backwards. "Wasps!" he called, both arms windmilling around his head.

Then one landed on Martin and in went its sting. The pain was so sudden and so sharp that Martin also cried out. As he began turning away, he saw Letitia suddenly jump back and then slap at her bosom.

They all scuttled back 50 paces, scratching skin and tearing clothes in their hurry to get away. There they came to a gasping, rubbing, scratching halt and looked back.

"I think we have left them behind," Carmen said while ruefully rubbing the side of her face.

It was Letitia who had fared the worst. With almost no clothes to protect her she had been stung a dozen times on her back, legs, arms and even on her left breast. Without thinking she held it up with her left hand and cradled it while rubbing at the sting with her right before realizing everyone was staring at her. Andrew fairly goggled as he watched. Then he hastily looked away.

Martin also stared and thought, *Poor Andrew. I can imagine just what he's thinking poor bugger!*

Then he realized that Carmen and Anne were both glancing at him and he blushed and looked away. But he wasn't very sympathetic.

Serves her right! She might wear clothes in future, he thought.

But he did concede that in the daylight Letitia was a sorry sight. The mud had dried and was flaking off, but her skin was blotched and mottled by sunburn and bruises and she was covered with red spots from mosquito and sand fly bites and her hair looked like a rat's nest. Her woebegone expression did elicit a twinge of pity from Martin. But there was nothing they could do to help her, so the march was resumed, detouring around the location of the wasp's nest.

They continued on, sweating and struggling through the undergrowth and tangling roots. The whole time Martin was aware of the noise and clicks from the forest and he even noted a few small white crabs with red claws. "They are the crabs that make that loud clicking noise I think," he observed.

They stopped and all looked at a group of four of the red clawed crabs. Andrew nodded. "They are," he said. "See that big right claw that some of them have? I think they are the males and they snap their pincers to make that sound."

"Why?" Anne asked, bending to peer at the crabs.

Andrew shrugged and then blushed. "To attract a mate I think," he replied.

"Wouldn't that also attract any predators?" Anne asked.

"Maybe," Andrew answered.

The group continued on. Martin noted more of the red and white crabs and also dozens of small purple and grey crabs.

Soldier crabs? he thought.

Suddenly Andrew sprang back, bumping into Carmen and almost knocking her over. "Snake!" he yelled.

Martin jumped in fright and peered at the foliage where Andrew was pointing. He glimpsed what he thought was a short length of the body of snake but then it vanished. It was almost the same colour of the grey green bark on the mangrove tree.

Anne gasped and stared as well. "Where is it?" she croaked.

"Gone now," Andrew answered. "It slid up into that tree."

"Where? Where is it?" Anne cried, her voice becoming almost hysterical.

Andrew shook his head and recovered his breath. "It's OK Anne. It has gone."

"What sort was it?" Carmen asked.

Andrew shrugged. "Not sure. Some sort of browny-green thing. Bloody hell! I nearly put my hand on it."

Martin saw him shudder and felt a twinge of anxiety himself. *A snake bite is the last thing we need now!* he thought.

Carmen peered up into the branches of the tree that Andrew had indicated. "Probably only a tree snake," she suggested.

"Don't care. The bloody thing gave me a fright," Andrew retorted. He resumed walking, detouring well away from the tree. Martin and the others followed.

After another half hour of struggling through the tangle they came to a panting halt and stood looking around. Thirst was the main problem and Martin already had a headache and gritty eyes and knew they were early symptoms of heat stress. Anxiously he looked at his friends to check them for symptoms as well and to his dismay they weren't hard to notice. To add to his worry there was no noise from any searching helicopter.

This is getting bad, he thought. He was now heartily sick of mangroves.

It was the attacking insects that drove them back into motion. A new type of mosquito began buzzing around and a small cloud of some sort of midge flew around their heads. These didn't bite but they were very annoying all the same. Martin began to feel not only thirsty but also light headed. His stomach grumbled and he realized they had not eaten since midday the day before.

We need food too or the heat illness gets worse, he thought, remembering a lecture at Navy Cadets on heat exhaustion. *You need food as well as water or you get cramps. And you need salt to make your nerves work properly.*

The word 'electrolyte' hovered in his mind and he gave a wry smile.

There was plenty of salt, dried and crusted on the trees and mud and even more in the nearby creek. But he also knew that drinking seawater caused salt poisoning.

It overloads the kidneys and destroys them, he remembered.

It was all very worrying. But then things abruptly got both worse and better. Martin's instinct for direction had been bothering him for a few hundred metres but now his eyes confirmed what he had been suspecting: the course of the creek was now east-west and cut directly across their front.

The friends struggled out onto the bank of the creek and when Martin looked to his right he was dismayed. Fifty metres to his right the creek joined up with the main creek again. It could be clearly seen, 25 metres wide and full of dark green water.

"We are on an island," he said.

"We are," Andrew agreed.

"So we have to cross this creek," Carmen added.

Martin looked down at the creek and felt his stomach tighten with fear. The creek was about 25 metres wide from bank to bank but only about 5 metres was full of water. On each side grey mud sloped down to the channel. The mud wasn't steep, but it glistened with water and looked soft and slimy. The water was a muddy grey-green.

Anything could be lurking in that! he thought, his chest tightening with apprehension.

Andrew shook his head. "This is going to be tricky. Getting down to the water will be easy, you just slide on your bum, but getting up the other bank might be difficult," he commented.

"Like yesterday when we got out of the boat," Anne added.

"Yes," Andrew agreed.

Carmen gestured at the creek. "Well, too bad. The sooner we get across the better. The tide is coming back in."

It was too. Martin now noticed a distinct flow moving floating leaves and sticks along, and in the direction he thought was upstream.

It has been coming in for about three hours now, he thought, noting that it was almost 7 o'clock.

Andrew studied the creek then shook his head. "It might be easier to cross when it is full of water," he suggested.

That idea made Martin feel queasy with fear. He opened his mouth to object, but Carmen beat him to it. "No fear little brother. I am not swimming that when it is full of water. It must be twenty or twenty-five metres across."

"But that mud is going to really difficult to climb," Andrew replied.

Carmen shook her head vigorously. "It might be, but when the creek is full there could be anything swimming along it. At the moment it is unlikely that any croc is lying on the bottom in that shallow water."

"But..."

"No buts little brother. We are crossing now," Carmen insisted.

Martin agreed with her but that did not stop his chest tightening up with anxiety. As he looked both ways along the creek, his eyes searching for any sign of a crocodile his whole being began to cringe.

This is going to be a test! he told himself.

Chapter 13

THE CREEK

Carmen faced them. "We must cross that," she said, pointing to the creek.

Letitia stared at the water, obviously aghast at the idea. "I'm not swimming that!" she cried.

That annoyed Martin. "Well don't! Stay here and let those men catch you," he snapped.

That upset Letitia even more. "Oh, don't be horrible!" she wailed.

"Then don't be so unrealistic. We can't stay here," Martin retorted, guilt at hurting his sister's feelings adding an edge of anger to his voice.

Letitia sniffled and then pointed at the creek. "Well you go first then."

At that Andrew interrupted. "No! We all go at the same time," he said.

"But what if there are crocodiles?" Anne queried, voicing all their fears.

"There almost certainly are," Andrew answered. "But they aren't right here. If one person goes in the splashing and vibrations will alert every croc for hundreds of metres and they will come to investigate. That means they will catch the second or third person."

Carmen nodded. "That's right. The shorter the time we take the safer we are. If we all go at once by the time the crocs wake up to the fact that lunch is crossing the creek we will be across and up the other side."

That made sense to Martin, but he still hesitated. His nerves were now so highly strung he found he was trembling. As soon as he realized this, he felt a flush of shame and summoned up some of his remaining willpower to steady himself.

For another minute or so the friends stood and stared at the muddy green water. Then Carmen shook her head.

"Come on, the longer we stand here the more likely it is that a croc will hear us and come to investigate. Let's get this over with. Line up side by side and on my command slide down and get across."

They did so but with varying degrees or reluctance. Martin found he was terrified but made himself give Letitia and Anne a reassuring grin. When they were all standing side by side Carmen looked both ways along the line and then said, "On the count of three. One. Two. Three!"

Not wanting the others to think he was scared Martin forced himself to step forward. As directed, he dropped onto his backside, lifted his legs and pushed himself forward. His efforts were more successful than he expected, and he found himself slithering out of control at high speed. To his horror he discovered that he could not have stopped himself even if he had wanted to. The slope was so slippery that he just went down it in one rapid slide to splash into the creek.

That was a moment of real terror. Even as he hit the water Martin hurled the rifle and began to flail with his arms and feet. Despite efforts to avoid it he went right under water which added to his fears. An attempt to open his eyes when underwater was instantly regretted and the process reversed but not before more stabs of near panic went through his already overstressed body and salt got into his already sore eyes and stung them fiercely. Then his boots struck the bottom and sank into the ooze.

For a moment Martin feared he would be stuck in the mud underwater and either drown or be caught by a croc. Driven by sheer desperation he used his arms to breast stroke as hard as he could and to his intense relief found his feet pull free of the suction. A moment later his head broke surface.

Almost blinded by the stinging salt he struck out towards the blurry grey slope ahead of him. He reached it within a few strokes, much quicker than he had expected. As his hands encountered the slime of the mud, he clawed at it in a frantic attempt to climb up.

Then he remembered the rifle, blundered into it in fact, and he grabbed at it. The rifle had landed butt first and Martin could only be thankful. He pulled himself clear of the water using it as an anchor. Then he dragged it clear and drove the butt into the mud a metre further up the slope and began to repeat the process. A glance showed Andrew doing the same thing with the shotgun except that it was so coated in globs of mud that it was hard to recognize as one.

On either side the others were also clawing their way up the slope, except for Letitia who was still splashing in the water. Martin glanced back at her to check that she was alright but when he saw her start to drag herself face first up onto the mud he continued climbing.

It turned out to be easier than he had expected. By not trying to stand but instead by lying on their front they were able to drag and push themselves up to the drier mud without sinking in deep. In the process they became plastered with another layer of mud, but Martin barely noticed. He was just glad to be across and safe. With a gasp of relief, he hauled himself onto the flat mud at the top of the bank and then looked around to check on the others. He saw that they were all up and were either already on their feet or getting up, except for Letitia. She was still squirming and hauling her way up, and in the process providing yet another embarrassing spectacle. Her buttocks were wobbling wildly, and her front was dragging in the mud and she was splattering and flinging so much sloppy mud around in her near hysterical motions that she was getting coated by gobbets.

Several of these struck the others and Martin took one fair in the mouth. The sudden shock and bitter taste of salt and grit caused him to cry out, then regret opening his mouth. Spluttering and spitting he tried to wipe the muck away, swearing and calling his sister names in his embarrassment and irritation.

But at least Letitia was up. Both Anne and Carmen reached down and helped her to her feet. Then they all stood and stared at the caked layers of mud clinging to her front. Big dollops began sliding down her front. Letitia wiped at it and then shrugged.

By now it seemed that her appearance was just taken for granted and Andrew stared with fascinated interest before realizing he was. Red-faced he looked away and began scraping mud off the shotgun. Then he paused and cupped his hand behind his ear. "What's that noise?" he queried.

Martin heard it at once and felt a chill of fear stab through him. The sound was a mixture of slapping noises and outboard motor sounds.

"Someone coming up the main creek in a boat," he said.

Andrew nodded, a grim expression on his face. "We need to get moving," he said.

But even as he spoke the noise increased and Martin glimpsed movement out in the main creek. His heart skipped a beat and he gasped as the terror gripped him. Through eyes that were stinging and blurred he focused on the image of a boat powering into view, its bows slapping at the pattern of ripples.

And in the boat was a man. Even as Martin focused, he saw the mop of hair, black eye patch and unshaven face of Long John Silver. Silver turned his head and saw them at once. His mouth opened and he swung the tiller to turn the boat into the creek.

"Here they are!" he shouted. "Here they are!"

"Run!" Carmen cried.

She turned to do so but then saw that Letitia was standing gaping open-mouthed at the boat. Instantly she grabbed at Letitia's arm and pulled her to follow.

Martin turned and nearly pushed Anne over in his hurry to get into the trees. Hastily snatching at her shirt, he held her up until she had her balance and then followed her as she scrambled into the tangle, impeded by the thicket of aerial roots and narrow mangrove trunks.

Silver shouted again as he turned the boat and aimed it into the creek. Martin heard the engine slow and as he began to follow Anne into the forest he got a glimpse of Silver reaching down and picking up a gun. Whether it was a rifle or a shotgun he did not have time to see but the sight of it sent his heart hammering and he dragged himself over a tangle of roots, heedless of the scratches that resulted.

The others were also forcing their way into the tangle and a glance showed them all moving in among the trees. Letitia was whimpering and complaining as her bare skin was scratched but Martin felt no sympathy.

Serves the silly bitch right! he thought.

Crack! Bang!

A shot snapped through the leaves and Martin almost voided his bowels as the fear swamped him. Then Long John Silver shouted again, "Here they are! Get moving you guys!"

More of them, Martin thought. As he scrambled deeper into the shadows his mind turned that idea over and he knew it was obvious. *That man Joel has gone to get some more from the trawler and they have landed and are tracking us,* he deduced.

That was a terrifying notion and spurred him on. Carmen and Andrew had obviously reached the same conclusion as Andrew gasped, "There are more of them. They will be on our trail as soon as they can cross the creek."

There was another shot, but Martin had no idea where it went, although the sound caused him to flinch and his heart to skip a beat. Carmen came to a panting standstill when she was baulked by a big tangle of roots. "Anyone hit?" she gasped.

Martin looked around. All the others were there, and all were looking at each other. No-one answered so they continued on, now skirting the more difficult patches of scrub and mangroves.

"Keep running," Carmen warned. "They aren't far behind us."

Fear and despair flooded through Martin. The idea that in their weakened state they might outrun fit men with guns seemed hopeless, but he forced himself to keep moving. By now he was taking great gulps of air and his heart was hammering fit to bust. And both Anne and Letitia were falling behind. Martin slowed and looked back. There was no sign of the brightness along the creek bank, but he did hear the boat's outboard motor and then distant yells.

"They are still a fair way behind," he gasped, cheered by the notion.

"They are not that far back," Andrew replied. "And they can cross by boat."

"No, they can't," Carmen croaked. "They will still have to slide down and then crawl up the same as we did. It will take them a few minutes."

The image of their pursuers getting soaked and splattered with mud cheered Martin some more and he growled, "Serves the buggers right!"

"I hope a crocodile comes along," Anne added.

Her ruthless comment surprised Martin and caused him to experience again the horrifying images of Corey being mangled. He shuddered and shook his head.

"Oh, slow down!" Letitia wailed. She came to a gasping standstill and leaned on a tree, head down.

Martin stopped. "Keep going you guys. I will stay with her," he called.

But the others also stopped. Carmen shook her head. "We all stay," she replied.

"Keep walking," Andrew croaked. "Even if you can't run then walk."

They did, falling into a single file between him. Martin urged Letitia into line ahead of him, and he and Anne came last. "We need to try to hide our tracks," he said.

"How?" Anne croaked. "In this mud we leave tracks like an elephant."

"Speak for yourself," Carmen replied. Then she nodded. "But you are right. Everyone try to walk as flat footed as you can to minimize the pressure. We have to make the attempt, or they will catch us in a few minutes."

"And change direction every hundred metres," Martin suggested. So they did that but when Martin looked down he saw that they still left a fairly obvious trail.

If we don't break contact, we are done for, he thought grimly.

That got his mind working in an attempt to come up with a strategy. *If we can't run can we hide?* he wondered.

But it took him only a short study of the trail they were leaving to show him that hiding wasn't an option.

Maybe we should split up? he wondered.

But those thoughts quickly led him back to the same moral dilemma as before. In his heart he wasn't willing to leave his sister to her fate, even if it meant him losing his life. Some dark and brooding thoughts about death and whether there was anything after it then occupied his mind.

As they pushed their way through another muddy thicket his stomach was gripped by apprehension and he felt a sense of impending doom that made him fretful and then angry.

If only we can get this rifle to work! We could fight back, or at least scare them off, Martin thought.

He looked down at the rifle and noted that some of the mud was now dried and was a light grey in colour. He began to brush and rub at it as he walked behind Andrew. The others followed, Letitia in front of Anne this time. Carmen came last. They went straight on through the mangrove forest, Andrew keeping direction by the sun.

After a couple of minutes Carmen questioned this. "Which direction are we heading Andrew?" she asked.

"I am trying to go south," Andrew replied.

"Shouldn't we going west?"

Andrew shook his head. "No. The sea is to the north of us at the moment and the nearest farms should be south," he explained.

Martin thought about this, trying to picture the chart. *Yes, he's right,* he decided. *If we go west we will run into that big creek again.*

Once again, the mangroves became a problem with large areas of trees with aerial roots that were almost impossible to climb through or over. The usual scuttling small crabs and insects drew the eyes and clicking and rustling sounds filled the ears. The salty, rotting vegetation and 'seafood' odours assailed the nostrils and Martin began to hate the experience.

"I hope I never see another mangrove as long as I live!" he muttered.

"Amen to that!" Andrew replied as he detoured around yet another dense clump of roots.

As they walked Martin kept looking for another puddle he could wash the rifle in, but he noted that the mud seemed to be firmer, a sort of spongy clay rather than mud, and that it was getting drier.

Then a zone of brightness appeared ahead that indicated that there was a clearing of some sort.

I hope it isn't too big, Martin thought. But as he walked he saw that the brightness was extending right across their front. *I hope not!* he thought.

Abruptly they reached the edge of the trees and his worst fears were confirmed. Extending for several kilometres ahead of them was a vast salt flat. It was totally devoid of any cover and there was not even a heat shimmer yet to distort visibility.

Oh bloody hell! I hope we don't have to cross that, Martin thought.

Andrew obviously thought the same as he said, "Strewth! If we try to cross that we will stand out like flies on the ceiling. Those men will spot us from miles away."

Anne looked anxiously around. "But what other choice do we have?" she asked.

Martin stared at the vast, open expanse of dry mud and salt and felt his stomach churn with apprehension. After looking around he noted that the mangroves ended at what was obviously the bank of the main creek only a hundred metres to their right. To their left they trended southeast in a long, gentle curve.

"That way," he suggested.

Carmen looked and then nodded. "I agree. If we keep close to the edge of the mangroves, we will be able to hide in them if anyone follows us."

"But they might spot us," Andrew replied, glancing anxiously back into the forest.

Carmen shook her head. "They might but they will be able to track us easily enough as it is. I think it is our best option to get quickly out of this area."

Andrew nodded. "OK," he said and without further debate he turned left and started walking fast beside the edge of the mangrove forest. The others followed.

As he walked Martin glanced at his watch and noted it was only 0720. *This could be a long day,* he thought, licking dry lips that were starting to crack.

This time he went last, putting Letitia just in front of him. That bothered him a bit as he watched her muddy buttocks wiggling and wobbling but at least she was not being looked at continually by the others. However, despite not wanting to he could not help looking and noted that she had several cuts and quite a number of scratches on her bum and on the back of her legs. These were covered with hundreds of red dots where insects had bitten her.

Poor old Sis! She will give up nudity after this, he mused.

While walking—trudging—along, Martin kept looking behind and at the sky. He was hoping that a rescue helicopter would appear but was also aware that were moving directly away from the most likely search area.

He also kept brushing at the mud on the rifle and from time to time gently tried to work the bolt of the rifle. To his great satisfaction he felt it move slightly so he persisted, blowing off grains of dry grit and mud and rubbing at the exposed working parts.

We might need this, he thought.

Out on the flat, dry mud the going was easy and they made good time, only delayed by exhaustion. This seemed to hit with redoubled force after a while and Martin deduced that was the effect of the adrenaline wearing off, leaving them feeling quite down. As if to emphasize this his stomach gave a loud grumble and he found his tongue sticking to the roof of his throat.

We certainly need water soon, he thought, aware he had a bad headache and that is vision kept going blurry.

His eyes became so sore and gritty that he had to resist the temptation to rub at them and he found he had trouble making them water.

We are dehydrating fast, he thought.

Information from a Sea Survival Course at Navy Cadets tossed around his consciousness to remind him that without water in the tropics a person doing hard physical exercise could suffer serious heat illness within half a day.

Longer if we rest in the shade and don't talk, he thought.

But there was no chance or resting. Fear of the men kept them moving. Again, Martin licked his dry and now cracked lips and then looked up at the sky. It was completely cloudless and already the heat was building with the promise of it being a scorcher of a day.

The edge of the mangrove forest continued to slowly curve around to the south. After ten minutes Letitia muttered that she needed to rest, but was ignored. Then she wailed she could not keep walking.

Carmen glanced back over her shoulder but did not stop walking. "If we stop, we die! Keep moving!" she snapped.

Letitia let out another whimper but did as she was told. Martin began to worry that either she or Anne might collapse from exhaustion or heat stress. That was how he starting to feel and only the fear kept him forcing himself to go on.

Suddenly Andrew stopped. Martin saw that the mangroves had ended. He walked forward to join him and looked around the end of the forest. To his dismay he saw that the open ground now extended right across their line of march to the east as well. The forest trended back northwards for what looked like a kilometre or more.

Chapter 14

FLY ON THE CEILING!

Martin stared at the vast expanse of bare, open mud flat and felt a chill of desperation clutch at his heart.

Bloody hell! What do we do now? he wondered.

Andrew looked that them in turn with eyes that were red-rimmed. He bit his cracked lips and looked worried.

"The mangroves have come to a point. If we go on beside them we are hidden but will be heading back towards the mouth of the creek where we started from."

Martin turned and again stared at the miles of open salt flats and felt his chest tighten with apprehension.

"Do you think we should try to cross this open ground?" he asked, wording it that way to suggest the military meaning of no cover.

Andrew looked grim and nodded. "Yes. If we go back northeast we could be trapped and cut off against the sea."

"But what if those men see us and chase us?" Anne asked.

"Then we have to move faster," Andrew replied.

At that Letitia shook her head. "Oh no! I can hardly walk now. I need a rest."

"And a feed," Anne added.

Andrew shrugged. "You can stop if you like, or you can keep following the mangroves, but I am going south across these salt flats."

Carmen looked worried and frowned. "But what if those men have another rifle?" she asked.

"Then we are in real trouble," Andrew replied. There was a hint of desperation in his voice. "Come on, we can't afford to stand and argue."

With that he turned right and headed out onto the bare open mud flat.

Martin glanced at his sister who was sagging with exhaustion and looking ready to drop.

Bloody hell! What do I do? he thought.

Then he gently took her arm. "Come on Sis. Let's do this together," he urged.

To his relief, Letitia nodded and began plodding out across the mud flat. Martin sighed and moved with her, holding her arm and trying to encourage and comfort her.

But being out in the open made him feel very exposed. *Like being naked,* he thought, casting a quick glance at his sister as she walked along beside him.

He noted that the coating of mud on her skin had now dried and was starting to flake off or turn to dust. Patches of red raw skin were showing through and more insect bites. Then he shrugged. Somehow her female curves did not seem to matter anymore.

Within a couple of minutes, they were over a hundred metres out on the flat. Martin kept glancing to his right rear to try to catch a glimpse of any pursuers. He also frequently twisted his head to look to the west and north in the hope of seeing the rescue helicopter.

We are right out in the open now, he reasoned. *From the air we must stand out like flies on a white ceiling.*

But there was no sign of the helicopter, so he plodded on, dusting the rifle and trying to ease the bolt loose as he did. Clearly in his mind was the idea that he might have to use that rifle, if the worst came to the worst.

Another five minutes of walking had them nearly half a kilometre out onto the flat. Martin stared ahead and noted a distant line of trees and scrub, but these looked to be several kilometres away.

This is getting hard, he thought. By now he felt so weak and dizzy he was scared he might actually collapse.

And Letitia was starting to stagger. She suddenly bumped against him and then grabbed at his shirt. "Sorry," she muttered thickly.

To his concern Martin noted that her tongue looked swollen and her eyes were not only red but had dark rings of exhaustion under them.

Then the sound of the helicopter sent his hope soaring. They all stopped and looked back in the direction the sound was coming from. But almost at once Martin's hopes began to ebb. The sound was only a distant a vibration and the machine was obviously a long way away. Then his eyes picked it out, a tiny speck in the far distance. And it was flying away from them!

Andrew shook his head and swore.

Carmen muttered something, then said, "It is searching the mouth of the Haughton. They have no idea we are so far away."

That made sense to Martin. *They will be looking for bodies or wreckage washed out on the outgoing tide,* he thought, but wisely did not say. Those thoughts caused him deep concern at the agony of anxiety his parents must be going through. *They must be beside themselves with worry.*

Suddenly he stiffened. A spurt of fear sent adrenaline into his veins. *Is that movement?* he wondered.

Blinking and rubbing at his eyes to clear the blurred vision he stared back at the edge of the mangroves off to the northwest. And it was. At the point where they had come out of the mangroves, about a kilometre away, were two men.

Martin tried to call a warning but it came out as a croak and he had to work his throat to moisten it. Then he pointed. "Two men," he said.

"I see them," Andrew agreed.

Carmen shook her head and gestured the other way. "Let's move!"

They did. Turning their backs on the men they began to hurry away from them, fear fuelling their urgent efforts. Andrew now changed direction to walk directly away from the men. Martin understood why. If they continued on south the men could walk diagonally across and their courses would converge.

That will shorten the distance and they are fresh and probably fitter, he decided.

None of the others questioned the decision. Martin decided that Letitia had not even noticed. *She has a terrible sense of direction at the best of times,* he remembered.

But he stayed with her, holding her arm and urging her to walk as fast as she could. As he did, he kept glancing back and what he saw chilled him with apprehension. The men were following, hurrying across the mud flat in pursuit.

A sweeping glance showed Martin that there was nothing ahead of them for several kilometres and then only a dim line of trees, either more mangroves or scrub. The line of scrub they had been heading towards was now on their right front but did not extend all the way to the distant line of trees. Far to the left were the mangroves they had come from. These were now further away than ever and offered no hope. They obviously could not regain their cover before the men cut them off or caught up.

And they were catching up, and fast! To his dismay Martin saw that the men were noticeably closer, close enough to see that both carried weapons of some sort.

Shotguns hopefully, Martin thought.

He resumed gently working on the rifle, letting go of Letitia to do so.

After ten minutes Letitia gasped that she could not keep going. She slowed to a staggering plod. Martin bit his lip and stayed with her, his guts churning with a mixture of fear and despair. Anne also slowed. Then both Carmen and Andrew slowed as well.

Martin looked around and saw that the men were now only about half a kilometre behind. The distant line of trees, distinct now in the clear morning air, looked to be about 2 kilometres. The line of scrub to the right was much closer but still over a kilometre away.

We have no hope of reaching cover before those men catch up, Martin thought. *They are nearly within range now.*

But they didn't give up. The sight of the men gave them all a spurt of terror that enabled another 300 paces to be covered in as many minutes.

But then Letitia stumbled and fell. Grimly Martin grabbed her and pulled her to her feet. She raised her dark-ringed, red-streaked eyes and said, "Keep going! Leave me."

That act of courage sent a surge of warm appreciation and affection through Martin. "No way!" he replied.

He put his arm around her waist and began to walk. She clung to him, and they hobbled slowly on. But the men were 100 or so paces closer, perhaps only 400 metres behind and their features were becoming clearer. One looked to be Joel the Grizzly and the other was tall and thin and had a mop of mousy hair and a beard.

The deckhand off that trawler? Martin considered.

Then Letitia stumbled again and half fell. Martin clung to her. "Come on Sis. Keep trying," he urged.

She groaned and gasped and raised terror-filled eyes to his. That helped firm his determination and he hauled her upright. For a moment he even considered trying to pick her up. As this thought crossed his mind he looked back and saw that one of the men was standing still and had his right elbow sticking out sideways.

He's aiming a rifle! Martin thought. Even as the fear began to surge, he began to crouch and drag at Letitia. "Down! Get down!" he croaked.

Crack!

The snap of the passing bullet was so close he felt it just above his head. That sent him flat and Letitia went sprawling. Awareness that he would almost certainly have been hit in the back if he hadn't crouched sent waves of cold and hot terror sweeping through him. A glance showed all the others lying flat on the dry salt pan.

Gasping with fear Martin, stared at the men, his whole body quivering. He expected another shot but to his dismay he saw both men start walking again, hurrying across the open ground towards them.

Bloody hell! We are pinned down out in the open, he thought. With his heart pumping frantically he tried to think of a plan. And then it came to him that he still had the rifle. *It must have a bullet in the magazine or that man would not have tried to reload to shoot the croc,* he reasoned. In desperation he gripped the rifle and gave the bolt a savage wrench.

Clack! Tinkle. The bolt came open and the spent cartridge case went flying to land nearby. A spurt of intense satisfaction and determination surged through Martin. He glanced into the open breech and saw the gleam of shiny brass down in the magazine. Fired by the determination to save the others he pushed the bolt forward hard. To his intense relief it picked up the next round and pushed it into the breech. The bolt snapped shut with a reassuring click.

Martin now raised the rifle into the 'lying unsupported' position, his elbows resting uncomfortably on the gritty surface. Snuggling the butt into his shoulder he aimed the weapon at the man with the curly mop. He had done the shooting and Martin was sure he was the more dangerous of the two. As he steadied the rifle and squinted through the old open 'iron' sights on top of the barrel, Martin was assailed by the moral dilemma and absolute reality of what he might have to do.

Do I fire a warning shot and hope it will scare them off? he wondered. What fuelled his concern was not knowing if there were any more bullets in the rifle. *If it is my only bullet and that plan doesn't work, we are dead,* he reasoned.

He bent sideways and glanced to see if the magazine could be easily detached but then hesitated. Then he glanced at the men and knew there wasn't time. The men were now less than 300 metres away.

Probably only two hundred or so, Martin thought. As the dread churned in his stomach, he bit his lip and then grimly made his mind up. *I must save the others,* he thought.

He did not articulate the moral dilemma clearly but swirling in his almost panic-stricken mind was the moral issue of killing, of whether it was right to take another person's life to save others. He was sure that if it was just to save himself, he couldn't. But a glance at Letitia and Anne and at Andrew's anxious face made his mind up. Even though he knew that the act would irrevocably change his entire life, probably destroying his mental health and giving him regrets and haunting nightmares as long as he lived, he determined to shoot.

Carefully he wiped each hand on his shirt and then took a firm grip. Then, perversely, he began to sweat and the perspiration made his hands slippery despite the clinging grit and he had to wipe them again. Steadying himself he lined the man up through the sights. The tip of the foresight was steadied on the man's chest and then lined up with the top of the 'U' of the backsight. Through Martin's mind ran the words of his Navy Cadet instructors at the rifle range. He now muttered these to himself, all the while trying to calm his trembling.

"Take aim. (*Have to blink, blast the blurred vision!*). Take up the slack in the trigger pressure. Breathe in (*the foresight will drop*). Breathe half out (*the sight should come back up*). Squeeze the shot." (*Don't hesitate or you start to shake. Damn it, I am shaking!*).

Bang!

The butt punched back into Martin's shoulder. For a moment his vision was obscured by the puff of smoke and his sore eyes. Then he saw that he must have missed. Regret and relief both flitted through his mind along with the instructor's caution.

Open the bolt immediately or the heat will expand the used cartridge case and jam it in the breech.

Desperate to succeed Martin wrenched the bolt back. To his relief it moved and came open, flicking the spent case onto the dry mud.

A glance down showed him that there was another bullet in the magazine and he closed the bolt with grim satisfaction. Determined not to miss the next time he raised the rifle again. Only to find that hitting his target would be very much harder!

To his surprise and intense relief, he saw that both the men were now running away as fast as they could run. And they were dodging and weaving as they did!

"I've done it!" Martin cried in surprise.

Andrew grinned. "That made the bastards jump!" he called.

"I missed," Martin replied.

Andrew shook his head. "Never mind. They will be more careful now. Let's get out of here."

He and Carmen began scrambling to their feet. So did Anne and Letitia but Martin stayed down, still holding the rifle. "You go. I'll cover you," he said.

"No, come on!" Letitia cried. She began staggering and stumbling away across the salt pan.

But Martin shook his head. "I'll follow once you have gone a hundred metres," he said. "Now get moving!" He kept his eyes on the men as the others dithered for a moment and then began moving.

Martin turned to call after them and pointed. "Go right. Go to that scrub. It is much closer."

Andrew looked back and waved then changed direction, calling on the others do to do the same. As they did he waved at them and shouted to keep spread out.

It was as well that he did because the man with the rifle threw himself flat and rolled over to face back towards them. The other man kept running. Martin eyed the tiny dark shape on the shimmering white surface and bit his lip.

He's going to shoot again, he thought.

A glance over his shoulder showed that his sister and friends were at least another 50 metres further away.

That makes the range for that fellow at about three hundred and fifty metres, Martin thought.

Three hundred was the longest range he had ever fired at but he knew, from talking to the army cadets at his school that snipers routinely fired at ranges of a thousand metres or more.

Is he that good a shot? Martin wondered, squinting through the sights at the man.

Then it came to him that he could not take the risk of not giving covering fire. *He might still hit one of them,* he reasoned. So he steadied the sight on the man and took the 'first pressure'. Then his instructor's words again crowded into his mind.

If you are unsure of the range aim low. Aim at the bottom of the target and watch for your fall of shot.

So Martin did and with a half gasp he tried to stop his shaking and squeezed the trigger. As he did he saw a puff of smoke from the man's rifle and he cursed himself for being too late.

Bang! Crack! Boom!

Martin's mind registered the sound of his own shot, the vicious noise of a bullet passing and breaking the sound barrier as it did and then the sound of the man's rifle. His eyes also registered a spurt of dust right in front of the man and then how the tiny, prone shape seemed to twitch.

Did I hit him? Martin wondered as he reefed open the bolt and then rammed another bullet into the breech.

Even as his heart went into his mouth with dread—he knew now that he feared killing someone else far more than he feared being killed himself—he saw the man roll sideways and then aim at him.

My turn! Martin thought, the terror almost paralysing him for a second.

Cringing in anticipation of being hit he made his choice between shooting back or moving. He moved, rolling sideways and then scrambling to his feet, the terror gripping his whole being.

As he did the man fired and the bullet cracked close past him. It was so close Martin flinched and then began to run. With panic clutching at his throat he dashed sideways. But his mind was still functioning.

Don't run in a straight line, jink! he told himself. So he did, suddenly swerving to the left and then back to the right.

It was lucky that he did because another bullet cracked past, fearfully close. It was obvious that the man was a reasonable shot.

But not used to targets that move, or shoot back, Martin thought with grim satisfaction. But he also knew he was running a terrible risk so he suddenly swerved again and threw himself flat.

A glance showed him that his friends were now at least another 150 metres away and he was surprised to note that how small and distant they looked.

They will be safe soon, he thought. So he squirmed around to face the man and lifted the rifle ready to shoot again.

But having aimed he hesitated. The range was now 400 or more metres and the target was quite a small one.

Do I fire and possibly waste my only bullet? Martin worried. He decided not to. *I will only shoot if he tries to follow.*

Crack!

Martin actually saw the puff of smoke as the man fired but was shocked to find his face splattered with grit before he could even react. For sure his teachers and instructors had told him that bullets travel faster than sound and so fast you can't react but it was a mind-numbing shock to experience the reality of it. Much too late he flinched and rolled aside as the fear flooded back.

Shaking so much with reaction that he could not hold the rifle steady Martin did not dare fire back.

Bloody hell! That was close, he thought.

Blinking and wiping at his left eye he tried to clear it of grit and stinging salt. Only when he had cleared it enough to get some blurry vision restored did he note the ploughed up mud about 5 metres in front of where he had been lying. Whether the bullet had embedded itself in the mud or ricocheted he could not tell.

Shivering with fright and reaction he gasped deep gulps of air and again steadied his rifle. A swift glance over his shoulder informed him that his friends were another hundred metres away.

They are safe for the time being, he thought. *As long as I can hold this bloke up.*

Calming himself he braced to face another shot. By now he felt so drained from the nervous reaction that he became quite calm.

All I can do is wait, he thought.

He lowered the rifle to ease the strain in his trembling fingers and then lay as flat as he could to make the smallest possible target.

But a minute went by and no shot came. Cautiously Martin raised his head and stared through his blurred and stinging eyes at the tiny shape that was the man.

Did I hit him and he has died? Martin wondered, dread clutching at his heart.

There was no way of knowing. But the man was still lying there and not moving in pursuit so Martin decided he must wait, at least until his friends had reached the safety of the distant scrub.

Chapter 15

HEAT AND FEAR

Five minutes of awful waiting dragged by, each one seeming like ten. Every few seconds Martin looked over his shoulder to check where his sister and friends were, and each time felt satisfied that his tactic was working.

They are nearly safe, he noted.

Then he turned his attention back to the man. There had been no sign of him moving and the worry that he had indeed been hit and killed really shook Martin. As the guilt built in him, he began to pray, to beg forgiveness for the evil act.

To add to his worries, he again saw and then heard the search helicopter, but it was still many kilometres away, doing low circles over the mangroves. After a time, it vanished in the haze that had begun to build.

Oh! Why don't they widen their search? he thought, shaking his head in exasperation.

More minutes dragged by and he saw his friends and sister vanish into the belt of low scrub. In the other direction he saw Grizzly Joel reach the distant mangroves and vanish from sight. As he did another worrying thought crossed Martin's mind.

He might go back to that trawler and get reinforcements.

For several minutes Martin lay there, too afraid to get up and run. While he lay there, he chewed over the enemies options. But after considering the people he had seen on the trawler he decided that they probably only had two more men on it.

There was the bearded bloke who is the captain and there might be an engineer. Those females will be the cooks and deckhands, he reasoned.

Somehow, he could not imagine the females taking up guns to start a manhunt. *So that means two more at most. But how many guns can they muster? Surely a trawler doesn't carry an arsenal?*

A glance at his watch showed him it was a couple of minutes to 9 o'clock. That was a surprise. It felt like much more time had passed.

Then Martin became aware that he was hot. The dry salt and gritty mud was heating up as the sun rose higher and he found he was perspiring. It wasn't much but it was just enough to make tiny beads of perspiration trickle down into his eyes. These set them stinging again.

This is bad! I am dehydrating fast, he thought. The notion of being an egg on a hot plate made him glance up, hoping for cloud.

There was some but it was all very high level. "Alto Cirrus," he muttered through lips that were now dry and cracked. His tongue felt swollen and he swallowed to try to moisten it but without success. He was also aware that he had a blinding headache and that his vision was continually going blurry. The sun was so hot that the metal parts of the rifle became uncomfortable to touch.

I can't stay here much longer. I will be fried, he thought. Apprehension gripped both his chest and stomach and he felt his stomach growling from hunger. And he felt exhaustion. *Lack of food and too much stress,* he decided.

Once again, he studied the distant shape of the man. To his surprise he found it hard to see. Everything seemed to dance and shimmer and he blinked and then carefully wiped at the corners of his eyes to clear them. But then he realized it was not only his eyes.

That is a heat haze, he told himself.

Looking around he saw that the whole vast mudflat had taken on a 'watery' appearance with the more distant objects looking blurry and as though they were floating on a shimmering line of white water. He also noted that the sky off to the east also looked whitish and hazy.

Then Martin looked back and noted that the man was no longer visible in the heat shimmer. But as he strained his eyes to focus them the man reappeared, still prone. Then he vanished from view again.

If he is hard to see then so am I, Martin reasoned. He decided that moving was worth the risk. *He will have trouble aiming and I can't stay here anyway,* he told himself.

So he took several deep breaths and braced himself, ready to spring to his feet to run.

But just as he tensed to do this, the man's shape changed and became taller. Martin stared hard, the anxiety pounding in his veins. His tired mind realized that the man had stood up so he lifted the rifle and held it ready. Then the man vanished in a wave of shimmer and Martin had trouble tracking him to aim. When the man's shape did become visible again Martin shook his head with relief.

He's running away! he thought.

For a few more seconds Martin watched to confirm that the man really was going in the opposite direction and then he slowly and painfully got to his feet. The effort required worried him, and he was dismayed at how weak he was and how sore his muscles felt. Every one of them seemed to ache and he had to blink to clear his eyes.

Turning around he began walking south towards the line of scrub, the tree tops now just visible as blurred shapes above the mirage shimmer. So stiff and sore did he feel that it took him a couple of minutes walking to warm up and loosen his over strained muscles. And by then he was aware that he was plodding rather than walking and that he was even having trouble keeping his balance.

Once he did stumble and he hastily dropped the rifle butt to steady himself. For a few seconds he stood there swaying before the dizziness passed. Then, as he leaned on the rifle, he remembered the safety catch.

You bloody fool! You could have shot yourself by accident, he berated himself.

A wave of shivering passed up his body and he picked the rifle up and clicked on the safety catch. Then he set himself to the task of walking that kilometre.

As he did movement ahead attracted his eyes and he blinked and tried to focus. Fear surged and then abated when he saw that it was Andrew. He was hurrying back towards him.

Good man! Martin thought.

That bucked him up and he made the effort to straighten up and to walk as normally as possible.

Andrew reached him within five minutes. Martin nodded, unable and unwilling to smile with his cracked lips.

"Thanks mate," he croaked.

Andrew also nodded. "Thought you might need a hand," he suggested, holding up the shotgun. "What are the men doing?"

"Grizzly Joel ran away and has gone back to the mangroves and the other bloke, the one with the mop head, has just run off as well."

"They've given up the chase?"

Martin shook his head. "For the moment maybe but I reckon they will collect the other two men on that trawler and try to catch us up or cut us off," he replied.

The two plodded slowly across the salt pan. The glare from the dry salt was almost blinding and the heat now seemed to rise in waves. Martin found he was gasping and staggering and then he realized that Andrew had grabbed his arm to steady him.

"Thanks mate," he muttered thickly.

It took them ten long minutes to walk to the line of scrub. As they got closer Martin saw that it was dry coastal savannah on a low sand dune. The trees were mostly spindly little things or twisted eucalypts which offered sparse shade. Underneath them was a thin matt of dead leaves and twigs amid tufts of wiry grass and prickles.

These he discovered when he joined the girls in the shade of the biggest tree in the area.

"Ouch!" Martin cried as he sat on some.

Wincing with pain he levered himself up and passed the rifle to Carmen so he could pluck at the burrs that had embedded themselves in his fingers and buttocks.

"Bloody Bindi Eyes!" he cried.

Having pulled several from the back of his shorts he carefully checked the ground for more before sitting down, or rather slumping down. Now that he had re-joined the others and reached what felt like relative safety the energy just seemed to drain out of him. For a few minutes he just sat and recovered his breath, ignoring their questions.

Then he described what had happened out on the mud flat, omitting his thoughts and emotions. Letitia shook her head. "You are wonderful," she said. "You are so brave!"

Martin would have blushed if he had had the energy. Instead he made light of his actions. But inside he knew he had passed one of his life's great tests and he wasn't sure if he was satisfied or appalled.

I deliberately tried to kill another human being, he thought.

The knowledge that he could do that he found very disturbing. But it also calmed him. Nothing would ever be quite as bad again.

I know what I am capable of now, he thought grimly.

After he had finished his description they sat in silence for a few minutes. Martin checked for prickles and then lay back on the dead leaves and closed his eyes. But the sand was too hot for comfort and he soon sat up and bent over forward instead. The heat seemed to come in waves and what little breeze there was felt like it was coming from the open front of a furnace.

We aren't out of the woods yet, he thought.

Groaning with pain he sat up. "We should move before those men come after us again," he suggested.

Carmen shook her head. "Not in this heat. We will end up with heat stroke in an hour. We are all on the edge of heat exhaustion now. You look like a grilled chop."

"I certainly feel like one," Martin agreed, making an attempt to smile at his own weak joke. But he could only agree although he had the niggling fear that they might not last just sitting in the shade either. "Should the fittest of us go for help and the others stay here?" he suggested.

They debated this for a while. Martin saw that it was now 10 o'clock and that worried him even more. Another hour had gone by and that meant the men could have travelled quite a distance. He wished he had a map to plan with and made an effort to concentrate his throbbing mind to remember it. But all he was sure of was that there were farms somewhere to the south and a settlement called Mud Crab Landing somewhere to the east. But which one to aim for?

They also discussed this. Andrew used a stick to draw a rough map in the sand. "What about a compromise? There must be a vehicle track from this Mud Crab Landing place. If we go southwest we will either come to the track or a farm."

Martin liked that idea. "I agree. Let's try that."

Letitia looked up and nodded but then said, "Can we just rest a bit longer please? I feel completely exhausted."

This was also agreed to but not without some trepidation on Martin's part. *The longer we delay the more time those men have to come up with some other plan to catch us,* he thought. He felt sure they would not just give up.

So they sat and sweltered. The heat was so intense that the dry leaves crackled when they moved on them, and Martin felt he was shrivelling like them. He closed his eyes against the glare and then brushed at the bush flies that had begun to cluster and annoy. The flies did not buzz but landed on him and crawled into the corners of his eyes or up his nostrils. To exclude them he had to keep his mouth tightly closed.

The flies were annoying everyone but then Letitia let out a gasp of pain which startled Martin so much that he sat up and opened his gummed and gritty eyes to look. He saw that Letitia was brushing at her bosom.

"Eeek! Aaargh! Oh! Oh, get off me!" she cried, scraping at the top of both her breasts with both hands.

"What is it?" Martin queried in alarm.

Carmen answered. "A hairy caterpillar," she said.

Even as she did another one dropped from the branch above and landed full on Letitia's left shoulder. She let out more shrieks and sprang up, brushing at the caterpillar.

"Ow! Aaargh! They hurt!" she wailed.

The friends quickly moved out from under that tree and into the shade of another nearby. After a careful check for more of the furry little creatures, they stood and Martin was treated to the spectacle of the whole group examining Letitia's bosom. He was both embarrassed and resigned. Even Andrew stared at the angry red welts that had appeared where the hairy caterpillars had been. Letitia didn't help by cupping each breast in turn and lifting it up to look.

As he stood there in the dry bush while burning with embarrassment Martin experienced a sudden chill and for a moment he wondered if he was going to faint. Then he realized that it was a cool breeze and that they were in shadow. Glancing up he saw with surprise and relief that a layer of stratus cloud had come sliding across the sky from the east.

"Oh! That's better," he sighed.

With that help they picked up a little and when Carmen suggested they get moving he agreed. As before Andrew led, then Carmen and Anne with Letitia behind her. Martin came last, looking back to check if there was any sign of pursuit. There wasn't. The heat shimmer had gone off the salt flats and he could see the mangroves on the other side quiet clearly.

So what are those men doing now? he worried.

The sand rise was only a few metres high and a hundred metres wide but moving through the dry scrub on it was unpleasant. The tufts of wiry grass stuck into them, especially Letitia, and there were prickly bushes, green ants and even a snake.

As they all jumped back and stared at the reptile when it slid across into another clump of grass Anne asked Andrew what type it was.

"Dunno. Some, sort of browny, greeny, olive coloured thing."

"What type is it?" Letitia asked fearfully.

Again, Andrew shook his head. "No idea. It might be a brown snake, or it might be a taipan. Or it could just be some harmless tree snake."

"Can't you tell?" Letitia asked.

"Not unless you count their scales," Andrew replied.

He explained the belly scales and the need for a count across the diagonal around the snake to be able to accurately determine what type.

"Except for the obvious ones like death adders and pythons and so on," he added.

Then he explained how many snake species changed colour to suit their local environment.

"I read that king browns, which are actually black snakes, can be dark brown or light brown or even a golden colour to grey," he explained.

Carmen shuddered. "Remember that horrible great mulga snake in the Northern Territory Wildlife Park near Darwin Andrew? It was a king brown type wasn't it?"

"I think so," Andrew answered, while still eyeing the long grass. Then he started walking to detour around the clump. "Come on. It's gone."

They continued on for another 50 paces, startling several birds as they did. Then they came to another wide stretch of mud flat. Beyond it was another line of scrub and more salt pan.

"What are those stick things?" Anne asked, pointing to tall thin posts which stood in a line across the distant mud flat.

Martin focused his eyes and at once his spirits lifted. "Poles for electricity or telephone wires," he answered.

Suddenly Carmen grabbed Andrews sleeve and pointed to her left. "Look! Houses!"

Martin looked and several kilometres away to the east he saw the glint of sunlight reflecting off corrugated iron roofs.

"Mud Crab Landing?" he suggested.

"Has to be," Andrew agreed.

Anne nodded. "Then let's go there. There must be people and then we are safe," she said.

So they hurried forward out onto the mudflat. At first it was easy going and they just plodded along but all too quickly they began to tire and go slower. Hundreds of tiny purple and grey soldier crabs were moving out on the flat and these scuttled out of their way or fled down holes at their approach. Several heron type birds stalked off or flapped away as the group got closer.

The nature of the mud flat began to change. Small clumps of wiry salt water grass were encountered and then whole stretches of it. The grass was interspersed with a ground cover of a plant with dark green and purple leaves. This scrunched when trodden on. A few small clumps of mangroves struggled for existence. The sun came out again with what felt like redoubled force and the heat shimmer re-appeared. The buildings did not seem to be any closer.

Grimly trying to moisten his throat Martin put his head down and plodded on. When he next looked up, he estimated that the houses were still at least 5 kilometres away.

Further than we thought, he decided, noting that the buildings were nestled amid scrub and dark trees that looked like mangroves.

He had never been to Mud Crab Landing, but he had been to several other similar localities. This one looked to be just a small collection of weekend fishing huts and he was worried that there might not actually be anyone living there.

But it is Saturday so there might be, he reasoned. Then he shook his head. *Saturday! We have been on the run for twenty-four hours. Poor old mum and dad will be frantic by now!*

Once again, he scanned the sky behind him searching for the rescue helicopter. There was no sign of it but he did note that the clouds were building up. A 360 degree sweep of the horizon brought home to him just how flat the country around Bowling Green Bay was. The only mountains he could see were the massive bulk of the Mt Elliott Range and it was at least 15 kilometres away and hazy blue with the distance.

Licking his cracked lips, he looked ahead and then frowned. A distinct line of grass and a scattering of small trees appeared to stretch right across their front between them and the houses.

What is that? he wondered.

The line was only a few hundred metres ahead, and as they got closer he studied it with some concern. Then realization burst on him and he gasped with dismay.

It was another creek, and it was full to the brim!

Chapter 16

TESTED AGAIN!

As they approached the small ridges of mud that marked the actual bank of the creek Martin's fears were confirmed. It was a creek and it appeared to meander right across the mud flat for many kilometres in both directions. It blocked the direct route. *Damn!* Martin thought, then gave at wry grin at the pun.

As they reached the bank of the creek the group came to a halt and the others also gasped in dismay. "Another creek!" Anne cried, her voice almost cracking with fear.

The creek looked to be only about 10 metres wide but it was brimming with greenish muddy water and there was an obvious current flowing up it. A glance in both directions revealed that it did not appear to narrow anywhere along its length before the actual water was hidden by the bends.

For a few minutes they just stood there, drooping with exhaustion and demoralized by the new test they had to face. Then the heat began to get at them. Martin blinked and shook his head.

Bloody hell! I don't need another test of courage like this, he thought as he eyed the muddy water. *There are liable to be crocs in this creek as well. They like to nest in the long grass.*

To add to Martin's concern he noted that the creek was so full it was starting to overflow its banks in places and shallow streams of water were starting to spread out across the mudflats.

Of course! The tide is coming in again, he realized.

Turning to Andrew he said, "What time is high tide Andrew?"

Andrew looked thoughtful and then replied: "Most of this month there are four tides a day, and I think this tide is around midday."

Anne looked surprised. "Oh, I thought there was only one of each every day," she said.

Andrew shook his head. "No. It depends on the phase of the moon. Sometimes there are only two but often there are three and sometimes four," he explained.

Carmen interrupted. "Never mind the lesson! The sooner we cross the better. We will do it the same way as last time, all at once but no diving in and splashing. Just ease yourself in," she said.

Martin looked at the muddy water and felt his stomach tighten with fear. Knowing that there might be crocodiles had a whole new edge now that he had seen a man mangled to death by one. Swallowing and trying to mask his terror he moved carefully forward. Then he hesitated, considering what might be the best policy with the rifle.

Can I throw it that far? he wondered. He eyed the far bank and wasn't sure. Then he thought about how hard it had been to clean the rifle. *If I do throw it, it will get covered in mud again. I will carry it.*

That decided him He held it in his right hand and lowered himself in, his whole body cringing with apprehension. As he did his boots slipped on the slippery slope and he slithered in until only his head and the arm holding the rifle were still out of the water. Then he glanced to check what the others were doing. The others were scared too and he saw Letitia standing on the bank looking very anxious.

"Come on Sis. Swim with me," he called.

"I'm scared!" Letitia wailed, crossing her arms over her bosom and hunching up.

"We all are. Come on. It's only ten metres," he replied.

Whimpering and sobbing she began to make her way down into the water. Then she slipped and fell in with a big splash. Martin groaned and shook his head and then raised himself so that he was in the water up to his chest. As soon as he saw that Letitia had started swimming, he pushed out with his feet into a side stroke posture. The rifle he held at its point of balance so that it was up out of the water.

Instantly he discovered that it was much harder than he had anticipated. The problem was the footwear. They prevented his feet turning to the right angle to give thrust. He swam as hard as he could but found it difficult to keep his head above water. Then the splashing and small waves generated by the others slopped salt water into his mouth and he found himself spluttering and spitting as the stinging liquid burned in his throat. He was also dismayed at quickly his strength seemed to drain away. The fearful notion occurred to him that he might have taken on something beyond his ability.

As he struggled across Martin was aware of the others splashing their way across as well. Carmen and Andrew both swam easily and quietly, Andrew holding the shotgun above his head in the same manner as Martin was holding the file.

They are both divers, Martin reminded himself.

A glance showed Anne dog paddling to his left.

How is Sis going? he thought.

He glanced back at where Letitia was splashing across on his right. That fleeting glance was enough to tell him there was a problem.

Sis is in trouble, he thought.

She was. She gurgled and then choked. Then she tried to cry out and in the process swallowed some water. "Glug! Glug. Gasp! Hel… Help! C... C... Cramp!" she cried.

Martin met her eyes and noted the terror in them just as her head slipped out of sight under the water.

Bloody hell, Sis is drowning! he thought.

An urgent pulse of anxiety gave him a reserve of energy and he at once got rid of the rifle. The decision was made in a split second and with all the strength he could muster he acted on it. He swept his arm down and then up, flinging the rifle as hard as he could towards the far bank.

It landed with a splash close to the bank but by then his focus was on Letitia. He saw the water boil into foam and then her hand appeared. A moment later her head came up. Her mouth opened and she tried to breathe in but instead sucked in water as well. This set her coughing and she splashed frantically to keep her head up.

Martin turned and reached across just as she slipped under again. But he was just too late and she vanished from view. His immediate response was to duck his head under and swim down. As he did, he opened his eyes but all he could see was muddy gloom and the salt water stung fiercely. None of this was helped by the fact that he had not had time to take a full breath of air or by the fear of crocodiles that was almost paralysing him.

Then his clawing fingers encountered her struggling form and he at once entwined them in her hair and began kicking upwards. He could at last tell which way that was by the relative shades of light and dark.

As he went up Martin felt Letitia strike his legs with her arms. Then she grabbed at his left ankle and a pulse of pure fear ran through him. Several times in the past he had almost drowned and he remembered doing exactly that to Andrew when he had dived in to Ross River to save him. Stories from Life Saving instructors of would be rescuers being drowned by the people they were trying to save swirled in his mind to add to his terror.

Suddenly Letitia let go but then she clawed her way up his body, grabbing at his clothes and pulling and then pushing him down. He just had time to gulp a breath before his head was pushed under. Now it became a real battle for survival and Martin's will to live came to the fore. Savagely he pushed at Letitia, shoving her legs away. Then he tried to break her grip on his neck while kicking upwards with all his might.

By using his utmost strength, he managed to get his face clear of the water long enough to get more air.

"Let... glug... Let go, you silly bitch!" he gasped. "I've got you."

Then he went under again, his face enveloped by her breasts and then her lower body and thighs. Desperate to live he dug his fingers hard into her stomach and then into her groin. She twitched and then moved away and he was able to get his arms free and used them to stroke with.

Once again, he got his head above water and found himself looking into her panic-stricken eyes at a range of only a few centimetres. With an effort he trod water and kept a grip on her. After sucking in more air, he croaked, "Relax! I've got you. Just float and I will tow you."

Something must have sunk in as she suddenly went limp and Martin was able to grab her and turn her around. Determined to get ashore as quickly as possible he put his right arm over her shoulder from behind and grabbed her tight, clutching her under the armpit in the process. Then he began side stroking.

It was only five more metres and both Carmen and Andrew appeared beside him to help. A few strokes later Martin felt the ooze of the bottom and thankfully scrabbled to get a firm footing on the muddy slope. While doing this he did not release his grip on his sister.

I'm not going to lose her now! he told himself.

The others helped. Anne was out on the bank by then and she grabbed his shirt and both Andrew and Carmen helped push both up so that they slithered onto the 'dry' flat.

Only then did Martin let go. Satisfied Letitia was safe he lay back and sucked in great gulps of air. Great wracking sobs convulsed his shivering body and he felt so exhausted that all he could do was lie there. Letitia lay next to him, sobbing and wheezing. The others crowded round.

Carmen bent over Letitia. "You alright Letitia? What happened?"

"C... C... Cramp," Letitia croaked.

For a couple of minutes they stayed as they were until Martin's breathing returned to normal and the worst of the trembling had stopped. Then the glare of the sun in his eyes got him to roll onto his side and then to push himself up to his hands and knees. He stayed that way for another couple of minutes as great shudders of emotion and reaction coursed through his body.

"Oh, bloody hell! I thought I was a goner then," he croaked.

Then he vomited. It was painful as there as little to come out except a dribble of seawater and then a trickle of acid bile which burned in the back of this throat.

Letitia also rolled over and was helped into a sitting position. She was shivering and sobbing, and only after another minute did she look at Martin with great red-rimmed eyes.

"Oh thank you Martin! You saved my life," she whispered.

Martin could only shrug and feel slightly embarrassed.

Andrew had been staring at Letitia and suddenly seemed to realize he was. He quickly looked away and then said: "I think we should move away from here. We are a bit too close to the water for comfort."

Martin looked at the creek and noted that it was now spilling over the bank in an ever-spreading shallow flood.

A croc could just slide right out and grab us, he thought.

He shuddered and then struggled to his feet and stood there shakily. Then he remembered the rifle.

"Did you see the rifle?" he asked Andrew.

Andrew shook his head. "No. I saw you throw it but it landed in the water."

"Oh bugger! We need that," Martin said, moving closer to the bank and staring at the swirling muddy water. There was no sign of the weapon and through his mind ran the ghastly idea of going back into the water to try to find it.

Is it worth the risk? he wondered.

Determined to get it he began to lower himself back into the water. Carmen looked appalled and hurried over and grabbed at his shirt. "Martin! What are you doing?" she cried.

"Looking for the rifle," he croaked.

143

"Don't be stupid! We have made so much disturbance that every croc for hundreds of metres must know we are here," she snapped.

"But we might need it. It saved our lives back there," Martin answered.

Stubbornly he continued to lower himself in. When he was in chest deep, he began groping in the mud with his hands.

Then Letitia joined Carmen and she reached down and took hold of his shirt and pulled.

"You are crazy! A croc could get you. Get out please," she yelled.

Both she and Carmen began dragging at him. Martin did not resist. His boots and hands had been feeling in the slimy mud, but his mind had been focused on waiting for the terrible crunch of monster teeth into his arms or legs. His whole body was tingling with terrified anticipation, so he was actually relieved to be pulled back out of the water.

Letitia stood over him, her breasts wobbling close to his face. "That was silly! Don't you take risks like that again!" she cried. The she sobbed and suddenly enfolded his head into her arms and bosom and began to sob. "Oh, Little Brother, I need you alive!"

Martin was embarrassed and managed to squirm free. He sat up and Letitia knelt beside him, her breasts quivering only centimetres from his eyes.

Bloody hell! he thought. *Why have a got a sister like her?*

But he did love her and was glad she had acted. But he was also very conscious suddenly of her sexuality and her semi nudity.

She is my sister. I shouldn't have thoughts like that, he told himself.

So he rolled onto his hands and knees and groggily levered himself to his feet. "Let's get going then. When we get to those houses, we should be safe."

Martin began plodding towards the distant buildings. These were half hidden by the heat shimmer, but the silver roofs seemed to beckon and offer safety, so he made the effort to put one foot in front of the other.

The others followed in a straggling group. All had their heads down and looked how he felt, on their last legs. From time to time Martin glanced around and he noted that the line of telephone posts was much closer. They shimmered and wavered in the heat and appeared to be growing out of silver water.

The heat became even more unbearable. It burned at the top of his head so that he started putting his hand over the crown of his hair in a largely futile attempt to protect it. He found his vision blurring again and had difficulty swallowing. His tongue felt swollen and his headache moved to the 'blinding' stage so that he began blinking and squinting in the glare.

I feel ready to drop, Martin thought, anxiety gripping him.

A glance at the others showed that they were all staggering and reeling as they plodded on. The prospect of heat stroke became a distinct possibility.

Will we make it? he wondered. The buildings still looked to be 2 or 3 kilometres away.

Worse still they encountered salt water. This was slowly spreading right across the flat. Martin rubbed his eyes and studied it. He noted with dismay that large parts of the mud flat were covered with water.

The tide is still coming in, he realized. *Oh, this could get unpleasant!*

The idea of walking through water across a vast swamp where saltwater crocodiles lived made him shudder. There were a few tufts of saltwater grass but stepping on them had little appeal.

That is where snakes might live, he thought.

The water made the mud soft and they had to slow down even more as they splashed their way through it. To begin with, the water was only a few centimetres deep, more a nuisance than anything, but it hid holes and deeper gutters and in their weakened state this soon led to stumbles and falls. Once again it was Letitia who provided the spectacle when she slipped and fell flat on her back.

Then she had trouble rolling over and getting to her feet. She ended up coated with mud, but she then decided this was a good policy and began smearing it on herself.

"Cover my back please. It will stop the sunburn and keep the sand flies off," she said.

So the girls slapped mud on her back and buttocks and smeared it down her legs. She smeared it all over her front. Andrew watched for a while and then shook his head and kept on walking.

Just when Martin thought he couldn't endure the heat anymore, another big cloud came over and gave them some very welcome shade. Relieved he plodded on, his head drooping from exhaustion.

Suddenly he shivered and he realized it was from a cool breeze. Then a light drizzle of tiny raindrops landed on his skin. Lifting his head Martin saw that a light shower of rain was sweeping across the flat towards them from the east.

"Rain!" he thought, or cried, he wasn't sure which.

We might make it!

Chapter 17

MUD CRAB LANDING

The rain misted over them. It was only a gentle drizzle but one that instantly cooled the skin and which brought hope. Martin felt his spirits lift. It was such a relief! He wiped the salt and mud off his face and then very gingerly dabbed at the corners of his eyes to clear the gunk and grit from there. The others did likewise and then they stood there grinning at each other.

But it wasn't enough to really wet them, much less give them a drink and an attempt by Andrew to suck the moisture out of his shirt sleeve resulted in him grimacing and spitting.

"Too much salt still," he explained.

They resumed walking, buoyed up by the damp coolness and the apparent closeness of the buildings. But the misty rain soon ended and the sun came out again, harsh and hot. Martin looked around and saw more dark clouds out to the east. There were curtains of rain under them and he fervently hoped one of them might come their way.

At least there is a cool breeze, he told himself.

But they were now wading rather than walking. Midday had arrived and the tide was still on the make and the whole mudflat was now flooded to between ankle and knee deep. It became quiet awkward to keep their footing and Martin found he had to slide his feet rather than lift them.

Anne then voiced one of his remaining fears. "What will we do if a crocodile comes swimming along?" she asked.

Several times Martin had looked anxiously around, aware that crocodiles could also be sliding or swimming across the flat. But he wasn't too worried as he did not believe they would.

There would be nothing for them to eat so why would they? he reasoned.

But it was one thing to be rational and quite another to be splashing across a vast wasteland of muddy salt water! And not a tree anywhere.

Carmen replied that it was unlikely. She sounded annoyed and Martin decided that was because Anne had alarmed them, particularly Letitia.

There were a few clumps of grass and some patches of slightly higher ground that were also covered with grass or the purple ground cover but even these were soggy and awash and Martin did not enjoy squelching his way across them, mainly because of fear of snakes.

Then a real rain shower arrived. It began as a heavy downpour that swept across and drenched them. While it did they just stood and opened their mouths and looked up. It was wonderful, but also cold! And it was all but impossible to get a proper drink as not enough drops fell in their mouths. But it did rinse the sweat off their skin and out of their clothes so when Andrew tried his sucking method again he nodded with satisfaction.

Martin tried it as well and the effect was immediate. The sweet water at once eased the constriction in his throat and his cracked lips felt instantly better. After sucking at one sleeve he changed to the other. Then he noticed that Letitia was trying to lick the drops off her skin.

"Suck my shirt Sis," Martin said.

Gratefully she moved over and bent to suck at it. As she did Martin noted that the rain was washing the mud and grime off her so that her bare skin was again revealed. Once again he was astonished at the number of bites and scratches on her sun burnt skin. Then his eyes noted the welts on her skin from the hairy caterpillars. These had now puffed up into blisters the size of 20 cent coins.

"Holy mackerel Sis! Look at those blisters," he commented.

Letitia did and gasped. The others stopped drinking and moved to watch. Carmen bent over and studied the blisters and frowned.

"From those hairy caterpillars. You must have an allergy. Do you feel sick?"

"Not from that, just from being exhausted and sunburnt," Letitia said.

They all bent closer to study the welts and Letitia gently brushed at them with her other hand. "I think my skin is just sensitive," she commented.

Then it struck Martin how surreal the situation was. *Here we all are, Andrew included, examining Sis's body and none of us thinks it is odd!*

But the same idea must have occurred to the others at the same moment because Carmen suddenly straightened up and shook her head and Anne blushed while Andrew looked away.

To change the subject, Martin said, "We had better keep walking. Let's get his over. Those buildings are still a couple of kilometres away."

So they resumed wading but this time in drizzle which at first cooled them and then threatened to chill them. As they made their way slowly along Martin and the others kept sucking at their shirt sleeves to get more water. It wasn't much but already he felt much better.

Then his stomach growled loudly, so loudly the others looked at him. "Just hungry," he commented.

Then his stomach moved again and before he could control himself he did a loud fart. The embarrassment made him blush crimson.

Andrew chuckled and then said: "We all need a good feed Martin. You don't have to voice your complaints so loudly."

Martin had to grin and the others smiled. They plodded on, each one sending out a ripple of small waves with each step. To make it harder there were crab holes which they stumbled in and the mud itself was softening as it became wet and they started to sink in.

The drizzle eased off but the sun did not return as the clouds now covered most of the sky. Martin was glad of that but he was irritated by how his boots were now sinking into the mud so that it took an effort to break the suction to pull each one clear. Every step became an effort. The others were having the same difficulty and several times Letitia fell over.

For some distance Martin had observed a few sticks or posts protruding from the water a few hundred metres to his right and now he noted that there were also what looked like rocks and that these were in a distinct line.

What is that? he wondered.

As they waded slowly on he saw that their course and that of the lines of rocks and posts would converge about a kilometre ahead. He studied the pattern more closely.

They are in two distinct parallel lines, he decided. Then it dawned on him what he was looking at. *Those posts mark a vehicle track!*

Pointing to them, he said, "That is a road over there."

"Road? Where?" Letitia queried.

Andrew looked and then nodded. "I was looking at them and wondering what they were. I thought they might just be an old fence."

"No," Martin replied. "I reckon they are marker posts so vehicles can stay on the track when it is covered with water."

"You are right," Carmen agreed. "Let's get on it. It should be easier going than this mud."

"And a car might come along," Anne added.

Andrew made a face. "I wouldn't be driving my car through miles of salt water," he commented.

They turned right and sloshed across the posts and rocks. These were lined up 10 or 20 paces apart and in two rows about 5 metres apart. It was at once apparent that Martin's supposition had been correct. The posts did mark a vehicle track, and this was topped with stones and gravel that formed a firm footing.

"Ah! That's better!" Andrew said as he turned left and began walking along it. They still had to wade rather than walk but the going was certainly easier.

As Martin reached the track he looked the other way and noted that the posts and rocks extended off to another of the low, scrub-covered sand dunes about 2 kilometres to the south.

"Should we split up and some of us go the other way in case there isn't anyone at this Mud Crab Landing place?"

Carmen looked and then shook her head. "No. We will stay together. If there isn't anyone at the town, we will come back this way and find a farm."

Martin accepted this and they set off, wading as fast as they safely could. Then more rain came sweeping in from the east, gentle rain but drenching and cooling. He was able to suck moisture while he walked.

After twenty minutes of wading, the buildings, now half hidden by the rain and the scrub, looked to be only about a kilometre away. The water extended to within a few hundred metres of them, ending on a low rise covered with the long grass and stunted trees of the coastal scrub.

But the submerged road did not run straight. It curved quiet a lot and twice ran up over low rises that were almost clear of water.

"They must have followed the firmest going in the old days and then added some gravel to that," he commented.

"Which means the road gets used a lot and there must be people here," Anne added.

"There is electricity anyway," Andrew added, pointing to the line of posts supporting wires that was now also converging on their route.

"Possibly telephone," Carmen suggested. "They probably use generators for beach huts."

Having visited several similar beach communities Martin could only agree. Most were a very mixed collection of very old shacks built by weekend fishermen and new, very modern homes that were lived in.

As he got closer to Mud Crab Landing Martin studied it and then counted the buildings. *Only nine buildings,* he counted. *And only four look like houses or shacks. The others look like sheds.*

One of the houses looked new and had the shiniest roof and there was a large new shed made of grey steel near the left-hand end of the settlement. But details were hard to make out from that distance as the trees and bushes and rain hid much of the place.

For some time, Martin had observed that there was a line of trees coming from the right front to end at the buildings. There were more trees on the left.

The seaward side, he told himself, remembering that he was now walking north. *And those trees are along the bank of Mud Crab Creek.*

There had to be a creek, he knew. Why else would there be a fishing settlement? And the name suggested there was a boat ramp or hard of some sort.

Maybe even a wharf? he mused, noting what looked like a couple of masts behind the largest shed at the north end.

At 1135 they finally reached dry land. The settlement was on a large flat area of sand covered with long grass, bushes and straggling and stunted trees, either ironbarks or paperbarks. The sand rise was only about 2 metres but was obviously clear of the highest tides.

As he trudged thankfully up the short rise Martin saw that the buildings were still about a hundred metres away through the thin screen of scrub and that the place was more spread out and bigger than he had at first thought.

Right on top of the rise the vehicle track split into three. The centre track went directly on for another hundred metres to a large area of bare ground beside what was obviously the bank of the creek. A dense growth of mangroves lined the far bank.

That is where the boat ramp will be, Martin decided.

After walking another 50 paces Martin noted that there were a few more buildings than he had at first seen. Away off to his right, nestled in among some trees about 150 metres away was an old house made of unpainted timber. It had a shed or boat house near it which looked to be right on the bank of the creek. To the left of that was an open area and then another old house, one with a veranda all around it and an open-fronted garage or shed made of rusty corrugated iron half hiding it.

To the left of the house, between it and the large open are on the creek bank was a shack made of timber and corrugated iron. Several vehicle tracks criss-crossed through the bush near it. Closer to the centre track, only about ten metres to the right of it, and fronting the large open area was another shack. This one was made of rusty corrugated iron and had iron shutters instead of windows. It was surrounded by weeds and looked derelict. There was even an old car body rusting behind it.

To the left of the track was a large shed, also very old and made of bush timbers and corrugated iron. It had piles of junk and several upturned boats against its side and back walls. The left-hand vehicle track went to the left of this big shed and led to the new house and the big new shed made of grey steel sheeting. The grey shed was right at the river bank and the new house was 50 metres back from it on the other side of another vehicle track that ran northwards parallel with the creek from the open area and into drier bush behind a patch of mangroves. Another couple of shacks were just visible through the trees and presumably this track led to them.

As they approached the big rusty shed Martin saw that another vehicle track went left across the rear of the building to join the left-hand track near the new house. More junk, rubbish, old car tyres and a rotting timber dinghy lay in the long grass at the back of the big rusty shed.

As they reached the back corner of the big rusty shed Martin studied the corrugated iron shack on the right.

It looks all closed up, he thought.

They came to a stop at the right front corner of the big rusty shed. The open area stretched out ahead of them. Martin looked to left and right for signs of life. But nothing moved.

"Which way will we go?" he asked.

Carmen pointed left. "To that new house. These others all look derelict."

Andrew nodded. "I agree. It doesn't look like anyone lives in this shanty here," he said.

Letitia looked anxiously around. "I think I will stay here if you don't mind," she said.

Martin looked at her and nodded. "I agree. I'll stay with you Sis. We don't want you arrested for walking down the main street with nothing much on."

"Huh! Main street!" Andrew scoffed, indicating the bare open areas and sandy vehicle tracks. They all laughed, their good spirits revived now that they had reached civilization.

Carmen turned to Letitia. "I agree Letitia. You wait here out of sight and we will get help and then bring you some clothes."

Andrew pointed to the left. "There is a wharf on the other side of that grey shed. I can just see the mast of a boat. There might be people there," he said.

Carmen looked and nodded then said: "House first. I would rather contact a woman. Let's go."

She led the others around the front of the big rusty shed, leaving Martin and Letitia waiting at the corner. Letitia hunched over and appearing, for her, quite concerned.

"I feel very exposed here," she said, looking anxiously around.

"We will watch from the back of this shed," Martin answered.

He led her back and around behind the shed. They walked along the sandy track between the piles of old timber, rusty iron, old cars tyres and three upturned boats to the far corner. Here they were able to view the house from behind the shelter of the shed but were not visible from any other building.

A minute later they saw Carmen, Andrew and Anne walk up to the front door of the new house. It was, Martin noted, the sort of house that was normal in one of Townsville's newer suburbs, made of concrete block with concrete rendering and with a Colourbond steel roof. It looked very modern and out of place.

Carmen knocked and they heard her call out. Nothing happened and Martin noted that all the windows on the house were closed. But as it had air conditioners along the side wall, he presumed that was normal. When nothing happened, Carmen knocked again. Again, they waited.

Martin saw the front door swing open but then to his astonishment Carmen stepped back, her mouth agape and her hands going up. Andrew and Anne also looked frightened and both took several steps backwards. Martin felt a stab of fear.

Something's wrong, he thought.

A moment later exactly what was wrong was revealed. From inside the house appeared a large woman dressed in a pink and grey floral dress. She was a large woman with scraggly black hair. And she was holding a shotgun which was pointing at Carmen!

Ma Baker! was Martin's first thought, the movie image of the murdering American gangster flitting into his consciousness. But a more careful look indicated that this woman was more slatternly. She wore rubber thongs on dirty feet and had a cigarette hanging out of the side of her mouth.

"Git yer hands up or I'll shoot!" she called.

Andrew and Anne did as they were told. Carmen moved back to stand beside them. Just once did she start to turn her head towards where Martin and Letitia were crouching but then she looked the other way.

'Ma Baker' then yelled loudly: "Hey Tony! Marcus! You git here. Quick!"

This call was directed towards the big grey shed so Martin edged forward to look at it. Letitia joined him, looking over his shoulder as he crouched behind a pile of old pallets.

From there they watched in astonishment as the back door of the grey shed swung open and a man came out. The man also had a gun, a pistol, and he pointed it at Carmen!

Martin felt himself chill as the fear stabbed through him. Behind him he heard Letitia suck in a sharp breath. He turned to her.

"Shh! Something's wrong," he whispered.

Then another man appeared around the near end of the grey shed. He also had a gun, a rifle this time. The men closed in behind the three friends who stood in shocked disbelief. Tony, a tall, thin man with black hair and a black moustache snarled at the friends.

"Keep your hands up. OK Ma, we got 'em covered."

Ma Baker kept her shotgun levelled on Andrew. "One move an' I'll blast yer. Now, where are the other two?" she demanded.

On hearing that Martin felt another stab of apprehension. *These people were expecting us,* he thought. His mind went into overdrive. *We have walked straight into a trap!*

Letitia crouched lower. "Martin, these people are part of the same gang. What will we do?" she whispered.

Chapter 18

WHAT NOW?

Martin's mind raced. *What do we do now?* he wondered. He saw that there was no chance of rescuing the others. Not with three people with guns guarding them. The real question was whether he and Letitia could get safely away.

This was given added urgency when he heard Ma Baker shout angrily. "Joel, git out here."

Martin risked a peek through the pile of old timber pallets. To his dismay he saw 'Grizzly' Joel appear around the end of the grey shed. The man hurried towards the group standing out in the open. As he did Martin realized that he could see the stern of the vessel at the small wharf on the other side of the grey shed. With a shock he realized it was the square stern of a trawler and now he noted that the tops of the booms that spread the nets were just showing above the roof.

The trawler! It is here! he thought, his mind racing. Then the deadly implication struck him like a blow. *This is the gang's base!*

The surge of fear he experienced almost paralysed him and what he heard next sent his emotions into a mix of panic and terror. Ma Baker yelled angrily at Joel.

"You said there were five of them?"

Joel stopped near her and nodded. "There were. We had plenty of time to count them. There's another boy and a half naked girl," he replied.

"Half naked girl?" Ma Baker cried in astonishment.

Joel nodded. "Yeah, well, she's only wearing a skimpy bikini. I think she was sunbathing near where Corey shot them fisheries rangers. I seen her several times quite clearly and for sure she's not wearin' much. She's got… she's got…" He gestured with his hands to indicated large breasts.

"Big tits you mean?" Ma Baker cried. "Well she shouldn't be hard to find. Get moving! Tony, you and Marcus go and find them. Joel and I will take these three into the shed and tie them up."

Martin felt the adrenaline spurt into his blood stream and he almost voided himself.

They are coming for us! he thought.

Turning he met Letitia's eyes. "They know about us. We must hide. Quick, get back!" he hissed.

He scuttled back past Letitia, his eyes flicking frantically around in the hope of finding a place to hide. Near him against the back wall of the shed were the piles of timber, some sheet iron in a stack, rusty old machinery and two aluminium dinghies resting upside down on baulks of timber.

Under one of those boats? he wondered. Then he shook his head. *No. Too obvious.*

To their right, on the other side of the sandy vehicle track, scattered on the edge of the triangle of dry scrub, were more piles of junk, some old car tyres, a timber dingy upside down on timber beams, some sheets of rusty corrugated iron and odd items of rusty machinery and chain.

By now Martin was in such a state of anxiety that he was starting to fluster and his eyes kept going out of focus.

Must hurry! Must hurry! he kept telling himself.

He was very aware that the men might appear at the corner of the shed at any moment. A glance behind also showed that he and Letitia would be very visible from the house if they crossed the sandy track to the old dinghy or piles of junk

But there was also a huge risk of continuing on. *If we try to run to that next shack, we will have even less cover,* he decided.

A glance to his right front showed the glint of water beyond the end of the scrub, very open scrub that offered almost no cover.

Even so there was more chance of hiding in it than in the smaller pieces of scrub between the shacks and vehicle tracks further along. So, hammering heart in dry mouth, he swerved to his right and scuttled across towards the old dinghy. But even as he got closer the same considerations flashed across his mind.

Too obvious. But where else could they hide?

Martin knew he had only seconds left so he dashed between the boat and a stack of old timber and junk and into the long grass beyond. The grass wasn't very long and was patchy with areas of bare sand. Worse still there were almost no bushes among the spindly and scattered iron barks. But it would have to do. Flinging himself behind the biggest clump of grass he could see Martin croaked, "Down!"

Letitia came down beside him and at once let out a stifled yelp. Martin understood why. He had landed on a patch of the burs and even the grass and creepers were prickly and spiky.

"Shhh!" he gasped as he screwed his body into a ball and tried to draw his legs in behind the clump of grass.

Next to him Letitia lay on her front and hunched up. She let out a couple of quiet whimpers and he could hear her breath rasping in her throat, but she had enough self-control to be silent.

Peering back through the sparse growth of grass Martin was appalled to see that he and Letitia may as well have been lying out in the open. There was very little cover and most of the grass wasn't even long enough to hide a prone person.

They will spot us for sure, he thought, the dread churning in his stomach.

But it was now too late to try to find somewhere better so he just lay there and prayed, ignoring the prickling pain from the bindis.

Because there they were! Into view around the far end of the shed came Tony and Marcus, guns pointing and eyes questing. The two men stopped for a moment and Martin saw their gaze sweep the whole area. Then they moved to the boats at the back of the shed and looked under them.

Thank God we didn't try them! Martin thought.

But then he saw Marcus point directly at him and his blood froze with terror. The icy hands of panic made the hair on his scalp prickle and he stared in horror as Tony turned to follow the pointing finger and then began to walk towards him.

Oh my God! They've seen us! Martin thought, his whole body starting to quiver with terrified anticipation.

The men walked towards him but then stopped and Martin stared but barely dared hope. *They have stopped at that old boat just there,* he thought.

The men spoke to each other and then Martin saw Tony slide the pistol, a Colt automatic from the look of it, into the waistband of his trousers. Then he bent and lifted the side of the old dinghy while Marcus aimed his rifle.

Suddenly Tony dropped the old boat and sprang back. The movement was so sudden that Martin flinched.

What the? he started to think. But then his question was answered as Tony danced backwards, his face a mask of alarm.

"Snake!" he yelled.

Marcus sprang back too. "Where?" he cried.

Tony stopped dancing and whipped out his pistol and pointed it. "Big brown bastard. Taipan I reckon. He was coiled up under the boat and nearly got me," he explained.

Taipan! Martin thought, and shuddered. The Taipan was reckoned to be amongst the deadliest of all Australian snakes. *One of the deadliest in the world. What can one drop of their venom kill? Is it 600 sheep, or 200?*

Anyway, he decided it didn't matter. A person who was bitten by one had almost no chance of survival unless they were injected with anti-venom within minutes.

Then Tony yelled again and danced forward, pistol at the ready. "There it is! There it goes!" he yelled.

"Where? Where? Oh, I see it! Get out of the way so I can shoot," Marcus shouted.

"Too late. It's gone into that big pile of junk," Tony replied. He lowered his pistol and shook his head. "Shit! That gave me a fright."

Martin lay there watching, his whole body shaking with fright. The men were only 10 paces away on the other side of the old boat.

If that snake comes sliding out this way we are in trouble, he thought, his eyes now flicking to the pile of timber and other junk to his right.

Then, to his vast relief, Marcus said, "Come on, never mind the bloody snake. There'll be one in every pile of junk in this place. Let's find these kids."

As he said this Marcus turned and looked towards the rusty old shack on the other side of the main track. Then he started walking that way. Tony looked at the pile of timber and junk for a few more seconds then shook his head and walked after him, muttering and shaking his head as he did. The men vanished from view around both sides of the rusty old shack.

As they did Martin slumped down and began to tremble. *Oh bloody hell! That was close!* he thought.

Then he became aware of Letitia quietly whimpering beside him. She was also shaking and looked utterly terrified and miserable. He reached across and patted her back, and when she gasped and flinched he realized that the palms of his hands had a dozen burs embedded in them. She let out a gasp of pain and arched her back.

"Sorry!" Martin whispered. He rolled onto his side and set to work to try to pull the burs out, resulting in more pain as their prickles stuck into his fingertips.

"They are all over my front," Letitia whimpered.

Martin glanced around. The two men had reappeared beyond the rusty shack and were now walking off towards the old houses further up the creek. As they walked, they could be seen looking in all directions.

They are wondering where we have got to, Martin thought. *And when they have searched those buildings they will come back and do a more thorough search.*

So while he pulled out more prickles and watched his sister lie on her side and try to do the same his mind turned over the options.

If they use their brains and track us by our boot prints they will find us quickly. But for sure they will now search the bush. So where can we hide?

He lifted his head and looked the other way towards the house. It was just visible through the trees and long grass.

If I can see it then anyone there will see us if we start walking around, he mused. For a fleeting second, he considered trying to hide in or near the house. *They won't think to look in their own HQ,* he reasoned. But then he shook his head. *Too risky. But equally they might not look where they have already searched,* he decided.

His first thought was to get under one of the boats behind the shed but then a better idea came to him. *That old wooden dinghy just here. They aren't likely to look under it again.*

But there was the snake to worry about. And when he put his idea to Letitia that was the first question she asked. Martin shook his head and tried to look convincing.

"It won't come back, not while we are here. It will be more scared of us and will stay in hiding," he said. But in his mind he was very anxious and added, *I hope!*

Time was now important. The men had reached the first of the old houses and were searching around it.

That Ma Baker will be finished tying up Andrew and the others soon and might come back to the house, he thought.

That meant he and Letitia had to get under the old dinghy before then. Having decided that, he got to his hands and knees and started crawling towards the old dinghy, taking care to avoid the prickles as much as he could. Letitia grumbled but followed.

When he reached the boat, Martin raised his head and looked carefully in all direction for any sign of the enemy. They were nowhere in sight.

Be quick, he told himself.

So he got to his feet and put his hands under the gunwale of the boat and lifted, his heart hammering with anxiety as he did. He was tensed ready to spring back if the snake had returned but an anxious look showed no sign of it, other than some slide marks in the soft dry sand under the dinghy.

"Get under, quick!" he hissed.

Letitia looked fearfully under the boat and then at the nearby pile of old timber and junk but then did as she was told. Martin then told her to hold the boat up while he got under. She turned and put her hands above her head to take the weight. She managed this but with some difficulty. Martin just had time to slide in under before she let it drop back onto the two baulks of timber that were keeping it about 10 centimetres off the ground.

Under the boat there was just room to sit up but it was awkward, so Martin lay full length on the sand and eyed the nearby grass and rubbish, the possible proximity of that snake very much in his mind. Letitia was afraid of it as well and whispered to him, asking what they would do if it slid back. All Martin could do was pick up a short length of timber that lay half under the boat and hand it to her.

"Use this," he instructed.

Letitia grumbled but then lay back and resumed trying to pick the bindis off herself. Martin watched for a second, embarrassed yet again by being confronted at close range by his sister's female parts. Instead he lay flat and peered out from under the boat. He could only achieve this by lying on his side and using one eye, but it allowed him to see most of the rear of the shed.

Letitia muttered and then said, "Help me please Martin. They hurt."

Martin didn't want to but after making a wry face he rolled the other way and studied her body as she lay on her side. She was gingerly plucking at several burs which were embedded in her left buttock.

"Help me with these please," she said.

"But you are my sister," Martin replied, again experiencing very mixed feelings, and disturbed by how the sight of her was causing him distinct sexual thoughts, even arousal.

"So you have seen me often enough," Letitia replied.

So very carefully he reached forward and plucked out several of the burs. Then he started on her belly. They were still involved in removing burs when the sound of voices sent Martin's anxiety level shooting back up. He resumed his watcher mode and soon after that he heard the crunch of boots on sand. The boots and lower legs of Marcus and Tony came into sight.

"Buggered if I know where they can be hiding," Marcus grumbled.

"Out in the scrub there probably," Tony replied. "We will just check here again and then see what Ma wants us to do."

At that Martin's terror went sky-high again. He tensed ready for discovery. But the men walked to the boats at the back of the shed and looked under them again. Finding nothing they straightened up and Martin saw Tony glance towards the old boat.

If he sees our boot prints, we are done for, he thought.

But instead of scanning the ground Tony looked towards the wood heap and said, "I wonder if that bloody snake is still in there?"

"Never mind the bloody snake! Let's go and search that bush behind the house and then back along beside the road," Marcus replied.

To Martin's great relief, the men walked off towards the house and he lay back, trembling and gasping as the tension eased out of him. Then his stomach gave a loud grumble and sent shivers of fright through him.

Bloody hell! It's lucky that didn't happen while they were here, he thought.

Letitia was lying clutching the piece of plank and staring towards the pile of timber.

"What will we do now?" she whispered.

Martin had been thinking about that too. "We could try to sneak away," he said.

"Which way?"

Martin pointed towards the old houses. "If we can get to those old houses, we can get into the trees along the bank of Mud Crab Creek.

They will give us cover and Mud Crab Creek goes all the way to the Bruce Highway," he said.

"Won't they be able to track us?" Letitia asked.

"Probably, if they think of that," he agreed. "But first I am going to see what has happened to the others."

"Martin! No!" Letitia gasped.

Martin shook his head. "I have to. We can't just leave them. I might be able to set them free," he answered.

"That's madness!" Letitia hissed.

"Maybe, but I have to do it. I won't be able to live with myself if I don't try," he retorted.

"But what about me?" Letitia wailed.

"Shhh! Not so loud!" Martin cautioned. "You just wait here. You will be safe enough."

"But what about the snake?"

A spurt of pent up anger surged through Martin. "Never mind the bloody snake! The only snakes you have to worry about are one-eyed trouser snakes and you see enough of them!" he snapped.

"Oh Martin! Don't be horrible!" Letitia gasped.

"Listen Sis, you have no idea how embarrassing it is for me when every boy in the school thinks of you as the school bike and when they call you the morgue."

"The morgue?" Letitia asked in puzzlement.

"Where all the stiffs go!" Martin grated.

Letitia was shocked. She looked hurt and began to cry. "I'm sorry," she muttered. "But I like it and I need it."

"Then get a steady boyfriend and be more discrete," Martin replied, now sorry he had said what he had.

Then it began to rain. Martin heard the heavy drops start thrumming on the bottom of the upturned boat. Trickles of water begin running off onto the sand. Then he heard the sound of running feet and Marcus and Tony went hurrying by.

"Bloody rain!" Marcus cried. "We will keep looking later."

At that Martin clenched his jaw.

Now is my chance, he thought grimly.

Chapter 19

VERY RISKY

Martin knew what he was planning to do was very risky, but he was now determined.

I will save the others if I can, he told himself.

"Lift the side of the boat for me Sis," he instructed.

Reluctantly she complied and he slid out into the rain. For a moments Martin crouched behind the old boat, his eyes searching for signs of the gang. But there was none. The heavy rain seemed to have driven them inside. Then an idea came to him and he paused for a few more seconds while he cupped his hands under an angle in the boat's hull where the rain water was pouring off in a steady flow. Lifting the handful to his mouth he drank the fresh water with intense satisfaction.

He kept drinking until he felt bloated. *We may not get another chance to drink for some time,* he reasoned.

He bent down and whispered, "Sis, drink while you can."

Letitia replied with a muffled "Yes," and her hands appeared under one of the trickles. Feeling much happier Martin turned and crawled away through the grass and scattered trees. He went directly away from the boat back to where he and Letitia had been hiding earlier and then continued on parallel to the main vehicle track.

He had thought about the route to take and realized it needed to be quite circuitous. So he moved as fast as he safely dared on hands and knees, enduring the prickling and spiky grass and avoiding the bindis and 'bull heads' as much as he could. Every few metres he paused behind what cover there was and glanced back to check that the men were not in sight.

After about five minutes, Martin was at the apex of the triangle of bush at the point where the vehicle track to the new house forked off the main entrance track. Here he again paused while he peered along that track to decide if it was safe to cross. As he lay there the rain eased off to a fine drizzle and he was able to see the new house quite clearly.

Better not cross here, he thought.

So he turned left and crawled across to the main entrance track. A quick look along it showed no enemy so he quickly slid across and then turned right parallel to it and made his way through the grass to the edge of the mud flats, or what would have been the mud flats if the tide had not been in.

What he was now confronted with was a vast lake of salt water extending off into the distance. Crossing it were the power line and the rows of posts marking the vehicle track. Looking to his left he studied the line of trees that lined Mud Crab Creek and then wondered if he should not just go back and get Letitia and try to take her to safety.

Then guilt over running out on his friends gripped him and he swallowed. A wave of hunger and dizziness caused him to shake his head. With the awful doubt that whatever he did would be the wrong decision he decided to press on with his plan.

So, do I crawl on the sand or try to swim in the shallow water? he thought.

His plan was to make his way northwards in a big clockwise semi-circle past the new house until he came to Mud Crab Creek and then to creep south beside the creek to the wharf area. A glance behind showed him that his own tracks were very clear in the soft, wet sand.

If I go along just below the bank beside the water my tracks will be as plain as day, he thought. That decided him to opt for the water, despite the risk of crocodiles. *They won't be sliding around in this shallow water,* he told himself. *There is nothing for them to eat.*

But even so he hesitated, and his gaze swept the sheet of water. It appeared to be just a vast pond with a few wind ruffles on it. No obvious 'logs' or ripples showed. Summoning up what felt like the last tiny bit of courage he had left he took a deep breath and crawled down over the bank and into the water. To immediately take another deep breath! The water felt quite cold and the shock took his breath away.

For a few seconds he paused while his mind and body adjusted. Then, from down at water level, he did another careful study of the surface for any sign of crocs. There was nothing, but another gust of wind made him shiver and he lowered himself deeper so that only his head was sticking up. The water was barely deep enough to cover his body, but he was glad of that. Even so, it was a terrifying place to be with images of the giant croc mauling Corey swirling in his consciousness! With another deep breath Martin summoned up his determination and began crawling and sliding to his right.

Within 5 paces he discovered it was easier just to pull himself along by his hands and to let his feet trail or drag behind, depending on the depth of water. He crossed the line where the entrance track went down the slope and under the water and then kept on for a few more metres.

Then his hands encountered something hard and scaly and rough and he experienced such a jolt of fear that he paused. His hands touched the object again and his mind told him it was only a rock marking the side of the track.

Not a croc, he reassured himself.

Martin again scanned the water before moving forward again. The feel of the cold, slimy mud he found revolting and these emotions were not helped when his fingers encountered small stones, shell fish and other hard objects. Each time his heart leapt into his mouth in fright.

He had only moved about ten metres past the entrance track when the sound of voices sent a spasm of fear through him.

The men! They are out looking again, he thought.

And they were close! The nearest cover was a small muddy inlet in the bank to his right. It was only about a metre deep and he could only just slide his upper body and head into it.

As soon as he had pulled himself in against the overhanging tufts of saltwater grass Martin glanced back to check that his movements had not sent obvious waves rippling out across the lake. To his consternation he saw that they had but there were also a few wind ruffles and he hoped that the men would not notice.

To his dismay Tony and Marcus both appeared on top of the bank back where he had slipped into the water. They were looking down and had obviously followed his tracks. Marcus frowned and then looked out to scan the lake.

"The tracks go into the water here at the road," he said.

Tony swore and then said, "Bugger! They might have got away."

Marcus nodded. "I reckon. They came in along the road so they know about it. And they had time to get a fair distance during that rain." He shielded his eyes and stared into the distance. Martin knew that if they looked in his direction they must see him, so he pressed himself further into the mud and grass.

Tony also peered out from under his hand as more drizzle fell. "What'll we do?" he said.

"Go back and tell the boss," Marcus said. With that he turned and walked out of sight. Tony followed. Martin realized he had been holding his breath and he slowly eased it out and then took a deep gulp of fresh air. His heart was hammering so much he had trouble hearing and he trembled as the tension eased out of him.

Oh, bloody hell! That was close! he thought. Then another horrible thought came to him. *If they follow our tracks back, they will come to the old boat and find Sis.*

To check he took the risk of being seen and raised himself up to peer over the top of the grass. To his great relief he saw that the two men were walking quickly along the left-hand vehicle track towards the new house.

Sis is OK for a bit longer. Time I got moving, Martin told himself.

So he slid back into the shallow water and resumed his progress. Now he went faster, familiarity with the environment at least easing his fears if not inducing the proverbial contempt. It took him only seven minutes to drag himself about 300 metres so that the new house was now 150 metres to his right rear.

Towards the end he found it harder to progress as the water became shallower so he took the risk and moved up onto the sandy beach just below the bank and moved on hands and knees, but not without frequent anxious glances to his left to ensure that no monster was going to rush out of the slime and attack him.

By 1335 he was in the open savannah bush again and near the vehicle track that led north from near the grey shed to the two shacks. He could see them more clearly now and both looked derelict and unlived in. Up until then here had been a faint hope of someone living there who might help but he now dismissed this. Instead he lowered himself back into the long, wet grass and continued crawling.

A minute later he came to a vehicle track which led to the two shacks. It was easy to cross unseen as it wound through the trees and all he had to do was brush out his tracks. Another 2 minutes of careful movement had him at the bank of Mud Crab Creek.

Creeping right to the edge of the bank Martin looked down at the water, noting that the sandy bank dropped steeply into deep, dark green water.

The tide is going out, he noted, seeing the movement of mangrove leaves and the long mangrove seeds which were bobbing along vertically in the flow. The stream looked to be about 50 metres wide.

To his left was bush for about a hundred metres to the first of the shacks. There was more open scrub to the second shack. Beyond that appeared to be mangroves. These hemmed the creek in. The creek trended to the right to a point where it curved left and vanished from view. Martin knew that the sea must be somewhere in that direction. The other bank, from left to right as far as he could see, was a dense forest of mangroves growing out of black or grey mud.

Martin looked to his right and decided that the wharf and grey shed were a bit over a hundred metres from him.

I can get a lot closer, he thought, noting that the bush extended almost all the way and that a cluster of 44-gallon fuel drums stood right on the edge of the bush. The trawler was tied up, bows to the sea, at a small but solid looking timber wharf.

As he started to crawl towards the grey shed it began to rain again, a steady, drenching downpour that quite chilled him, causing his skin to come out in goose bumps. But the rain was welcome as he was able to lick drops from leaves and it covered any sounds he made.

And it will keep those mongrels indoors, he added.

But the rain eased to a few spits by the time he had covered the distance. As he got closer Martin became more careful and it took him ten minutes to cover the last 50 metres. Cautiously he crawled on his belly right in behind the fuel drums until he found a spot from which he could see the wharf and trawler clearly.

There was nobody in sight, so he now studied the trawler. Then he got something of a shock.

That isn't the same trawler, he thought. *How big is this gang?*

The trawler was the same design and even had a dark blue painted hull and generally similar colouring, but its number was EXJ 52 and on a faded and peeling name board above its wheelhouse windows was the name *Marlin Magic.*

Definitely not the same trawler, Martin mused, noting the streaks of rust and oil smeared paintwork.

Then an oddity caught his eye. Lashed to both bulwarks appeared to be long rolls of blue canvas. These were lashed tight with gaskets but from the end of each lines led down to small pulleys secured to the timber hull and then back up to cleats on the bulwarks.

What are they? he wondered.

Martin now shifted his focus to the grey shed. His aim was to get inside to try to rescue the others. But he was looking at the end of it and no doors or windows were visible. He began to study a possible route along the muddy bank to the end of the wharf but knew it would be a terrible risk to try to use it.

Anyone on that trawler who looks at the creek bank would see me, he reasoned.

He was still tossing up whether the risk was worth it when he heard the sound of a vehicle engine. It was coming from beyond the shed, so he quickly crawled along to the right hand end of the fuel dump and peeked through between the last two drums. The ground here was soaked with diesel and the reek made his empty stomach bilious, but he shook his head and concentrated.

From where he lay the new house and the sandy area between it and the grey shed were clearly visible. And he could also just see the end of the old rusty shed and the piles of junk behind it. The old boat was not visible, but he prayed that Letitia was still there and safe.

Into view along the left-hand track came a dark grey SUV. As it did Ma Baker, Tony and Joel appeared from the far end of the grey shed and stood waiting. The 4WD came to a stop in the middle of the clearing and out of it climbed a big, burly man in late middle-age. He had sunglasses on despite the overcast and was wearing a pair of good quality grey trousers and a white shirt and tie.

The Boss? Martin wondered.

"Maybe," was his answer when the man went and gave Ma Baker a hug and a kiss on her cheek. "Now explain what the bloody hell is going on here," the man demanded to know in a voice that betrayed a slight European accent.

Italian? Martin speculated, as he studied the man's complexion and dark curly hair.

It was Joel who did most of the talking. Martin could not hear most of it but several times 'The Boss' exploded in anger.

"Crabbing! What were you and bloody Corey doing crabbing? You were supposed to be here getting this tub ready for sea."

Joel looked both downcast and quiet anxious. "Corey wanted some crabs Mr Barberini," he explained.

"So he has to shoot two fisheries rangers! I don't believe this! How stupid can the man be? Well go on."

Joel went on to explain how they had chased the friends in their boat as Corey did not want any witnesses. Again, Mr Barberini erupted angrily.

"Bloody fool! So instead he sets out to commit mass murder! This gets worse and worse. No wonder you didn't want to explain the details over the phone! Well, go on."

Joel did and when he got to the bit where the giant croc had killed Corey Mr Barberini shook his head and then said in a savage voice, "Lucky for him! It saved him from being a meal for the crabs instead."

At that Joel visibly blanched and Martin decided that disobeying orders in this gang could have very nasty consequences, which did nothing to ease the apprehension he felt. Joel then continue his explanation, describing how he had spent the night in the tree then sunk the teenager's boat before going out to the trawler to get reinforcements.

"Tyler an' me tracked them through the mangroves and found them out on a big claypan," Joel explained. "But they had a rifle and shot at us, so we backed off."

"A bloody rifle! Where did they get that?"

"Off Corey I think Boss," Joel explained.

"And now they have walked to here, but you only caught three?" Mr Barberini said.

"Yes Boss."

Mr Barberini looked around the settlement and shook his head. "So two have got away, one of them a boy who possibly has a rifle and the other a girl?"

Tony answered that. "Yes dad," he said.

Martin eyed Tony anew. *Dad? Is Mr Barberini his father?*

Mr Barberini swept his arms apart. "So where did they go?"

Tony looked uncomfortable. "We think they snuck away during the rain and headed back along the road towards the highway," he explained.

Mr Barberini shook his head. "I've just come in along that and I didn't see anyone or any footprints in the mud. So where are they?"

"Hiding in the mangroves maybe?" Tony suggested. He also looked quite anxious.

You would be, with a father like that, Martin decided.

Mr Barberini again looked around. "Alright. I will question these kids you have captured and you two will go and search the whole place again. And Ma, you get on the phone and call Angelo. Tell him we need him here as quickly as he can get here. No ifs and buts or excuses, and tell him we need his dogs."

Dogs! Martin thought, fear lancing through him.

Chapter 20

HUNTED

Martin felt the fear slither in his empty stomach.

Dogs! They will soon find us, he thought in dismay.

For a few moments despair overwhelmed him and he just lay there shivering and quietly sobbing. Then the instinct for self-preservation kicked in and the thought crossed his mind that he had a chance to get away.

If I go now, I might get clear before they get these dogs, he thought.

But which way? Crossing the creek into the mangrove forest would be the fastest and possibly the best option but one look at that murky deep green water killed that idea. Fear of crocodiles was too strong.

And the bloody things will be lurking in that, or at least along the banks somewhere, he thought.

For a few minutes he weighed his chances of diving in and swimming across before a croc heard him and came to investigate. Then Martin shook his head.

Too risky. Besides, I will make a lot of noise and those men might hear me.

So that meant returning the way he had come. As his mind reviewed that route Martin flushed with shame. He realized he had been considering abandoning Letitia to her fate.

You gutless coward! he thought.

Deeply ashamed of having had such thoughts he determined to return at once to see if she was safe. So he backed away from the fuel drums and crawled back the way he had come through the long grass and dry bush.

Crawling as quickly as he safely could he back-tracked across the vehicle track and across the flat sandy scrub-covered dry land, only to get another shock. A lot of the water was gone!

Martin stared at the mud flats in astonishment. *How could all that water possibly vanish in such a short while?* he wondered.

Then a glance at his watch told him that he had actually been away from it for more than an hour. It was now 1445hrs. And it wasn't all gone. There were still plenty of puddles and ponds but it was obviously draining away quickly as the tide ebbed.

I will have to crawl all the way in the grass, he decided.

But that was a daunting and worrying prospect as the grass wasn't all that tall and it was very prickly. Unless he took real care he found he was constantly placing his hands or knees on prickly grass or vines that were so sharp that the small leaves and prickles stuck through his clothing or punctured the skin on his hands. The other choice was to crawl along the narrow sandy beach and that would leave him very exposed and also leave very clear tracks in the wet sand.

After moving for about a hundred metres Martin came to a shivering, shuddering stop. He lay flat and trembled, his stomach rumbling and squelching from hunger and his while body feeling drained and weak. For perhaps a quarter of an hour he just lay there, utterly exhausted and demoralized.

Then it began to rain again, a steady, drenching drizzle and his morale dropped even more. Another ten minutes went by before he found he was shivering violently from the cold.

I'd better move or I will die from exposure, he told himself.

So he summoned up what strength he could and resumed his painful progress. It took him nearly an hour to return to the old boat. As he approached it he lifted his head behind a tree and looked cautiously in all directions for the men. They were nowhere to be seen.

I hope Sis is alright, he thought. As he hadn't heard any commotion, he thought she was.

At the boat he hissed and whispered her name and she answered at once. Martin sighed with relief and moved to get under the boat with her. That took several minutes as he was too weak to lift it. In the end, Letitia helped by pushing up from inside. Thankfully he slid under.

Letitia at once hugged him tight. "Oh Martin! Thank God you are back! I was so scared!" she said. "Those men came back again."

"They didn't find you though," Martin observed.

Letitia shook her head and sobbed onto his chest as he lay on the dry sand, thankful to be out of the rain.

"No," she agreed. "They half lifted the boat and I was sure I was going to be found but then they started talking about that snake and they dropped the boat."

Martin had forgotten the snake. He glanced uneasily towards where his feet lay close to the bow of the boat.

"What did they do then?" he asked.

"They walked around all the piles of rubbish and looked at the tracks we had made in the sand. I was sure they would find me then but they both walked off following them. I was so scared that you would be found. Oh! Oh, I am so glad you are safe."

"So am I," Martin agreed. He then described what he had seen and heard. At the mention of dogs Letitia sucked her breath in sharply. "Dogs! Then we are in real trouble," she gasped.

"'Fraid so," Martin agreed.

"So what do we do?"

Martin could only shrug and shake his head. "We must try to get away," he replied.

"When?"

"Now. We need to put as much distance between here and us as we can," he replied. He was then shaken by such a tremble that Letitia held him tight.

"You are so cold," she whispered.

Martin was, but he was suddenly very conscious he was holding his scantily clad sister and that made him feel very uncomfortable.

"We'd better get going while this rain lasts," he replied.

"What about Carmen and Andrew?" she asked.

Martin shook his head. "Nothing we can do. They are in a shed guarded by at least four gang members. Now help me lift the boat and let's go."

It took both a physical and an emotional effort to leave the relative security of the upturned boat, but Martin told himself it was a false sense of security.

As soon as a dog starts sniffing around here it will find us, he told himself.

So they crawled away from the boat and slithered across the main vehicle track. As Letitia followed Martin turned. "I will brush out our tracks," he whispered. "You keep going."

Letitia did as she was told, and Martin brushed out their tracks as well as he could. Then he turned and followed, noting that her bum was sticking up. Hurrying past her on his stomach he told her to get lower.

"You might get seen otherwise."

"But it hurts!" Letitia protested.

"Then wear bloody clothes in future!" Martin snapped back. He was angry as well as embarrassed. He resumed crawling and as he did he kept lifting his head to look for the men.

None were visible and the rain persisted, coming in short, heavy splatters with gusts of wind. The pair moved across behind the rusty shack and then crossed another track where the power line came in from the mudflats. Martin then angled away from the two old houses and took a route close to the edge of the mudflats. He followed this until they reached the edge of the close country lining the bank of Mud Crab Creek just beyond the last of the old houses.

With a feeling of intense satisfaction, he crawled into a thicket of long grass, trees and prickly weeds.

Made it! he thought.

Sighing with relief he continued crawling into the thicket. As he did, he glanced back to check on Letitia. She gave him an encouraging smile which changed to a grimace as she encountered a prickly bush. There were lots of those but the type of grass changed. The soil in among the trees was sandy and covered in a deadfall of leaves and sticks. In places there were whole thickets of head high weed with little burrs on them. They had to either push through or under these or detour around them.

It was slow going, but once Martin was satisfied they weren't visible from any of the buildings he stood up and dusted the sand off himself. Letitia did likewise and they continued creeping away. 1530 came and went and Martin noted that they had only moved about 200 metres.

But we are now in good cover, he thought. That made them safer from the men, although they were leaving tracks in the sandy leaf litter. *But not safe from dogs.*

Martin estimated that they had at least 5 kilometres to travel to reach a farm but he wasn't sure. All he felt like doing with his drained and scratched body was flopping down to rest but he urged it into motion and then had to encourage Letitia to try as well. Several times she stumbled and after the third fall she just lay on the leaf litter sobbing and shaking her head.

"I can't do it! I can't!" she wailed.

"You must!" Martin replied. A feeling of desperation clutched at his throat and he tried to get her to rise. But she insisted on a rest so, against his better judgement, they lay there for ten minutes.

Only then was he able to persuade her to get up, almost dragging her to her feet. He saw it was 1625 by then.

And we have barely covered a kilometre! he thought.

They struggled on for another hour, pushing through patches of dense scrub, being stung by wasps, scratched by prickles and thorns. Once Letitia cried out and Martin saw beads of blood appear in a line down the side of her left breast. She stopped and held the breast up to study it and then wiped it.

"Oh, I hope I don't get a scar," she muttered.

Their eyes met and Martin blushed as he had been staring in wonder. "Sorry!" he muttered. Quickly he turned away and continued pushing his way through the tangle.

Next, they were frightened by a black snake which went sliding across near his feet. It vanished under some sheets of paperbark that lay in dense carpet under the trees.

Then Letitia detoured to avoid a log that Martin clambered over and she walked into a spider's web. This time she let out a genuine shriek of fear.

Frantically brushing at her face and front she danced up and down and made spasmodic jerking motions with her arms and legs.

Martin stared at her and shook his head. "Shhh! What is it?" he asked.

"A spider, a great big spider! Get it off me! Where is it?" she cried.

Martin put his hand to his chest. His heart had jumped in fright at her cry and was now hammering rapidly.

"I can't see it," he replied. "Now stop the noise or those men will hear you."

At last Letitia did but then she just staggered a few steps and fell on the sand. Martin hurried to her and knelt down.

"Did it bite you? Are you all right?" he asked anxiously.

Letitia nodded and lay back. "No. It didn't bite me. It just gave me a fright. Oh, let me rest for a minute."

Martin glanced anxiously back. By his calculations they had only travelled about 2 kilometres and he was fretting.

"OK," he reluctantly agreed.

So he sat down beside his sister and lay back to suck in deep lung fulls of air. As he lay back he noted that only a few drops were spattering down.

It has stopped raining, he thought.

It was the sound of a motor that jerked him back to wakefulness. Muzzy in the head and with gummed up and bleary eyes he sat up.

What? Where? Oh, bloody hell! We have gone to sleep, he told himself. Looking around he saw that everything appeared gloomy. *Twilight,* his mind said and his watch confirmed it. It was 1820!

Bloody hell! We have been asleep for a couple of hours, Martin thought, dismay flooding in. The thought of pushing through that horrible dense dry scrub in the dark was very daunting.

Then he noted the motor noise again. His first thought was that it was an outboard and that the men were coming up Mud Crab Creek which he had glimpsed on his left from time to time. But then his ears and mind settled on the sound coming for the other direction.

A vehicle, Martin decided.

The thought uppermost in his mind was that it might be bringing the dogs. That idea sent stabs of fear through him. Bending down he shook Letitia. She was lying on her side, her thumb in her mouth and her face relaxed like a little girl's.

Shaking his head in fascinated shame he shook her again. "Wake up Sis!" he hissed urgently. She groaned and opened her eyes and then rolled onto her hands and knees.

Without waiting for her Martin pushed through the bush to the west, knowing that the mudflats were somewhere to his right. They were, only about 25 metres away, and he quickly found a gap in the bushes where he could look out across them.

Out in the open it was much lighter, and the sun was just dipping below the horizon.

About an hour to last light, Martin told himself as he noted this. Then an upward glance showed a dense layer of clouds and he revised it down by twenty minutes. *But plenty of time for men with dogs to track us and catch us before it gets dark,* he reasoned. *A man can walk a kilometre in ten minutes, and we are only two or three from the buildings.*

About half a kilometre away the lines of posts marking the vehicle track stood up from the vast flat expanse of mud, saltwater grass and salt pan. Beyond, just visible in the haze and drizzle, was the distant bulk of

Mt Elliott. The mountain's upper slopes were lost in dense clouds and showers of rain.

Moving along the vehicle track from his left was a small truck, a 1- or 2-ton flat bed with boxes and cages on the back. Martin couldn't see any dogs in the cages, but it certainly looked that type of vehicle.

It will be at the gang's hideout in a few minutes, he thought. *We must get going.*

He was about to push his way back through the bushes when he heard Letitia call out, asking where he was. Softly he called back:

"This way. Out here."

With muttered grumbles and curses Letitia appeared, brushing green ants off her front.

"What is it?" she asked.

"The dogs I think," Martin answered, pointing to the now distant vehicle. "Let's move!"

He waited another minute until the vehicle had vanished from view around a curve in the line of trees and then pushed his way right out onto the mudflat. Logic told him that the dogs would find them anyway so tracks no longer mattered.

We need to move as fast as possible, he told himself.

He had been hoping to find a sandy beach on the edge of the mudflat. There was for short stretches, but it was very narrow and in many places bushes overhung it so that as he and Letitia hurried along they had to detour out onto the soft mud.

It quickly became apparent that this was not working very well as a plan. The mud was softer than he had expected and in places still had puddles of water on it. In fact, the pools and small streams became more and more frequent until much of the mudflat was covered. The water wasn't deep, varying from ankle to knee but it slowed them down.

After about 300 metres of sloshing along, dragging his boots clear of the sucking mud at every second step, Martin came to a panting, sweating stop and wiped his face.

This is not good, he thought.

Looking around in the rapidly deepening twilight he noted that the line of posts marking the vehicle track were now only about 300 metres away. The posts were poking up out of water.

That must be firm for vehicles to drive along, he reasoned.

Pointing to it he said, "We will walk along the vehicle track. They won't see us in the dark."

"But what if a vehicle comes along?" Letitia asked anxiously.

"We lie in the mud and hide. We will see the headlights from a long way off."

"Won't they see out footprints in the mud?" Letitia asked, looking anxiously around in the gloom.

Martin shook his head. "The track is under water. Come on."

Without waiting he started sloshing across the mudflat towards the vehicle track. He knew it was a risk, but he told himself that all of the gang were now behind them.

We should be alright, he hoped.

But within 20 paces he was wading. There were holes and gutters, but he and Letitia were both so wet and muddy that he just ignored the falls and being wet.

Letitia splashed along behind him, falling several times and making a good deal of noise.

"What about crocodiles?" she queried in a quavering voice.

It was almost fully dark by then, the last of the sunset mostly hidden by the thick cloud layer and the moon not yet up. Martin felt a stab of concern and his stomach churned. Anxiously he looked around the vast wasteland.

If a croc attacks, we have no hope at all, he thought.

There was not a tree they could climb. But he didn't want to frighten Letitia by saying that so he snapped: "Too bad! They don't walk around on the mudflats, so hurry up." He was annoyed at her bringing the peril to the front of their minds.

After five minutes of wading and slipping they reached the line of posts. As soon as he passed the first post Martin felt his boots step onto firm gravel and his spirits lifted.

This is better, he thought. Turning left he waited till Letitia joined him and then began wading along the track.

The gravel and stone track was much easier going and the water was only ankle deep although the road was rough and they both frequently stumbled on larger rocks. The stones obviously hurt Letitia's bare feet and she frequently cried out in pain or whimpered. But she kept gamely limping and hobbling along.

The track also curved continually, following the firmer ground, so they had to watch carefully they did not wander off it when the posts were a long way apart.

They did a couple of times and each time they came to a shivering, sweating standstill, gasping and trembling with weakness. Martin was dismayed at how exhausted he felt.

Bloody hell! I hope we have enough energy to make it, he thought.

And it was hot. Martin was amazed at how humid and sticky he felt. Except when a short shower or rain set them shivering. He tried to lick some of the rain water off his skin and clothes but could only rinse his sore eyes and moisten his lips. Worse still Letitia kept crying out as she stubbed her toes on rocks and she developed a distinct limp.

There were also several small rises which went up above the level of the water. At first Martin was relieved to get onto 'dry' land but then he realized that they were almost certainly leaving tracks. So he detoured to walk beside the track until it went back down into the water.

As they walked Martin continually turned his head to look back, anxious to catch the earliest possible glimpse of any headlights. Ahead all was dark as the last of the daylight faded, leaving a dim blackness across the whole skyline.

Half an hour of steady plodding brought them to another rise, larger this time and sandy. It was covered in a sparse growth of prickles, weeds with burs and spiky grass. As before Martin detoured off the track but quickly became disoriented as the moon was hidden by the overcast. Then he had trouble finding the 2-wheel ruts again.

When he did, he stopped to listen, staring in all directions. There was a breeze, annoyingly just strong enough to make hearing difficult. Cupping his right hand to his ear he listened again.

"What is it?" Letitia asked, stopping beside him.

"Vehicles. I think I can hear traffic on the Bruce Highway," he replied.

They both listened intently and then, as the breeze died away for a few seconds, the sound of distant heavy vehicles came clearly to them. Martin felt his spirits lift.

Not far now, he thought.

He had been hoping to see lights but there was still no sign of anything but the black water and black background.

They resumed walking, going down into the water again. And then wading. The water was still mostly only ankle deep, but occasional patches were deep enough for the water to reach their knees. When they lost the track, the water was thigh or waist deep and the bottom was soft, sucking mud.

After another ten minutes of steady movement, Martin again stopped to listen. Puzzled he frowned and strained to hear over the breeze. He had been expecting to hear traffic noises, but this was different. And then Martin glimpsed the flicker of moving lights. The lights came and went, flickering behind a screen of trees.

At last! he thought. He wasn't sure how far away they were but he estimated only one or two kilometres. *Another twenty minutes to half an hour,* he decided.

Then, clearly above the wind, came a loud toot. "A train!" Martin cried, recognizing the sound of a diesel locomotive's air horn. He watched with a mixture of relief and dismay as the locomotive's lights went flickering past in the distance.

"Is it far? Can we stop it?" Letitia asked.

Martin shook his head. He had remembered that the main north coast railway was between the sea and the Bruce Highway.

"No, we can't!" he snapped as tiredness and exasperation swirled in him. "Keep walking. We still have a few kilometres to go." With a heavy heart he watched the lights flicker out of view away to his left front.

Letitia moaned but resumed moving forward. By now the fear of crocodiles had quite dulled so he and Letitia just sloshed along, occasionally murmuring comments or encouragement to each other. Also, the vehicle noises became obviously closer and then the skyline ahead changed to a darker mass which resolved itself into a line of trees against the dark grey sky.

Not far now, Martin told himself, his hopes going up another notch.

They came to another sandy rise and Martin noted that trees were growing out of it.

This might be the end of the mudflats, he decided.

He had often been along the Bruce Highway between Townsville and Ayr and did not remember any mudflats between the Haughton River and the Pioneer sugar mill near Brandon.

Suddenly, four very bright lights sprang into blinding action from about 25 metres in front of them. The lights shone directly on them. As his eyes closed in automatic reflex to the blinding glare Martin's heart leapt with fright and he threw his left hand up over his face to shield his eyes. Squinting against the glare he noted that two of the lights were vehicle headlights and between them and a bit higher up were two powerful spotlights, the sort used by shooters.

A man's voice called loudly from behind the lights: "Stand still! Hands up or you are dead!"

Martin's heart leapt in terror.

Oh no! We are caught!

Chapter 21

DESPAIR

M artin felt the terror clutch at his heart.
Oh no! We have walked into a trap! he thought.

For a fleeting moment he considered running to try to get away. But a glance behind him revealed that there was nowhere to hide. The vast sheet of shallow water on the mudflat was brightly illuminated by the lights. If the man had a gun, and Martin was sure he would have, there was no hope at all. Reluctantly his hands went up, even as his hopes plummeted.

The man called again: "Keep your hands up. Now walk up here."

Seeing no other option Martin did so, the fear of violent death almost paralyzing him. Letitia waded forward with him, sobbing and shaking as she did. They made their way up to the front of the vehicle.

The man now moved into the lights. *Only one,* Martin noted, but he had a shotgun and it was levelled on them. He told them to stop and then ran his eyes up and down Letitia.

"Well, well! What have we here?" he cried in amazement.

Then he chuckled, an evil lascivious sound that sent chills of apprehension through Martin and which reduced Letitia to tears.

The man then held something out to Letitia. "Here sweetie, tie his hands behind his back with these."

Letitia just stood there and sobbed until the man strode across and slapped her. As he did, he let go of the gun with one hand and Martin tensed, hoping for a chance.

Is he on his own? he wondered.

But the man was too alert and too far away. He slapped Letitia again and snarled, "Tie him up I said! Do it now or it will be the worse for you."

Letitia lifted her terrified face and Martin looked into her tears filled eyes. For a few more seconds she just sobbed and trembled and then she held the thing up and Martin saw it was a plastic cable tie. Giving her what he hoped was an encouraging grin he turned and placed his hands behind his back. Disobedience would obviously result it violence.

Letitia was shaking so much that she had trouble getting the thin end of the plastic tie through the small fastener on the other end. She was crying and having difficulty seeing. The man stood behind her and twice hit her and snarled to hurry up.

Martin wanted to whisper 'Not too tight' but did not dare. *If the man hears me he will tighten it right up,* he thought.

So he did what he had read all the heroes in stories did and tried to hold his wrists apart so that the resulting fastening was slightly loose. In this he was almost successful but then the man moved past behind him and shoved him towards the vehicle.

"Get in the back!" he snarled.

Martin found himself dragged, shoved and pushed until he hit his head on the roof of the vehicle, a 4WD 'troop carrier' of some sort. Then his shins and knees struck the bottom of the door space. Quite excruciating agony caused him to cry out. The pain was so intense he almost collapsed but the man grabbed his shirt with one hand and pushed him hard so that he went sprawling face first onto the back seat.

For a few seconds blind rage boiled in Martin and he was tempted to lash out with his boots against the man but before he could the man moved away and slammed the door, hitting Martin's boots with it as he did. All Martin could do was squirm and struggle to get himself around and up where he could see. As he did the fear slithered in his belly and he would have thrown up if there had been anything in his stomach.

The man returned to Letitia, who still stood brightly illuminated in the headlights. Martin feared the worst and he was right. The man chuckled and then pawed at Letitia, fondling her breasts and muttering about how good 'it' would be.

He's going to rape her, Martin thought, disgust, dismay and despair all welling up to choke him with fear and rage.

But the man suddenly stepped back and looked down. Disgust showed on his face. "Oh, bloody hell! You weak bitch! Go and wash yourself," he snarled.

Martin saw that Letitia had voided herself, a slick of brown streaming down the inside of her legs. He felt a mixture of revulsion mixed with thankfulness. At least for a few more minutes she was safe from violent sexual assault.

Letitia covered herself with her arms and hunched up then backed down into the water. Once there she crouched and washed herself, staying doubled up. In the glare of the lights Martin could see that she was obviously terrified and ashamed.

As he watched her a fury at his own impotence rose in Martin and he struggled with the cable tie until he flopped back exhausted. Sweat poured from him and he sobbed with helpless anger.

Then the man pulled out a mobile phone and began talking on it. The only words Martin clearly heard were: "Got them Boss. Yes."

Once he had finished the phone call the man snarled at Letitia to get in the vehicle and Martin felt a tiny surge of relief. At least she was being spared, for the moment. But as Letitia climbed into the front passenger seat and the man moved to the driver's seat Martin felt despair flood in with redoubled force. They were both now prisoners in the crook's vehicle and he suspected it might be very difficult, if not impossible, to escape.

But surely they won't murder all of us! he thought, clinging to that faint hope to keep gibbering terror of death at bay.

The vehicle's engine was started and it was driven forward into the water. Martin managed to get into a sitting position but with his hands behind his back he found it hard to stay that way as the vehicle bounced and bumped over rocks and potholes. The man was obviously familiar with the submerged track as he drove quite fast, the way clear because of the posts.

With every minute Martin's hopes slid lower and the dread gripped him. He began to shake with fear as thoughts of death and dying crowded his mind. It was all so horrifying and unreal that he wished he could just black out and not have to face it.

How can I? he wondered. But then he gritted his teeth and determined to at least die like a man. *I'm buggered if I'll give these crooks the satisfaction of seeing me beg,* he vowed.

But easier to say than to do! As the lights of the buildings at Mudcrab Landing came into view the fear built to parlayzing proportions and Martin found he was praying and trembling, and he had to use all his willpower to stop himself whimpering. Letitia, he noted, just sat in the front, sobbing and bouncing with the movement of the vehicle.

Her hands aren't tied. Why doesn't she try to get free? he asked himself.

But he knew why. The man had a shotgun and even if it was leaning up on the seat between him and Letitia Martin could not see how she could grab it and turn it in time. For sure the man would really hurt her if she tried.

Within ten minutes, the vehicle came to a standstill on the sandy area between the grey shed and the new house. A group of people showed for a moment in the headlights: Mr Barberini, Ma Baker, Tony, Joel and a man Martin had never seen. They were all grinning and Mr Barberini called, "Well done!" as the engine was switched off.

Martin and Letitia were both dragged out. As they were Tony exclaimed loudly: "So she was almost naked! Holy mackerel, she looks like a goer this one."

At that Ma Baker spat and then snarled, "You just keep yer filthy thoughts to yerself boy! You is getting' married to Maria next month so don't you go catchin' some stinkin' disease off some trollop that runs around in the nuddy."

"Yes Ma," Tony answered, but to Martin's ears not very convincingly.

From the way the other men ogled Letitia in the torch light he felt with a sickening certainty that rape was very much on their minds.

Poor Sis! he thought. First she would be violated and then she would die!

Joel stepped forward and shone a torch on Martin's face. "Yeah, this is the one who had the rifle and shot at Tyler and me," he said.

The Boss also shone his torch in Martin's eyes. "So where's the rifle kid?" he snarled.

Martin trembled with apprehension and felt his gut tighten up. But there was no way he was going to answer. The result was what he expected, a savage, stinging blow to the side of his face, delivered by Tony.

"My dad asked you a question you little shit! Answer him."

Martin stood there shaking and half stunned but then he pressed his lips together and braced himself for another blow. Inside him the fear slithered and churned and, to his own shame, he knew he was weakening.

The Boss shook his head. "We are wasting time. It doesn't matter where the bloody rifle is. He doesn't have it and even if he has hidden it he can't get away now. Get organized and get moving. That cyclone is starting to turn our way."

"Where is it now Boss?" Joel asked.

"At eight it was about two hundred and fifty kilometres northeast of Cairns and it is now a Category 3," Mr Barberini replied.

"That's a long way away. That's about four or five hundred K's from here," Tony commented.

Mr Barberini shook his head. "Don't you believe it son. We are already in the edge of it. We need to get both trawlers well out of the area before it gets worse," he said.

Tony gestured to the buildings. "What about here?"

"We will shift what we can in case it does comes this way," Mr Barberini replied. This started a general discussion on what to move and how.

The Boss ended the talk by snapping, "Stop the gabble eh! Put this pair with the others and get that trawler moving."

It was Joel who answered. "Yes Boss," he replied. "But we'll have ter wait. The tide is out. We should'a gone hours ago. You could just dump this pair in the creek."

"Not in any creek. Some bloody crabber will find their bodies that way. Now get moving."

Joel spread his hands. "But Boss, we'll have to wait for the tide. We will have to wait."

The Boss turned on him angrily. "Shut up and do what you are told! Just get to Bowen as quickly as you can before this cyclone affects this area; and on the way get rid of the evidence."

"Yes Boss."

On hearing this Martin felt chills of apprehension lance through him. *Get rid of the evidence! They are going to murder us and toss our bodies into the ocean.* It was too horrifying to contemplate and for a moment he entertained wild thoughts of making a run for it.

But the other man had him in a tight grip by his right arm and he had no chance. Instead he was shoved hard and told to get moving. As Martin stumbled across the darkened clearing the Boss turned to the man who had captured them and said: "Thanks Angelo. We owe ya. You can get going now."

Martin and Letitia were pushed and dragged over past the grey shed and onto the wharf beyond. The trawler was still tied up there and looked to be floating much lower. A dinghy with an outboard lay astern of it.

Tide is right out, Martin thought as he was lowered down over the gunwale by a man he then recognized as Marcus.

Marcus dragged him roughly over the gunwale so that he fell onto the deck near the nets.

"Where will we put 'em skipper?" he asked.

To Martin's surprise Tony answered. "Up on the foredeck in front of the wheelhouse with the others. We can keep an eye on them there," he instructed.

Marcus now looked towards Letitia who was being helped down by Joel.

"What about lovey here?"

Tony snorted. "Huh! Do you want a go with her do ya?"

In the dim light from the wheelhouse Martin saw a look lascivious desire show on Marcus' face. He leered at Letitia and then reached out to fondle her left breast.

"Yeah, I reckon," he said.

Letitia tried to pull away but was held by Joel. Tony grinned and said: "Do what ya like."

At that Letitia cried: "On no, please!"

"Shut up slut! We'll do what we like," Tony replied harshly.

That obviously stung Letitia's pride as she straightened up. "Then you'd better use a condom," she snapped.

At that Marcus snorted. "Huh! A condom! You don't need to worry about getting' pregnant, ya stupid troll."

Letitia bit her lip and hung her head. Marcus reached out and took her arm to lead her away. She licked her lips, shook her head and muttered: "It wasn't that. You don't want to get herpes or HIV do you?"

At that Marcus swore and pushed her away. "You are just sayin' that ya bitch!" he snarled, obviously angry but unsure.

Letitia shrugged. "Don't complain later you weren't warned," she said.

There was a short pause while the men looked hard at Letitia. Martin was both shocked and full of admiration.

Has Sis really got a sexually transmitted disease? he wondered.

She was so promiscuous that he thought it possible. The notion of STD's caused him to shudder in disgust and anxiety and he guessed that the men were having the same reaction.

I just hope they don't have any condoms, he thought.

Marcus tried to put a brave face on the situation. "I'll get some and we will give you what ya deserve," she snarled.

Tony nodded. "She can go with the others until we meet up with the *Jolly*. They've got plenty. Then we can sample the goodies," he said.

Disgust and anger seethed in Martin and he turned to glare at Tony. "You low mongrels!" he grated.

Whack! Tony struck him hard in the face with the pistol he had in his right hand. The blow half-stunned Martin and sent him reeling back. He tried to lash out with his boots but missed. The result was sharp blow to the back of his head from Marcus.

"Get moving you!" he snapped.

Martin was hit again and then shoved hard. His head throbbing, he stumbled and would have fallen if Marcus had not grabbed his left arm and held him tightly.

"That way!" he snarled. Martin was again shoved hard and he staggered along the narrow deck between the gunwale and the bundled-up fishing nets.

As he did Tony called from behind: "And tie the little turd's legs up so he can't make a run for it."

"OK skipper," replied Marcus.

He followed Martin, gripping his left sleeve tightly and urging him to move. It wasn't far, only 10 metres forward past the low deckhouse and the wheelhouse to the foredeck.

This was only 5 metres long and had a small winch, a hatchway and the usual cleats and bollards and a couple of thick ropes on it. Along the port gunwale were Andrew, Carmen and Anne. They were sitting in a row with their hands behind their backs and their feet tied together and secured to cleats or other fittings.

In the dim light Martin saw that his friend's faces were drawn with anxiety, but they did not speak while the gang members were present. Martin, his head still spinning from the blow, was shoved down and his legs roughly bound with rope. The rope was then wound around a nearby bollard. A sobbing Letitia was told to sit next to him.

As she did Marcus again grabbed her left breast. "Later girlie," he hissed. Letitia cringed and whimpered.

Carmen strained at her bonds. "You low scum!" she cried.

Marcus jerked his head up and sneered back. "Shut up bitch! You'll get a go too," he retorted.

"You are just a revolting animal," Carmen replied.

For a moment Martin feared that Marcus would stop what he was doing and go and bash Carmen, but he just glared at her then went on tying Letitia up. When he had finished, he gave Carmen an insolent look and then deliberately twisted Letitia's left nipple until she cried aloud in pain.

That attracted Tony's attention. He leaned out of the door of the wheelhouse and scowled. "Stop that Marcus! You can have her later. Now ease off fore and aft!"

"Yes skipper," Marcus replied. He then stood and went to ease off the mooring ropes.

Carmen shook her head. "What a low creep!" she muttered, just loud enough for Marcus to hear.

Marcus paused to glare back then went on with his work. Martin could only admire her rebellion.

The mongrels will do what they want anyway so we may as well make it hard for them, he thought.

Martin then nudged Letitia. "Buck up Sis! We will get out of this somehow," he whispered.

Letitia sniffled but met his eyes and nodded. Martin then studied how Letitia had been tied up.

But not as securely as me, he noted.

That gave Martin a glimmer of hope. *Maybe she can get free and release us?* he thought.

Tony then said, "You keep watch Marcus while we get tea organized."

All three men went into the wheelhouse and the door was closed. In the faint light Martin saw movement behind the windows and knew that Marcus was there watching them.

Time began to drag. The friends discussed ideas on how to escape but no plan produced much as they had to first get away. That meant getting the knots untied but they were so securely bound that none of them could wriggle free or get their fingers near any of the knots. After half an hour of straining and trying Martin began to despair. He slumped down and sat hunched in the darkness, shivering and terrified.

As the time dragged by with nothing happening exhaustion took over and he dozed. He was aware of someone shining a torch on their bonds but then he drifted off into a restless sleep full of nightmares and terrifying images of ghosts and death. A truly fearful image of a rotting corpse rising from the darkened sea to grab at him jerked him to trembling, sweating wakefulness. Hunger and cold both afflicted him.

He knew that the men were waiting for the tide.

That is about two in the morning I think, he decided.

The others were also having a bad time and he could feel both Anne and Letitia shivering as they pressed against each other for warmth. Time dragged slowly by. Joel came and checked their knots were still tight and then withdrew to the wheelhouse as a drizzle of rain started again.

The friends exchanged a few words, but it was apparent to Martin that they were all gripped by dread and were exhausted as well and they lapsed in and out of sleep, with frequent bouts of trembling. The drizzle stopped and the night air became hot and humid again. Mosquitoes began to attack in swarms. That was real torment as none of the friends could do more than writhe and jerk to try to stop them settling to bite. Martin gritted his teeth and set himself to endure the continual pin pricks. Beside him Letitia squirmed and whimpered.

The hours dragged slowly and painfully by until at last the wheelhouse lights came on. Martin jerked his head up and stared through his sore eyes. Tony and Marcus appeared inside. The men bent forward and were obviously looking at something and discussing it. Then Martin saw Marcus nod and move to open the wheelhouse door.

At that moment the wheelhouse lights went out and a few moments later the trawler's diesel engine rumbled into life. The whole vessel vibrated and then Tony leaned out and called, "Let go aft!"

By twisting his head Martin noted that Marcus was on the wharf casting the springs and aft mooring line off the wharf pilings. He then scrambled back aboard and on seeing the height of the rail in relation to the wharf Martin deduced that the tide was coming in again. Marcus hauled in the dripping hawser and then hurried forward in time for the order 'Let go forward!'. Marcus loosened the mooring line and flicked it clear of the bollard, then dragged it on board. In the process cold drops of water were flicked onto Martin and his friends and he could only shudder and quietly curse. The engines rumbled louder and the dark bulk of the shed appeared to move away.

We are moving, Martin noted.

Twisting his head, he stared into the darkness ahead and what he saw reflected the blackness now clouding his mind. Terrified at the prospect of being murdered he began wracking his brain for a way of escape.

A brief shower of rain chilled him even more and he looked around to try to keep some situational awareness. Andrew and Carmen were doing the same and Carmen nodded upwards with her head.

"No navigation lights," she commented.

Martin looked up and saw that the regulation white masthead light and the red and green port and starboard lights were not showing. "Sneaking out?" he suggested.

He twisted his head to study the creek and noted that the trawler was creeping along in the darkness with a dark wall of mangroves only 10 to 20 metres on either beam.

How on earth are they going to navigate this thing out into the bay?.

From his limited knowledge of Bowling Green Bay, he understood it to be mostly very shallow water, numerous sand banks for many miles out from the coast and certainly their experience a couple of days before had shown that.

The crook's navigation secret was soon revealed. Andrew hissed: "A light!"

Martin looked around and saw that ahead of them, just where the creek appeared to open out into the open sea, a tiny red light had come on. The light was low down on the water and appeared to be shimmering. As the trawler came closer the reason became obvious. The light was on a small buoy.

As the trawler approached the light, two more came on further out. Andrew shook his head. "They must have some sort of radio-controlled command to turn the lights on when they want them," he suggested.

The cunning mongrels! Martin thought. Mounting small radio-controlled lights would be no particular problem. *Even I could do that,* he mused, thinking of his radio-controlled ship models.

The trawler passed the first light port side to and then turned to line up on the next marker. This one was set on a post set in the seabed. As the trawler passed between the ends of the mangroves the wind increased noticeably and the trawler began to pitch. It was a mild movement but told Martin that they were now out in the bay.

More lights came on ahead, marking a zig-zag course along what was obviously the deepest channel. The dark line of the low coastline quickly receded and was lost in the darkness. Overhead was heavy overcast, just an occasional faint glimmer of moonlight showing that the clouds were moving fast.

Wind is from the east, Martin noted.

That made sense to him. Being a North Queenslander, he had a fairly extensive knowledge of tropical cyclones and knew that the giant revolving storms rotated clockwise.

So if the cyclone is north of us the wind should be coming in from the east, he told himself.

Not that it matters! he thought bitterly. *We will be dead long before we have to worry about that.*

For the next fifteen minutes the trawler made its way northwards, turning frequently. As it passed each light the light was switched off. This left a total blackness for a few minutes until Martin's eyes adjusted again to the darkness. He could just make out Tony in the wheelhouse but there was no sign of Marcus or Joel.

Joel must be the engineer, Martin decided.

There were more light showers of rain and the wind gusted from time to time, chilling him. His body began to tremble from the cold as much as the over-exertion and fear and he felt terribly weak.

Oh, how can we get away? he wondered. He did not think their bodies would be thrown into the bay. *They might wash ashore then. They will drop us in deep water out at sea,'* he thought.

That caused more terror and gut-twisting anxiety and again he tried to think of an escape plan. With all his strength he tried working his hands and feet free and could see that the others were doing the same. But no luck.

Then the nightmare took a turn for the worse. Martin heard voices in the wheelhouse and then the door banged open and out came Marcus.

Oh no, what does he want? Martin thought anxiously.

Marcus had a pistol in his right hand and he walked straight over to Martin and put the muzzle to his head. Martin cringed and the fear flooded his whole being.

I am going to die! He is going to shoot me! he thought. He tensed himself to face the awful reality.

Instead Marcus moved the muzzle away and then struck him on the left side of his temple with it. "Not yet, you little smart arse," he jeered. Then he turned to Letitia and showed her the gun. "Any trouble sweetie and I use this."

Martin winced from the numbing pain of the blow. He found he was trembling and gulping as though he had been drowning. His whole body reacted and he shook uncontrollably for a minute or so. While Martin slowly recovered his wits, Marcus slid the pistol into his waistband and then knelt next to him. He drew a wicked looking fisherman's knife which he held in front of Letitia's terrified face.

"You are lucky sweetie. I found a condom. Now just do what you are told, or else," Marcus said in a purring tone that caused Martin's skin to come out in goose bumps.

Marcus slid the point of the knife slowly down the side of Letitia's face and neck. She flinched and tried to draw away.

"D... Don't... Don't hurt me please!" she wailed.

Marcus chuckled and slid the knife back into a sheath on his belt. Then he untied Letitia's feet.

"You'll love it. Now get up," he ordered.

He stood up and hauled an unresisting and visibly shaking Letitia to her feet. She stood there trembling and crying and then cried aloud that she had a cramp. For a minute or so she stood there shaking until Marcus slapped her hard.

"Stop the nonsense!" he snarled.

Gripping her left arm tightly he roughly pushed her aft along the deck. Martin watched them vanish beyond the wheelhouse and felt his stomach churn with disgust and nausea.

Oh poor Sis! he thought.

Chapter 22

LETITIA

As Martin watched Letitia being dragged away, ghastly dark thoughts of rape and violation crowded his mind. He experienced such a surge of white-hot anger he was sure he would have struck Marcus dead if he had been able to. Then he slumped down in despair, the misery bringing tears to his eyes.

The others looked similarly upset and Martin noted that Anne was crying and that Carmen looked darkly angry. But there was nothing he or they could do. Despite straining with all his might, he could not work himself free. So tight were the bonds that he was losing feeling in his limbs and particularly in his hands.

The trawler continued weaving its way out towards deeper water and once again Martin looked around in the vague hope that they might meet someone else.

Not likely to, he told himself. With a cyclone in the offing people would be foolish to be out in small boats. *Or even in big ones,* he added as a larger than usual wave sent the bow sharply up and then a small shower of spray blew across them.

A look at the dark water gave Martin the impression of waves about a metre high. The wind also seemed to have increased slightly.

Maybe 20 knots? he speculated.

Once again, he scanned the horizon as far as he was able but all he could see was darkness. He had been hoping to see the lights of Cungulla but there was nothing but darkness, so he deduced that they were still too far away.

Over the curve of the earth, he thought, his knowledge of nautical affairs leading to the deduction that from such a low height his visibility horizon was only about 5 nautical miles. *Bowling Green Bay is nearly twenty nautical miles wide and we are over near the east side of it,* he told himself.

Suddenly a stab of light over the starboard bow of the trawler caught his eye.

What is that? he wondered. Then the flicker of light came again and Martin noted a distinct beam visible against the low clouds. *Ah! The lighthouse on the seaward end of Cape Bowling Green!*

For a few seconds Martin watched the distant light coming and going as the light revolved. A faint uplifting of hope then slumped again.

Not that it can do us any good, he thought grimly. He knew there were no manned lighthouses on the Queensland coast anymore. Beyond the light was the Coral Sea. *And that is where we are most likely to be thrown overboard,* he told himself. *And hopefully already dead,* he added as he dreaded the notion of drowning.

The trawler pitched sharply again and more spray wet him. He hunched lower and brooded on what death was going to be like. Then movement caught his eye and he glanced to his right. To his astonishment he saw a person hurrying along the deck at a low crouch. Then, as the distant beam of the lighthouse swept around again, it provided just enough illumination for him to see it was Letitia.

Letitia! What?

He got no further. Letitia scuttled over next to him and crouched down. In her right hand she held a pistol and in her left a knife. She placed the pistol on the deck and glanced over her shoulder at the nearby wheelhouse. Placing a finger to her lips she went, "Ssssh!" and began to cut at the ropes at Martin's feet.

As realization and hope surged Martin leaned forward. "Hands first," he hissed.

Letitia nodded and moved to reach behind him. It was an awkward angle to Martin rolled over on his side with his head on Anne's lap. Letitia was then able to reach behind him and began slicing at the cable tie. But she was trembling so violently that it was obvious she was having trouble. A sharp little nick told him that she was cutting him as well so he shook his head.

"Careful Sis, don't slice me open," he whispered.

Letitia muttered something and nodded, then reached behind to feel at the cable tie before placing the point of the blade between it and his arm. She started an upwards sawing motion. Martin almost cried aloud as his hopes shot up. Within seconds the plastic was cut and his hands were free! Martin wrenched his arms apart and moved his hands to the front. Sharp pains shot up his forearms and through his wrists. He began rubbing and chafing at his numb hands to restore the circulation. Letitia moved to cut at the ropes holding his feet.

But this rope was much thicker and she quickly came to a panting, trembling stop. Martin stared at the ropes in the darkness.

"Might be quicker to untie them," he suggested.

Letitia nodded and she placed the knife on the deck and began feeling along the rope.

That worked. Martin was able to help, despite the aching stabs of pain that throbbed up his lower arms. The rope came loose and he was able to start easing his right foot out of the coils.

"Start getting Anne free," he whispered.

Letitia nodded and picked up the knife. She crawled over to Anne past Martin's feet and as she did she groaned. His heart went out to her and he vowed that the gang would pay for hurting his sister. While she sawed at Anne's bonds with the knife Martin freed his feet and began rubbing and massaging to restore the circulation.

By then Anne's hands were free and she bent to start on the knot around her ankles. Martin shook his head.

"No Sis. I will untie her feet. You cut Carmen and Andrew's hands free," he said.

Letitia nodded and moved to crouch in front of Carmen. At that moment the wheelhouse door banged open. Martin looked up in fright and saw Tony leaning out to squint at them.

"What's going on there?" Tony asked.

Martin acted without conscious thought. He turned, scooped up the pistol and went into a crouch facing Tony at a range of about one metre. Tony's eyes widened with astonishment and then fear as he took in what was happening. Martin pointed the pistol at his face.

"Hands up!" he croaked.

Tony goggled and then jumped backwards, pulling the door shut as he did. Martin tried to stand up to follow but a sudden cramp sent searing agony down his left leg and the calf muscles refused to function. For a few seconds he half stood, leaning on the bulwarks for support while he hit at the offending muscle with his left fist.

Tony's face appeared at the wheelhouse windows and Martin forced himself to his feet. Holding the gun up he shouted, "Open the door and put your hands up!"

But Tony shook his head. Martin aimed the pistol but then found he could not make himself pull the trigger. As he wrestled with his conscience and body his mind speculated on whether the pistol was loaded.

And is it cocked and does it have its safety catch on? he worried.

Noises behind him caused Martin to glance over his left shoulder and he saw that Letitia was staring at him but that Andrew had snatched the knife off her and was cutting at the bonds around his ankles. Carmen's hands were free and she was struggling to untie her ankles.

A feeling of desperation welled up and Martin again faced Tony. "Open the door and put your hands up or I will shoot!" he shouted.

But Tony just shook his head and ducked down. Martin kept the gun pointed at him but still could not make himself pull the trigger. To his dismay he saw Tony scuttle out of sight down a companionway that led below. Furious and frustrated Martin slammed the pistol into the glass of the window pane. This broke and he hammered it again until a sharp little pain in the palm of his hand made him pull back.

Andrew appeared beside him, knife in hand. "What happened? Where's he gone?" he asked.

"Below, to the engine room I think," Martin replied. Then he turned to face Andrew and stammered, "I... I couldn't. I couldn't shoot him."

Andrew nodded. "That's alright mate. Nor could I. Now let's get weaving."

"Where will we go?" Martin queried. In his mind he had half formed the plan to seize the trawler and to use it to take them to safety. "Can we use this boat?" he asked.

Carmen stood up next to him. She shook her head. "Not if that man and a couple of others are below. We might not be able to shoot people in cold blood, but I wouldn't put it past them."

"What about the radio?" Anne asked.

Martin knew the trawler must have a marine radio. A call on that would bring help quickly.

Carmen tried to open the wheelhouse door. "It's locked," she said.

Again she tried, putting the weight of her shoulder against it. Still the door didn't budge

"I'll break the window," Martin said, waving them aside with the pistol.

Carmen shook her head. "No. If those men are just down that

companionway then we would be at to much risk. We have to get off before they can get guns and organize a counter attack."

That notion sent stabs of fear through Martin. He knew the men had more guns but not where they were stored.

"How?" he asked.

Carmen pointed aft. "There's a dinghy towing astern. Get into that. Come on, move!"

Martin took one more look through the broken wheelhouse window, but in the darkness could see very little. A dim glow showed the location of the companionway leading below and at any moment he expected to see the shape of a person appear in it.

Then I will have to shoot, he thought. The idea made him queasy.

By then Andrew had gone running aft and Carmen had shoved Anne and Letitia past her.

"Come on Martin!" she hissed.

Martin did, still gripping the pistol and wondering if it was loaded. It was a short distance to the rear of the deckhouse, and as he hurried past its lights came on inside, showing brightly through the small portholes. Martin paused and risked a peek. What he saw sent more shards of fear stabbing through him. Tony was pulling guns out of a locker helped by Joel. As he did Tony was glancing over his shoulder towards the companionway to the wheelhouse and telling Joel what to do.

They've got guns so they will be after us in a few seconds, Martin thought.

The fear sent him hurrying aft. When he got there he almost tripped over a person lying on the deck. It was Marcus. He was sprawled at the aft end of a hatch cover near the nets, his trousers and underpants around his ankles. Letitia stood nearby as Andrew and Carmen hauled the dinghy alongside by its painter.

Martin bent forward to peer at Marcus, wondering if he was unconscious or dead. "What did you do Sis?" he asked.

"I went all sobby and limp and just sat down so that he thought I wasn't going to give any trouble and when he slid down his duds I kicked him in the nuts," Letitia explained. "Then I hit him on the side of the head with that steel thing."

She pointed to what looked like a steel bar or spanner lying on the deck. Martin bent to look more closely at Marcus. "Is he dead?" he asked.

"Don't know! I hope so!" Letitia cried.

Then she began to sob and was shaken by a storm of trembling. Martin started to straighten up to comfort her but Anne was quicker. Instead an idea flashed through Martin's mind and he bent and grabbed Marcus's trousers and reefed them hard. Marcus did not resist and Martin was in no mood to be gentle so he pulled hard, half lifting Marcus and dragging him across the deck until the trousers came free of the man's boots. As the trousers came off Marcus was half rolled on his side and he groaned loudly.

Good. He's not dead, Martin thought.

Martin turned to Letitia. "Take these. I'll get you a shirt." With one eye on the wheelhouse Martin bent and placed the gun down and with trembling fingers tried to unbutton Marcus's shirt. But he couldn't. His fingers were too stiff and he was too scared.

Then Andrew interrupted. "Never mind that! Get into the boat."

He grabbed Letitia and led her to the side. Martin picked up the gun and stood up, then followed, moving backwards ready shoot until he reached the side. A glance showed the dinghy bobbing alongside, Anne already in and Carmen climbing down. Letitia tossed the trousers down into the boat and threw her legs up over the gunwale and was helped down. Andrew followed, scrambling nimbly into the stern.

Martin hesitated for a moment over what to do with the pistol. He didn't want to give it up but needed both hands to climb down. He went to slip it into the front of his waistband but then the notion of a loaded gun pointing at his private parts and lower belly made him wince and he changed his mind. Instead he slid it into his waistband at the back, hoping it wasn't loaded as he did. Then he swung a leg over the rail and turned to drop into the boat. It wasn't far, only 2 metres, but it was bobbing on the waves and he didn't want to miscalculate.

As he hung there waiting his moment the wheelhouse door banged open and Martin waited no longer. He sprang into the centre of the dingy, bending his knees to take the shock. But in the darkness he lost his balance and fell heavily, knocking down Anne and Letitia as he did. For a moment he feared he was going to capsize the boat but Carmen was standing up holding on to the trawler and she quickly shifted her balance.

As Martin squirmed desperately to get right way up he saw Carmen let slip the painter and shove the boat away from the side of the trawler.

Spray showered over them as they rocked through the trawler's wash and Martin tasted the salt. Then he saw the stern of the trawler slip past, the wake churning white in the darkness.

A dim figure appeared on the side deck of the trawler and came hurrying aft at a crouch, the head and shoulders only visible. Martin struggled upright, ignoring the bumps and bruises and the way he was shoving at Letitia and Anne. Driven by the urgent desire to protect his friends he grabbed at the pistol and pulled it free. Then he lifted it up and pointed it. As he did he pulled the trigger.

Bang!

The pistol went off. It bucked much more than Martin had expected. He had no idea where the bullet went but he did hear a man cry out indicating fright and he saw the head at the trawler's transom vanish.

By the time Martin had regained his balance and was seated ready to aim properly the trawler was a good 50 metres away and vanishing into the night at a good 10 or 15 knots. There was a brief flash and then the report from a pistol at the stern near the nets but that shot also missed.

But it caused near panic. *We have to get moving or they will just turn and run us down,* Martin thought.

Obviously Andrew thought the same as he crouched at the motor and worked on it.

Oh hurry up! Hurry up! Martin thought as he saw the silhouette of the trawler, now 75 metres way, begin to change shape.

"They are turning Andrew," Martin called over his shoulder.

He found his mouth dry and licked his lips and then wiped his wet hands on his clothes to get a better grip on the gun. As he saw the trawler swing hard around to port and start back towards them Martin felt the fear rising and a feeling of desperation tinged with panic made him shiver.

Damn! he thought. To manage to get away and then to be left drifting helplessly! *It's enough to make man grind his teeth!*

Suddenly the trawler slewed to starboard and appeared to lean over. *What happened then?* Martin wondered.

Carmen knelt and shielded her eyes. "Has it stopped?" she asked.

Martin squinted into the darkness and tried to decide. The dark shape did not appear to be moving. He shook his head.

"I can't see a bow wave. I think it has," he replied. Hope began to crawl back.

"He has run aground," Andrew said.

"You sure?" Carmen queried.

"I think so. We are still in shallow water. Look near the trawler, you can see white water. I reckon that is from waves breaking on a sand bar."

Martin stared and noted the faint pattern of dappled white, but he did not really dare to hope lest he be disappointed yet again. But after another minute or so there was no doubt the trawler was not moving.

But nor are we, he thought.

Anne sat up and turned. "Oh Andrew, can you get that motor going?" she queried, her voice cracking with anxiety.

Andrew shook his head. "No. I can't see what the problem is," he replied.

"Then they might catch us again!" Anne said.

Martin bit his lip and felt sick. It seemed like a nightmare that never ended. Once again, he studied the dark shape of the trawler.

We are well within rifle range, he decided.

But how visible were they? Uncertain he stared hard, wiping his eyes as they watered in the cold wind. The waves were enough to make the boat toss about and from time to time water slopped aboard. Then he stared again and frowned. Did the trawler look further away?

He thought it did, so he used his raised finger to measure the trawler's mast and then repeated the exercise several more times over the next few minutes. A surge of hope again filled him and he did another measurement, just to be sure.

Then he said: "That trawler is further away, I am sure."

Andrew also raised a finger to measure. Then he nodded. "We are drifting on the tide," he commented.

"And the wind," Carmen added.

Martin did some calculations and then experienced a feeling of dismay quite disproportionate to the situation.

We are drifting back inshore! he thought.

Andrew obviously worked out the same thing as he said, "We are being carried back towards the coast by the incoming tide," he said.

"That's not good is it?" Anne asked.

Andrew shook his head. "No. We could just end up in the mangroves again," he agreed.

Anne gasped and cried, "Will we end up back at the gang's hideout?"

Andrew again shook his head. "No, because we won't go directly back along that winding channel into Mudcrab Creek. The wind is blowing is sideways as well," he explained.

"When is the top of the tide?" Anne asked.

Martin looked at his watch. It read 0245. "About now," he answered.

"What happens then?" Anne asked.

"The outgoing tide should take us out to sea," Andrew answered.

Anne shook her head. "But won't that take us back to that trawler?" she asked.

Andrew shook his head. "Probably not. There is a fair bit of leeway from this wind," he said.

Martin looked at the dark lump that was the now distant trawler and tried to compare its position with theirs using the lighthouse to give him a bearing. He saw that they were indeed now to the west of the trawler.

The wind is from the east, he reasoned, as another cold gust struck them.

The minutes began to drag by, the boat rocking and tossing on the fretful wind waves. Every few minutes Martin, Andrew and Carmen all measured the angles and distances to the trawler and after about twenty minuets Martin noted that the lighthouse was now shining to the left of the trawler instead of the right.

We are certainly drifting crabwise, he thought.

But then he noted that the trawler was definitely more distinct.

But we are also drifting back closer to the trawler, he thought. *If we drift too close, they could shoot us!*

Chapter 23

TERRIFIED

Martin licked his lips and shivered. There was no doubt: they were drifting back towards the trawler. And to make matters worse the movement was painfully slow. That meant that they would be close to the trawler for longer.

This is not good, he thought, the fear swirling in his empty stomach.

He looked at his watch, crouching low to hide the tiny light in the watch from the trawler. To his surprise he saw that is was already 0320.

It will start to get light in an hour or so, he thought. That would make things even more dangerous.

Andrew interrupted his thoughts by saying, "Start bailing guys. This tub is starting to fill with water."

They did, using their hands and a bucket. The bottom was full of fishing gear, rods, small nets, pieces of cloth, and the trousers Martin had taken. He picked them up and held them out.

"Here Sis, put these on," he said.

Letitia did so, with a lot of squirming and wriggling. Then Carmen handed her a buoyancy vest. "And this too," she said. "It will help keep the wind off you." She then passed a second vest to Anne.

Letitia tried. She did a lot of wriggling and in the process almost poked Martin in the eye with her boobs. Then she snorted and said, "I can't do it up. My tits are too big."

Martin could not help but look. He found himself staring at Letitia's breasts from a few centimetres away. The image that flitted through Martin's mind as she turned to show the others was of the big guns on a battleship.

Carmen was scandalized. "Oh Letitia! The poor boys didn't need to know that."

"Sorry," Letitia muttered, while straining to pull the vest closed. But it was no good.

Anne called to her. "Here Letitia, you try this one. It's much too big for me." She slid off the vest she wore and passed it across.

Letitia slid hers off, again almost poking Martin in the eye as she did. Then she picked up the other vest and began to squirm to get her arms through the sleeve holes

Again, Carmen shook her head. "Letitia! Poor Martin is getting an eyeful," she chided.

Letitia shrugged. "Huh! He sees me with nothing on almost every day," she commented.

"That's a bit unfair," Carmen answered.

"He doesn't mind," Letitia replied.

"He might," Carmen suggested. "Anyway, you shouldn't tease him. He is at that age."

Letitia grunted and buckled up the vest then thanked them. "That's better. It cuts out most of the wind," she said. Carmen nodded approval and helped Anne to put on the second vest.

Another ten minutes dragged by, and there was no doubt now that the tide was on the ebb. They drifted slowly along and the trawler came closer all the time.

Andrews studied it and then said: "It is still hard aground."

Carmen nodded. "And we are still making a bit of leeway."

Even as she said this there was a sharp report and Martin jerked his head up to stare at the trawler.

What was that? he wondered.

He soon found out. This time there was a loud *crack!* just over his head and then a distinct *thump!*

"They are shooting at us," he said, the fear leaping at his throat.

"Oh my God!" Anne wailed.

"Get down! Lie flat," Andrew ordered.

It was as well they did as the next bullet snapped past very low overhead. Martin cringed and felt a stab of pure terror.

How long can this go on for before one of us is hit? he wondered. His whole body seemed to be a quivering mass of fear and he felt an intense urge to run.

"Martin, can't you shoot back?" Letitia asked as she lay beside him in the cold, smelly water that was slopping around the bottom of the boat.

Martin had forgotten the pistol but a glance at the trawler and moment's thought made him shake his head. "The range is much too great," he replied.

"It might scare them though," Letitia said.

Martin shook his head. "I'd rather save the bullets until we drift even closer." He estimated the range at about 150 metres.

Whang!

That bullet struck the boat and he flinched and felt the fear wash through him in an icy wave. Cold water sprayed up over the side and he shuddered.

"Anyone hit?" Carmen called.

"No," they replied. Then another bullet struck the water close alongside and showered them with icy drops. Again, Martin flinched and he cringed lower and began to pray.

Two more shots struck the water nearby and a third snapped through the air seemingly just above his back. Then a fourth bullet hit the boat near the bows and he felt the shudder of its impact. Anne screamed and then hunched back.

"Anne! Are you alright?" Martin called.

"Y... Y... Y... yes. It just g... g... g... gave... gave me a f... f... fright," Anne replied.

Two more bullets hit the waves, one close enough to again shower spray into the boat. Martin felt his whole body trembling and knew he was terrified. Swallowing to keep the bile down he raised his head to look and noted that the trawler now looked further away and that its silhouette had changed. A tiny flicker of hope grew.

We are past it. We have drifted out past the trawler, he thought, noting that the lighthouse was now well to the left of the trawler.

There was one more shot and Martin saw it throw up a spurt of white a good 50 metres short of the boat. Then he eased himself up.

"I think we are safe," he croaked. He sat on a thwart and stared at the trawler, his whole body trembling with cold and fear. The trawler now looked to be 300 or so metres away. In the darkness it was hard to tell.

One by one the others got up and they all looked about. Andrew stared at the trawler then grunted before saying: "Back to bailing people. We have shipped a lot of water."

They had too. The boat felt quite sluggish and the water was ankle deep in the bottom, sloshing back and forth. Martin resumed scooping it up, flinging it to leeward. As he did he studied the waves and decided that they were slightly bigger than they had been. His rational mind told him that as they drifted further from the lee of Cape Bowling Green the wind would have more effect.

So the further west we go the worse the waves will become, he thought. That was a worrying thought as in his mind their nearest safety lay at Cungulla on the western side of the bay.

"Which way are you planning to go when you get the motor going Andrew?" Martin asked, while thinking 'if'.

"Where is the closest place?" Andrew replied.

Martin brought the chart to mind for a moment. "Alva Beach," he said.

"Where's that?"

"On the seaward side of Cape Bowling Green, at its base," Martin answered. "Probably about ten nautical miles."

"And that place we tried to reach the other day, Cungumbla or whatever?"

"Cungulla. About twelve I think. It might depend on the sea state," Martin answered.

Andrew looked thoughtful. "Yes, it's getting pretty rough, and we are still in the lee of the cape," he said.

"Cungulla then."

Andrew nodded. "If we don't sink first. Keep bailing," he ordered. This was caused by another wave slopping aboard and swilling around the bottom.

Carmen dug around in the litter in the bottom and then groped in the small locker under the aft thwart. "This boat seems to lack the basic safety equipment required by regulations," she commented.

"What are you looking for?" Andrew asked.

"I started looking for more lifejackets and then it occurred to me that there should be a radio and an EPIRB," Carmen answered.

Martin felt like smacking himself. *An EPIRB!* he thought.

By law all small boats registered in Queensland and which were going to travel more than few nautical miles from shore were supposed to have one of the radio beacons which would transmit a distress signal and their position via satellite to the authorities.

But there wasn't one. Nor was there a radio. That puzzled Martin. "This is the boat that chased us isn't it? I saw those men using a radio."

"There isn't one here," Carmen replied.

They all looked and then they bailed. They also got colder and wetter as the waves grew even larger and the spray came aboard more frequently. Martin began to get anxious about them sinking. In the darkness he was sure they were a long way from land.

We could just end up drowning, if we don't die from exposure first! he thought, shivering both from the cold and fear.

Anne suddenly gasped. "What's that?" she cried, pointing over the side.

Martin looked and saw a distinct boil of white foam about 25 metres away. For a second he thought it must be some large sea creature, a whale or something. Then he saw that there were other large areas of sea foaming white and he realized what he was looking at.

"It is waves breaking in the shallows," he answered.

That was whole new hazard. They looked around and Andrew pointed to more areas of white water on their starboard side. "You are right. It is the waves breaking on the sandbars," he added.

Anne whimpered and Martin felt like doing so. *If we go aground and get swamped we are done for!* he thought.

His heart began to hammer, and he looked fearfully in all directions. But the only other thing he could see clearly in the darkness was the revolving beam of the lighthouse. And it looked to be directly upwind of them and several miles away.

We will never swim against these waves to reach that, he thought. It was a chilling prospect.

But then he realized that he could actually see a faint grey area low to the east. *Dawn. It will be daylight soon,* he thought.

A check of his watch confirmed this. It was 0510.

"Daybreak," he said, pointing.

And a particularly cold and forbidding daybreak. The wind was strong and chilling and the waves were growing and continually slopping more water into the half waterlogged boat. But even so it cheered them. As the pale grey was tinged with a watery pink Martin was able to see much better the situation they were in.

He saw that their boat was bobbing along in a deep gutter on the outgoing tide and that the force of the current was taking them clear of the dozens of sandbanks on both sides. The shallows appeared to extend off in both directions for vast distances.

We can't just head directly for Cungulla, he noted gloomily. It was obvious they would have to detour far out into the bay to find deep enough water. *Maybe we should try for Alva Beach?*

Looking astern Martin picked out the trawler in the half light. It was now several miles astern and looked to be side on and still stationary. That was a relief. Next, he looked southwards beyond the trawler, expecting to see the shore line they had come from but to his surprise it was not visible. *Out of sight over the curve of the earth,* he decided, noting the haze and spray that was also obscuring visibility.

To the east, and only about 2 nautical miles away, was a hard line emerging against the lightness.

"Cape Bowling Green," he said, pointing to it.

It showed up as a low, dark, lumpy line which he knew were sand dunes before an irregular line of trees marked the main part of the cape. The lighthouse stood up among the last of the trees near its seaward end. For a long-distance northwards from the tip of the cape a confused pattern of white water and breaking waves indicated a large area of shallows.

Martin knew that the cape was nothing but a long, low sand spit 15 kilometres long and in places only hundreds of metres wide with mangroves and mud flats on its western side. He had never been there, only seen it on the map. But he had been to Alva Beach and he now put his theory to Andrew about having to detour well out into the bay to reach Cungulla safely.

Andrew studied the sea and nodded. "You are right. It might be easier to go around the end of the cape to this Alva Beach place," he commented. He then bent to the outboard motor and started working on it. As the light rapidly improved he was able to see what he was doing.

In between bailing the others watched him. Martin kept bailing in an attempt to warm himself but he felt terribly worn out. But he also saw that they had floated out past the most obvious lines of breakers and were now in deeper water.

We will be level with the tip of the cape soon, he observed.

Suddenly the outboard motor spluttered and blue smoke puffed out. Martin felt his heart leap with hope and he grinned. They all grinned and Andrew tried again. This time the outboard burst into a healthy roar and they all grinned again.

Oh thank God! Martin thought. *Now we can get to safety.*

Andrew settled to steering and at once the motion of the boat improved. With steerage way he was able to pick a course that saved them from the worst of the waves so that many fewer broke aboard.

Carmen looked up from bailing. "Which way are you going Andrew?" she asked.

"I am going to head northeast to check out what the sea is like on the outside of the cape," Andrew answered. "If it isn't too rough we will go round it and head south to Alva Beach."

Carmen turned to look in that direction and then shook her head. "It looks pretty rough to me," she commented.

It looked pretty rough to Martin too. Out beyond the tip of the cape the horizon was a jagged line of waves, and as they moved further from behind the lee of the cape they began to encounter quiet big waves. Some of these were breaking on sand bars and in shallow water and it all made for very confused and dangerous boating.

Then an object out past the cape near the lighthouse caught Martin's eye. "Look! A ship!" he cried.

They all followed his pointing finger. Anne gasped with relief and Letitia let out a shivering sob.

Carmen shielded her eyes and stared at the distant vessel. "It is heading north," she commented.

"Making for Townsville?" Andrew suggested.

As he said this they hit a large wave as it was breaking and spray showered over them. A large amount of water poured aboard.

Carmen shook drops from her face and hair. "You just watch your steering and try to avoid things like that," she snapped.

"Aye aye ma'am!" Andrew retorted with a grin.

"If we can reach the ship they will save us," Anne said.

Carmen nodded. "Yes, they must have a radio," she agreed. She bent to bailing but looked up every few seconds. So did Martin, his anxiety now that the vessel might be too fast and that they might not be able to catch up with it.

It is a converging course but they are larger than us so can cope with the waves better, he thought.

For the next ten minutes they bailed, and Andrew concentrated on steering to avoid the worst of the waves, quartering the largest. But they had to slow down as the waves became bigger and bigger. Worse still the waves now had an unpredictable pattern, coming in at right angles to the now strongly gusting wind.

"Refraction," Andrew explained. "As waves hit the coast they curve around capes and headlands so as to hit the coast close to square on."

"Will we catch the ship?" Anne asked. She looked pinched and blue as the first rays of the sun illuminated them.

"Not sure. I hope so," Andrew replied. But he looked very worried and Martin's thoughts mirrored that.

Then Martin blinked salt spray clear of his eyes to see better. "That is a trawler," he said.

"I don't care if it's the *Titanic*, as long as we catch it," Andrew replied.

Carmen stared at the vessel. "It's turning to port. It's heading into the bay," Carmen said.

It was. Martin stared hard at it and his hopes went up even more. The trawler, now about 2 miles north of the tip of the cape and well clear of the boiling white water in the shallows that extended from it, was definitely turning their way.

"Have they seen us?" Anne queried hopefully.

Carmen shook her head. "No. They couldn't see such a small object in such a rough sea. They might be just trying to get into sheltered water in the lee of the cape. That ocean looks very rough."

The trawler went west for about ten minutes and then it abruptly turned to port again and headed directly for the boat. Martin stared at it but did not dare voice his hopes.

Letitia did though. "It is coming this way! It must have seen us! We are saved!" she cried.

It looked like it. Andrew slowed the boat to maintain steerage and concentrated in keeping clear of any obviously shallow water and on breasting the waves with minimum fuss. Martin bent to bailing again as the boat was again half full.

But his arms quickly grew tired and he stopped to get his breath. Panting and trembling with the over-exertion he looked up. The trawler was now bows on and obviously in the same deep water channel as them.

Won't be long now, he thought, deciding that the trawler was only about a nautical mile away.

And then he froze. Something about the trawler looked familiar and he stared, wiped his eyes and stared again.

It's got a blue hull, he noted.

Up till now he had not been concerned, knowing that there were dozens, if not hundreds of trawlers, working along the North Queensland coast. But now a niggling suspicion grew. Frowning, he squinted and tried to read the numbers and letters painted on the hull. But they were mostly obscured by the bow wave and by the bursting spray the trawler was throwing up as it met bigger waves.

It was one of those bigger waves that tossed the trawler's bow high when it was about half a kilometre away. Martin stared and felt as though he had been drenched with ice. Clearly visible was a white letter 'K' and behind that the numerals 3 and 4.

"Oh no!" Martin cried. "I think that is the crook's other trawler."

"Other trawler?" Anne queried, her expression disbelieving.

Martin bit his lip and nodded. "Yes. The one that chased us the other day had a registration number staring with a 'K'. The one aground astern of us starts with 'EXJ'," he explained.

Carmen nodded. "Martin's right. There are two trawlers. This is the one with our friend Long John Silver on it."

A comment he had overheard from Mr Barberini clicked in Martin's brain. "She is called the *Jolly Roger*."

"How do you know that?" Andrew asked, his eyes on the approaching vessel.

Martin shrugged. "I overheard them mention a boat called that," he explained. "I thought it was on its way to Bowen."

Carmen nodded. "They must have called this one back to help. Andrew, turn around!" she said.

Andrew looked grim but he didn't hesitate. Picking his moment, he swung the boat through 180 degrees. In those big waves it took some skill, but he managed it, the boat completing the turn before the next big wave arrived. Then he opened the throttle and headed them back the way they had come.

By then the trawler was only about 400 metres astern and Martin had no doubt. A thin man with a woolly mop of mousy fair hair appeared at the bows.

That is the man who shot at us on the mudflats, Martin thought, the terror flooding back as he saw that the man had a rifle.

"Get down! He's got a gun," he croaked. Next to him Anne sat petrified, her face showing shock and fear. He pushed at her. "Get down Anne. He will shoot."

He did. The shot snapped close alongside and threw up spray. Martin felt his bowels loosen as the terror kicked in. He lay as flat as he could, half on Anne.

Crack!

Another shot snapped overhead. Andrew bit his lip and kept glancing astern. "He's having trouble aiming because the trawler is pitching so much in the waves," he said.

"Then it will get more deadly as we move into calmer water," Carmen suggested.

Andrew nodded. "Yes."

Martin looked around and felt so scared he could hardly speak without his face muscles quivering. "We can't go back along this channel. The other trawler is there," he said.

They all looked ahead and the other trawler seemed to leap into focus, still side on and sitting almost high and dry on the now exposed sandbars. The channel was now very obvious as the tide was even lower.

We will have to go right past that other trawler,' Martin thought.

It was an appalling prospect. Looking around he noted several shallow channels and deep-water gutters leading in behind the lines of sand bars towards the cape.

"We need to get ashore," he cried, pointing towards the cape.

Carmen nodded. "I agree. Andrew, see if you can find a deep-water channel heading in that direction."

"Not yet," Andrew replied, his face calm but grim. "If we turn now we will be beam on to these big waves. I will..."

At the sound of a bullet snapping close past he ducked and grimaced then went on.

"As I was saying, I will wait till we are inshore of this line of breakers."

If we live that long! Martin thought, his whole body cringing in anticipation.

Chapter 24

SWAMPED!

Another shot struck the water close astern. Martin looked back at the trawler and saw the man cock the rifle.

Tyler, that's his name, he remembered.

But Tyler didn't shoot. Instead he stood there watching. A tiny flicker of hope grew in Martin's chest.

The trawler has slowed down, he noted. That was sensible in such shallow and confined waters.

"Aren't they taking a risk following us into this narrow channel?" Anne queried.

Carmen nodded. "They are, but they probably know the channel pretty well if it leads to their base at Mudcrab Landing. Besides, the tide is now so low they can see the main channel clearly," she answered.

By this time Andrew was crouching to study the waters ahead. The boat was moving slightly faster than the trawler and also faster than the waves and as it went over each crest it went surfing down the front. Once they nearly lost control and hung on the edge of a broach, causing Martin to suck in his breath in fear.

Carmen shook her head. "Careful Andrew!" she cautioned.

"Sorry. Get ready. I am going hard a-port in a moment. Keep bailing you guys, we are hauling a lot of water," he answered.

Martin did as he was told, his eyes flicking around to keep track of the situation. At a word of warning Andrew abruptly turned them to port and they headed off eastwards through a deep-water channel which wound its way towards the cape. To the left were breaking waves and foam and to starboard were hundreds of sandbars that were mostly exposed or just awash.

Now they were heading directly into the wind and a pattern of small wind waves caused the bow to buffet hard against each one. Cold spray flew up constantly and the hull hammered hard at each one. From time to time a larger ocean wave that had survived breaking on the sandbars to port washed across to cause a horrible, heart-in-mouth roll.

Then the boat struck the bottom when it was in the trough between two larger than usual waves. The sudden jolt sent a gasp of anxiety through Martin and he looked back and saw dirty brown water mixed with silt swirling up. The propeller was pushed up by its safety guard but Andrew at once pushed it back down again.

If the motor stops it will be a disaster, Martin thought.

They struck the bottom several more times as the water shallowed. Martin stared anxiously ahead, estimating they still had about a kilometre to go. Then he glanced back, and felt his heart skip a beat. "Look! That trawler has stopped," he cried.

They all stared astern and then Martin felt his heart give another skip. "They are launching a boat," he added.

That was desperately bad news. Martin had somehow thought that getting ashore would mean that they were safe but now he realized that they were in the same situation as two days earlier.

Except that now we definitely do know too much! he thought grimly. That the gang meant to kill them was all too obvious.

The boat sped on, still bumping into wind waves and scraping the bottom from time to time. Martin studied the way ahead and noted that there was another channel coming in from their left through a gap between two sand banks. It looked to be about half a kilometre from the beach which was no longer a dark silhouette but had taken on a pale creamy tone. The lighthouse was just to the left of their course and the mangroves started again near there.

I hope we don't have to fight our way through mangroves again, he thought.

Another glance behind showed that the people on the trawler were definitely hoisting out a boat. It hung from one of the booms and was swung out over the side even as he watched.

At that moment the boat seemed to leap up. Martin lost his balance and tumbled forward. So did Anne and Letitia. Then the boat fell forward and landed with a hard thump which sent up a huge sheet of spray. There were cries of alarm and Martin saw Andrew wrestling with the steering as the bow rose.

"Hang on!" he shouted.

Martin just had time to raise his head to look. He saw that the waves had suddenly become much higher and steeper and he knew this was characteristic of waves as they entered shallow water. And these waves were coming in on their beam as they motored across the second channel.

Splat! Swoosh! Whack!

The boat rolled and pitched violently, and suddenly dirty brown water poured over the bows and port gunwale in a massive waterfall. Within seconds the boat was swamped. The flood engulfed Anne and Letitia as they struggled to get up and even sloshed into Martin's face causing him to choke and splutter. Bitter tasting salt went down his throat and his eyes stung. He clung on grimly while his heart hammered with fear.

Worse still the boat did not rise to the next wave. This just broke over them, the force of the water almost wrenching Martin from his grip. It did drag Anne away and Letitia was knocked over again, her scream cut off to become a choking gurgle. Then the sound of the motor stopped.

Oh no! Martin thought, blinking and looking around. *Full to the brim,* he thought just before the next wave struck them and swamped them again.

It was instantly obvious to him that they had no hope of bailing the boat out, or of restarting the motor. And Anne was being carried away by the wind and current. She was already 10 metres away.

I must save her, he thought.

With that in mind he stood up, then lost his balance and fell heavily on Carmen and Letitia, bruising himself and going under again.

Andrew dragged him up. "Get over the side. Swim for it!" he shouted.

Martin nodded, spluttering and coughing too much to speak. As he put a foot on the now submerged starboard gunwale he glimpsed Anne. She was now about 25 metres and three waves away. With all the strength he could muster he sprang into the sea towards her, the boat sinking as he did.

But within seconds it became a desperate battle just to keep his head above water. The waves were so large that he went swooping up and down and even hit the bottom with his feet in the troughs. And several of the waves broke, tumbling him over. The strength of the waves and the current came as a horrible shock and Martin quickly revised his plan of saving Anne to wondering if he could preserve his own life.

Swimming with all his remaining strength he struck out across the flow, aiming for the tiny white pencil of the lighthouse. It was hard going and he quickly tired. Worse still he several times sucked in water as well as air and had to come to a coughing, panting stop while he trod water and tried to restore his breathing.

As he went up and down on the waves Martin noted other heads in the water near him, Letitia with her life jacket floating high and Andrew and Carmen both breast stroking determinedly across the waves.

Where is Anne? he wondered.

A quick look around on the next rise revealed her to be about 50 metres away and close to a sandbar. She was swimming but not very strongly. It was obvious that her buoyancy vest was saving her.

"OK, she should be safe. Now save yourself," Martin told himself.

After looking around to orientate himself he again struck out towards the lighthouse. But after being slapped in the face by a big wave he realized that he was starting to swim upstream against the bigger waves, so he changed course more to his right and swam partly with them.

That was easier and his tired mind and blurred eyes noted that the large areas of shallows and sand bars were closer with each stroke. Redoubling his efforts, he struggled as hard as he could, despite feeling utterly drained. His arms and legs began to feel as though they were made of lead and he knew his efforts were becoming very feeble. It was all he could do to keep his head above water to gasp breaths of air.

Andrew and Carmen both went past, Andrew towing Letitia by the straps of her buoyancy vest. They called encouragement and that helped. Martin made what he felt must be his last effort before he was totally drained of energy, and his feet touched bottom again.

Twice he was washed off his feet, but he struck out in desperation and once he reached water too shallow to swim in he dragged himself up out of it. Sobbing and gasping he crawled on hands and knees up onto an exposed sandbar. That was a massive relief, tempered by the strong wind which began to instantly chill him and by the fact that it was whipping up particles of sand which got into his eyes.

Flopping down on the wet sand Martin lay there gasping, trembling in every limb. For a minute or so all he could do was shiver and shake and gulp in lung fulls of cold air. Then Andrew and Carmen staggered past dragging Letitia. They dropped her and fell to the sand, Carmen to lie on her back, chest heaving as she sucked in great breaths and Andrew kneeling on hands and knees, shaking and head sagging. Letitia rolled half onto her side and gave a couple of convulsive twitches before spewing.

Seawater and bile trickled from her mouth and she then lay with her eyes closed while coughing and spitting out more. The mucous dribbled down the side of her face.

At least Sis is safe, Martin thought. *But what about Anne?*

Anxious and ashamed he lifted his head and looked around. To his mixed dismay and relief he saw Anne lying in shallow water about 75 metres away. She was face down and not moving.

Oh God no! I hope she hasn't drowned, he thought.

Summoning up what seemed like his last reserve of energy Martin rolled over and then pushed himself up to hands and knees and then to his feet. For a few seconds he stood there, swaying like a drunken man. Then he forced his trembling legs to move and he tottered over to where Anne lay, splashing through a knee-deep gutter on the way.

She was alive. As he reached her Martin saw her chest rising and falling and noted that she was trembling violently.

Thank God! Poor kid, he thought.

Falling to his knees Martin patted her on the back and told her she was safe. As he did his eyes roamed back to where the other three lay on the sand. Then he looked back towards the bay, and felt a spurt like he had been given an electric jolt.

The boat was in the water beside the trawler and people were climbing down into it!

They will be here in a few minutes. We have to get away from here, Martin thought. Then his mind moved faster. *Pistol!* he thought.

But his groping hand found nothing tucked into the back of his waistband. Clearly it has slipped out during that desperate swim to shore.

"Bugger!" he swore, his stomach turning over with apprehension.

The boat began moving away from the trawler and even as Martin watched it turned towards him. With that the terror flooded back in and with it a spurt of adrenaline. Grabbing Anne he shook her.

"Anne! Anne! Get up! Here come the men," he croaked.

Anne stirred and lifted her head. Her face looked sickly blue under the pale skin and wet hair was plastered over her face.

"What?"

"The men. They are coming in a boat. Get up!" Martin cried, pulling at her arm as he did.

He saw the fear flood into her eyes and she whimpered and shuddered.

Then she reacted and with an obvious effort pushed herself to her hands and knees. Martin stood and helped her to her feet. Then he looked around to check what his friends were doing.

Andrew was sitting and watching so Martin pointed towards the boat. "Run Andrew, run!" he called.

Andrew turned and looked towards the boat. A moment later he sprang to his feet like a cartoon character and began yelling at Carmen and Letitia and pulling at them. As both stirred and began to move Martin got Anne moving as well. The pair staggered across the wet sand like two drunks leaning on each other to hold each other up.

They came to a wave filled gutter about 25 metres wide and Martin stopped. Glancing back, he saw a white bow wave at the front of the boat. It was now forging through the rough water towards them. That overcame any scruples and Martin urged Anne into the water. They waded, splashed and stumbled across, the water luckily mostly only thigh deep although a couple of waves came up to their chests and nearly bowled them over.

Then they were up on firmer dry sand again and were able to stagger and stumble along with relative ease. Off to their left Martin saw Andrew and Carmen supporting Letitia between them as they also floundered across the gutter.

The line of mangroves looked to be about 500 metres ahead. Between them and the mangroves was mostly just flat sand plus a few puddles and shallow water gutters. A quick look over his shoulder showed the boat to be only about a kilometre behind and coming on fast, throwing up big bursts of spray as it buffeted across the turbulent water.

Oh my God! It is catching up fast! Martin thought.

He began to despair of them escaping. But he kept on trying. Another, shallower gutter was waded and they hurried on. The other three took a converging course and with 300 metres to go the two groups joined up. For a moment they came to a gasping standstill and Martin looked back to estimate their chances.

He saw the boat was now in the second, deep channel where their boat had been swamped and he hoped the crooks would also capsize, but it didn't. But it did turn to quarter the waves and that took it more to the south. Then the boat turned again, and Martin saw that there was another deep water channel running eastwards roughly parallel to the course they were taking across the exposed sand flats. The boat turned into this.

"They are going to beat us to the shore," Martin commented, bitterness and despair mingling in his voice.

"Keep going. If we reach those mangroves, we have a chance," Carmen cried.

It looked to be a slim hope, but Martin nodded and urged Anne to start walking again. Run they could not, a shambling stumble being the best they could manage. As they moved Martin kept glancing sideways, to keep tabs on the boat. What he was watching for was when one to the people in it raised a rifle to shoot.

Then we will be in real trouble, he thought grimly, remembering the last time that they had been pinned down on the mudflats.

To his surprise he saw that there were only two people in the boat but one of them was Tyler with the mop of brown hair. That knowledge sent shivers of fear through him. Certain that Tyler would shoot to kill Martin hurried on, ready to call a warning and throw himself flat at any second.

But then it occurred to him that Tyler was actually conning the boat so couldn't use his rifle. The other person was a man with a black eye patch.

What's his name? Martin wondered.

Carmen informed him by gasping to Andrew: "There's your mate Long John Silver in the bows."

Martin nodded to himself. *Silver, the pirate we had a fight with on Endeavour Island,* he remembered.

Silver was looking in their direction and Martin could see that he had a gun. But to Martin's surprise he made no attempt to shoot. The boat drew level about 300 metres to their right and then moved ahead.

Martin grimly forced his weakening legs to keep moving, ignoring the pain, cramps, cold wind and sand in the eyes in a desperate bid to reach some sort of cover before Tyler got ashore. The line of trees seemed to dance provocatively and frustratingly near, yet far. But they were making progress and the distance fell from 300 to 200 to 100 metres before the boat ran aground on the edge of the mangroves about 400 metres to their right.

"Run! Run!" Martin croaked as he saw Long John Silver scramble ashore. After 10 paces Silver tossed a small anchor onto the sand. Tyler followed, rifle in hand and his head turned their way.

They ran. It was lung-bursting, gut wrenching and heart busting effort but they all ran. Martin saw Tyler go down on one knee and raise the rifle, but he kept running.

"Keep running!" he cried.

If we get pinned down in the open, we are finished. Moving targets are harder to hit, he thought, but the terror still coursed through him.

Crack!

The shot went between them and that sent another burst of energy into their legs.

Missed! Martin thought, glancing around to check that Anne and the others were keeping up.

They were, but she and Letitia were both staggering and weaving with exhaustion, eyes wide with fear, mouths agape, breath coming in frantic pants.

Crack!

Missed again!

And they were into the mangroves. These grew out of a mixture of sand and hard mud and had buttress roots not aerial roots, a fact that Martin instantly appreciated. That meant they were able to hurry into the relative darkness without having to climb over an ensnaring tangle.

But can we get away? he fretted, fearing that Tyler would just run along the beach and then follow their tracks.

Chapter 25

CAPE BOWLING GREEN

Martin slowed to help Anne but as he hurried deeper into the mangroves his mind raced. He knew that the mangroves were just a thin belt of a few hundred metres at most before they came to the sand spit that was the 'dry land' of the cape.

How can we hide in this? How can we lose those mongrels in this? he worried.

And then his anxiety went up another notch as he noted patches of sunlight ahead. They were already approaching the other side of the mangroves! A quick glance behind showed daylight in that direction as well. Looking left and right for possible hiding places Martin felt his hopes slide down. The mangroves all had thin trunks, too thin to hide behind. And there was nowhere else to hide.

Oh God! What can we do? he fretted.

The others also came to a gasping stop and looked frantically around. Then Andrew shook his head. "Keep going," he gasped.

There seemed to be nothing else for it so they did, staggering and stumbling on for another hundred paces until they reached the other side of the trees. As they did Martin noted that it had begun to rain again. All the trees were rustling and bending to the strong wind. Cold drops showered down, making it hard to see.

Blinking the drops from his eyes Martin paused in the edge of the trees to look at what lay ahead. It was more or less what he had expected, sand dunes with sparse cover. The group came to a standstill again and looked around and at each other.

The dunes were between 3 and 5 metres high, nothing much really, and on this side, in the lee out of the wind, they were studded with small bushes, tufts of wiry grass and festoons of some sort of spiky vine.

A hundred metres to their left the top of the lighthouse showed above the dunes. Anne pointed to it, her anxious face asking the question her gasping body could not manage.

Martin at once shook his head. "No good. There won't be anyone there. We need to go the other way. That is the direction of Alva Beach," he croaked. As he did he shivered, both from reaction and cold. He was quite surprised at the strength of the wind, even in the lee of the dune, and the rain was slashing in hard and heavy, making it harder to see.

"But those men are that way," Carmen objected.

Martin shook his head. "Maybe. But they are just as likely to try to follow our tracks," he replied.

"But we can't outrun them! We are exhausted," Letitia said. She looked haggard and pale.

Martin shrugged. "What other choice do we have? We can't go left. If we do we run out of trees just past the lighthouse," he answered.

Andrew nodded. "Martin's right. Come on guys, let's make it hard for them. Get moving Martin," he said.

Martin sucked in a big breath, and set off to his right, walking fast on the sand just outside the edge of the trees.

Speed matters, he thought. *The trees will just slow us down.*

Luckily the rain had wet the sand and it was fairly firm and easy to walk on, but the downside was that they left a very clear trail.

That bothered Martin and caused anxiety to clutch at his throat, but he could not think of any way to erase them. So he hurried ahead, skirting to the right and then around to the left into a small hollow behind another dune. Ahead were two small bushes about 2 metres apart, like a doorway between the slope of the dune on the left and the trees on the right. Beyond them was a dip and then another, slightly larger dune which half blocked their path.

As he hurried between the bushes Martin felt his right ankle get snagged. Before he could stop himself he tripped, falling forwards. He was just able to break his fall with his hands before rolling on the wet sand.

"Bloody hell! What the?" he cried.

A glance showed him that he had tripped on an old length of rope, flotsam that had obviously been washed onto the cape. Other bits of human litter lay nearby: old plastic bottles, a rubber thong, several pieces of sawn timber grey with age.

"Watch that rope," he said as he was helped up by Andrew.

Dusting the wet sand off his hands and forearms he resumed his hurried progress. His every urge was to run but he was unable.

And the girls have no chance, he thought, glancing back and noting their drawn faces and heaving chests. One of his fears now was that one of them would collapse.

Anxiety was now squirming in him like black maggots and he experienced the nightmare sensation of trying to run but being unable to while some terrible thing was catching up. But the terrible thing was real! It was two armed men with murder in their hearts and the fear was so all-consuming Martin could hardly think straight. He knew he was on the edge of both collapse and panic.

Fifty paces on Martin rounded the end of the next dune and then came to a gasping halt when he spotted movement on the dunes ahead. Blinking to clear his eyes from the driving rain he felt the fear clutch at his throat.

It was Long John Silver.

The man was about a hundred metres away and had just run up onto the top of a larger sand dune. He was just visible through the rain but even as Martin put up his hand to stop the others, he saw Silver's head turn.

Silver's mouth opened and he yelled, "Here they are!"

Bowel loosening, mind numbing fear swamped Martin, almost paralysing him.

"Back! Go back!" he croaked.

With that he turned and fled, pushing at Letitia in his frantic desire to escape. They ran. Despite their exhaustion and weakness, they ran, or rather stumbled and lurched.

As he ran, his heart pounding and his breath coming in great gulps Martin felt the despair gripping him like a black fog.

Where can we hide? How can we get away? he thought.

Then Andrew, who was two ahead of him, went down. Martin and Letitia stopped to help him and Martin saw that he had tripped over the same piece of old grey rope that he had. Carmen glanced back and then turned and came hurrying back.

The plan just fell into Martin's head. "Stop! I have a plan," he cried.

Andrew scrambled to his feet, gasping for breath and wide–eyed with fear. "What?" he croaked.

"You and Carmen grab that rope and hide behind those two bushes. I will stay here until Silver appears and then run. When he chases me wait till he is close and then pull the rope up and trip him. Then get his gun. Find something to hit him with," Martin said.

Letitia was aghast. "Martin, it will never work. Don't be silly! Run!"

But Andrew looked thoughtful and Carmen nodded. "Worth a try," she said. "We can't outrun them. But I will do the running and you grab him."

Martin shook his head vigorously. "No. The running is the riskiest bit. He might shoot. Now quick, don't argue! Get down. Letitia, you and Anne go on until you can just see me and then wait. When you see Silver let him see you then run on around behind the dune. Go!"

To his relief they did. Andrew and Carmen went to each side of the narrow gap behind the bushes and crouched down. Carmen began tugging at the old rope while Andrew picked up several pieces of old driftwood and tested them. Martin stood facing back towards the enemy, his chest heaving and his stomach so tense it was like a tight ball of worms.

And there was Silver! The man came running into view, an unbuttoned yellow rain coat flapping in the wind, and as he did Martin felt a spurt of pure terror. Silver had a submachine gun.

Heckler and Koch 9mm, Martin thought, even as he wondered if he had left his run too late.

Absolute fear got him going. He turned and fled, sprinting between the bushes and barely noting Andrew and Carmen crouched behind them. Ahead he saw the anxious faces of Letitia and Anne and then their expressions changed to fright and they also turned and fled.

Now Martin felt his whole being cringe as he ran, expecting bullets to punch into his back at any second. Instead he heard Silver's voice shouting, "Stop!"

Nerving himself to ignore the threat Martin ran on, reaching the curve of the dune 25 metres further on before snatching a quick glance back over his shoulder.

He was just in time to hear Andrew cry "Now!" and see Silver run between the bushes. The rope went up and Silver tripped and went down. He went down so hard and so fast that the submachine gun went flying from his grip to land ten metres closer to Martin. Even as Silver swore and made to rise Andrew dashed over and whacked at his head with a piece of driftwood. The rotten old wood splintered and broke but Silver dropped flat on his face. Andrew hit him again and then leapt on his back.

As he did, Martin noted that Silver was carrying a back pack.

The gun! Martin thought.

Skidding to a stop he turned and raced back, his boots flinging sand up as he did. His hands stretched for the gun, reaching it a moment before Carmen.

"I've got it!" he cried. "Get under cover and help Andrew hold him."

Carmen nodded and turned to do so. Martin dashed back to the bushes, his mind alive with fear and the worry about where Tyler was.

He is the more dangerous of the two, he thought.

Reaching the bush Carmen had been hiding behind he crouched down and peered through the leaves.

He was just in time. Into view came Tyler, rifle held in both hands, running as fast as he could on the wet sand while he followed Silver's tracks. Martin knew that they could not repeat the trip trick but was resolved to save the others by using the submachine gun.

Raising it to his shoulder he sighted along the top of the barrel at the running man.

Fifty metres, too far; forty metres, still too far, Martin thought.

He was waiting for 25 metres but then Tyler suddenly skidded to a stop and hefted the rifle to his shoulder. Martin thought Tyler had seen Andrew or Carmen, but she was hunched behind the other tiny bush, her face a determined mask and in her hand another piece of driftwood.

Martin aimed but then found he could not bring himself to just shoot the man. While he hesitated Tyler suddenly shouted, "You two girls, stop!" and Martin knew he had seen Anne and Letitia. As Tyler aimed his rifle Martin stood up, weapon aimed, and yelled at the top of his voice: "Hands up! Drop the gun or I shoot!"

Tyler hesitated and gaped at him in astonishment and then the rifle barrel moved to aim towards the bushes.

Bang!

Martin did not flinch. He had no idea where Tyler's shot went but he was now grimly determined. He sighted and pulled the trigger.

Blat! Blat-a-tat-a-tat-a-tat!

The submachine gun hammered and kicked. Martin had never fired an automatic weapon and was quiet taken by surprise at the vibration and kick. The barrel jerked up and he stopped shooting, his vision obscured by rain drops and oily smoke.

And Tyler was down! But he was moving, and moving very fast. Martin saw that he was rolling sideways on the sand and still holding onto the rifle. Martin quickly aimed the submachine gun again and again pulled the trigger.

Blat-a-tat-a-tat!

This time Martin was better prepared and he kept a tighter grip. But the gun still bucked and the target, a fleeting, moving one, was quickly obscured by the smoke and his own blurred vision. Then Tyler went down.

I hit him! Martin thought, relief mingling with dread. He blinked to clear his eyes and took a better grip on the submachine gun.

Tyler scrambled to his feet and started limping away. As he did he cast terrified glances back towards Martin. Martin then saw that Tyler was bleeding from his right buttock and lower back and that he had no rifle in his hands.

"Stop! Come back! Stop!" Martin shouted.

But Tyler didn't. Instead he broke into a shambling, hobbling run. Martin sighted the gun on Tyler's back and tensed, but then couldn't bring himself to pull the trigger. Inside he locked up, trembling and torn. Instead he shouted out "Stop!" but Tyler ignored him and darted to his right and vanished into the trees.

Martin turned to find Carmen beside him. "I couldn't shoot him," he explained. "He is unarmed and I just couldn't do it."

Carmen patted his shoulder and nodded. "Nor could I. Where's his rifle?"

"Somewhere there on the sand," Martin said.

Carmen went to move but as she did a yell of alarm from Andrew made Martin jump with fright and he glanced over his shoulder.

It was Silver. The pirate had begun to struggle violently and had thrown Andrew off his back. Andrew clung on to Silver's backpack, but this came loose and Silver rolled over and shrugged it off then went to scramble to his feet. Andrew swung the backpack and struck Silver in the ankles, bringing him down. But he was up in an instant. By then Carmen had turned and raced over. She grabbed at the tail of the flapping raincoat. Silver was dragged off his feet again.

Silver tried to stand but the coat dragged at him and came half off one shoulder. Shouting with rage and swearing he then slid his arm free of the coat and turned to lash out at Andrew with his boot. Andrew took the blow on his forearm and rolled aside to avoid another kick. In the process Silver let the raincoat slip right off and then reached behind and whipped out a knife.

Anne screamed. "Lookout! He's got a knife!" she cried.

The blade flickered as it swung. Andrew rolled aside. Carmen threw the coat, but it missed so she snatched up a piece of driftwood. As Silver sprang forward to attack Andrew, she swung it with all her might. It came down across the pirate's wrist and the blade went flying.

Silver turned to glare at Carmen with his good eye. "Bitch!" he swore.

As he did Martin noticed that his face had several large bruises on it and a cut that had been dabbed with antiseptic. Then Silver jumped aside, his eyes flickering left and right. He glanced at Anne and Letitia hurrying back and then his gaze fixed on Martin. For a second Silver's mind could be seen at work, calculating his chances with the submachine gun.

Martin stared back and dithered. He fidgeted with the gun and aimed it at Silver. "Hands up!" he called.

But Silver ignored him. Instead he turned to face Andrew. But Andrew had snatched up the knife and now adopted a fighting posture: thumb on the blade; blade sideways to slide between the ribs; knife and hand in line with his forearm. Silver studied the situation for a second and obviously thought better of it. He then glared around him and began backing away.

Martin felt terribly stressed. "Stop! Hands up or I shoot!" he cried.

Silver turned to sneer at him. "You wouldn't be game!" he retorted. With that he turned and ran towards the nearby mangroves.

Andrew sprang forward then yelled, "Shoot Martin, shoot!"

But Martin couldn't. He just shook his head. "I can't," he admitted.

"Shoot him in the legs then," Andrew cried.

But Silver was gone. He dashed in among the mangroves and within seconds was just visible as a shadow flitting through the trees.

Andrew swore. "After him!" he cried.

"But why?" Letitia cried. "Why don't we just get out of here?"

"Because that boat of theirs would be very handy," Andrew answered. With that he hurried down into the mangroves.

Carmen gestured to Martin to follow. "I'll see if I can find that rifle Tyler dropped and then follow you," she said. "And Martin, put that safety catch on."

Safety catch? Martin felt embarrassed and slightly foolish.

He lifted the sub machine gun and looked at it. Having located the safety catch he clicked it on. By then he felt utterly drained but he forced himself to walk slowly down among the mangroves. The others followed. He found it a relief to get into the shelter of the trees and out of the wind. All he wanted to do was lie down and he found he was shaking so much he had difficulty keeping his balance. Reaction set in and he felt awful, both physically and emotionally. What particularly distressed him was the knowledge that he had tried to kill another human being.

The walk through the mangroves only took four minutes. It was only 0620 when Martin reached the edge of the sand flats again. Andrew was there, hands on hips, swearing and looking frustrated.

"Too late!" he muttered.

Martin saw Silver running across the sand flats about 200 metres away. He was now only the same distance from the boat and Tyler was already there, pulling the bows around to face the bay.

"We could still catch them," Andrew said, but without conviction.

"You might be able to but I couldn't," Martin replied. "Besides, what would we do if they just ignore me again?"

Andrew had no answer to that. Instead he turned to Martin and clapped him on the shoulder. "You did bloody well mate. That was real good work," he said.

Martin glowed at the praise. "You had the harder job," he replied. "I wouldn't have had the guts to tackle Silver."

Andrew chuckled. At that moment Carmen, Anne and Letitia joined them, Carmen carrying the rifle. Andrew pointed. "There they are Car. Have a go with the rifle."

Carmen shook her head. "It's all full of sand. Might be a bit risky. I will clean it first."

So they stood and watched as the two pirates dragged the boat into the shallows. The motor was started but the tide had obviously dropped even lower as it soon ran aground. The two men had to jump out and then push and drag the boat into deeper water. It gave Martin some sardonic amusement to watch and he was tempted to fire a few shots just to frighten them and speed them on their way.

Better not, he decided. *We might need the ammo.*

Silver tripped and floundered in the shallow water and Andrew chuckled. "Your mate Silver isn't having a very good day Car," he commented. "And he looks even uglier than usual."

"What do you mean?" Carmen asked.

"Didn't you see his face? All the bruises and cuts from where you whacked him with the anchor the other day?" Andrew replied.

Carmen gave a tired smile. "Serves the mongrel right. I'll break his head next time."

The friends stood and watched until the boat was out into a deeper channel and obviously heading for the anchored trawler. Anne then said, "What will we do now?"

"Walk to Alva Beach I guess," Andrew replied.

That idea was instantly both appealing and daunting to Martin.

Fourteen or fifteen kilometres. Am I up to that? he wondered..

Chapter 26

NASTY SHOCKS

The friends stood and watched as the two crooks made their way back to their trawler in the small boat. To their relief they saw the boat hoisted aboard and the trawler began moving, heading south along the channel towards the grounded trawler. Deciding they were safe for the moment the friends began making their way back through the mangrove forest. As they did Martin noted that the whole forest was shaking and rustling from the force of the wind and rain drops continually showered down as big drops, keeping them soaked.

Carmen then said, "I wonder what Silver had in his backpack?"

"Where is it?" Andrew asked.

"Back where he dropped it I suppose," Carmen answered.

So they backtracked to the hollow behind the dunes and Carmen picked up the backpack. Quickly she unclipped it and her face changed to a delighted smile. She held up a packet of sandwiches wrapped in plastic.

"His lunch," she suggested.

"Good," Andrew said. "Share them out Car."

"Don't let them get wet," Anne commented as Carmen began unwrapping the sandwiches.

Martin noted the yellow plastic raincoat now caught against the mangroves and held there by the force of the wind. "Shelter under that," he suggested. He walked across and picked it up then held it with Letitia gripping the other side to allow them all to huddle out of the rain and wind. Martin found that an instant relief.

There were four sandwiches, so Carmen gave them one each and they broke off a bit each to give to her as her portion. The sandwiches were corn beef and pickles with a slice of cheese and Martin felt himself salivating even before he lifted the food to his mouth.

The food was good but there was more to come. Carmen found a second packet of sandwiches and these were also shared out. Then she produced two chocolates.

Even better! Martin thought.

They were dark energy chocolates and that was just what he needed. So the friends sat in a huddle under the raincoat and ate all of one chocolate.

"Save the other for later," Carmen said.

She then took out two plastic bottles of spring water. These were also shared and then, at Carmen's insistence, immediately refilled. This was done by using the plastic raincoat to catch the rain drops and to channel them down into the necks of the bottles. She insisted they all have another drink and then yet another until they felt bloated.

"You never know how long the rain will last," she cautioned as the bottles were refilled again. They were then placed back in the backpack along with the chocolate.

"That's better," Anne said. "Now what do we do?"

"Walk to Alva Beach," Andrew answered.

"Let's have a rest first. I'm exhausted," Letitia said.

Carmen nodded. "Yes. A short rest will do us good."

Martin half agreed but anxiety about the men made him mention them. "What if they come back with reinforcements?" he said.

Andrew looked doubtful. "They won't," he replied.

"They might," Carmen said.

"So we should have someone on sentry watching them," Martin suggested. As he did, he checked that the SMG was still on 'safe'.

Carmen nodded. "Yes, but no-one goes off on their own. We will all go and watch. It's only a few hundred paces and we will get better shelter down among the trees than here."

Martin could only agree with that because even in the lee of the dune the wind was strong and the rain lashed at them. The wind was strong enough to even lift some of the grains of wet sand off the dunes and these were very uncomfortable on the skin. He would have dearly loved to put the raincoat on but instead offered it to Letitia.

She shook her head. "I've got a vest. Carmen, you take it," she said.

Carmen was reluctant but both Andrew and Anne supported this so she nodded and gratefully pulled the raincoat on. Andrew pulled on the backpack. Then the group walked slowly back through the mangrove forest until they could just see the trawler through a gap in the trees. Despite the ground being either wet sand or hard mud they just sat down with their backs against trees.

We are soaked from the rain anyway, Martin thought.

The friends stood and stared across the sand banks and channels to where the two trawlers were just visible. They were too far away for any details to be clear but Martin thought that both were now facing north.

Andrew agreed. "Probably trying to tow the other one off," he suggested.

"We will watch for a while," Carmen said.

No roster was organized as Martin understood that they would only be resting for half an hour or so. For a few minutes he studied the distant trawler, noting that it was almost hidden from view by rain and a haze of spray flung up by the breaking waves.

It looks pretty rough out there, even in that narrow channel, he thought. Of the small boat there was no sign.

Glad to be on 'dry' land and with no sign of the crooks Martin sighed and closed his eyes.

It was another one of those horrible dreams where he started off on a big yacht out on the bay in bright sunshine but then it became gloomy and the yacht shrank to a small skiff that tipped over in the wind as a storm blew up. As he struggled to right the boat it turned into a surf board that was half awash and then dark shapes began flitting through the dark green water near him. And it was cold, and very wet.

And he was cold and very wet. And he was shaking. Martin opened his eyes to find that Andrew was shaking him.

He cried, "Wake up! Wake up! The tide is coming in."

It was too. Martin jerked fully awake and found that cold water was swilling around his legs and buttocks and around the tree trunks. "Bloody hell! What?" he cried.

"Tide," Andrew repeated.

Martin swore and levered himself to his feet. He felt washed out and muzzy and was trembling from being cold but the cold rain quickly woke him fully. The others also climbed to their feet with various groans and cries to indicate sore and stiff muscles or exhaustion.

"What time is?" Letitia asked.

Martin looked at his watch, and got a shock. "Bloody hell! It's ten thirty!" he cried. They had been asleep for nearly three hours.

Looking around he saw that shallow waves were surging in among the trees and that the sea looked even rougher. The whole of Bowling

Green Bay appeared to be one vast tumble of breaking waves; dirty brown water mixing with white foam.

Then awareness of the situation burst in Martin's mind. *The crooks! The trawlers, where are they?* he thought, the anxiety swilling in him to make him nauseous.

One glance was enough. To his surprise both the trawlers were still out in the bay. They were just visible as dark lumps amid burst of white spray and showers of rain and did not appear to be moving.

"The trawlers are still there," he commented.

The others all looked and Anne said, "I wonder why? What are they doing?"

"Waiting for orders?" Andrew suggested.

"Or the tide," Carmen added. "They would need high water to tow that stranded one off. Come on, let's get going. We are wasting time now."

That there was no point in delaying was brought home to Martin by a wave that washed in knee deep. With hardly a word the group set off back to the sand dunes. This meant wading and sloshing slowly as by the time they reached the dunes the water was knee deep nearly all of the time and water was lapping out past the edge of the mangroves. Along the way Martin rinsed the sand off the submachine gun.

Might need it yet, he thought.

As the group came out of the shelter of the trees the wind and rain struck at them with redoubled force. It was cold and unpleasant and Martin hunched against it, trying to pull his neck down into his soaking collar. For a moment he was jealous of Carmen in her plastic raincoat. He also noted that she had slung the rifle, obviously thinking the same as him.

"Bloody cold," was all he said. He could see that the others were all shivering as well and he worried about hyperthermia.

The sooner we warm up the better, he thought.

There was obviously no reason to delay there so he turned right and started walking south, skirting the edge of the mangroves to stay in the lee of the dunes. The others followed in a straggling line of cold and worn out figures.

But the food and rest had picked them up and once his muscles had loosened and warmed Martin felt much better.

Just tired and bloody cold, he told himself. But his spirits were on the up. *All we have to do is walk for a few hours and we will be safe,* he thought.

The friends trudged slowly along, slipping or stumbling from time to time. The wind and rain lashed in from their left and grains of sand blown off the dunes found their way down the back of Martin's collar to irritate. Several grains got into his eyes, causing him discomfort until he blinked them clear.

After about a quarter of an hour they stopped for a toilet break. Martin and Andrew went on ahead to allow the girls privacy and then waited till they re-joined. Carmen made them all have a drink. Then the water bottles were refilled.

Another hundred metres along Martin noted a large red sphere the size of a basketball on the sand to his left. He detoured to check that his supposition was right and found it was. The red ball was one of five that were attached to an old fishing net that was half buried in the top of the beach.

Letitia stared at the red plastic ball. "What is it?" she asked.

"A buoy," Martin answered. "It holds up fishing nets." He gestured to the old net that lay in a straggling line on and under the sand.

"Ghost net?" Carmen suggested.

Andrew looked and then shrugged. "Might be," he agreed. "Off a fishing trawler anyway."

"What's a Ghost Net?" Anne asked.

Carmen gestured out to sea. "Fishing boats from places like Taiwan and other countries string out huge nets dozens of kilometres long in the open sea to catch large quantities of fish. Sometimes the nets break loose and they just drift around the ocean until they wash ashore."

"That's awful!" Anne cried.

Carmen shrugged. "It is, but they often do it out in international waters where Australia can't police what goes on. Never mind the world's environmental problems. We've got plenty of our own." With that she turned and resumed walking.

The trudge continued in driving rain. The belt of sand dunes varied in width and at one stage the friends walked through a long dip between two parallel dunes which had she-oaks growing on them. Martin liked that as it was a pleasant change and even gave a small amount of shelter from the wind which was now starting to really get on his nerves. It wasn't just sighing through the trees it was howling.

They came out onto a low stretch where the dunes were only a few metres high. At this point water was washing up out of the mangroves on their right and there was a low dip in the line of dunes. This allowed Martin a glimpse to the east out to the Coral Sea and what he saw amazed him. The sea was just a seething mass of big waves that were rolling and crashing in. The waves were breaking in huge smothers of foam and almost washing right across the narrow peninsula.

Andrew hunched himself against the wind and squinted to his left at the sea. "Getting bloody windy!" he called.

"Certainly flogging in," Martin agreed.

Carmen heard them and added: "That cyclone must be closer."

"I hope not!" Martin replied, a small spurt of anxiety changing his optimistic mood.

They walked on, passing into the lee of another big dune. Soon after that they stopped for a 10-minute break, all huddling under the raincoat.

Letitia looked downright miserable. "Have we got far to go?" she asked.

Martin did not want to lower her morale but then decided that the truth was what was needed. "I think we have only come about one kilometre. We still have thirteen or fourteen to go," he replied.

Letitia gasped and looked appalled. "Is that all! Oh my God! At that rate we will take all day to get there," she said.

Andrew nodded. "Probably. So let's keep moving. If we sit here we will get cold. The sooner it is over the better."

So they pushed on, Letitia reluctantly. It was slow going and very unpleasant as the sand was blowing off the big dune in showers, irritating and getting into their eyes, mouth and nose. For nearly another hour they plodded slowly south, each step taking an effort. Martin found his muscles protesting but worse still he was starting to suffer chafe between his thighs and under his armpits. Sand and salt combined with the wet cloth to make every step painful.

At 1130 they had another 10-minute break and then plodded on. Martin estimated they had covered about 5 kilometres and he found that dispiriting.

If this chafe gets much worse I won't be able to walk at all, he thought.

Their path was then blocked by a large dune which had been pushed by the wind so that it was slowly smothering the mangroves. The lee slope was much too steep for them to walk on, so Andrew led them up the side onto the crest. It was hard work just climbing the 5 metres to the top, and once there the wind tore at their clothing and buffeted at their bodies.

By unspoken consent they stopped on top to get their breath back and all turned their backs on the tearing wind. That meant they were looking west. Martin noted that they could see out over the tops of the mangroves and that they could see Bowling Green Bay. Then two small objects half hidden in spray several kilometres away caught his eye.

"There are the trawlers," he said, pointing.

They all stared. Martin noted that one was facing away from the other and that they were a few hundred metres apart.

"What are they doing?" Anne asked.

Andrew answered. "I reckon that second trawler, the one we just ran into, is trying to pull the other one off the mud."

That made sense to Martin and when, after about five minutes, the two trawlers began moving in different directions he glanced at his watch to confirm what his eyes told him. It was 1245.

"Top of the tide," he commented.

"And they've managed it," Andrew added.

That seemed obvious as the left-hand trawler, the one they had been put on at Mud Crab Landing, headed northwards past the one that had come in to help. It started moving the other way, going south.

"Where are they going?" Anne asked.

Martin pointed to the left-hand trawler. "That one, the one with the 'K' on it, looks like it is heading towards Mud Crab Landing."

"What about the other one?" Anne queried.

"Looks like it is heading north out into the bay," he said. Then he shook his head. "That isn't a good move in this weather."

"Why not?" Letitia asked.

"Look at the sea! If they head out from behind the lee of the cape they are going to run into really rough waves," Martin replied. A glance over their shoulder confirmed this, the Coral Sea looking like a churning welter of spray and big waves.

Andrew nodded. "I read an account by an old coastal skipper named

Cummings that the only safe place for a small vessel to be in a cyclone was right up a mangrove creek. 'Mudskippers' we are, he said."

Carmen nodded. "That's what that trawler on the left is trying to do," she added.

"Looks like it," Andrew agreed.

Martin bit his lip. "He's game, to try to follow that winding channel in this weather," he said.

"You are right. But it is a better option than staying out in the open," Andrew agreed.

The friends stood and watched as the two trawlers drew slowly apart. The vessels were almost hidden by the spray and haze as even in the shelter of the cape the waves were building and the water looked to be just a froth of brown and dirty green flecked with white.

Andrew pointed at the left-hand trawler. "That one has stopped."

Martin stared at it and then lined the trawler up with a mangrove tree. After a minute or so he nodded. "I think you are right. But I reckon he has run aground. See how the bows have come around this way?"

They all stared but the distance was too great to see any real details and it was becoming progressively colder. Heavy rain began again, mostly blotting out the scene and hiding both trawlers.

"Let's push on," Carmen said. "The sooner we get to safety the better."

So they turned and plodded on along the crest of the dunes, even though this exposed them to the full blast of the wind. They had no real option. To their right the sand sloped too steeply to walk on and the mangroves were flooded while to their left the waves were pounding in across the beach to wash half way up the dunes. The sea now presented a fearsome spectacle and Martin began to worry that they might be in danger if a really big wave broke while they were on one of the lower parts of the dunes.

They had to wade a small area of flooded swampland and then found more big dunes ahead. Once again they struggled up, to halt, puffing and sweating on top. Here they drained one of the water bottles and Carmen insisted they refill it, using the raincoat she wore to catch the water.

"This is a blow-out," Anne commented.

"Do you mean the wind or the event?" Andrew replied with a weak grin.

Anne gestured to the sand dunes. "These sand dunes. See how it has this horseshoe shape with the highest point heading inland into the mangroves and the tails near the sea?"

Martin looked and noted what she was describing. Anne went on, "We learned about them in Geography from Mr Wickham. They are the opposite of the sand dunes in the desert. Those are called 'barchans' and their tails are downwind."

"I wish we were in the Sahara Desert right now!" Andrew commented.

Having drunk and refilled their water bottles the group slid down into the belly of the blow-out and then skirted its upper edge as the waves were washing right up inside it. On the other side they struggled up and over into more normal and lower dunes studded and faced with She Oaks.

Just before 1300hrs they climbed up over another dune and found themselves faced with flooded mangroves. The dunes ended and in front of them was a churning welter of water washing right across the peninsula and on into the mangroves. By common consent they came to a standstill and Martin stared down at the obstacle in dismay.

Bloody hell! How do we get through that? he wondered.

The others all had the same thought and said so. Carmen gestured to their left. "Well, we can't go along the beach. Those waves will just wash us away."

"Or pound us to pulp in the mangroves," Andrew agreed.

"Can we detour through the mangroves?" Anne suggested.

They looked and Martin felt his hopes slide even lower. The water in the mangrove forest looked to be several metres deep and was sloshing violently back and forth and swirling around the aerial roots with every wave.

"That looks too bloody deep, and too dangerous," he commented.

"And don't forget the crocs," Andrew added.

"So what do we do?" Anne cried. She looked haggard and afraid.

Carmen pointed back the way they had come. "Go back and find shelter," she said.

"Why not just shelter somewhere here or among those trees back there?" Anne protested.

Carmen looked deeply worried. "Because I don't think this dune is high enough and there isn't any proper shelter," she replied.

"Not high enough!" Anne cried, looking around.

So did Martin and as he did he noted a big wave break half way up the side of the dune. Spray joined the rain to drench them. "I think you are right," he said to Carmen.

"But. but!" Anne gasped. "But why?"

Now Carmen looked grim. "Because I think that cyclone is heading straight for us and if it does it could bring a storm surge that might wash right over these dunes at high tide."

Martin felt a sudden chill grip his complaining stomach.

Oh, bloody hell! he thought.

He had grown up in North Queensland and every year there were cyclones, but he had never really been through one yet. Several times Townsville had been on the edge of one but even that had been frightening.

Now the thought of being caught in such an exposed location by one chilled him with fear.

Chapter 27

CYCLONES

Letitia echoed Martin's fears. "But where can we find shelter?" she cried.

"The lighthouse," Carmen answered.

"Back there! All that way!" Letitia cried.

Anne was visibly appalled. "Oh! Oh, I don't think I can walk all that way," she added.

Carmen pressed her lips together and shook her head. "Too bad! We have to try. We can't stay here. Let's move."

"Ooh!" Letitia wailed. "Can't we at least have a rest for a bit?"

Carmen shook her head. "No. We need to move. It has taken us nearly three hours to get here and it will take as long or longer to get back. We don't want to be caught out in the open in this weather when it gets dark," she said.

With that she turned and struggled back up the side of the dune, her boots slipping and pushing sand down at every step.

Martin felt sorry for Letitia, but he agreed with Carmen. The next big wave reinforced this when it washed so far into the trees and so high that it almost reached them. He also scrabbled back up the steep slope. The others followed.

But Letitia kept wailing and wasn't convinced. "How could it be that cyclone? That man back at Mud Crab Landing said it was hundreds of kilometres away, somewhere off Cairns."

Carmen stopped on top of the dune. "When was that? What did he say?"

Martin answered. "It was that Barberini bloke. He said to that Tony mongrel to get going because at eight last night the cyclone was two hundred and fifty kilometres northeast of Cairns."

Andrew joined them. "So, if that was at eight last night, which was... er... was seventeen hours ago, it could be at least two hundred kilometres closer to us or more. That is if it is moving at ten kilometres per hour, which is an average speed."

Anne looked puzzled. "Ten kilometres per hour? Don't they blow a lot harder than that?"

Andrew looked at her with a puzzled look on his face. Martin was confused as well but then he grasped what she meant. Shaking his head, he said, "No, that is the speed of the whole system as it moves across the surface of the earth. That isn't the wind speed," he explained.

Andrew nodded. "That's right. They aren't even classified as cyclones until the wind speed reaches 60 knots, which is about 120 kilometres per hour."

Carmen braced herself against a sudden strong gust. "And that's what it feels like now. Come on, we can talk while we walk." She continued moving across the sand dune.

Martin and the others walked with her. But Anne was still puzzled and said, "But why do you think it is coming here? Wasn't it heading for Cairns?"

Martin then remembered that Anne's parents were Commonwealth public servants who had only recently been transferred to Townsville from Canberra.

She obviously doesn't know much about cyclones, he thought.

To explain he said: "It was but their course is quite unpredictable. Cyclones are huge spinning systems. They are influenced by all sorts of things, like the earth's rotation and the upper level winds and the temperature of the ocean and ocean currents and so on. They are like one of those spinning tops little kids play with, the whole system can wobble and change course."

Anne looked thoughtful. "But why do you say it is coming here?"

Andrew answered. "Because the wind has been consistently from the east all day and getting stronger. If the cyclone was crossing the coast north of us the wind would swing round to the north and then get quickly weaker. This is slowly changing to southeast and getting much stronger. I reckon we are right in its path."

Carmen nodded. "I agree. I think it is coming down the coast and because the coast changes direction at Townsville from a north-south alignment to a southeast direction this is the part of the coast most likely to be in its path."

Martin agreed. "I read that most cyclones hit the Queensland coast between here and the Whitsundays."

"Do you know what category it was?" Carmen asked.

Martin nodded. "The man said Category Three."

"It must be that now, right here," Andrew said.

Anne frowned. "Category?"

Martin answered her. "Yes. They are rated according to their wind strength. I forget the fine details, but the weakest is Category One and the strongest is Category Five. I think then the wind is up around two or three hundred knots."

"Oh, that's impossible!" Anne cried.

"No, it's not," Andrew replied. "The jet streams in the upper atmosphere often blow at five or six hundred knots."

"Oh, they do not!" Anne said.

Andrew looked annoyed at not being believed. "They do. Aircraft fly through them all the time and that gives us the measurements," he said.

Anne looked very thoughtful. "But surely the wind won't just blow us away? Why can't we just shelter here?"

"Because of the possible storm tide and storm surge," Martin answered. He had read about this and the knowledge now bothered him.

"Storm tide? What is that?" Anne asked as they slid down the far side of the dune.

While Martin gathered his thoughts, he noted that their foot prints from the outward journey had almost been obliterated even though the sand was soaked.

"It is all to do with barometric pressure. Did you ever do that experiment in science where you turn a glass upside down and push it down into a bowl of water and the air pressure keeps the water out of the glass?"

"Yes."

"And then you insert a plastic tube into the glass while it is upside down in the water and suck some of the air out and the water in the glass rises above the water in the bowl?"

Anne nodded. "I think so, but I didn't pay much attention."

"Well that is what is happening on a grand scale except the cyclone is the glass. In the eye of the cyclone the barometric pressure drops so that higher pressure air flows in to replace it. That is what starts cyclones off in the first place," Martin explained.

Andrew butted in. "That's right. When the sea is hot."

"Over 23 or 24 degrees," Martin said.

"Then the air above it is heated as well and it rises, lowering the air pressure at the surface over that area of ocean. Then the cooler air flows in but as it flows it gets turned from blowing in a straight line by the rotation of the earth," Andrew said.

"Coriolis Force," Martin explained. "When an object tries to move in a straight line across the surface of a rotating sphere it gets deflected."

Andrew nodded again. "To the right in the Northern Hemisphere and to the left in the Southern Hemisphere."

"And if the air pressure is low enough and the wind speed high enough centrifugal force stops it just flowing into the centre and it becomes a circular flow pattern with an 'eye,'" Martin explained.

Andrew continued: "And it if stay over warm water and the wind builds into a proper circular pattern it become a cyclone or hurricane."

"Hurricane?" Anne said, "Aren't they in America?"

Martin nodded. "That's what they call cyclones in North America and the West Indies. They call them typhoons in East Asia and the Indian Ocean."

Anne still wasn't satisfied. "But if it is still hundreds of kilometres away why are you so worried?"

Again, Martin realized she did not understand. "We are in the thing now. Cyclones are gigantic circular storms that can be hundreds of kilometres across. They can cover half of North Queensland in one hit. They don't just suddenly arrive. The wind just gets stronger and stronger."

"Oh, I thought they just came down out of a cloud and blew houses and things away," Anne answered.

"No. What you are thinking of are tornadoes. They are really destructive, but they only cover small areas," Martin answered.

He then had flashback to a few years before when a tornado had ripped through the centre of Townsville during the night. His own home had been spared but the nearby trees had been blown down and other houses had lost their roofs.

Andrew agreed. "Tornadoes might blow one or two houses apart in a block and leave the ones on either side quite untouched."

"They do," Martin agreed. "You see it on TV, and I saw the suburb of Vincent after that one that hit us."

Letitia let out a cry and nodded. "Oh yes! I remember that. That really wrecked a lot of homes but all in a line across two or three suburbs."

Carmen had been listening and added: "And tornadoes usually only last a few minutes or a few hours at most, but cyclones can go on for days."

"Days?" Anne queried, looking quite scared.

Martin nodded. "Yes. Days. This one has been going for at least three days now and it still hasn't crossed the coast."

"Why does that matter?" Anne asked.

Andrew answered. "Cyclones depend on a continual heat exchange to keep the air pressure low. That comes from evaporation over warm seawater. The hot sea is their energy source so to speak. When they move onto land their fuel supply is cut off and they start to die."

"But how does this affect the tide?" Anne continued.

"Well the lower air pressure has a sucking effect, or maybe the higher air pressure has a pushing down effect, or both, but the result is that the sea level inside the cyclone is raised above normal level," Martin said.

Carmen cut in. "By a few millimetres for every Hectopascal of pressure," she added.

Martin nodded and blinked more rain drops clear of his eyes. "So the sea can rise several metres above its normal level. And as the storm moves the winds push waves in front. They are the storm waves."

"That's right," Andrew agreed. "The winds are so strong they pile the sea up in front of the storm and these become the storm surge. I read that the sea level can be up to three or four metres higher than normal. Worse still, waves of three or four metres will be whipped up on top of that. That means rough water six to eight metres above the normal level."

"And they can be moving at thirty or forty knots," Martin added.

"Oh you are just trying to scare me," Anne cried.

I'm scaring myself, Martin thought, glancing at the seething fury of the waves off to his right.

"No we aren't!" he said. "Just trying to make you understand why we have to get to somewhere higher."

"Yes," Carmen agreed. "These dunes are mostly only three or four metres high and if the cyclone hits at high tide the waves could wash right over them."

"But some dunes look higher than that," Anne protested.

"They are," Carmen agreed. "But they are very exposed. There is no shelter and even if the waves don't get us the wind will. We will be sand blasted and will just die of exposure."

It was all very sobering and helped Martin to find the energy to keep trudging up and down the sand hills. His chafing was now so painful it was just a continual sharp ache, but he said nothing about it.

Andrew didn't help by continuing to talk about storm surges. "I read that there was a storm surge that hit the city of Galveston in Texas in 1906 and it destroyed half the city and killed 6,000 people."

"Oh, that can't be!" Anne gasped.

"It can," Andrew retorted. "It isn't the wind or flying objects that cause most of the deaths in cyclones. It is water, either floodwater from all the rain they bring or from storm surges. The biggest natural disaster in human history was caused by a storm surge. That was in Bangladesh back some time like 1973 or thereabouts. It drowned hundreds of thousands of people."

Anne looked very pale and thoughtful, but she doggedly kept plodding along. After another half hour Carmen allowed a short break and then urged them on. Martin groaned at the effort and pain of getting up and forcing overworked muscles back into action. The fact that the cape continually curved to the left was no help either as their objective was never visible.

The rain and wind increased, and Martin became certain the cyclone was heading their way. Another hour of walking had him hanging his head from exhaustion and hunching himself to try to minimise the wind's blast. Despite this he clung to the submachine gun, fear of the men still lurking at the back of his mind.

They came to the low, swampy section and found it was now awash and almost waist deep. When they came to a halt Carmen shook her head and strode straight in. "We have to cross," she said, "And we can't get any wetter!"

"That's for sure!" Andrew agreed, following her.

Martin took Letitia's hand and led her in. Anne clung to her and the three waded across. The water was cold and the back and forth surge of the waves made it difficult to keep their feet but they managed it.

As they came up onto the next line of dunes the rain eased off and Martin stared out to sea, both thrilled and appalled by the sheer majesty of the spectacle. Huge waves were pounding in and the ocean was just one great maelstrom. A long line of dark clouds spanned the horizon from left to right.

As the friends slogged slowly along Andrew gestured with his head towards the sea. "We are in for a real drenching I reckon," he said.

Martin could only agree. The wall of dark clouds and rain was racing towards them at quite frightening speed. He felt his chest tighten as the fear clutched at his heart and he shook his head and prayed. Then the first rain arrived, accompanied by even stronger gusts of wind that almost blew them off their feet. They found it hard to walk a straight line and the blown sand began to sting their skin. Heavy showers blotted out the view.

After a few minutes there was a lull and then more rain showers swept over them. Out to sea more were visible. Martin glanced that way and then blinked to clear his eyes. A dark object smothered in white foam had caught his eye.

He squinted and then pointed and yelled, "Look! A ship!"

Out to sea, several miles away, was a vessel. It was heading south and was pitching wildly in the huge waves. At each wave huge bursts of spray hid it and it often vanished into the troughs.

Andrew shielded his eyes. "Is that the other trawler?" he asked.

They all stared but Martin could not decide. It was too hard to see clearly and too far away. "Whoever he is he is in real trouble," he commented. At that moment several rain squalls blotted out the vessel and then swept in over them. Heart in mouth with apprehension for the people on the vessel Martin kept glancing that way. Then he blinked, stopped and clutched at Andrew's sleeve. For a fleeting second, he glimpsed the image of a storm-tossed, old-fashioned sailing ship with torn square sails. Then it was gone.

Andrew looked quizzically at him. "What?"

Martin did not know what to say because an image had flitted through his mind and with it a legend and then a name.

"I thought I saw a ship," he replied.

"We did, that trawler," Andrew answered.

Martin swallowed as a deep chill seemed to grip him. Goosebumps broke out all up his back, arms and head. For a moment he did into want to explain but then he said, "No, another ship, a sailing ship and it was going east."

"Sailing ship!" cried Carmen, turning to stare out to sea.

Andrew scoffed. "Fair go Martin! How could it be sailing east against this wind?"

Then Martin began to shake as his mind reeled. He was keen maritime historian and loved reading stories about ships and the sea and he also made model ships. So he was very familiar with the various ship types over time. And this image had been of a square-rigged sailing ship from centuries ago. Once again, he squinted into the wind and rain and then he began to shake.

Letitia noticed this and grabbed at him. "Martin! Are you alright?" she cried.

The others all turned to look. Martin found himself trembling so much he could hardly make his mouth work. Letitia moved to face him and held him with both hands. "What's wrong?" she shouted above the now roaring wind.

"Van... Van der Dekken," Martin gasped. Then he felt foolish at saying such a thing.

"What?" Anne asked.

"Who you mean," Andrew answered. "Martin, did you say vanderdekken?"

Martin could only nod and shake. "Yes," he moaned. To his embarrassment and shame superstitious dread gripped him and he shivered, the goose bumps again engulfing him.

Anne looked quizzically at him and then at Andrew. Andrew shook his head and glanced out to sea then said, "Cornelius van der Dekken. He was the captain of a Dutch ship back in the 16th or 17th Century. He was on a voyage from the Netherlands to the Spice Island, Indonesia, and he ran into storms off the Cape of Good Hope."

"Cape of Storms Diaz named it," Carmen interjected.

Andrew nodded. "According to legend the winds kept blowing van der Dekken's ship back every time he tried to round the cape and he vowed to keep on trying until Doomsday. The story goes that Providence tired of his persistence and condemned him to keep trying until the end of time."

As Andrew said this Martin shivered and stared out at the boiling grey sea. He swallowed and licked his lips and squinted to check if he could see any sign of the sailing ship.

It definitely looked 16th or 17th Century in its rig and design, he thought. Having made a model of the Dutch East Indiaman *Vergulden Draak* he was familiar with the type.

Carmen then added to his emotional turmoil by adding, "He is called the *Flying Dutchman* and according to old sailor legends to see his ship was an omen of certain disaster."

They all looked out to sea and at that moment the last of the rain squall swept away leaving a clear view to the tumbling horizon.

Anne stared hard, then said, "I can't see any sailing ship."

"Nor can I," Andrew added. "I can't see that trawler anymore either."

Martin felt his whole body freeze with dread and he stared hard until his eyes watered. But Andrew was right, there was no sign of any vessel of any sort out on the raging sea.

Carmen bit her lip. "Oh dear! I hope it hasn't been sunk," she said.

Letitia then surprised Martin by crying, "Well I hope it has!"

"Letitia!" Carmen gasped.

"If it was those horrible men who tried to rape me I hope they are dead," Letitia shouted.

Carmen shook her head. "They might just have been poor fishermen trying to outrun the storm," she said sadly.

That was an appalling thought for Martin but he half agreed with his sister. But what really shook him was the doubt about whether he had seen anything.

Did I see the Flying Dutchman? *Or did I just imagine it?* he wondered.

But even as he did the image of that storm-tossed ship with sails in tatters sprang into his mind again and he was sure it was a Dutch 17th Century ship.

Andrew didn't help by pointing out to sea and saying, "The *Yongala* went down in a cyclone just out there."

"What was it?" Anne asked.

Andrew answered. "The most famous shipwreck in North Queensland," he said. "The *Yongala* was a four thousand-ton steel steam ship, three hundred and fifty feet long, and she vanished in bad weather on a voyage from Mackay to Townsville back in 1911 or 1912."

"1911," Carmen put in. "The *Titanic* was 1912."

Andrew nodded. "Anyway, she went down with all hands, a crew of about 70 and 40 passengers."

"Forty-eight," added Carmen.

"And the wreck wasn't found until about fifty years later when a Royal Australian Navy minesweeper that was clearing mines after World War 2 located the wreck."

"The HMAS *Lachlan* in 1947," Carmen said.

Andrew nodded. "Thanks Sis! I'm telling this story. Anyway, the *Yongala* is one of the best dive sites in the world. It is a major tourist drawcard for this region."

Carmen nodded. "We were going to dive on it back in July when we were doing our Open Water Diving Course, but the weather was too rough."

Martin knew that both Carmen and Andrew were qualified divers and he then remembered that they had been involved in locating the wreck of a coastal steamer which contained their grandfather's body.

He said, "That ship you found, the *Merinda*, she went down in a cyclone too, didn't she?"

Both Andrew and Carmen looked uncomfortable. Carmen nodded and said, "Yes, back in the 1950s."

Letitia asked: "That's when you found your granddad's body wasn't it?"

Both Carmen and Andrew nodded and Martin sensed they did not want to talk about such a sensitive topic.[2] To change it he said: "There was a big steamship called the *Waratah* that went missing in a storm off South Africa back about that time and she was even bigger than the *Yongala*."

Carmen shifted the slung rifle to her other shoulder and began walking. "Come on, let's keep moving. I'm getting cold."

As they resumed plodding along Andrew called across the group, "Well come on Martin, tell us the story."

Martin didn't want to because he had just remembered that the story of the *Waratah* also included the legend of the *Flying Dutchman*. But he shrugged and told it anyway.

"The *Waratah* was a 16,000-ton steel steamship. She sailed from Durban in July 1909 bound for Capetown but she never arrived. She spoke to the steamer *Clan MacIntyre* the following day and was never seen again. There had been a typhoon out in the Indian Ocean and bad

[2] Read *Davy Jones's Locker* by C.R. Cummings

249

storms, and it was presumed that a freak wave struck her and that she foundered."

What he didn't add were the legends of passengers disembarking at Durban because of premonitions and of the story that the people on the other ship had allegedly seen the *Flying Dutchman* in the storm. The conversation shifted to freak waves and their prevalence off South Africa because of the meeting of warm and cold ocean currents combined with the configuration of the seabed and continental shelf and the effects of the Roaring Forties.

The conversation flagged after a while as the sheer effort of walking came to dominate their thoughts. It became a slow, gruelling slog and Martin began to worry that his sister might collapse.

And so might I, he thought, feeling the drain of energy each step seemed to cost. *Oh, I hope we come to that lighthouse soon!*

Chapter 28

THE LIGHTHOUSE

Within ten minutes Martin felt ready to give up. The wind and rain flogged at them and he felt battered and exhausted.

I don't know how much more of this I can manage, he worried. That got him casting anxious glances at the others, particularly at Letitia.

But she was plodding silently along although she looked thoroughly miserable and drained. So did the others. The expression 'drowned rats' crossed Martin's mind. Breathing in deeply he summoned up the effort to keep going. Conversation died away to almost nil as the sound of the wind screeching through the trees and off the sea made shouting necessary to communicate.

They came to another low section of dunes. This had not really been a problem on the southward journey, but it was now awash with surging, scummy foam. This brought them to a halt, and they flopped down on the wet sand and stared at it for a few minutes while they mustered the energy and courage to tackle it.

Anne shook her head. "Do we have to cross?" she asked.

Carmen answered. "Yes. This area is too low. It is nearly underwater now. We must make the effort. Here, hold on to the rifle sling and we will go together."

Anne nodded and struggled to her feet. Martin levered himself up and then helped Letitia to her feet. He was still gripping the submachine gun and found comfort in having something solid to cling to. Andrew led the way, judging his moment to when a big wave had begun to drain away.

Martin and Letitia waded in as the ebb reached its lowest point. As they splashed and sloshed across in knee deep, flowing water Martin anxiously eyed the next big wave. It was already coming in from his right and he hoped they could get across the dip before it broke. But they did not manage this and the breaking wave swept them off their feet.

The sudden dunking in the cold water, accompanied as it was by a sense of powerlessness, shocked Martin. He found himself hanging on to the submachine gun with one hand while he dug it into the bottom as an anchor. With his other hand he clung to Letitia. But she was simply torn from his grasp. Unable to get up he was appalled at the strength of the water and experienced several icy stabs of real fear as he was dragged and tumbled along as though he was of no consequence. To his added horror he was brought to a stop by the mangroves. That both hurt and terrified him.

Unable to raise himself because of the water pressure all he could do was cling on and hold his breath. This was made difficult as he was half bent around at least three small trees. Sharp knobs and twigs were poking into him. Then the pressure eased as the wave began to ebb.

As the wave receded Martin was able to get his head above water to breathe and as soon as he could he scrambled to his feet and looked around for Letitia up. She rose spluttering and gasping and seemingly unable to move a few metres away. Fear of a repeat now urged Martin to move. He had heard of people in floods being drowned because they were caught against fences by the pressure of the water and he had no desire to suffer that fate in the mangroves. Spurred by his instinct for self-preservation he grabbed Letitia's vest and started wading across the waist deep outflow, dragging her with him.

Andrew and Carmen were just ahead and they had Anne between them. An anxious glance to the right showed the next wave curling in and Martin forced himself to hurry, sloshing and slipping the last few metres to the next dune. He scrabbled up the side of this, hauling Letitia in his wake. They were just in time as another wave surged in and broke in a smother of foam. The water swept into the dip and against the mangroves.

It was obvious to Martin that the mangroves were now just a death trap.

Except maybe up a big tree like the one we spent the night in, he thought. But all the mangroves in this area seemed to be thin, spindly things only about 4 or 5 metres tall.

Urged on by Carmen and Andrew the group struggled on along the line of dunes. They came to the area where there were several lines of parallel dunes with sheoaks growing on them and received another blow their hopes. Martin had been looking forward to it as a possible refuge, but he now saw that it was deeply awash between the dunes and that already several of the sheoaks had been either broken off by the force of the wind or were being undermined by erosion and were leaning.

There was nothing for it but to push on along the line of dunes furthest from the sea. This gave them some respite and they had another 20-minute break before being urged back into to motion by Carmen and Andrew. Martin now had to keep holding Letitia's hand, and when she threatened to collapse he walked beside her with his arm around her waist and hers over his shoulder.

It all became just a mind-numbing, exhausting nightmare of plodding along with the wind and rain lashing them on their right-hand side, the grit stinging and spray soaking them all the time. Then Andrew got his foot tangled in the remains of the ghost net. He tripped and ended up kneeling on hands and knees swearing until helped up by Carmen. The group continued on, slogging past the ghost net and as they did Martin noted numerous other bits of flotsam, rubbish and driftwood.

At last the lighthouse came into view. At first it was just a flicker of light in the gloom of the storm and then the top appeared above the next dune.

Safe! Martin thought. *We have made it.*

Only to reach the lighthouse and get another almost stunning blow to their hopes: the door was locked and the sides were unclimbable!

After staring at the padlock and the steep, white sides of the lighthouse the friends flopped down in a huddle in what little lee the structure provided. This wasn't much as, being circular in cross-section, the wind curled around it to swirl in a vicious back-eddy.

For nearly twenty minutes the friends did nothing but huddle and try to recover their breath and energy. Martin found he was trembling violently, both from the cold and from over-exertion.

What will we do? he wondered.

It was obvious they were still in danger as waves were breaking half way up the side of the dune and the sheoaks on nearby dunes were all awash or bending in the storm. A glance at his watch told him it was nearly 1600hrs.

That took us over three hours! he thought.

Andrew now shook himself and stood up, leaning on the side of the lighthouse and staring up. "We have to get into this thing or we will die of exposure," he called.

He picked up a piece of driftwood from the lee of the dune and hammered at the padlock but all that happened was the wood splintered and broke. He then kicked at the door in his disappointment and frustration and began swearing. Suddenly he was screaming and pounding on the door with the balls of his fists. He ended up standing there, leaning on the door and sobbing.

Andrew's momentary breakdown shocked and alarmed Martin and he scrambled to his feet. So did Carmen. She levered herself up and joined him in examining the padlock. Martin tried to break the padlock with the butt of the submachine gun, but it was quickly obvious the gun would break long before the large, heavy duty padlock would. The rifle butt also made no impression. The friends stood there, huddled and shivering and looking at each other in dismay.

Then they moved out with their backs to the storm to stare upwards. The lighthouse was made of steel and was about 5 metres in diameter at the base and tapered to about three just below the light. There was a circular platform with steel railings just below the light, but this was at least 5 metres up.

"I wonder if we can get up to that platform?" Andrew said. "That will at least get us up away from the waves."

A shivering Anne joined them. "Can't we just stay here?"

Carmen shook her head and gestured to the wave that was breaking half way up the dune. "The tide is half out, and the water is already this high. If this storm goes on until high water, we are liable to be in real trouble."

"When is high water?" Anne asked.

Martin thought, now thankful he had taken the trouble to memorize the tide tables for the weekend. "About 2200hrs tonight," he replied.

"Oh, what can we do?" Anne wailed.

"What about that rope we tripped Silver with?" Martin suggested.

Andrew nodded but looked thoughtful. "Maybe. It looked too short and was pretty rotten, but we can try it. I'll go and get it."

He hurried off into the lee of the dune. The others returned to huddle with Letitia, pressing together to try to get some protection and warmth.

Andrew returned ten minutes later, dragging the sand encrusted rope. "Not nearly long enough," he said. "But strong enough."

Martin saw that the rope was only about 4 metres long. Then his memory clicked, and he said, "I saw some nylon rope just back along the beach. Maybe if we add that?"

The others nodded so Martin handed the submachine gun to Andrew and levered himself up. Then he staggered out into the full blast of the storm. The wind was now so strong that he could barely keep his feet. Only when he got into the relative lee of the dune was he able to make progress.

It took him ten minutes just to find the rope. It was entangled with a lot of rubbish and driftwood on the surging edge of the surf. Going down into the foam called for a bit of courage on Martin's part as the sea by now was a fearful thing to approach. The rope was blue and thin, only about 5 millimetres in diameter, but being nylon he knew it would be strong enough to support their weight. Better still, it was at least 10 metres in length.

After untangling the rope, not without a fair bit of difficulty and a couple of drenchings to thigh depth, Martin rolled it up around his hand and elbow and made his way back to the lighthouse.

Carmen and Andrew both got up to examine it when Martin arrived. Carmen bit her lip and looked doubtful. "Looks a bit thin. I doubt if we can climb this. We will slip and it will cut into our hands."

"What if we tie knots in it or loops?" Martin suggested.

This was done, small loops being made every metre. This shortened the rope by about a metre so Andrew tied it to the old, thick rope to maintain the length.

As he tested the sheet bend securing the two pieces of rope Andrew nodded with satisfaction. "Now we have to get it up there," he commented.

He squinted up at the platform and was obviously calculating how to get the rope up over the railings. As he did a blast of air made him stagger and he almost fell over. Martin noted that the wind was coming in savage gusts with flurries of soaking rain and the friends had trouble keeping their balance.

Andrew picked up a short length of driftwood and tied the end of the rope to that and then went out into the full blast and tried a heave. But the wind was now so strong that the driftwood was just flung out of his hand and instead of going up it flew hard and fast to strike the side of the lighthouse right next to Anne.

Andrew wound the rope up again. "We need something small and heavy that the wind won't just blow away if we are going to get this up over the railing."

That puzzled them, but then Martin said, "What about the submachine gun?"

He didn't really want to risk damaging it but it was the only small, heavy object they had, and not even a very small one. But he could see that they were all getting worn down by the cold and constant battering of the wind. This was now shrieking through the remaining tree tops so loudly the friends had to shout to make themselves heard. And the waves looked to be even higher. It was also becoming quite dark as more black clouds piled in and the rain increased to a solid downpour.

Andrew accepted the idea. He picked the gun up studied it. Then he removed the magazine and had Martin place it in the backpack he was still wearing. Next, he checked the gun was unloaded and safe. The rope was then passed through the trigger guard and tied to the body. Having checked the knot Andrew made Letitia and Anne both get up and move away to the side. After tying a bowline around his waist with the other end Andrew then coiled the rope and held the submachine gun suspended from his right hand.

Moving at least 5 metres upwind of the lighthouse he shouted: "Stand away!"

Then he began to swing the submachine gun in a backwards circle. The gun became a dark blur and Andrew slowly increased the length of rope it was spinning on until it was almost touching the ground. Then, with a strong underhand fling, he cast the gun upwards.

The submachine gun flew up but was immediately caught by the wind and thrust forwards. It struck the side of the lighthouse about a metre below the platform with a vicious clang and came thudding to the wet sand.

Undeterred Andrew coiled his heaving line again and moved another 3 paces further away from the lighthouse. Bracing himself against the force of the wind he repeated the process. As Andrew let go and flung the gun upwards Martin found that he was mumbling prayers and that his heart was in his mouth with anxiety.

It worked. The gun landed on the platform. They cheered but then found they had another problem. To use the rope, they needed the end back down to them but only after it was around one of the upright stanchions holding the handrail on the platform.

So Andrew had to pull the gun down, jumping clear as it fell heavily.

Then he tried again, moving two more paces back from the lighthouse. This time he was able to get the gun to swing up and drop over the top of the rail on the platform. Better still the gun slid right across the platform and ended up dangling on the other side, banging against the steel with hard metallic sounds as it swung in the gale.

But the rope was now too short to reach back down to them, so Andrew had to haul the gun back down to try yet again. This time he stood to the side so that the gun went up between the rail and the platform. It then slid over the curve of the platform to hang down. By lowering the gun under control, they were able to just join the two ends near ground level. So that the tope did not blow up out of their reach Andrew stayed in the bowline.

But they were quiet unable to climb the rope. As Carmen had predicted it was too thin and hurt the hands too much. Even with the loops it was very difficult. Andrew managed to get up about 3 metres before he dropped back down.

"Too hard," he commented. "It is cutting into my hands so that they stop functioning."

Martin tried but found the same thing. He then stood there ruefully examining the red welts in his skin and rubbing his shaking hands together.

Anne joined them. "What can we do? It's getting dark," she cried.

It was too. Martin saw that it was now 1720hrs and he was amazed. *Where did the time go?* he wondered.

The idea of being stuck there in the dark with a cyclone in the offing was deeply worrying and he wracked his brains for a solution. Suggestions such as tying people to the rope and the others hauling them up were rejected as the rope was too short.

We need more rope, Martin decided, thinking hard to remember where he might have seen some among the flotsam washed up along the beach.

Then it came to him and he clicked his fingers. "The Ghost Net!"

Andrew and Carmen's faces lit up. "Yes!" they cried. "Come on, let's go!"

Carmen found Anne willing, but Martin had to urge Letitia to get up. "Come on Sis. We have to do this. You won't want to just give up. If you do you will die here."

"I don't care!" Letitia wailed.

"Yes, you do! I love you and I will miss you, and think how it will hurt mum and dad," Martin retorted. He then added, "And thinks of all the boys whose hearts you will break if you aren't around. Now get up!"

She did, with help from him. Staggering like drunks in the gale they stumbled off into the lee of the dune. The others were a few metres ahead but in the drenching rain, haze and gloom they looked like shadows at even 25 metres.

The net took some finding. Martin was afraid it would be underwater, but the red floats had kept it up and the waves had washed it mostly free. But freeing it meant getting soaked and it took all their strength to drag it clear of both surf and sand. Then it was half a kilometre of straining exertion to drag it back along the dunes to the lighthouse.

By the time they had plodded back, dragging the 50 metres of net, they were all exhausted and shaking. Carmen made them all sit in the relative lee of the lighthouse and then allowed them all to share out the remaining chocolate.

"We need the energy now," she said. "So rest for ten minutes then we will rig this net so we can climb up."

The chocolate was bliss. Martin sat with his back against the cold steel of the structure and savoured the taste. Then he tried to ease the trembling out of his over-stretched muscles. He felt utterly drained but knew that the real crisis was now upon them.

The tide must be even lower but these waves are nearly reaching the top of the dune now, he noted.

He also thought that the wind was stronger, but he felt so battered and buffeted that he just felt numb and was not sure. But the rest did him good. When Carmen called on them to get up, he was able to do so.

The submachine gun was untied and slipped into the backpack. Then the net was tied to the thin rope in its place and they set to work hauling the net up. This took their combined efforts and led to some swearing and ill-will. Letitia was reluctant to get up and help but at Andrew's angry urging she did.

But they could only get the net as far as the base of the platform before it snagged and would not move. The remainder of the net was caught by the gale and billowed away from them and began flogging back and forth. It took all of their strength to hold it.

Andrew stared up and then said, "You all hold the rope and I will climb up and free it."

They did, Carmen slipping into the bowline at the end and with the others holding either the thick rope or the loops in the thin one. Andrew then tried to climb the bundled-up length of net that hung down. But he could only use his arms. His boots just kept slipping on the wet nylon. He had to slide back down.

"I can get a good grip with my fingers," he explained. "But my arms aren't strong enough and I need my toes. Have to take off my boots."

"Don't lose them," Carmen cautioned. Andrew nodded and sat to take off his gym boots and socks. The socks were thrust into the boots which were then tied together by their laces and added to the backpack.

"All of you put your boots in the backpack," Andrew instructed.

This was done and then Andrew tried again. This time he went up easily, despite the swaying and surging of the netting and when he reached the platform and hauled himself up onto it Martin felt his hopes rise.

We might do it yet, he thought.

But there was more hard work in the dusk before they did. They had to keep hauling until Andrew had several metres of the net up on the platform. He leaned over and yelled for the rope to be let go and he tied it around a steel upright.

"OK, up you come!" he shouted.

Anne went next, helped by Carmen and Martin. He knelt to give her a step up and Carmen and he then pushed her bum, legs and feet until she was up the first 3 metres. Andrew leaned down to help and encourage and to Martin's relief she made it safely, being dragged out of sight by Andrew.

Martin turned and gestured to Letitia. "OK Sis, you next," he yelled.

Letitia came and stood there, looking up and looking scared. Martin knelt on all fours to again provide a step up and Carmen held her steady. Letitia then tried to lift herself. But her muscles just trembled and she only got up 2 metres before sliding back down.

"Oh! I can't!" she wailed.

At that moment a wave broke and washed right to the base of the lighthouse, drenching Martin's legs. He stared at the swirling water aghast and then felt sickening dread clutch at his heart.

We are running out of time! How can we get her up there? he wondered.

Chapter 29

FOAM AND FEAR

Martin swallowed to ease his fear and then braced himself again. "You have to, Sis! Step up on my back and jump as high as you can and grab on to the net," he shouted.

After a few moments of dithering and sobbing Letitia did. As she sprang up Martin stood up and also pushed upwards, his hands clawing at the net. But as he went upwards the top of his head met Letitia's bottom coming back down. The blow was hard and felt as though it had broken his neck but although suffering waves of pain Martin gritted his teeth and clung on. Finding a grip with his toes as well he shoved hard upwards.

It worked. Letitia was able to get one hand higher and then the other and then move her feet, helped by Carmen. Martin stayed under her, shoving at her buttocks and thighs and taking much of her weight. In the process he could feel his muscles burning with lactic acid and he bit at his lip, drawing blood.

Then, just as he thought he was going to have to give up the weight came off and he was able to haul himself higher. He found it very hard to keep his grip as the netting swayed and flogged about in the wind and several short lengths of rope whipped at his face and bare arms. Grimly he clung on and moved first one limb and then the other.

This is what it must have been like for the old sailors in sailing ships when they had to go aloft during a gale, he thought.

To his surprise he found the base of the steel platform just in front of his eyes and then he was looking into Anne's eyes. She grabbed at his shirt and helped him to get higher. Reaching up onto the net as it went across the platform he curled up and got a leg around a stanchion. After a few more seconds of straining and pulling he was safe on the steel deck of the platform.

Rolling aside Martin lay on his back, gasping and trembling. Carmen came scrambling up and crawled over him, flopping down half on him, the rifle barrel whacking at his shoulder. The platform was only a metre wide so they were now all packed onto it, and on the windy side.

Andrew crawled over. "Move! Get up!" he shouted. "We need to get this net up."

Carmen knelt and yelled back, "Isn't there a door into the lighthouse?"

Andrew nodded. "Yes, but it is locked from the inside."

"Door?" Letitia croaked.

Andrew gestured to the glass section of the lighthouse which was just above their backs. "So the maintenance workers can come out here to clean the glass and repair things."

"Could we break the glass?" Letitia asked.

Andrew shook his head. "I doubt it. It is made to withstand storms. Anyway, that's not a good idea. We will use the net instead."

Martin went to croak 'why?' but then his mind told him. *It will make a shelter and will also stop us being blown off.*

Even as he squirmed onto his front and went to rise a gust of wind pushed him against Carmen, confirming in his mind the safety problem they had.

A glance over the side showed water and foam swirling around the base of the tower. It looked a long way down even though he knew it wasn't. And up here the wind definitely was stronger. It was howling and hammering at them so that they had to cling on the whole time. Letitia stood up and let go of the railing and the wind plucked her away instantly. She slipped and struck her face on the steel upright and only a convulsive grab by Andrew stopped her slipping over the side.

She was pulled back and Martin held her, while she sobbed and wiped at the blood which trickled from her split lip and nose. Then he gently but firmly pushed her away and moved to grasp the net.

Urged by Andrew they crouched and took hold of the net. Martin saw that Andrew had tied the rope to a stanchion on the other side of the platform. Now he instructed them to haul the net up.

"Up over the railing and across to where I've tied it on," he shouted.

They did but it took ten minutes of straining, gasping effort, clawing and pulling. Martin found he was sweating despite the rain and the chill wind. It took all their efforts to drag another 10 metres of net up over the rail. As they did, Andrew slipped Tyler's knife out of his belt and cut off the red floats. Martin wasn't sure if that was a good idea.

We might need them, he worried.

But they kept snagging and hitting at them. As each float was cut off the wind instantly snatched it and it vanished downwind so fast it diminished like a cannonball fired from a gun. Within a second it had become a pinpoint and then became invisible in the rain and gloom.

As he strained at the net Martin was repeatedly bathed in bright light as the light in the glass top section was still functioning, revolving automatically to spell out the signature 'shorts' and 'longs' that identified the place. Several times he glanced in through the curved window and once he was momentarily blinded. He found it vexing and unreal to have such a normal piece of machinery quietly functioning just there but to be trapped outside in the storm.

The bundled-up net was dragged doubled up bit by bit across the platform on top of the section that was already there. On the other side Andrew again looped it through the railings and led it back up onto the platform. But this time he made his way around the other side of the lighthouse, unrolling it into the lee of the structure.

It took another twenty minutes to pass the net back around the same stanchion and then back through one further downwind and back again to make a low barrier of netting on both sides of the tower. The other end was then secured firmly so that it did not flog loose in the wind.

Andrew then gestured to the netting in the lee of the tower. "We will all get in here, inside the net so it breaks the wind and keeps us from being blown off," he explained.

What a good idea! Martin thought.

The net now made a fence about a metre and a half high and in its bundled-up state the small mesh net had so many layers that in many places it was almost solid.

As he waited for Carmen to climb in between the sections of net Andrew was holding Martin clung on and took the opportunity to look around. His watch told him it was now 1825 but it was so dark and gloomy it felt later.

Sunset is in about ten minutes, he thought.

Then he gave a short, sharp bark of a laugh at the notion of 'sunset' in such a storm. The whole sky was just black and grey clouds and to the west it was black and grey walls of driving rain. In the distance lightning flickered. It was so wet that water continually trickled into his eyes and down his face, even when he had his back to the rain.

From up on the platform Martin found that he could see out over the now mostly submerged mangroves. Where it should have been miles of exposed sand flats as the tide went out was now just a seething boil of foam and surf until it was lost in the gloom.

I wonder if that trawler is still out there in the bay? he thought. His imagination then saw it being battered and rolled and he felt sorry for the people on it. *If they didn't get to shelter they are in real trouble.*

But so were they. A squinting glance the other way, into the wind's fury, showed a fearsome sight of huge, boiling seas thundering in to smash at the dunes. Already most of the sheoaks on the other dune were either broken off or bent over and even as he looked, he saw the ferocious undertow scouring the sand from among the roots of a big tree at the end of the dune. It made him very glad they had not opted for trying to seek refuge in the trees.

We would be dead now if we had, he decided.

Under Andrew's direction Letitia was helped into the shelter at the right-hand end nearest the stanchion. Once she was seated Martin climbed in behind her, his back to the wind and his left shoulder touching the steel side of the tower. Letitia was then moved to sit so that she was against his legs where he could put his arms around her. Andrew went next, his back against the closed door and with Anne in front of him. Carmen was at the left-hand end on the other side of the tower.

The relief was immediate. As soon as he ducked his head below the level of the netting out of the direct blast of the wind Martin felt better. Being enclosed by the net also made him feel more secure. For the first time in hours he allowed his tense muscles to relax.

That's better, he thought.

But perversely he also noticed the tiny jets of cold air that were forcing their way through the gaps in the rolled-up mesh.

"Boots on," Carmen called. She had Andrew unpack the backpack and he carefully handed the boots and gym shoes and socks one at a time to their owners.

Martin pulled on his socks and gym boots and was at once glad. *That will help keep my feet warm,* he thought. At that moment, they felt numb and frozen.

Once that was done Andrew put his arms around Anne and drew her against him. "We will change over from time to time," Andrew shouted, "Like penguins in Antarctica."

Martin managed a smile at that as he visualized nature programs he had seen on TV of Emperor penguins standing in a huddle on the ice and slowly shuffling in the blizzard.

And it feels like a blizzard, he thought as he shivered in the cold.

The irony of them being only 19 degrees south of the equator and being lashed by a 'tropical' cyclone caused him to give a wry smile.

Letitia snuggled against him and he held her tight. She was just a big, wet bundle of clothing and life jacket so there was nothing too intimate in the embrace, not that he cared.

We must get warm, he told himself.

Her exposed arms felt icy and he did his best to rub and cover them. She responded by patting his hand and putting her left leg over his right.

Darkness slowly set in. As it did, Martin peeked out to study the sea below. To his relief, he saw that it had not risen any higher.

In fact it looks like it has gone down a bit, he thought, noting that not as many waves were breaking right up onto the dune now.

They all had a drink and Carmen struggled around in the net to use the raincoat to catch more water to refill the bottles. She then made them drink again and had the bottles refilled a second time. Then they settled down again.

Over time they all pressed closer together, snuggling into a huddle that helped shield each other from the worst of the wind and rain. Martin began to experience some sensations of warmth.

But now I need a pee, damn it! he thought.

He held on as long as he could, but even in that extremity he was too inhibited to just do it in his clothes. He wriggled and got Letitia to move so he could get downwind of her.

"What are you doing?" she asked.

"I need to do a pee," Martin admitted.

Andrew heard this and chuckled. "Downwind please," he called.

Martin tried to stand to get his penis above the level of the netting barrier but when he did the wind buffeted him so much he was nearly blown over the top. Then his numb fingers had real difficulty in unzipping his fly. Gasping at the force of the wind he clung on to the rail and then glanced to see if anyone was watching.

"Don't look!" he cried in embarrassment.

And the downwind theory only partly worked. The air turbulence around his body was such that a lot of the urine was blown back and onto him and the others. Burning with shame he vowed to just do it next time. He then lowered himself back down in front of Letitia. She edged back against the tower and put her arms around him and hugged him to her.

"Thanks, Little Brother," she croaked.

Then time began to drag. Conversation in the normal sense was impossible as the wind was now roaring, the sound resembling that of a large jet engine at take-off or sometimes like an approaching freight train as a severe gust approached. They could only huddle and shiver.

At 1930 Carmen ordered them all to stretch and then to work their legs and arms to warm them. "Don't get all frozen and just slip away in the cold," she warned.

Martin returned to sitting against the steel tower with Letitia in front of him. Carmen was allowed into the middle between Andrew and Anne and Letitia moved so that Martin was on the right. They all had another drink and settled again.

Martin sat with eyes closed most of the time, opening them only when some unusual sound aroused his curiosity, and fear. Once something metallic struck the other side of the lighthouse with a vicious *whang!* It vanished into the night with a spine-chilling whir. Martin flinched and pondered on what it might have been and where it might have come from.

The wind is off the sea so did that piece of metal come off a boat or off the Great Barrier Reef?

For a few moments his mind filled with the images of the trawler plunging its bows into the huge waves and then of there being nothing but big waves.

Did it sink? Or did it survive? he wondered.

The notion of people being trapped and drowned in a foundering vessel made him feel ill and he spent some time thinking about what death might be like. Then he prayed.

By 2100 there was no doubt about the tide. The sea had receded. The waves were still smashing in, but they were now only swilling around between the dunes and not breaking right over them. Even the shrieking of the wind seemed to have settled to a steady roar.

Maybe we will make it, Martin thought.

More time dragged. Martin was allowed to move back in to the centre at 2230 and he found himself holding Anne. They both sat in silence and tried to get comfortable and warm. He was more hesitant at holding her tight than his sister.

He woke from a restless slumber to find Anne sobbing on his chest. "What's the matter Anne?" he asked.

Anne looked up, her tears and strained expression very clear in the reflected light from the beam. "I can't stand it anymore! I just want it to stop!" she cried.

"We all want that," Martin replied, holding her tight and patting her. "It will be OK. We are safe up here."

"But it's gone on for hours! How much longer can it go on?" she cried.

Martin was tempted to lie but then shrugged. "It is a cyclone. It could take another day to pass," he replied.

"Oh! Oh, that's not possible! Oh, I can't stand that!" she wailed.

Anne became almost hysterical and kept sobbing and wailing about the wind stopping. Martin allowed Carmen and Letitia to move in to hug her and he slid to the outside again.

I wish it would bloody stop too! he thought, grimly wondering if they would all die from exposure before it did. A check of his watch showed it to be only 2345.

Once again, he closed his eyes against the cutting wind and pressed against Letitia. Dark and anxious worries kept crossing his mind and he bit his lip and prayed for the night to end.

But the waves were so big! They were bursting over the bows of the ship. Martin clung to the railing at the front of the quarterdeck and stared in horror as the bows pitched violently down into the back of a huge wave. Vast plumes of white spray went bursting upwards either side of the bowsprit. Then he looked up to check that the sails were holding in the storm. To his dismay he saw that the main topsail was just flapping tatters and that the furled mainsail was being torn from its reef points.

"Captain!" he croaked.

When the captain did not answer Martin turned to look at him, and was instantly gripped by paralysing terror. The captain was standing on the windward side of the deck, holding a backstay. He was a bearded man in old-fashioned clothes: thigh boots, leather pantaloons, fluffed sleeves showing from under a leather jerkin. The captain's beard was a pointed 'van Dyke' style.

As the icy fingers gripped Martin's skull and held him paralysed with fear his mind told him that the ghostly figure was Cornelius van der Dekken.

The Flying Dutchman! his frightened mind cried.

Then he saw that the captain was a ghost, and so was the ship. To his stunned horror Martin saw that he was standing on the quarter deck of an old-fashioned sailing ship which was running before the storm, and the waves were truly monstrous.

We will be pooped or broach, he thought as he noted a huge monster of a wave building and sweeping up astern.

The wave struck and Martin was engulfed in cold water and foam. The whole ship trembled.

And he woke from his nightmare to find he was in the middle of a real one! There was water and foam and the tower was shuddering!

Aghast Martin blinked spray from his sleep-gummed eyes looked around. To his horror he saw that foam was swilling around the platform!

The water drained away and Martin saw in the beam of the lighthouse that the foam and rain where being whipped past horizontally.

I've been asleep, he told himself. As the beam swept around again he looked at his watch and saw that it was 0100. *The tide is coming in again!* he thought.

With that he turned and looked over his shoulder. He was just in time to see the next huge wave come breaking in. To his horror it looked to be higher than the tower! Then it broke in a welter of spume which came surging around the tower just below the platform, spray and foam showering up to soak him again. Once again, the whole lighthouse shuddered from the impact and Martin felt his stomach churn with fear.

Oh my God! The cyclone is heading right for us, he thought. *And it will be high tide in two hours!*

Chapter 30

NOTHING BUT WAVES

For a few moments Martin experienced such extreme terror that he was left breathless and gasping.

If the waves are breaking this high and it still isn't the top of the tide we are done for! he thought.

Another huge wave struck the lighthouse, shaking the entire structure. Martin raised himself to peer down and saw that a massive amount of water was just pouring across what had once been the sand dune below. Then it surged and swirled and began sucking back with a fierce undertow.

That they were right in the path of the cyclone was obvious to Martin as the wind was now screaming so loudly his ears felt numb and he had to swallow to ease the pain in them. When he tried to lift his head to look over the barrier of netting the wind struck at him with physical force so that he quickly ducked down again.

For several minutes Martin sat there, hunched in a trembling ball while he fought down his fear. But every time a wave broke and the tower shook, he felt the sour bile rise in his throat and his stomach tightened and churned. He was very scared, and knew it.

Lighting cracked down behind him and he risked a look. As another bolt flickered down it lit up the whole scene and the word 'surreal' flitted across his mind. The ocean was such a tumbling maelstrom he found it truly terrifying to look at. Sucking in great breaths from anxiety he lowered himself back under cover.

Suddenly something long and black lunged up over his head and there were snapping and cracking noises. Martin cried out in fright and winced, his heart leaping into his mouth and hammering. Then something thin, lots of thin, wet, straggly things, stroked and then whipped at his cheek. Screeching in panic he brushed at them and then reached up.

Leaves! Needle leaves off a sheoak. And the long black thing was a branch from a tree! Martin stared in astonishment as the beam illuminated it. Then the wave subsided and the branch went with it, crackling and making groaning noises as it did. A moment later it was gone.

He knew what had happened. *One of the trees in that other line of dunes has had its roots eroded and it has been torn loose by the force of the waves.*

Slowly his hammering heart slowed, and he perversely felt thirsty. He glanced towards Carmen, but her face was covered by the yellow hood on the plastic raincoat. Andrew was slumped with his head down on his chest. Anne's he could not see but next to him was Letitia and she lay with her mouth half open and looking awful.

Oh my God! Has Sis died? he wondered, the anxiety tightening his chest again.

Thrusting her aside so he could kneel in front of her he shook her. "Sis! Sis! Wake up!" he shouted.

Her head lolled sideways and his concern grew. In the noise and rain, he could not detect any rise or fall to her chest and there was certainly no chance of hearing her breathe. He tried to feel for a pulse in her neck, but his fingers were too numb. What he did detect was that her skin felt like ice.

"Sis! Sis! Wake up!" he screamed, shaking at her.

To his immense relief she half opened her eyes and let out a low moan. That spurred Martin to act. Desperate to get her awake and warm he slapped her face. Her eyes jerked open and she looked surprised and then puzzled. Martin felt a surge of guilt because he knew that in his anxiety he had hit her much harder than he meant to.

But it worked. Letitia looked hurt and rubbed at her cheek as he called and shook her.

"Wha...? Whatsa matter?" she mumbled.

"Wake up and get warmed up!" Martin shouted.

His efforts to wake her woke the others. Andrew opened bleary eyes and lifted his head. "What is it?" he asked.

"High tide," Martin replied, still shaking Letitia while urging her to move her legs and arms.

Anne and Carmen both groaned and moved and then sat up. Carmen rubbed her eyes and looked around, blinking in the harsh light of the rotating beam.

"What's this about the tide?" she asked.

The next wave answered the question, breaking so high that water gushed over the platform, swirling around their buttocks and legs.

Andrew swore and looked down in dismay. "Bloody hell! That's high," he cried.

Urged by Martin they all sat and worked their arms and legs until they were wide awake and had eased their cramped and chilled muscles. Letitia gasped with fear at the next wave. This shook the whole lighthouse so much that there was no doubt. "What is that?" she asked.

"Just a big wave," Martin answered. But terror flooded his mind.

I read somewhere that this is the third the lighthouse on Cape Bowling Green. The other two were washed away by the sea.

He knew that the lighthouse was constructed on a concrete base which just rested on the sand dune and now his imagination took over as the next wave caused the structure to tremble.

If the waves scour the sand away from around the concrete base the tower could collapse, he thought. Then he corrected himself. *No, it's a steel cylinder. It won't collapse, but it might just topple into the sea.*

He realized that if that happened there would be no hope for any of them because all he could see out in the beam of the lighthouse were churning waves and flying foam.

Andrew added to his concern by shouting, "This lighthouse feels a bit unsteady. I hope it's strong enough to withstand the storm."

Martin wished he hadn't said that as the girls all looked very anxious and then another wave slammed into the tower and the entire structure shuddered.

Much more of this and we will be in the sea, he thought.

He told himself he had never been so terrified in his life and being surrounded by a dark ocean that was whipped into a fury by the cyclonic winds did not help. It seemed to sum all of his darkest fears.

The fleeting image of the 17th Century sailing ship came to him and he shuddered in unison with the lighthouse. *Was that an omen? Did I see the Flying Dutchmen? Does that foretell our doom?* he wondered.

Carmen took a peek over the rail and then bobbed down. "We must be right in the path of the cyclone. This water is at least five metres higher than normal," she said.

Martin nodded. "I think so," he replied.

Another giant wave burst, showering them with almost solid water. The lighthouse shuddered and Martin was sure he felt it move. Andrew cried out in fright and then said, "When is high tide?" he asked.

Martin looked at his watch and saw that it was now 0150. "At about 0230," he shouted back.

Andrew bit his lip and shook his head. "That's nearly an hour. I hope it doesn't rise much more or we will be washed off this thing."

"If it doesn't wash away," Carmen added, voicing Martin's fear and causing them all to look scared.

But there was nothing they could do but crouch and huddle together and pray. And it did get worse Almost every second wave began to break onto the platform, smothering them in water and spray. The force was so strong that Martin knew that they would have been washed helplessly over the side but for the net.

Like an ant in a washing machine, he thought.

As it was, they all got washed against the net and spent some time regaining their upright positions and grip.

Worse still the lighthouse began to obviously sway. It not only shook and shuddered, but it moved in a semi-circular motion that sent tremors of terror through Martin.

This can't last much longer, he thought.

He was now so battered and numbed that he just wanted to slump down. Being weak from lack of food and over-tired added to his distress and he was sure he was now hallucinating from time to time. His vision blurred and returned to focus and he found he was croaking a prayer as he panted for breath.

Then the biggest wave so far broke and the water cascaded onto the platform. Its force was so sudden and strong that Martin found himself scooped up and washed away, even as he convulsively tightened his grip on the netting. He felt his legs slam against the steel railings and other people's legs and arms hit against him.

When the water drained away, he found both of his legs were poking out through between the railings in a very painful position. Worse still Letitia was half over the edge head first. He was just in time to reach down and grab her life jacket and then he hung on for grim death. She slid mostly out but then Carmen, who was sprawled astride the rolled-up netting, reached out and grabbed her from the other side and Anne grabbed her hair and they all pulled. Letitia screamed but was hauled back into the embrace of the netting shelter.

Shocked, shaking and gasping Martin dragged himself back in, aware that lighting was arcing down nearby. He was sucking in great gulps of air and was shaking so much he could barely control his limbs.

One more like that and we are finished, he thought.

Kaa—rack!

A massive bang came simultaneous with a vast flash of light. Martin jerked as he was stung and the stench of iodized air and burnt plastic assailed his nostrils for a moment. They all cried out in fright

"What the?" he cried.

"Lightning," Carmen shouted back, grabbing him and holding them down.

Another wave broke, smaller but still big enough to make the tower sway. Martin found he was trembling and sobbing and clinging to his sister. They all were. And they all clung to each other. As the tower shook again Martin glanced around and was again appalled. In the beam of the lighthouse all he could see in any direction were tumbling, churning waves amid the driving rain. It was the most awesome spectacle he had ever seen, and he shivered as the realization struck him of just how puny he was when matched against the forces of nature.

Another wave broke onto the platform but they were ready and clung on. It soaked them and left them spluttering and afraid but still on board.

This can't go on much longer, Martin told himself. He did not think he had the strength left to keep holding on.

Anne began sobbing and crying out for it to stop and Andrew hugged her and tried to soothe her, but Martin could see by his face that he was scared too.

More lightning cracked down nearby, causing them to cry out in fright and to flinch each time. One bolt struck the sea about 50 metres away and Martin stared aghast as it caused the sea to boil for a few seconds. But all he could do was cringe and hope! The rain seemed to increase in fury, flogging across horizontally so that Martin wondered where it might actually reach the sea. The tower shook and swayed. Fear made him ill and he felt himself weakening.

And then suddenly it stopped.

For a few seconds Martin did not comprehend what had happened. Then he became aware that the wind had died down to gentle gusts and that the rain had stopped.

What? What? his dazed mind wondered.

Then the roaring noise receded away from them and the next couple of waves only sloshed spray onto the platform. Cautiously Martin raised his head to look. The others did the same.

Anne looked around in wide-eyed fear and said, "What is it? What's happened?"

Carmen raised herself to look out over the railings and then answered. "I think we are in the eye of the storm."

The eye of the cyclone! Martin thought.

He had heard about it all his life and had read about such things and seen many satellite images of them but had never expected to find himself actually in one. Almost unable to believe that the shrieking wind had gone he looked out over the railings.

What he saw both thrilled and terrified him. In the far distance was a whirling wall of blackness that was moving away. In between were dancing, surging waves. Then he realized that he could see much clearer than if it was just illuminated by the beam from the lighthouse. The whole scene was a monstrous dapple of silver and black wave tops, all dancing and surging.

Then the answer struck him. *The moon!*

He looked up and there above them was the moon with a sprinkle of stars on either side.

Nearly a half moon, he noted.

He had read that the eye of a cyclone or hurricane could have clear skies but was astonished and fascinated to see it in reality.

Carefully he rose to his feet, clinging on tightly just in case the wind returned suddenly. He looked all around and saw that the scene was the same.

Nothing but waves in every direction, he thought.

As the implications of that sank in the fear came with it. To check he looked to where the sheoaks had been but there was no sign of them.

Just waves! he thought, shaking his head in awed disbelief.

Then he looked towards where he thought the mangroves grew but there were no tree tops visible in that direction either. Once again, he thought it was the most amazing and terrifying spectacle he had ever seen and it bothered him so much he had to sit down because his shaking legs seemed unable to support him.

Several minutes went by with the others slowly taking in the reality of the situation and commenting on it. But they were all too deafened and numb to say much and mostly just stared with varying degrees of fear evident on their faces. To Martin the lighthouse was like a ship adrift in a stormy sea with no land in sight!

After a few more minutes Martin noted the lightning growing more distant. It seemed to be flickering in two distinct areas among the blackness. Curious, he made the effort to orientate himself, using the nets tied across the platform as his North-South.

That lot of lightning to the west must be on Mt Elliott, he decided, but the mountains were lost in the swirling blackness.

The other grouping of lightning was more nearly south of them and he knew there were isolated mountains in that direction but not their names.

Andrew stood up and looked out to the north and northeast. Carmen looked up and asked, "What is it, Andrew?"

"Just looking for the other side of the eye," Andrew replied.

Carmen also stood and looked northwards. "How long do you reckon we have Andrew?" she asked.

Andrew shook his head. "Not sure. Depends on how big the eye is and on the speed over the water of the cyclone. The eye can be a few kilometres across or even up to a hundred. It depends on the barometric pressure. If it is say ten kilometres across and the storm is moving at ten kilometres per hour then it will take an hour to move over any given point."

"So we might have an hour?" Anne asked.

Andrew shook his head. "Don't know. We don't have the information. And we might just be in the side of the eye, like being on the chord of a circle," he explained.

"So it could all come back again soon?" Anne whispered.

Andrew and Carmen both nodded. Anne bit her lip and shook her head. "So what happens then?"

Carmen gestured northwards and said, "The storm starts again."

"Oh no!" Anne croaked. "I don't think I can stand any more of that!"

Martin didn't think he could either but he was a bit annoyed by her attitude. *What other choice do you have but to endure?* he thought, but didn't say.

Carmen then caused him another spasm of anxiety by adding, "And when the storm comes back the wind will blow from a different direction. If the eye passes directly over us it will start to blow from the west."

"Which way is that?" Anne asked.

Andrew pointed in front of them. "From that way. The opposite to the way it has been blowing. We need to move ourselves to the other side of the lighthouse and be ready."

They did this. It was slow and it was painful to move their cramped and stiff muscles, but they all stood up and then did some exercises to warm themselves before Andrew got them repositioning the net.

"We need some room on the east side of the tower," he explained.

So they set to work, untying and hauling the slippery wet bundle of netting so that it was moved to a different stanchion on the southeast side and then slid around to be hauled taut against the west side of the tower.

We will look bloody silly if theory doesn't line up with reality, Martin thought as he sweated and strained.

He was now so weak from lack of food that he had to stop every few seconds and the effort left him gasping and trembling. The others were in a like state but they got it done at last.

As they began to climb down into the new nest of netting Andrew looked out to sea. "What time is it Martin?" he asked.

Martin looked at his watch and as he did a shadow fell across them. Alarmed he glanced up and saw racing high level clouds starting to blot out the moon.

"Four fifteen," he replied.

And here it comes again! he thought, the fear churning in his gut.

Chapter 31

BATTERED AND BUFFETED

More shadows began racing across the dapple of waves. In the distance Martin clearly saw what looked like a grey-black wall of moving clouds, all racing to his right.

Here it comes! he thought.

There were a few gentle puffs of wind and they came from several directions. The view of the sea seemed to be swallowed at a fantastic pace by dark shadows closing in from the northeast and then a few gusts began to buffet the tower. To Martin's relief the gusts came from behind him, from the west or northwest. Lightning cracked down, illuminating a jagged horizon of huge waves, adding to his fear. A noise like the sound of a huge train approaching sent palpitations of fear through his heart and he tensed. Then the first rain drops began to hit them and he hunched down, trembling and frightened as the storm closed in again.

To arrive as suddenly as it had left!

One minute they were in gentle cool breezes with a bit of drizzle and the next they were engulfed in driving rain, the wind tearing past and curling in around the tower to buffet them.

Martin swallowed and felt the fear rise into his throat. He gripped Letitia tightly and began to pray. As he hunched there in terror a comment he had read once about generals preferring fresh troops for dangerous attacks flitted across his mind.

He is right. Once you know what you are really in for it is harder to face the prospect of doing it again, he thought.

He certainly felt like all his courage had been drained away or battered out of him, and when the tower began to shudder again the terror returned in full force, something like panic gripping his chest and throat. To have survived all that and to still be drowned!

The screaming, roaring wind now buffeted him so furiously that all Martin could do was curl up in a ball and endure. Speech was impossible and the hearing was so overwhelmed that he felt numb. And it went on and on!

Stop! Please stop! his mind cried. Or did he call it aloud?

He wasn't sure, but he could feel Anne quivering against his left side and Letitia shaking in his arms so he knew the others were as scared as he was.

But it didn't stop. Ten minutes went by, then another and another. Martin felt numb and chilled and was sure his heart could not stand much more. But then a tiny corner of his mind told him that this time things were a bit different. To divert his thoughts from death and fear he forced himself to concentrate, to work out what had changed, other than the wind direction.

The first thing he noted was that solid water was not being flung up onto the platform. There was lots of spray and rain but not soaking wash. A peek at the sea helped him decide that the waves were not breaking as high. His intellect told him that would be so. Even during the lull of the eye he had noted that the weaves were dying down and losing their pattern.

The wind has to build up a whole new set of waves from the other direction, he reasoned. That led to the deduction that this would take time. *And the 'fetch' is much smaller. The wind has only got the width of the bay to blow up big waves, not the whole Coral Sea,* he told himself.

To test his theory he cautiously lifted his head and looked out. In the beam of the lighthouse he was able to get glimpses of a bursting, confused sea that was definitely not pounding in as huge rollers like there had been before.

There isn't that shuddering tremor through the sand, Martin noted. And best of all, the tower was not shaking and moving like it had been.

Maybe we have a chance? he dared to hope. He knew that the tide should be on the ebb. *Only down about a metre from high tide,* he remembered.

But still down. Driven by the desire to feed that hope he eased himself out from holding Letitia and moved to peer over the side of the platform. The moment he did he was glad he had. The sea was definitely at least a metre lower than he remembered it being an hour before. Certainly the waves were swirling around the circular lower tower but they weren't the same hammering brutes that had been shifting it off its base.

Once again Martin began to cautiously hope. He settled back down under cover and blinked the trickling water out of his eyes.

And even the rain doesn't seem as heavy, he thought. After observing it for a few minutes he was sure. *Definitely not as bad,* he decided.

That fed more hope. A check of his watch showed that it was coming up to 0500. *Low tide of about two metres in half an hour and First Light in ten or fifteen minutes,* he mused.

There was no sign of any lightening out to the east, but he became more hopeful with every passing minute.

The cyclone is moving onto the land, he thought. *Now it will start to weaken.*

And it did. Within twenty minutes he was sure that the wind had dropped a whole level. It was still roaring and flogging at them, but it did not have the maniacal screech that had dominated earlier.

The strongest winds are in the left forward quadrant of the storm, he thought. *And that has now passed us and is to the south, down there in Upstart Bay.*

From that came another deduction, that the west wind would be pushing the water out of Bowling Green Bay. To check he again got up and risked being blown over the side to have a look down. To his intense satisfaction he saw that he was right. Most of the tower was now visible and even part of the sand dunes and mangroves were being momentarily exposed. The waves were now washing in from the west and were not very well organized or very big.

And it was getting lighter. Martin looked around and noted that the complete darkness had gone, even to the west. Thunder still rumbled off somewhere inland but no lightning was visible any more. He began to dare to hope that the worst was over.

Maybe we will survive? he thought.

Another half hour went by and with it came the certainty that the worst was over. The rain stopped coming in drenching squalls and began to come in sudden bursts and as a flying mist that was as much a haze as rain drops. Visibility improved and the sea level continued to drop.

By 0630 the wind had weakened so that the friends could converse by shouting and best of all the sea level had subsided so that most of the sand dunes were now exposed. Watching waves break across the dunes and then scour sand away in obvious runnels caused Martin some anxiety but when the tops of the mangroves emerged, bending and flailing to the wind he was certain the worst was over.

The mangroves are breaking much of the force of those waves, he noted.

He also saw that many mangroves were broken off and were being piled up by the storm in a massive windrow that was washing back and forth, smashing off more mangroves as they did.

Nature's bulldozer, he called it.

By 0700 the visibility had improved so much Martin could see right out across Bowling Green Bay. It was a churning mass of white water but much of it was breaking waves.

The waves are breaking because the water is now shallow again, he told himself.

Then another thought came to him and he shielded his eyes and scanned the bay.

Is that trawler still out there? he wondered.

But he could see no sign of it. *Maybe they got back up the creek to Mud Crab landing?* he thought. Despite everything the men on it had done he did not wish them dead. *I would just like to see justice done,* he thought.

The sea, where it wasn't white foam, was a muddy brown and was full of debris. Hundreds of sticks and trees were bobbing in it and he realized that all the rain would be flooding rivers like the Haughton.

That will bring a whole lot more rubbish and snags down, he decided.

Then, through a sudden rift in the curtains of rain, Martin got a glimpse of Mt Elliott in the distance.

Ah! Good! Won't be long now, he told himself.

Shivering with cold and weak from lack of food he sat back down and hunched himself into a ball between Letitia and Anne. Both snuggled closer and he put his arms around them, not caring which parts of their anatomy he might be touching. Closing his eyes, he sighed with relief, and was asleep in seconds.

It wasn't a nightmare that woke him. It was the urgent need to pee. He put it off and put it off, half awake and half asleep and vaguely worried. But then he realized he was also thirsty, and hot.

Hot? he thought, forcing gummed up eyes open. To stare in astonishment.

The sun was out and the wind had died down to a strong gale. Overhead there was hardly a cloud to be seen although long streamers of rain clouds were visible to the south and southeast. These were still moving westwards at a rapid rate. Licking dry lips and rubbing at his sleep caked eyes Martin squirmed to a sitting position and looked around. Off to the south and southwest he could see masses of black and grey clouds and showers of rain.

That is the back of the cyclone. It has passed inland, he thought.

Slowly he eased himself free of the girl's embraces and pushed himself painfully to his feet. For a minute he stood there, bracing himself against the steel wall. He felt battered and drained and really just wanted to flop down again. But his mind told him they needed to move.

Stepping carefully over Anne he moved to the railings on his left. A searching look in all directions showed him that Mt Elliott was fully visible. So were the mountains on Cape Cleveland to the northwest. Looking at them made him wonder what damage Townsville might have suffered.

I hope our place is OK, he thought. Then his thoughts turned to his parents and he bit his lip. *They must be distraught. They will have given us up for dead by now,* he decided.

Bowling Green Bay was also visible, at least as far as the curve of the earth. The bay was now looking fairly normal, miles of exposed sand and shallow water. Thousands of dark lumps and shapes indicated trees and other flood debris. There was no sign of the trawler.

Then Martin wondered how long he had been asleep. A check of his watch showed it to be almost 1000hrs.

Holy Mackerel! I have been asleep for three hours, he thought.

Andrew and Carmen were stirring, which upset Martin as he wanted to do his pee before anyone else was awake. But when Carmen stood up and looked around his chance was gone. She and Andrew looked in all directions and then at their watches and also exclaimed at the time. Letitia and Anne woke up and began stretching.

Andrew then said, "Don't look Sis. I need to do a pee."

Carmen nodded. "So do I, so let's get down and we both can."

Letitia stood up and nodded. "Hurry up please. I need to go urgently."

So did Martin now so he helped Andrew and Carmen untie the end of the netting. They then hauled it back around the tower and let it slide down over the side. The netting reached the ground, so they all sat and took off their footwear and then Andrew, still wearing the backpack, led the way down. Carmen slung the rifle and slid between the railing and followed.

"Will it be safe?" Letitia asked as Martin began his descent.

"The net you mean? Of course," he replied.

"No, I meant what if the sea comes up again."

Martin was astonished. "The cyclone has gone inland Sis. There won't be another storm surge, not until the next cyclone."

"What if it comes back?" she queried.

"They don't do that. They can turn but that takes a lot of time and I've never heard of one just suddenly going into reverse. Now come on."

Letitia did, with a lot of 'oohing' and 'ohing'. Anne came last. "Do I unite the other end of this net?" she called down.

Andrew shook his head. "No. Just in case."

Anne came slowly down, shaking and obviously scared and weak. Carmen then pointed both ways. "Boys go east, girls go west."

Martin and Andrew grinned and walked a few paces down the face of the dune. As soon as the girls were out of sight over the crest Andrew stopped and unzipped his fly. Martin did likewise. As he relieved himself, he first noted that his urine was quite clear, which was good. Then he looked to the east and his mind boggled as he realized that nearly all the sheoaks were now gone. Only a few splintered stumps remained. Most of the sand dune they had been growing on was gone too, eroded by the waves. He found he could see far out to sea.

The sea now looked almost normal, except there was almost no surf. There was still a very strong wind but it was blowing offshore so that the waves were dancing away, sparkling in the sunlight. A few pieces of flood debris were visible but no ships or vessels of any kind.

The boys made their way back up to the lighthouse and waited for the girls to return. When they did Anne said, "What do we do now?"

Andrew at once pointed south. "We start walking. We need to get to civilization fast."

Letitia looked worried. "You said it was fourteen kilometres to this beach place?"

Martin nodded and answered. "About that."

"I don't now if I can walk that far."

That answer exasperated Martin a bit. "Then you will have to sit here and wait till we can get someone to come and rescue you."

"How long will that take?" Letitia queried. She looked battered and miserable and her mouth puckered.

Martin did a rough calculation and then shook his head. "Four or five hours to walk to the town but then it could take quite a while to get anyone to come here. It could be tomorrow sometime," he answered.

"Tomorrow! But I'm hungry!" Letitia wailed. "Why would it take that long?"

"Sis! The whole region has just been battered by a huge cyclone. The emergency services will be busy with rescues and the like," Martin replied, quite exasperated and astonished at his sister's mental processes.

Carmen agreed. "There will almost certainly be roads closed and probably no electricity and the phone lines might be down."

"And even some of the mobile phone towers," Andrew added.

Carmen nodded. "And with all the rain we've had there will almost certainly be a lot of flooding. So there will be people a lot worse off than us."

"So this is a self-help job, so let's go!" Martin snapped.

He was tired and irritable and just wanted to get it over. With that he turned and began trudging south along the crest of the dune.

The others followed. But Letitia still wasn't satisfied. "But what about that bit where the waves were washing right across? How will we get past that?" she queried.

"That was flooded because of the cyclone and the tide," Martin retorted.

"Isn't there still a tide?" Letitia asked as she puffed along in his wake.

"Yes. There will be a high tide in about two hours. But it will only be about two metres and it will take us that long to reach there anyway. We can wade or swim or wait," Martin replied.

Letitia looked puzzled. "Aren't high tides higher than that?"

Again, Martin was astonished. "Not necessarily. It depends on the sun and the moon. If they line up then you get very high tides, like spring tides and king tides. But this one will just be the sun, so it won't be that high."

"Why not?"

"Because the moon has more than four times the gravitational pull on the ocean than the sun does," Martin answered. "Now stop bellyaching and save your breath."

They plodded on in silence. After a few minutes of walking Martin realized that the sun had already dried much of the sand, making it loose and hard to walk on so he angled left down to the damp sand along the edge of the tide zone.

This put them mostly on the lee of the dunes from the west wind that was still blowing out to sea quiet strongly, but the other alternative was to try to walk along the edge of the mangroves on the inland side of the dunes and that had no appeal.

If there is going to be a boat or a plane we need to be out in the open here where they can see us, Martin thought.

With that in mind his eyes continually scanned the sea and the sky. He noted lots of drifting flood debris and that the clouds were rapidly thinning and drawing away to the southwest. The dim shape of a range of mountains appeared through the thinning haze to seaward. He pointed these out.

Andrew nodded. "Cape Upstart. We've been diving there. That is where we found the wreck of the *Deeral.* That gave us the idea that someone had been telling porkies about what really happened to our grandfather," he explained.

While they plodded on, he retold the story. Martin eyed the distant mountains and now realized they were joined to the mainland by a strip of flat land that was hidden over the curve of the earth.

Marching on the beach was slow going and they were all weak and feeling very battered, so they kept stopping every ten or twenty minutes to rest and to get their breath back. The temperature went up and the sun began to bother them. Now it reflected off the sand and off the sea and Martin found he had a headache and wished he had a hat.

And sunglasses, he thought, as he squinted to shield his eyes from the glare off the waves.

A bottle of water was shared out and Martin wished he could drink the whole bottle himself. He began to get a niggling notion that maybe thirst might become a problem before the end of the trek.

Sunburn certainly will be, he thought, sensing the sun's rays hot on his skin and noting how red his sister's already burnt skin looked.

The beach was strewn with logs and other driftwood plus more man-made rubbish: plastic bottles and pieces of plastic rope predominating.

Then, after they had been walking for about an hour and a half and had begun to reach the area of big dunes and low swampy areas, Martin noted an odd-looking shape on the beach ahead. But it wasn't until they got closer and it was too late to go another way did he realize what he was looking at.

That is a man, he thought.

Then he wondered if the man was dead. The man was lying on the beach face down with his feet being lapped by the rising tide. A sick feeling of apprehension gripped Martin and he wished he could somehow avoid the girls seeing.

He's not moving so he might be dead, he thought. *Oh, I hope not!*

Chapter 32

DIVINE RETRIBUTION?

But there was no avoiding the body.

The others had seen it too and Anne queried what it was. Carmen answered, saying it looked like a dead man. It then became an effort for Martin to make himself walk those last 50 paces. Dread and fear of death gripped him and battled with his concern for the person.

The friends came to a stop and looked down. It was a man and Martin felt his interest quicken, even as he felt almost paralyzed by superstitious fear. "That is Tyler off the trawler," he said.

Carmen bent and grabbed Tyler's lifejacket and rolled him over. Martin watched with ghoulish fascination as Tyler's arms flopped across. Tyler's eyes were wide and staring but he was not moving.

He looks dead, he thought. As he did he noted sand on Tyler's open eyes and he just knew he was dead. *Nobody could fake that. They would have to blink,* he reasoned.

Then Carmen did what he could not bring himself to do. She knelt and felt for a pulse and tried to detect breathing. After a minute she shook her head. "He's dead," she said with flat finality.

Letitia looked ill but then curled her lip. "Good!" she cried. She started walking again.

Martin shook his head, half agreeing with his sister. *Maybe justice has been done?* he thought.

Carmen then said, "Come on, lend a hand. We need to move him above the high tide level."

"Why? He's dead," Andrew replied. He looked very pale and green under the eyes.

Carmen made a face. "So the body doesn't wash away on the next high tide. The police will want to collect it," she answered.

Andrew nodded. "Come on Martin, give me a hand," he said.

He bent down and grabbed Tyler's lifejacket. Reluctantly Martin did the same. They then lifted Tyler's torso and dragged the body further up the beach. As he did this Martin was swamped by fear of death, compounded by fascination about what it might be like. It was all too real and too terrifying and he just wanted to get away from the body. He was also astonished at how heavy it was.

But Andrew was more matter of fact. "Roll him on his front," he said as they lowered Tyler back onto the dry sand well above the likely tide level.

"Why?"

"So the birds don't peck out his eyes," Andrew answered.

At that horrifying notion Martin involuntarily flinched and closed his own eyes. He almost spewed, would have if he had anything in his stomach. Feeling both nauseous and afraid he helped roll the corpse onto its front, all the while trying not to touch the actual body.

As they walked back down to re-join the girls Andrew gestured towards the ocean.

"So that was their trawler we saw yesterday."

Martin experienced flashbacks of massive waves and of the trawler driving its bows into bursting spray and then of it being blotted from view by walls of rain.

And that's when I saw the Flying Dutchman, he remembered. At that he began to tremble and would have collapsed if Carmen hadn't grabbed him.

"Are you alright Martin?" she cried.

Martin found he could not explain the superstitious dread that now gripped him, so he shook his head and said, "Just feeing a bit battered and weak," he answered.

"We all are. Come on, let's keep going," Carmen said.

By this time Letitia was several hundred metres ahead but they quickly caught her up.

By the time they had Martin was sweating. A glance upwards showed a clear blue sky with no clouds anywhere upwind of them. By common consent they halted and the other plastic water bottle was taken out.

"This is all we have," Carmen said.

Andrew shrugged. "So we need to drink it now. There is no point in walking till we collapse and then trying to revive people. We need to walk as far as we can as fast as we can."

Carmen nodded. "You are right, but I think water is going to become a problem. We have only walked about four kilometres so far."

At that Letitia let out a wail and Martin felt his stomach churn.

Still a long way to go, he thought. *Can I make it?*

They all had drinks until the bottle was empty. It was then placed back in Andrew's backpack. As Carmen did Andrew said, "You can take that submachine gun out Sis. I doubt if we will need it anymore."

Carmen pulled the submachine gun out and then hesitated. As she did Martin felt a distinct qualm about being defenceless. He held out his hand.

"Give it to me. I'll carry it."

"You sure?" Carmen queried. "It's just dead weight. We've got.. got Tyler's rifle."

But Martin had searing flashbacks to them being pursued and defenceless and he felt a deep need to be armed. He shook his head.

"It will be fine. Give me the magazine too, if we still have it."

They did have and it was also passed to Martin. He brushed sand off both and then inserted the magazine and checked the weapon was on safe. That done he nodded with satisfaction and resumed plodding along the beach.

His watch told him it was almost 1300hrs. *Near the top of the tide,* he thought. *And it is bloody hot!* Perversely he began to wish it would rain.

They passed several areas where much of the beach and dunes had been eroded so that there was only a narrow strip of sand between the sea and the mangroves. Here there were huge windrows of broken off mangroves all piled against the trees that were still standing.

Then they reached the low area where the waves had baulked them on their first attempt and Martin sighed with relief. Even at high tide it was dry. They plodded on out onto a wide area of flat sand with a few small, ankle deep rivulets flowing across it.

To the right there were no dunes and Martin glanced towards the wall of mangroves.

That is where we turned back, he noted. Then he frowned and looked again. *What on earth is that?*

Something large and shiny was reflecting sunlight from among the trees. Then it struck him. It was the side of a steel ship's hull. He stopped and pointed, mouth gaping in surprise.

"Look! A ship!"

They all stared and made exclamations of surprise. Now that he looked more carefully Martin saw that the hull was lying half on its side among the mangroves and it was painted dark blue.

The other trawler, he decided.

As they walked towards it he noted that there were bundles of blue fish netting wrapped right around the trawler's hull.

"It is the other trawler," he said. "And it has been rolled by the cyclone."

Anne let out a gasp and looked ill. Letitia shook her head and muttered something venomous that Martin didn't catch. Andrew and Carmen both hurried on ahead. Martin did not want to see any more dead bodies, but he knew he had to go and look.

There might be someone needing help, he thought.

When they reached the edge of the mangroves they halted. There was shallow water lapping around the tree roots but it did not look very deep.

But there might be crocs, Martin thought.

So he had a careful look before following Andrew, Carmen and Anne down into the forest.

As he did, Letitia stood and wailed, "I'm not going in there!"

Martin shrugged. "Suit yourself. Wait here then."

He really was past caring. With that he turned and kept wading. The water turned out to be only ankle deep and the mud was firm and spongy. And he hadn't gone 20 paces when he heard splashing behind him and a glance showed an annoyed looking Letitia following.

The friends had to push their way through the narrow belt of thin mangroves to reach the trawler but then came out beside it and there was no doubt. The painted number confirmed that. As he pushed through the last few trees Martin looked up and saw this on the starboard side of the bow, which was facing downwards.

Close up the trawler looked a fearful wreck. The steel hull was dinted and battered. In places the paint was gone completely, exposing shiny bare metal or streaks of rust. The bulwarks and railings were either gone completely or flattened and twisted flat. The wheelhouse was gone and only a few jagged splinters showed where the timber structure had been attached to the steel deck. The masts and booms were either gone or broken and tangled up in the nets. The nets were wrapped right around the hull and completely covered the propeller with a huge ball of blue mesh. More nets trailed astern along the lane of smashed mangroves that the trawler had made as it was washed right into the swamp from Bowling Green Bay.

Martin stared at the long, wide clearing of shattered mangroves and broken off trees and could actually see the open water of the bay in the distance. Looking at the wreck he felt an awful sense of tragedy. There was no sign of life and nobody answered their calls.

The friends waded slowly around the wreck, marvelling at the destruction and the awesome power of nature. Martin reached out and touched the cold steel and shook his head.

I am glad we weren't on board this, he thought, his mind conjuring up fearful images of huge waves and those terrible last seconds as it capsized and rolled.

They passed under the stern, noting the rudder bent almost double and then crouched to get under another net that was trailing astern and was snagged on mangrove stumps. As they made their way up the starboard side, which was only about 2 metres up, head height, Carmen pointed up and said, "We had better see if there are any survivors inside. They might need help."

"Bugger them!" Letitia snapped. "Let's just get away from here and keep going." Then she slapped viciously at some sand flies that had begun to bite her bare arms. "Bloody sand flies! I hate this place!" she shrieked.

Carmen just ignored her and called on Andrew to give her a leg up. Martin went to help and then crouched so that Andrew could climb up over his lower leg and back. But when Andrew turned and held out a hand to help him aboard, he shook his head.

"No thanks. You look," he said. What he actually meant was that he was dreading seeing another dead body and was ashamed of being so weak.

Carmen and Andrew carefully made their way along the sloping hull to the jagged opening where the wheelhouse had been. They then lowered themselves inside. As they did Martin noted that the fish hatch was gone from the stern and so was the winch. It was nowhere to be seen but had torn up part of the steel deck when it was wrenched loose. Once again, he felt sick at the thought of people dying as the vessel was rolled.

You would have no chance at all, he thought.

Suddenly he found he was trembling and gasping for air, the horrible images crowding his mind. Not wanting Letitia or Anne to see this he turned away and waded back to the stern of the trawler, pretending to be interested in the nets that stretched taut astern of it. For a minute or so he stood there, trembling in every muscle and staring unseeing into the distance.

Then his eye followed the long stretch of bundled up blue net that was stretched out astern.

It got caught on the mangroves I suppose, he mused. Then he noted a large black lump with odd black coils sticking up from it. *Is that the winch?* he wondered.

It was hot there, despite the strong wind that was funnelled along the cleared lane from the bay. Shallow water filled most of the cleared lane and tiny waves of about 5 centimetres in height were swirling in and lapping around the stumps and netting.

Martin shook his head and wiped perspiration from his face and was about to turn back to re-join the others when an odd shape caught his eye.

What is that? he wondered.

It was pale and sticking up through a fold in the netting. It was about 50 paces astern of the trawler and was down in the muddy water amid the stumps of the snapped off mangroves. Then it struck him: it was a hand.

Oh no! That is a person's arm sticking out there, he thought.

For a few seconds he felt so scared and bilious that he could only swallow and gulp air. Then he found his voice and croaked, "Help! I've found someone."

Driven by the urgent desire to help he began walking towards the arm, his gaze riveted on it as he threaded his way among the driftwood and shattered stumps.

Oh, I hope it isn't another dead person, he thought.

As he got closer more details became apparent. The arm was covered in mud and extended from a torn grey shirt. The person was wrapped in a bundle of fish net and looked to be all wrong as a foot and leg were sticking out at an odd angle. Worse still the person looked to be half submerged.

On reaching the person Martin knelt and gingerly pulled at the net. Through the mesh he could make out the person's head and he saw that it was half under water.

Luckily he is lying on his back, Martin thought, *so maybe he hasn't drowned?*

He was feeling extraordinarily fragile and squeamish and did not want to go on with what he was doing. But he made himself.

The person might still be alive, he thought.

So he studied the net and tugged at what looked like a loose edge. The net came free from the person's head just as Anne arrived. Martin instantly recognized him.

Long John Silver, he thought, noting the grey beard stubble and lined face.

The pirate had lost his eye patch and the empty socket was full of mud and filth. Martin eyed it and felt disgust well up.

At that moment Silver moved. He groaned as Martin tugged at the net and then his remaining eye came open. Martin started back in fright and then shuddered as he saw the eye glitter and stare at him.

"He's alive!' he cried.

Carefully leaning the submachine gun muzzle up against a stump he began tugging at the net while making sure that Silver's head was held up.

Anne stood next to him and shouted this information back. "Come and help," she added.

Martin turned to see if the others were coming. He noted Letitia standing near the stern of the wreck looking towards them. Andrew and Carmen were standing on the deck of the wreck looking and when Anne called they both jumped down and squelched quickly across to join them.

As soon as she saw who it was, Carmen sucked her breath in. "Silver!" she gasped. She unslung the rifle and leaned it on another stump.

Silver's eye moved and he tried to speak, then coughed. Mucous and a trickle of filth came out of his mouth. Then he coughed again and croaked, "Help me!"

Andrew pulled out the knife and hefted it. "I'd rather cut your bloody throat!" he snarled.

Anne was shocked. "Andrew! How can you say that? He's badly hurt. Help him please."

Andrew muttered and then knelt and began hacking and slicing at the ensnaring mesh. Tyler's knife was sharp and made short work of the nylon strands. As they fell away Martin and Carmen dragged the netting clear. As they did Martin got a better look at Silver's injuries. Apart from a lot of scratches and many bruises his left leg was twisted right back at an acute angle just above the knee. Wrapped tightly around it and strained hard was a greasy steel wire rope.

"Broken leg," Carmen said.

"Looks like a real mess," Andrew agreed.

Martin looked and felt nauseous. The leg was so twisted that it was obviously shattered in several places and the lower leg and foot were all black and blue and swollen.

"There looks like a lot of internal bleeding," he commented.

Images from First Aid lessons on how to treat shattered bones flooded his mind but he quailed at the thought of even touching such a horrible looking mess. Shaking his head he added, "I don't think the doctors will be saving that leg."

"No," Carmen agreed. "But a doctor is what he needs fast or he will die."

Martin was tempted to say 'let him' but then felt very guilty at such a thought. Instead he shrugged and helped drag the last of the netting clear. Then they stood and studied the steel wire rope.

Carmen bit her lip and made sucking and tut tut noises before saying, "This is going to hurt but we must get that wire off."

So saying she instructed Martin and Andrew to grab the wire and pull it to loosen the loop that was biting into the swollen flesh. Then she grabbed the leg and began to move it the opposite way. Silver's eyes went wide and he uttered a shriek of agony and then slumped unconscious.

Martin feared they were doing more damage and let go, cringing back as the man flopped back. "We could be doing more harm," he cried.

"Piffle!" Carmen cried. "No medical science is going to save that leg. If he hasn't got gangrene now he soon will have and they will have to cut it off anyway. Now grab hold and hang on while I get his foot out while he is unconscious."

Reluctantly Martin did as he was told, marvelling how Carmen could touch the horrible looking flesh. But she did and she firmly slid the foot free of the entangling loop of wire. "There. Now we need to get him up into the wreck."

"Why not the beach?" Andrew asked.

Carmen shook her head. "No shelter from the wind or sun. He needs shelter from the elements. I'd say he is suffering badly from exposure right now."

Martin looked at the pinched, drawn face of the unconscious pirate and could only agree. "Isn't there a risk we might cause more damage lifting him?" he queried.

Carmen nodded. "There is, but he can't stay here. The next high tide tonight will be nearly a metre higher than this one and this whole area will go under water."

"We could leave him for the crocs," Andrew muttered.

"Andrew! I expect a bit of Christian charity from you," Carmen chided. "Now go and collect some of those broken off mangroves and we will make a stretcher. Get moving."

Andrew stood up but then said, "What about the bodies?"

Carmen frowned and shook her head. "We will just have to put up with them," she replied.

"Bodies?" Anne croaked, her face pale.

"The two women who were on this boat are in the forepeak," Carmen replied. "They obviously got tumbled around and knocked out and then drowned. The hull is half full of water. They are still in there."

That was an appalling thought, but Martin found he was getting numb to the horror. At Carmen's direction he collected several straight lengths of mangrove trunk and he and Andrew very quickly fashioned a very strong and serviceable stretcher using nylon netting and ropes from the wreck. To trained cadets like themselves this was easy work.

The hard bit was getting Silver onto the stretcher and then lifting it up. In the process Martin had to touch the man's flesh and it made him cringe and feel revolted. Anne and Andrew helped but Letitia refused to come anywhere near them. Then the four had to hoist the stretcher up and stagger and slither their way across the 50 metres of mud to the trawler. In the process Martin banged his knee on a stump and also pulled a muscle in his inside thigh when his foot slipped.

They arrived at the side to the trawler gasping and trembling. Sweat poured off them and they had to put the stretcher down to rest for a few minutes before acting on Carmen's commands. "Hands on! Prepare to lift! Lift!"

Up went the stretcher and after a bit of muscle shaking straining it was hoisted over the bent bulwarks and lowered into the V-shape between the side and the sloping deck. The friends then rested. Martin felt utterly drained and very thirsty.

"I hope there is some drinking water in this hulk," he muttered.

"There must be," Carmen replied. "Now let's get him up and inside."

The friends hauled themselves aboard, leaving a sour looking Letitia standing on the mud in the shade of the stern. Just making their way along the sloping, wreckage strewn deck was difficult and as he sweated and struggled to keep his footing Martin noted that the wreck really stank. A disgusting stench that was a mixture of ship smells, rotting seafood and other, even worse odours, assailed his nostrils and made him feel nauseous.

Another ten minutes of staining and sweaty effort got the stretcher down inside what had once been the saloon or dining area. Here the stretcher was placed on a long bench against the lower bulkhead. The whole 'floor' was a revolting mixture of mud, wet clothes, rotting food and household items. There was no way to avoid stepping on this, but Martin was careful he did not tread on anything sharp.

"There!" Carmen cried, dusting her hands and then wiping perspiration from her face. "Now we need to get him to a doctor."

Chapter 33

SPLIT UP

"How will we do that?" Anne asked as she slumped down on the sloping end of the bench seat.

"We split up," Carmen said, looking at Andrew as she did.

Andrew nodded. "I agree. The two or three fittest walk to town to get help and the others stay here," he said.

Martin at once put his hand up. "I'll go," he volunteered.

"So will I," Andrew added.

But Carmen shook her head. "No. At least one of the boys stays here. And one of each pair of siblings should go. So you stay Andrew and I will go with Martin."

"Aw!" Andrew cried.

"No argument Little Brother. You can look after Anne and Letitia, and your good mate Long John Silver here."

"But what if someone turns up?" Andrew asked.

"Do you mean some of these crooks?" Carmen queried.

Andrew nodded. "Yes."

"Then you defend yourselves. You can have one of the guns. We will take the other," Carmen answered.

Andrew looked a bit miffed. "OK, but I would like the submachine gun. It would be best for close quarter fighting around a ship and in the mangroves."

Carmen nodded. "OK, and we will take the rifle."

Martin clapped his hand to his forehead. "The gun! I left it leaning on a stump out where we found Silver. I'll go and get it." He was finding the stench in the cabin almost unbearable and the knowledge that two dead bodies were floating in the nearby forecastle added to his strong desire to get out of there.

Carmen nodded. "OK, you do that while we rustle up some grub and drinking water."

Martin clambered over the table to get past them and then heaved himself up the splintered companionway to the open air. With a feeling of relief he sucked in some deep breaths of clean air and then moved to recover the weapons. After lowering himself into the shallow water he splashed his way aft.

Letitia was still standing in ankle deep water under the stern. "What's going on?" she asked in a petulant tone.

"I am just going to get the guns," Martin said, gesturing in their direction. "Then Carmen and I are going to walk for help."

"What do I do?"

"Stay here with Andrew and Anne."

Letitia looked hurt. "Why can't I come?" she cried.

"Because you aren't fit enough. You would just slow us down," Martin replied brusquely. He did not feel like arguing with her. "And I suggest you get aboard in case another crocodile comes along."

He had only just thought of them and the warning was effective. Letitia let out a little gasp and looked anxiously around, then waded forward to climb aboard. Martin also looked carefully in all direction before wading away from the relative sanctuary of the hull.

I will look a real goose if a croc appears now and me with no gun! he told himself.

For the whole 50 metres he kept looking anxiously in all directions, even though his rational mind told him that the water was too shallow for a croc to swim in unseen.

And those mangroves are too close together for one to quickly wriggle through.

The rifle and submachine gun were where they had been left, both resting on their butts and leaning half awash against stumps. Martin picked them up and set off back, hoping that the salt water hadn't done any real harm.

The mechanism didn't go under anyway, he reasoned.

He had seen plenty of photographs of navy Clearance Divers swimming with weapons so was confident the ammunition was waterproof.

When he got back to the wreck, Letitia was sitting on the deck. Martin passed the guns up and then climbed up to join her. Carmen, Anne and Andrew came out of the cabin and cups of water were handed to them. Sandwiches made of soggy bread were placed on the roof of the saloon.

"Plenty to eat so fill up," Carmen commented. "But eat quickly. It is nearly three o'clock and we want to get there in daylight."

Martin nodded and agreed. *I don't want to spend another night in the mangroves,* he thought.

Then he shuddered at the nightmarish images of the giant crocodile and the resulting night of terror. So he ate quickly, forcing down three sandwiches: corned beef and cheese with pickles. A small chocolate followed. Carmen showed him two more chocolates which she placed in the backpack, along with the two now refilled plastic water bottles. The others ate also, munching steadily between sips of water.

It was very hot by then, so Martin was glad to have another cup of water. A glance at the sky showed it to be clear of clouds. The wind was still gusting strongly from the west. Despite this he found he was perspiring just sitting there.

North Queensland summer back with a vengeance! he thought.

It was so hot that Carmen peeled off the plastic raincoat. She held it out to Letitia.

"Here Letitia, you put this on. It's too hot for me to walk in."

Letitia took it and draped it over her head and shoulders. There was some desultory conversation and Letitia again asked if she could walk with them. Carmen firmly vetoed this.

"No. We are both fit and we should get to the town in about two or three hours. You will just slow us down. You are safer here where there is food and water."

"But there are dead people, and that horrible pirate!" Letitia wailed.

"Oh, too bad! Stop whining, Sis!" Martin cried. "Just be thankful you are still alive. And you'd better get down inside out of the sun. You are horribly sunburnt."

She was too, but so were they all. Andrew agreed. "We will, once we have said goodbye."

Now very anxious to be gone from there Martin stood up and swung on the backpack. Then he picked up the rifle and said, "Pass me this after I get down."

He half expected Carmen to protest but she just nodded and stood up then moved to the side. Martin lowered himself and then dropped with a splat onto squelchy mud. Carmen followed.

Andrew passed down the rifle and held up the submachine gun with his other hand. "I'm going to strip this and clean it. You should do the same."

"While I walk," Martin replied.

He waved and then turned and started squelching towards the dry land. As he did, he noted that the tide had already receded so that the mud was exposed all around the wreck and in the mangroves.

By 1515 both he and Carmen were out of the mangroves and up on the dry sand. Martin sucked in a deep breath of clean air and felt much better.

Now we are really on our way, he thought.

The pair trudged the 200 paces across to the eastern side of the cape and then turned right and continued walking southwards along the beach. To their left was a calm blue sea dotted with floating debris but devoid of vessels of any sort.

By keeping on the damp sand just above the tiny waves the walking wasn't too bad and they made quiet good time for the first hour, covering perhaps 3 or 4 kilometres. The cape continued to curve slightly and by 1600hrs Martin noted in the distance some clumps of mangroves and white patches of sand dune showing above the heat shimmer that had developed over the beach and inshore waters.

That is more of the Burdekin Delta, he thought, knowing that the coastline was cut by the mouths of dozens of small creeks and also by the estuary of the mighty Burdekin River.

When he mentioned this Carmen looked anxious. "We don't have to cross the Burdekin do we? It will be in flood."

Martin shook his head. "No, it's near the southern end of the Delta. In fact I don't think any major streams cut through Cape Bowling Green," he replied.

Into his mind floated visions of the quaint settlement of Groper Creek on the south side of the Burdekin. All of the houses and even the shop there were built up on high stumps to be safe from floods.

I hope they are alright, he thought.

The walk now became a trudge, the narrow strip of glaring white sand bordered by the low dunes and mangroves to the right and the glittering blue sea to the left became monotonous and seemingly never ending.

They came to a stretch of coast where the beach had been washed away completely. In its place was a stretch of spongy mud studded with thousands of tree stumps. Piled in massive windrows that stretched for several kilometres were the trunks of the mangroves that had been broken off by the cyclone. It was another forbidding reminder of the awesome power of nature.

The mud was peculiar. It was hard yet springy. Carmen stopped to examine it on its seaward side where there was a vertical drop of a metre or so into the sea.

"This stuff is weird," she commented, as she broke off a lump.

Martin nodded. "My geography teacher said it is a sort of peat formed by the rotting vegetation being buried by the shifting sand which compresses it."

"So it might be coal one day," Carmen replied, tossing the lump aside.

"In a million years of so!" Martin added. Suddenly he felt very happy. The low land connecting distant Cape Upstart to the mainland was just starting to appear above the horizon as tiny dark lumps which he knew were tree tops.

Can't be too much further now, he thought, squinting into the glare for some sign of the town.

And then his mood abruptly crashed. They had been threading their way through the shattered stumps and piles of driftwood in the edge of the mangroves and now they came to a creek. The creek was only about 5 metres wide but it looked deep and sinister, being full off dark green muddy water that was slowly draining out into the sea.

Bugger! Martin thought.

He studied the creek and then scanned the mud and mangroves for any sign of a crocodile. There was none but he first tried walking to the right, to see if they could get across the creek more easily further in. But that just led them deeper into the mangroves where it was even more spooky.

Carmen shook her head. "We will have to risk it. You swim across and I will cover you with the rifle. Then I will throw the backpack across and follow you."

Martin was not keen. Nor did he want to get wet again. But he could only nod. Time was flying by and he saw it was nearly 1630.

Only three hours to dark, he thought.

Reluctantly he took off the backpack and handed the rifle to Carmen. He then moved to the edge of the creek and again anxiously scanned the water.

Go quickly, his mind told him.

But having seen a person killed by a crocodile he was now in mortal fear of the creatures and it took him a real effort of courage to slowly edge down into the water, holding on to a mangrove to keep his balance. He had been hoping that the creek would be shallow to wade but it wasn't.

Heart in mouth and hammering furiously he turned and cast himself sideways, then struck out for the other bank. He reached it in three strokes and scrambled hurriedly up out of the water, gasping and terrified. For a moment all he could do was stand and pant but then he saw Carmen waiting and got control of himself. At his nod she cast the backpack and he managed to catch it.

"Throw the rifle as well," he called. "Then I can cover you."

"No. Too dangerous," Carmen replied. Instead she slung the weapon and then launched herself into the muddy water. A moment later she was scrambling up the bank helped by Martin.

For a few minutes they both just stood and recovered. Then they had a drink and a toilet break before continuing on.

"1640. And still about five kilometres to go. Let's see if we can do it in an hour," Carmen commented.

They set off, wending their way through a belt of mangroves growing in sand. They came out on a long stretch of beach which was backed by low dunes and littered with hundreds of tree trunks and all manner of human rubbish.

There was more of the exposed peat to negotiate and then another section where the broken off mangroves formed another long windrow. It was sweltering hot there as the remaining mangroves cut out the wind. And Martin found he was tiring fast. Worse still his chafing was becoming almost unbearable and each step was a minor test of pain and endurance.

Oh, I hope I don't break down! he thought anxiously.

A glance showed Carmen doggedly plodding beside him, head down and hands gripping the rifle sling across her chest. She looked haggard, battered and sunburnt and Martin assumed that he looked the same.

I have had enough of this place, that is for sure! he told himself.

As he walked, he kept looking ahead, blinking in the glare to check on their progress. The whole cape kept its slightly curving course but often their view ahead was blocked by small headlands. They came to another stretch of beach about half a kilometre long which ended in a small 'point' of mangroves which were actually growing out of the sea.

As the trudged along Martin glanced to his right to where several big logs were lying along the high tide line.

Those aren't mangrove trees. I'll bet those have been washed down the Burdekin, he thought.

And then his gaze settled on what looked like a bundle of old clothes. His heart skipped a beat.

Oh no! Not another body! he thought.

But it was. Sick at heart he pointed to it and he and Carmen detoured and trudged across to where the body lay, entangled in the roots of a large tree trunk. As they got closer there was no doubt that the person was dead. A swarm of flies was buzzing around it and a host of tiny crabs went scuttling away from it at their approach.

It has begun to bloat, Martin noted with horrified disgust.

It was one of the things he most feared about dying and now he looked with fascination. This corpse was also wearing a buoyancy vest and lay face down. Martin halted beside it and looked at it, his heart hammering and throat dry with both fear and thirst. One look told him who it was.

"Tony, the skipper of the trawler that took us out from Mud Crab Landing," he said.

Carmen nodded. "Yes. Nothing we can do for him now," she said.

Turning she bent over and vomited. Then she wiped her mouth and looked at Martin with big, sorrowful eyes. Her face had gone deathly pale under her tan and there were dark rings around her eyes.

Martin also turned away. "Come on, let's get some help quickly," he said. He began striding along the soft sand as fast as he could go.

"Wait Martin! Wait! Slow down!" Carmen gasped.

She came hurrying after him and caught up after 50 metres. By then Martin was also panting for breath and was ashamed of his weakness.

"Sorry," he said. "Do you want to wash your mouth out?"

"Yes please," Carmen said.

So Martin halted and allowed her to dig out one of the water bottles. After rinsing her mouth she had a big drink and then handed the bottle to Martin.

"Drink the rest. We only have three or four kilometres to go," she said.

Martin did and then handed the empty bottle back to Carmen. She moved to return it to the backpack.

"Just in case."

As she did Martin stood with his back to the corpse. He looked southwards, wishing it was all over. He had a throbbing headache and felt sick, sore and very worn down. Then into the blurry fuzz of his vision he saw a dark object appear around the end of the point where the mangroves went down into the sea. Rubbing his eyes, he blinked again and then stared.

"A boat!" he cried.

Carmen did the backpack up and stepped aside to look. "A motor boat! We are saved!" she cried.

The pair stood on the beach and watched as the boat got closer. It was travelling only about a hundred metres out from the beach, just beyond the line of a long shallow sandbar. It was a small motor launch with a red foredeck and two people in it. Carmen began to wave and jump up and down and Martin did likewise. His spirits soared. The ordeal was nearly over!

Then Martin noted a thin black object sticking up between the two people and he felt a tiny tickle of concern.

That looks like the barrel of a gun, he thought.

Shielding his eyes from the sun he looked hard at the approaching boat.

Then his blood seemed to chill and drain away. Recognition burst on him like a wave of ice.

"It's the Boss! It is the gang leader, Mr Barberini! Run Carmen, run!"

Chapter 34

DOUBLE BACK

M artin fled, almost knocking Carmen over in his rush.
"Run!" he croaked again, the terror boiling in him.

Carmen stood for only another second before she followed him.
"Who are they?" she gasped.

"Bar... Barber... ini, the Big Boss," Martin gasped back; and that
looks like Ma Baker with him."

"Who?"

"H... H... His w... wife (pant)... I... think (pant)," Martin answered.

There was a shout from the boat and he cast a quick glance over his
shoulder. What he saw sent another spurt of fear drilling through him
and he tried to run faster on the sand. Mr Barberini was standing up and
shouting and he definitely had a gun.

Martin swerved around a log and raced on. Behind him he heard the
sound of the boat's motor burble and then roar. Another glance showed
him the boat's bow rising up on a curve of white.

They are accelerating! Oh no! he thought.

Panic was close but self-preservation helped his mind to work.
Changing direction, he began running up the beach.

"We can't out-run a speed boat," he gasped.

By now he had run nearly a hundred metres and already he was
weakening and gasping. The backpack thudded on his back but he
ignored it. It was too light to be worth wasting precious moments on.
Jumping a log he ran on.

Carmen followed, leaping over several logs to draw level with him.
The rifle was bouncing up and down, hitting at her back and shoulders.
"I could use the rife," she said.

"Not yet! Get under cover. Follow me," Martin cried.

A plan had formed in his mind and he now acted on it. Dodging
another big log on the high tide line he ran up onto the softer sand of the
low dunes. The mangroves beyond offered a tempting hiding place. But
even as he thought this he changed his mind.

I'm sick of mangroves and crocodiles, he thought.

Another change in the engine sounds caused him to again glance back. He saw that the motor boat had changed direction and was turning to come in to the beach almost directly behind them. The sea was calm and there was no surf so beaching would present no problems. And Barberini had the gun in his hand.

A shotgun, Martin noted with relief. *If we can get some distance, we have the advantage with a rifle.*

Sweat now poured into his eyes, further blinding him and he was sucking in great gulps of air. A painful stitch was developing in his right side and his arms and legs felt like they were made of lead. Prickling fear made his skin crawl in anticipation of being shot.

Once again Barberini shouted to stop and Martin took that as his cue. He suddenly jinked.

Boom!

His left arm, shoulder and buttock were struck sudden stinging blows, but he was still running and terror kept his arms and legs pumping.

But not for long. Suddenly he tripped and went down when near the top of the dune. He sprawled on the soft dry sand but was up in a moment, scrabbling frantically to get over the top and into some sort of cover. Beside him Carmen was sobbing and striving with all her might to run up the soft, yielding slope.

And he was over. Martin rolled across the crest and down the other side. In the process he rolled through several patches of bindis and over some of the nice-looking vine with the big green leaves, the vine with spiky prickles on it. That all hurt but barely registered on Martin's consciousness. Compared to being shot they were just irritating trivia.

Only 10 metres ahead down the slope were the mangroves. Carmen ran towards them but Martin had his plan in mind and called, "No! Follow me!"

Carmen hesitated and looked back. Martin pushed himself upright and glanced back over the top of the low dune. He saw what he was hoping to see. The motor boat had been beached and the Boss was leaping ashore, gun in hand.

Noting that the Boss was looking at him Martin turned right and began running northwards. Carmen gaped and croaked, "Wrong way Martin. The town is the other way."

"I know," Martin hissed back. "But I want to fool them. Let them see us and then we will duck down and double back."

"What about the mangroves?" Carmen queried as she started running behind him. As she did, she ran up the slope and looked over it to her right.

Martin made sure the Boss could see him as he ran, but he kept bobbing up and down, crouching to make it look like he was trying not to be seen. Stinging waves of pain were now sweeping through him, reminding him he had been hit by some of the shotgun pellets.

I hope they haven't done any serious damage, he thought.

Knowing that the Boss was in deadly earnest helped pump the adrenaline to keep Martin running. With his plan clearly in mind he went another 30 paces with his head showing from time to time and then he went down to the edge of the mangroves and abruptly turned back. Carmen did likewise.

Now is the real gamble, Martin thought.

The distance up to the top of the dunes from the boat was only a hundred paces and they were now about 50 north of the direct line.

We have to run back past that point before the Boss reaches it, he thought.

And in his haste Martin tripped again and went sprawling on the sand. Grit got into his eyes and he had sand adhering to the sweat on his arms and legs and face, but he just spat some out and blinked and got up to run. As he did, he snatched up a piece of driftwood in the desperate hope of using it as a weapon of last resort. He resumed running, bent double and keeping right down next to the mangroves.

Carmen obviously understood the mathematics of the situation as she also kept running as fast as she could. She also ran at a crouch, and as she did she unslung the rifle and hefted it ready to shoot from the hip.

Martin glanced back and saw her determined expression, her gaze questing the skyline of the low dune as they ran. At any moment Martin expected the Boss to appear on that skyline and he was gripped by mortal terror. It was just as well because his body was near the end of its tether and he was slowing down. His breath was coming in great sucking gasps and he could hardly see for the stinging sweat and grit in his eyes.

They passed the point which Martin judged to be directly up from the beached motor boat and there was still no sign of the Boss.

But that shotgun can kill at a hundred metres so we need to get a lot further away yet, he thought.

Now he was looking back over his shoulder as he scuttled along. He knew that their tracks would be instantly visible and that the moment the man reached the crest of the dunes the game was up. "Be ready to get down and shoot Car," he gasped.

"I am," she croaked back.

"I will do the shooting if you like," Martin added.

Carmen shook her head. "No. I am the senior rank," she replied.

We aren't at cadets! Martin thought.

But he accepted her lead and kept running. But he could not go on much longer and a sudden dip in the line of dunes gave him a place to stop. Scampering around the curve of the dune into the dip he threw himself flat and then crawled back up to use a clump of vine as cover. There were more bindis, which really hurt this time, and more prickles, but he ignored both.

Frantic to know what the enemy were doing Martin dragged himself the last metre and peered over the top, using the leaves for cover.

As soon as he did, he sighed with relief. The Boss had done what he hoped he would. Instead of running directly up the beach he had run diagonally towards the point where he had last seen them. That put him a good 75 metres to the north and near the crest of the dunes. Better still the man was obviously very unfit as he was struggling on the soft sand and not moving very fast. But he had the gun at the ready and he was looking around. Ma Baker was standing in the shallow water holding the bow of the motor boat.

Carmen crawled up beside Martin and slid the barrel of the rifle over the crest. She looked very pale and grim and her chest was heaving as she took great gulps of air.

"I won't be able to do any accurate shooting," she whispered.

Martin had heard that people who had been running found it hard to shoot well and now saw it to be true.

"A warning shot should do. We don't want to kill anyone," he replied.

Carmen pushed off the safety catch and raised the butt to her shoulder. Still gasping deep breaths, she took aim at the Boss. Martin blinked and kept his focus on the man.

"Wait till he finds our tracks and starts in this direction," he hissed.

"OK," Carmen gasped.

She dusted her hands and flexed her fingers as she took a better grip. Then she tried to steady her breathing.

At that moment the Boss stopped and looked at something further down the beach to his right. Abruptly he changed direction and began hurrying down towards it.

What the? Martin wondered. Then it struck him.

"He has spotted Tony's body," he whispered.

Then another, more a ghastly and infinitely more saddening thought came to him: not the body of Tony, but the body of his son!

The Boss came to a stop, looking down at the pathetic bundle at the log and Martin saw his shoulders droop and the gun was lowered to be held with one hand.

He has recognized him, he thought.

Despite the fact that the Boss was his enemy and was trying to kill him the sheer pathos of the situation struck Martin deeply.

The Boss turned towards the motor boat. "Hey Ma! You come here," he yelled.

Ma Baker shouted back, "Why? What is it?"

"It'sa Tony. It's our boy," the Boss replied.

Martin felt awful as he watched the shock of the statement hit the woman like a blow. She seemed to wilt and then she dragged the boat a metre higher and started walking quickly along the beach.

"How is he?" she cried, her anguish and dread apparent in her voice.

In reply the Boss just shook his head and Ma Baker began to wail and run. "Oh no! Oh no! My poor little boy!" she shrieked.

Martin exchanged a glance with Carmen. She looked sick and upset. "Poor woman," she whispered.

Martin could only nod. He was not only upset, he was hurting. The shotgun pellet wounds were now moving to the smarting stage and his blood was throbbing and pulsing. He reached behind his shoulder and then looked at his hand. The fingers were covered with dark red blood.

It is sad, he thought. *But that bastard just tried to kill me!*

By then Ma had run the hundred paces to where Tony's body lay and she went down on her knees and began weeping and wailing, her loud shrieks of grief carrying easily to Martin's ears.

"Oh, poor woman," Carmen muttered.

Martin half agreed but he was so stirred up by fear, exhaustion and horrible memories that he had very little sympathy left for her.

"Time we got going," he replied. He slid back out of sight and stood up.

At that moment the sound of raised, angry voices, came to him and he paused and risked another peep over the crest. What he saw astonished him. Ma Baker was now standing and she was punching at the Boss with the heels of her fists.

"You-a killed my boy!" she screamed. "You-a killed him. It is your fault! You ordered him to go outa into thata storm and now he is dead! It is your fault!"

The pair began a furious struggle on the beach, Ma trying to wrest the shotgun from the Boss while still hitting at him.

Martin was appalled, dread clutching at him. *Holy shit! If she gets that gun she might shoot him!* he thought.

Then the gun went off. The shattering bang made Martin flinch even though it wasn't aimed at him and was 100 metres away. For a second he thought that the Boss had shot her but then he saw that they were still struggling.

"Just went off by accident," he commented.

"Just as well it is only a double-barrel," Carmen added.

"Eh?" Martin cried. He had not noticed but now he saw that the shotgun was in fact a double barrel.

He has now got two empty barrels. I wonder how many other cartridges he has? he thought.

Then another idea came to him, borne to him by his cramping muscles, chafe and general weakness.

"Let's take their boat," he suggested.

Carmen looked at him and bit her lip. "It could lead to a real gunfight," she replied.

Martin shook his head. "He has fired both barrels. It will take him some time to reload and you can warn him off with a shot near him," he said.

Carmen glanced to their right. There, only a hundred paces away, was the motor boat.

"Right!" she agreed. "You push the boat out and get it going and I will cover you. Go!"

The idea of using the boat had double appeal to Martin: he wouldn't have to walk; and it deprived their enemies and meant they would have to. So he sucked in a deep breath and then scrambled over crest of the dune and sprinted down the beach.

He knew it was a terrible risk. If the Boss really had more ammunition he could reload in a few seconds and at that range, standing on firm ground, he could hardly miss.

We shouldn't have tried this, Martin thought, as he ran.

He was already regretting the impulsive decision. He knew that Carmen was aiming the rifle at the Boss but in his mind that only made it worse.

She might have to kill a man to save me, he thought. That was an appalling thought.

But it was done now so he kept running, glancing to his left at every second step. He saw the two people were still shouting at each other and wrestling with the gun. Then, as he reached the boat, he saw the Boss look in his direction and then reef the gun away from Ma's clutches.

He's seen me! The fat is in the fire now! Martin thought.

Leaning on the red plastic bow of the boat he shoved with all his strength. As he did he noted that the boat had a small windscreen at the back of the red plastic forecastle deck and that there was a steering wheel and that the boat had two seats but the one of the port side was facing aft.

Ski boat, he thought, having seen Letitia water skiing on weekends.

The boat slid backwards easily into deeper water and within seconds it was bobbing afloat. Martin kept wading out, pushing and cringing in anticipation of being shot. A glance to his left showed the Boss breaking the gun open and pushing Ma away. She also saw them then and stopped, staring at them, her huge bosom heaving and tears streaming down her face.

The Boss yelled at Martin to stop but in reply Carmen yelled back. Martin glanced behind and saw that Carmen had run down onto the beach and was only 10 paces behind him. She held the rifle up for the man to see.

"I've got a rifle and I will kill you if you try to stop us," she shouted.

The Boss's response was to turn and scramble over the big log near his son's body. He dropped out of sight behind it. Martin knew immediately what he intended.

"Car! Get aboard and let's go. He's going to reload under cover and then blast us," he cried.

With that he resumed pushing the boat out into the shallows. The waves were only ripples lapping in and the water was only ankle deep and then knee deep for 20 paces. Martin then remembered that the tide was going out and he hoped that the water wouldn't be too shallow.

Carmen came skittering into the shallows, rifle held high. She dashed past Martin and scrambled into the boat. Then she crouched in the stern and levelled the rifle to aim it towards the Boss's position.

"Get in Martin. Get the engine going!" she called.

Martin was pushing hard, his whole body cringing and his heart again hammering fit to bust as he pushed backwards towards the deeper water. Suddenly he found his feet slipping and finding no bottom. For a few steps he floundered and then, to stop himself going right under, he clung to the boat and heaved himself aboard.

Slithering onto the slippery plastic forecastle he managed to grip a cleat, which had jagged him painfully. Regaining his balance, he scrambled aft, water pouring off him and making the deck slipperier still. He climbed quickly over the windscreen and flopped into the driver's seat.

"Engine!" he muttered. "Must get the engine going."

His eyes scanned the dashboard of the ski boat and he got a shock. There were several dials or gauges, revolution counters and things but no on-off switch that he could see. Then, as his brow puckered in puzzlement, his eyes seemed to go out of focus and then back in, to concentrate on a keyhole.

"A key! This bloody thing needs an ignition key!" he gasped.

Frantically he looked around for it, heart hammering and almost in a fluster as he expected to be shot at every moment. But there was no key.

Oh my God! The Boss must have it, he thought.

The realization that he might have made a fatal mistake half stunned him and the fear rose up his throat to half choke him.

Martin lifted his eyes to the log where the Boss had taken cover and as he did he saw the man's head rise up above it and then the black line of the shotgun barrel swing up and over. Martin was about to call on Carmen to shoot when his view was blocked by Ma Baker. She was dancing with grief and rage and waving her fist at them. In the process she was blocking the line of fire. Then she began running towards them, screaming hate and obscenities.

"Mongrels! Interfering little turds! You killed my boy! You killed my son!" she shrieked.

Martin saw her running but for a few seconds was frozen with fear. *Oh my God! Here she comes!* he thought.

And the motor wouldn't start and they were only metres from the shore in shallow water!

We must get into deeper water! Martin thought.

Terrified of facing the angry woman's fury he knew he had to act. Heedless of the risk he stood up and jumped over port the side, putting the boat between him and the Boss. He landed in waist deep water. Luckily the bottom was firm sand so he at once grabbed the side of the boat and began to push.

But side on was not the most efficient way to do it and Martin quickly realized that. As the boat slid slowly past he stood and waited for the bow and then grabbed it and started to push hard with a direct thrust astern. As he did he glanced towards Ma Baker and to his horror saw that the awful woman was now only about 50 metres away. She was a frightful sight: fat wobbling, huge breasts bouncing, wild-eyed, hair streaming, mouth agape. And she was cursing and shouting horrible threats.

Panic welled up in Martin. *Bloody hell, if she gets hold of me I am in trouble,'* he thought.

Not wanting to be in the clutches of such an obviously enraged and large woman he pushed for all he was worth.

He was hoping for deeper water but to his dismay it became shallower and he found he was splashing in knee deep water. Then the water and sand right next to his right foot boiled in a swirl of sand and bubbles and he got a fleeting glimpse of a flat grey object as it flicked away.

"Sting ray! Oh bloody hell!" he cried.

The sting might not be fatal in the leg or foot but he was sure that the agony would incapacitate him and allow the woman to catch him. And she was now splashing into the shallows and only 25 metres away.

Dancing in terror Martin kept pushing. "Must get away!" he thought.

Oh, why doesn't Carmen shoot?.

Chapter 35

FEAR AND DISMAY

With fear clutching at his throat and holding his chest in a vice-like grip Martin pushed for all he was worth. Despite pains shooting up his arms and legs from overstretched muscles and the sharp stinging of his wounds and the embedded prickles in his skin and clothes he laboured with all the strength he could muster.

Gasping in great sobbing breaths he glanced over his shoulder and saw that Ma Baker was now running in the shallow water and only twenty metres away. Terrified of getting caught he let go of the boat and turned to defend himself. In his heart he knew that if she got hold of him it would be a fight to the death.

She will drown me, his frightened mind told him. And he sensed that there would be a lot of pain and scratching before he died.

Just as he turned to face the angry woman Martin saw her stumble. She floundered and then fell. Dripping and almost beside herself with grief and anger she was on her feet in an instant and came splashing towards him.

"I'm gunn kill ya, ya mongrel!" she shrieked.

But at that moment she ran into the deeper gutter and she floundered again, lost her footing and went right under. Martin saw his chance and immediately turned and went skittering after the still drifting boat. As he reached it he saw Carmen standing on the observer's seat. She had the rifle but wasn't aiming it.

Martin leant on the bow of the boat, pushing the propellers high. He didn't want them to dig in to the bottom and stop the boat. Then he shoved for all he was worth. As he pushed he glanced over his shoulder. The sight of a drenched, enraged Ma Baker wading after him while spluttering and screaming was enough incentive to summon up those last reserves of energy.

Then suddenly the bottom dropped steeply away and Martin found he could not reach it without going under. So he heaved himself half onto the bow and began kicking with his feet. As he did he looked back and his heart skipped a beat and then palpitated in fear. Ma Baker was splashing up onto the sandbar and was only 10 paces away!

Carmen climbed over the windscreen onto the forecastle, sending the bow dipping even more sharply down. Martin only managed to stay aboard by snatching frantically at the cleats; shiny, stainless steel cleats, he noted. Carmen lifted the rifle.

"Keep back!" she croaked at Ma Baker, her voice hoarse and breaking with fear. "Keep away or I will shoot!"

By then Ma Baker was only 5 paces away and reaching out with grasping hands, her eyes blazing and mouth working in rage. Martin kicked for all he was worth then pulled himself aboard so he could turn to fight.

Ma Baker almost got him. Her clutching hand reached for his foot just as he pulled it away. Then she grabbed at the bow of the boat. Driven by his instinct for self-preservation Martin kicked at her fingers and she lost her grip. Then she went down, floundering into the deeper water. One second she was there, screeching and clawing and the next she was underwater.

Martin squirmed around to get a better balance and to be ready to fight her when she surfaced. "Move back Car or we will capsize," he shouted. He was hotly aware that he must be a sitting target for the Boss. "Car, get under cover and get ready to shoot at the Boss," he gasped.

Carmen answered yes just as Ma Baker's head came clear of the water. She splashed and shrieked and then got water in her mouth and gurgled and choked. Coughing and spluttering she lashed at the water and it occurred to Martin that she looked like she was drowning.

Maybe she can't swim? he thought.

That was a cruel dilemma! *Do I try to rescue her, or let her drown?* he wondered.

But luckily, before he truly had to make that ghastly choice, she managed to get herself back into shallower water. She splashed her way back until she was in waist deep water and then she turned to face them.

"You murdering mongrels!" she screamed. "I'll get you! Come back here with our boat!"

"No fear!" Martin replied. The boat was still only about 10 metres from her and he was afraid she would make another lunge. Then he became aware that Carmen was calling him.

"Martin, get back in the boat. Get back under over in case that man shoots," she called.

That got Martin moving, and fast. Fear of being shot sent him scrambling back over the windscreen and into the empty observer's seat, Carmen having climbed into the driver's seat where she now had the rifle pointed over the starboard bow towards the Boss.

As Martin slid down, he looked back and saw that they were now a few more metres away from Ma Baker.

Good, the boat is still moving away, he thought.

Ma Baker stood there, soaked and distraught. She screamed, tore at her hair, howled ugly threats and swore crudely. With her great bulging body obscenely exposed by the wet dress and with her wet hair straggling over her face she was a frightful sight. To Martin she looked both appalling and terrifying, a mixture of extreme distress and fear.

We need to get away from here, he thought.

Once again his eyes scanned the instrument panel and then the deck and seats. But there was no sign of a key. Carmen, now also crouching low, turned to him.

"Can you get the motor started?" she asked.

Martin shook his head. "No. It's an inboard engine and it needs a key. One of them must have it," he replied.

He again looked towards Ma Baker and was relieved to see that she was now about 20 metres away. A further urgent search failed to find a key.

"If it was an ordinary outboard we could just start it with the self-starter," Martin said. "But I don't even know where the battery is."

"Under that," Carmen said, gesturing towards a covered engine compartment that took up half the stern section of the boat.

Martin twisted back to look and noted that the compartment had a cover that was held shut by a padlock.

"Not very trusting these people," he said wryly.

"I suppose if you are crook you think everyone else is like you," Carmen observed.

"At least we are still moving," Martin added.

He looked over the side and saw they were now in deeper water and 30 metres from the angry woman. He had considered getting over the side to swim to push or pull the boat but he wasn't keen on that idea. He had a fear, amounting to almost to a phobia, of all the horrible marine creatures that lurk in tropical waters and which either bit or stung.

Sharks, barracuda, sting rays, jelly fish, he enumerated.

Carmen looked around and then ducked down again. "You are right. We have a strong west wind and it is pushing us offshore and I think the tide is going out too," she said.

"It is," Martin agreed.

He also looked around and began to relax. Ma Baker was still waving her clenched fist at them and calling ugly names and threats but she was now 50 metres away. Martin was feeling safer with every metre.

The Boss's shotgun might reach us, but we are nearly out of range, he thought.

Several minutes crept by. The pair stayed crouched low and just watched. To Martin's immense relief, Ma Baker turned and began splashing ashore. The Boss stayed under cover and did not shoot and by the time Ma Baker reached him the boat was nearly 200 metres out to sea and safe.

Confident they could no longer be hit Martin heaved himself from the painful crouch and into the seat. "Phew! That was close!" he said.

"Definitely a devil and deep blue situation," Carmen agreed. She lowered the rifle and placed it upright in the corner. Then she turned to Martin. "Sorry Martin, but I couldn't have shot that woman. I was going to just hit her," she said.

Martin felt both guilty and relieved. "That's OK," he said. "I couldn't have done it either. I couldn't even shoot that mongrel Tyler when he was shooting at me."

"You did shoot though," Carmen said.

"That was to save you," he replied.

"You are wonderful man Martin," Carmen said.

Martin blushed and got all embarrassed. "Oh shucks! We were all in it together. I just hope we can get to help quickly."

That changed the subject abruptly. They both sat up and looked around. Martin noted that the sea was mostly very calm, the waves just little ripples. It was very blue except further out where it turned to a distinct brown colour. And it was dotted with hundreds of floating objects, logs mostly.

Then Martin glanced back at the shore and saw they were now 300 or so metres from the beach. They were so far out that Ma Baker was just an ant-like figure kneeling over her dead son. At that moment The Boss came out from behind his log and joined her.

But Martin forgot about them as the realization burst on him that he and Carmen had another problem, and potentially a serious one.

"We are being blown out to sea!" he cried.

He stared in all directions, hoping to see a boat or a ship. But except for the hundreds of pieces of flood debris there was no sign of anything on the water. Nor was there any sign of any aircraft in the now clear blue sky. And the further they got from the lee of the cape the stronger the wind became.

Martin noted that the distance to the shore had now increased to more than half a kilometre. He looked along the beach to the south, hoping to see some sign of the town of Alva Beach, or at least some people. But there was no sign of either. Then he studied the rate and direction of drift.

"We might just wash ashore on Cape Upstart," he ventured, pointing to the rugged range of mountains that was now standing up quite clearly across the bay.

Carmen looked doubtful. "Maybe," she said.

She then turned to searching the boat. Martin joined her. But they found very little. The most important items were a cane picnic hamper and a 4-litre drink container.

"This boat isn't carrying anything in the way of safety equipment," Carmen observed. "No life jackets, no food or water, no radio and no EPIRB."

"It's a ski boat," Martin observed. "They probably don't take it out into deep water."

"They are just slack crooks," Carmen replied. She then gave a big sigh and slumped down. "Give me a drink from the backpack," she said.

Martin did. The remaining water bottle was drained and that helped but the afternoon sun was blazing down and scorching them and he found he was perspiring and feeling feverish. And he was sore from his wounds and feeling battered, bruised and utterly exhausted. So he sat there and picked at the bindis and other prickles. Each time he pulled one off he got pricked and swore.

"Sorry," he muttered. "Is there a First Aid kit?"

Carmen shook her head. "Haven't seen one."

Gingerly Martin felt his closest shotgun wound. He found a hard scab of dried blood. The wound was a throbbing ache.

I hope the wounds don't get infected, he fretted.

Time slid past and Martin became thirsty and scared. He saw that the sun was now much lower in the sky and that they were over a kilometres from land. The distance was so great he could no longer see either of the Barberinis or even distinguish the particular piece of beach they were on.

1730hrs arrived and Martin noted that the amount of flood debris had increased dramatically. Looking over the side he saw that the colour of the sea had changed to a muddy brown. By following it with his eyes he noted that it formed a wide band that extended back to the shore several kilometres to the south.

"I think this is the flood waters from the Burdekin," he said.

Carmen looked. "I think you are right. And it is pushing us northwards."

That was bad news. Martin studied the situation and noted that they were no longer drifting towards Cape Upstart.

Bloody hell! If we miss the cape we will be out into the open sea, he thought.

Once again fear and dismay clutched at his heart and he felt wretched. Disgust was then added to fear as several dead beef cattle floating legs up drifted by. There were also tree trunks which were crawling with life; centipedes, small rodents and various bugs and lizards.

"I hope there are no snakes on that log there," Martin observed.

They drifted closer and he had to lean over and fend the log off. The relative movements lead him to deduce that the lighter boat had more windage and was heading almost due east while most to the flood debris was drifting northeast.

And Cape Upstart is now southeast of us, he thought gloomily. It seemed to him that they had escaped from one life threatening situation only to find themselves in another.

At Carmen's suggestion they checked the 4-litre drink container and found it was full of water. They both had a big drink and then sat back feeling better.

Suddenly Martin stiffened. He swung his head around and cupped a hand to his right ear.

"Listen!" he croaked.

Then it came to him faintly, the distinctive vibrating flutter of a helicopter. With hope surging he moved his hand to shield his eyes and he squinted northwest towards where the sound was coming from.

"A helicopter!" he cried.

And there it was, a tiny black shape the size of a pinhead silhouetted against the afternoon sky. It was coming from the north and even as his eyes picked it up he saw that it was flying down the length of Cape Bowling Green.

"There it is, just above the lighthouse," he added.

The tiny white stick of the lighthouse was just visible above the dark line that was the cape. Carmen sighed with relief and shook her head. "We could have just stayed there and they would have found us," she commented.

"Would have saved us a lot of drama," Martin agreed.

They watched the distant helicopter fly on southwards, obviously following the cape. Then it suddenly swung around, and they saw it circle low and then come to a hover. Martin felt even more hopeful.

"I think it has found the others on the wreck," he said.

After watching for a minute Carmen nodded. "I agree. Oh, that is good news! At least Andrew and the others are safe," she said.

The distance was so great that they could only speculate but the helicopter stayed there hovering for a good twenty minutes. Martin assumed it would land but conceded that landing on soft sand or mudflats that were awash might not be a good idea.

They will winch them up, he thought.

He then pictured the scene from the many TV news images he had seen. Suddenly, the tiny buzzing object began heading north, climbing as it went.

"They're heading towards Townsville," Martin said. He felt a stab of dismay. "Why don't they come and look for us?"

Carmen shielded her eyes against the glare reflecting off the sea. "They will have winched Long John Silver up and I would guess they are rushing him to hospital."

"Bugger him! He's only a bloody pirate," Martin growled his disappointment at not being immediately rescued growing.

"Be fair Martin. The others will have told the crew we are somewhere about. Anyway, the helicopter might be full up," Carmen said.

Martin knew all of this but it was still a sharp blow to his hopes. He slumped down and sat there brooding after the helicopter had vanished in the distance.

Time began to drag. It was still sweleringly hot despite the wind. Several times Martin had to help Carmen fend off floating logs and once he saw a whole string of 44-gallon drums go drifting by. There were more dead cattle in the stream as well and some of the tree trunks were huge and still had foliage on their branches. A seagull appeared and began fishing.

Carmen suggested another drink and then opened the picnic hamper. "Sandwiches," she said. She dug out two and held them up. "Ham and cheese and tomato or salad?"

"Ham please."

For the next ten minutes they ate, silently munching down the sandwiches. Two more were shared out. "There are two more left," Carmen observed, "and some biscuits. We will save them for later."

Feeling much better Martin sat with his back to the sun and then hunched down out of the wind which was starting to chill him. Once again he became cold. Overcome by reaction and exhaustion he dozed.

Carmen woke him about an hour later. By then the sun was low in the west, the sky blood red and streaked with yellows. Blinking and rubbing at sleep gummed eyes Martin looked up.

"What is it?"

"The helicopter is back," Carmen said.

Hope surged anew and Martin dragged himself to his feet to stare back toward the land. Shielding his eyes against the glare of the afternoon sun reflecting off the almost calm sea he stared towards the distant vibration of sound. But his first reaction was one of dismay, almost shock. They were much further from the land, 5 or 6 kilometres he estimated. They were so far out on the sea that the low line of the cape was almost lost below the curve of the earth's surface. Only a few high dunes and the tops of the mangroves were showing.

But there was no doubt about the helicopter. It came buzzing down from the north again, from the direction of Townsville. It flew over the lighthouse and the area where the trawler wreck was without stopping and then went lower.

"They are looking for us," Carmen said.

Martin watched the helicopter as it slowly headed south just above the distant line of trees and he began to get little prickles of concern.

"They don't know we are on a boat though," he replied. "They will be searching the beach."

The same awful idea obviously came to them both simultaneously as even as he thought it and looked towards Carmen she said, "They will see those horrible Barberinis."

This appeared to be confirmed when a few minutes later the helicopter again came to a hover almost directly in line with them to the west. They could see it as a tiny fly sized object silhouetted against the red of the sunset. It was obviously stationary.

Five minutes went by and the helicopter still hovered. Martin felt his stomach turn over.

"They might have found Tony's body too," he commented.

Carmen bit her lip and nodded. She stared and looked anxious and when another five minutes went by she shook her head. "I think they have. They are probably winching it up."

Another five minutes went by. The orb of the sun began to sink below the horizon. Then the helicopter suddenly began moving again. This time it flew off directly to the west.

The moment he saw the helicopter turn away alarm surged in Martin's chest. He sprang up and began waving.

"Hoy! Here we are!" he cried, knowing that calling out was futile at that distance. But the helicopter kept flying west, vanishing from view as it dwindled into the distance.

"Where are they going?" Carmen wondered aloud.

"Towards Mud Crab Landing," Martin replied. His stomach churned as his anxiety shot up. "Surely those people told the helicopter crew where we are?" he added.

"I wouldn't bet on it," Carmen replied grimly.

Again Martin's stomach churned with apprehension. He looked around the sea and sky for any sign of rescue.

Bloody hell! he thought. *It is getting dark and we are still being blown out to sea!*

Chapter 36

RAY OF HOPE

M artin swallowed as the fear churned in him. The wind was still pushing them east out to sea and the tide was ebbing in the same direction. The line of trees along the low cape began to vanish below the horizon. The sun slid lower, half then a quarter and then only a tiny piece, all blood red against the red sky. He shivered, hoping it wasn't an omen.

The old saw 'red sky at night, sailor's delight; red sky in morning, sailor take warning' flitted across his mind but he knew it was not relevant.

That was made up in the northern hemisphere. We don't need to worry about more storms for a few days, he told himself.

By now Cape Upstart was due south and he glimpsed more hazy hills further down along the coast.

There is a major coal port down that way at Abbot Point, he thought. But he knew there was no chance of any big ships being in the area. *They will all have cleared out when the cyclone warning was given. It will take them a day or two to get back.*

That was dispiriting and for a moment he wondered if he and Carmen would have to survive in the open boat for several days. Then the notion that they might just drift out to sea and die from lack of food or water came to him and he shivered and tried to push it out of his head.

Looking north he got more concerned. They were now so far out to sea that he could see rugged high land to the north of Cape Cleveland.

That is Magnetic Island, off Townsville, he thought. Having been there on picnics over the years only added to his feelings of anxiety and unreality.

One again Martin stared west, noting that the sun was now casting crepuscular rays upwards.

Is that a good omen? he wondered.

Then the sun slid out of sight and darkness came sweeping in from the east. As he watched the eastern sky darken Martin shivered with apprehension. He was reminded of the dark storm clouds racing in when the cyclone hit.

To survive all that and then to just die! he thought.

Then through the gathering gloom to the west came a flicker of light. Martin felt his heart lift with a spark of hope but then he shrugged.

That is the lighthouse on Cape Bowling Green, he told himself.

Vivid memories of that night of terror cringing among the nets while the cyclone buffeted them caused him to shudder and he came out in goose bumps. Then the vibration from heavy engines had them both on their feet and staring in all directions. Martin listened and then his heart sank.

"Aero engines," he said. "A big aeroplane and high up."

He spotted it then, a tiny dark silhouette against the last paleness of the sunset. Pointing to it he said, "An Air Force Hercules. Taking off from Townsville and heading south."

Carmen stared and nodded at the distant shape which became just moving, winking lights as the sky grew darker.

"Probably flying in relief aid after the cyclone?" she surmised.

It was both hopeful and disappointing. Martin sat back down and huddled out of the wind. This had dropped but was still quite chilly.

Next Carmen tried to open the engine compartment. Martin heard her working on the padlock and latches and sat up. "What are you doing?" he asked.

"Tyring to open this to get at the engine. I was hoping we might be able to short the electrical wires to get the motor going," Carmen answered.

Martin had heard of that. *It is how car thieves steal older cars without computer controls,* he thought.

He had never seen it done and wasn't sure how to do it. But it was a good idea and worth a try. So they did. For twenty minutes they punched, banged and thumped at the cover and the padlock. But nothing they had was hard enough or strong enough and they ended up sweating and puffing. Disappointed they sat back down again.

From time to time Martin and Carmen discussed the situation and also speculated on whether the helicopter had actually picked up Letitia, Anne and Andrew. "If they have mum and dad will know by now that we are alive," Carmen commented.

"Or that we were this afternoon anyway," Martin conceded.

He tried to imagine the emotions and reactions his parents might have been having over the last few days. He also wondered if his home had been damaged in the cyclone.

The wind died away until it was just a gentle breeze. Martin was happy with that as it meant their drift would be slower. It also eased his anxieties of being out in the open sea in a small boat with no motive power if the waves got bigger.

More aircraft, both propeller driven and jets, were heard and their lights seen. These were all high up and all climbed from the north and went off southward and were following a track well to the west of them. Having flown to Brisbane a few times Martin remembered that the usual flight path was over the town of Ayr which was well away from the coast.

In between aircraft the only sign of humans was the revolving light on Cape Bowling Green. But even this became faint as they continued to drift eastwards. Staring around the dark sea sent tremors of fear through Martin. Other than the lighthouse there was not a light to be seen in any direction.

Feeling both depressed and exhausted he hunched down and sat there praying, remembering and brooding.

A sudden bump woke Martin. For a minute or so he sat, blinking bleary eyes and with his heart hammering in fright.

Where am I? What was that? he wondered.

Then he remembered where he was and he looked at the sea. To his surprise it was flat calm. And it seemed very dark despite the almost full moon.

"What woke me?" he wondered.

"What?" murmured Carmen.

"Something woke me," Martin replied, levering himself up to stare at the dark ocean.

Then another sudden bump made the boat rock and his heart leapt into his mouth. Silly notions of sharks and crocodiles were replaced by the idea of a whale but then he saw a lumpy, dark thing floating beside the boat and he realized it was only a log.

Sighing with relief he leaned over and pushed the log away. Then he scanned the horizon, hoping to see a ship. But there was nothing and his hopes went down again. Now the only thing he could use to orient himself was the flicker of the lighthouse beam and it looked a long way away.

We must be ten or more kilometres out to sea, he thought.

A sudden swirl in the water and then a loud splash caused his heart to leap and palpitate. Then he realized it was a big fish jumping and he tried to relax. But his anxious mind added the afterthought that big fish are eaten by even bigger fish and he shuddered at the notion of ending up in the sea.

Sitting down again he asked Carmen for a drink and they enjoyed a cup of water each. They then relieved themselves with as much modesty as the situation would allow.

As she sat back down Carmen said, "What about some of that chocolate?"

Martin thought that was a very good idea so he slipped off the backpack and dug out the two chocolates. They were a real treat and he slowly dissolved each square on his tongue to get the maximum enjoyment from it. Then he lowered himself down to rest again.

Once more he slipped off into an exhausted deep sleep. There were dreams, but they were not nightmares and he came to a state of consciousness where he knew he was asleep and that he was uncomfortable. For a while he resisted the urge to shift but finally the discomfort was replaced by the stabbing pain of a cramp and this jerked him awake.

Still groggy and half asleep he rubbed at the sore muscles, noted that there was a cool breeze blowing on his face and that Carmen was asleep next to him. Once again he drifted into a deep sleep. The next time he woke it was when he dreamed that the boat was a large yacht which had suddenly shrunk to a small row boat and that the wind and waves were rising. In fact it was a dash of cold spray on his face that roused him.

For a minute or so Martin stared out, once again bewildered and lost. All he could see was darkness and then he realized he really was in a small boat. And the boat was rocking quickly, a short, sharp roll every few seconds. Small waves were causing this and he looked at the dark, rippling sea in horror, and noted that he had a definite wind on his face.

Where are we? he wondered, stabs of anxiety relacing the darts of pain in his muscles. *Are we right out to sea now?* he wondered, the fear growing with his imagination.

For several anxious seconds he looked wildly around, his heart hammering and his mouth dry. Then a sudden flicker of light showed in the distance. It was the beam of the lighthouse and to his enormous relief it did not seem to be any further away. It was showing just above the horizon and he stared at it while his heart slowed.

A ray of hope! he thought. And he needed it. He knew he was reaching the end of his endurance and he was afraid he would give up or go mad. *It is all too much! I just want it all to stop,* he told himself.

He sat there staring at the light for some time before he realized that the wind which had sprung up had changed direction and was now coming from the southeast.

The wind! It is blowing towards the land!

That realization sent another surge of hope through him and he hunched there hugging himself and trying to will the boat to be blown back to the shore.

Then things got even better. The moon, now down to the west, lit up a silver sea of rippling waves. Just being able to see better was cheering and when Martin glanced at his watch and saw that it was 0325 he felt even better.

Only a couple of hours to daylight, he thought. *And the tide is on the make so that should move us back towards the shore as well.*

It was all very heartening and he sat there trying to cheer himself up and feeling much refreshed. Carmen stirred and then sat up fifteen minutes later. She blinked and looked around.

"Where are we? What's going on?" she asked.

"We are just drifting still," Martin answered. "But now I think we are being blown back towards the shore."

Carmen sat up and joined him, then checked her watch. "Nearly four o'clock. It will start to get light in half an hour," she added.

It did. The pair just sat in the rocking boat, staring out at the rippling sea and then at the distant mountains and shore as the moonlight and then the first glow of dawn revealed them. As he watched the distant chunky shape of Cape Upstart become clearer Martin felt a distinct easing to the tension in his chest. A quick glance up at the fading constellation of Orion helped him orientate himself.

We are now north of Cape Upstart again. We haven't gone any further out to sea, he thought.

By 0500 he was feeling even better. By then it was fully light and he saw that Cape Upstart was definitely south southeast of them.

"We are being moved back towards the shore," he commented.

His eye caught on the bright white stick of the lighthouse as the first rays of the sun illuminated it and he smiled. It looked much closer and was like an old friend beckoning them. But then he looked again and did some hard thinking.

Oh bugger! he thought. *We are being blown to the northwest. We will miss the tip of Cape Bowling Green and will end up back in Bowling Green Bay!*

He put this to Carmen and she shrugged. "Better than being blown out onto the Great Barrier Reef," she commented. "It doesn't matter too much where we come ashore as long as we do."

Martin nodded but did not quiet agree. *We could end up back in those bloody mangroves,* he thought morosely, but did not say.

He knew that the prevailing wind along the Queensland coast was from the southeast so he set to work to try to calculate where they might make landfall.

Somewhere north of Cungulla, on Cape Cleveland probably, he decided.

Carmen watched a military transport aircraft that was passing overhead high up then said. "If we had a sail we would have some control."

That gave Martin an idea. "Let's stand up on the seats and I will use my shirt as a sail," he suggested.

It wasn't much but it made them feel like they had some control and Martin felt better even if the wind was chilly on his bare torso. He stood with his front to the wind and his unbuttoned shirt held wide at the hem by both arms so that the wind was caught in it. After twenty minutes of that he was sure that it was helping move them along. But it also made him certain they would just miss the tip of Cape Bowling Green. The lighthouse was now southwest of them. But it was also noticeably closer and he felt much happier.

We are only a couple of kilometres from land now, he thought.

Carmen then said, "You'd better button your shirt up Martin. You are getting very sunburnt."

He was too so he did as she said. Then they settled and had another drink and ate the last sandwich. The food and drink sent morale even higher and Martin relaxed and just watched as the wind and tide moved the boat slowly along.

By 0600 there was no doubt. The tip of the cape was visible as a line of small breakers some way to the left of their course. Ahead stretched the whole width of Bowling Green Bay. The far shore was still hidden over the curve of the earth but the mountains of the Mt Elliott range were standing up clear like a blue cardboard cut-out.

Then the shuddering tremor of a helicopter made Martin sit up and look to his right. To his intense delight he saw the machine at once and it looked to be flying directly towards them from the direction of Townsville.

At once he whipped off his shirt and sprang up onto the forecastle. Fearful that the people in the helicopter might not see them, or might think they did not need help, he began to wave his arms frantically. Carmen also waved her arms from the stern of the boat.

To Martin's great joy the machine swung to one side and came lower then began to circle around them. That made him certain they had been seen but he still kept on waving. Only when it circled even lower and he saw faces peering out at them did he stop and pull his shirt back on. A minute later the helicopter came to a hover directly overhead. He was just in time as the downdraft began to lash at them and he had trouble getting the buttons done up.

Down from the machine slid a crewman on the end of a winch rope. As he came lower Martin felt such a surge of joy all he could do was cry out and grin. The man was lowered until he was hanging just above Martin's head, the rotor downwash blowing him around. Carmen reached out and grabbed the crewman's ankle and guided him down into the boat. Martin moved to join them.

To Martin's surprise the man unclipped his harness and then spoke on a small radio. The harness was winched up and the helicopter flew on southwards.

The crewman pushed up the visor of the helmet he wore and as the noise of the helicopter's engine receded said, "Are you kids Carmen and Martin?"

"Yes!" they cried. Carmen heaved a huge sigh of relief. "Are Andrew, Anne and Letitia safe?" she asked.

The crewman nodded. "Yes. We picked them up yesterday and a man with a broken leg they said was a pirate. We took them to the Townsville Hospital."

"Oh thank God!" Carmen cried.

Martin grinned. *Safe!* he thought.

He then said, "Did you pick up two people on the beach south of there yesterday afternoon; a middle-aged man and a fat woman?"

"The Barberinis? Yes, and the body of their son," the crewman replied.

"Did they tell you we were out on the sea in this boat?" Martin asked.

The crewman shook his head. "Nope, not a hint. Your friends told us you were walking to Alva Beach so we thought we would find you somewhere to the south but when we didn't see you on the beach we assumed you had made it to town, or what there is left of it."

"Left of it?" Carmen queried.

"It is almost totally destroyed. The place has been hit by a Category Five cyclone you know and there was a four metre storm surge," the crewman explained.

"We know!" Carmen cried. "We were on the lighthouse over there during it. It nearly washed us away."

"On the lighthouse! Holy mackerel!" the crewman cried.

As they talked Martin felt a sudden change in his mood. The news that the Barberinis had not mentioned him sparked a sullen anger.

They wanted us dead! he thought. *The murderous mongrels!*

A sudden desire to see justice done was sparked in him. He looked at the crewman. "Where did you land the Barberinis?"

"They wanted us to put them down at a place called Mud Crab Landing which was where they said they lived but when we got there we saw that the whole place had been destroyed by the storm surge. And I mean destroyed! There wasn't a building standing and their home was just a pile of rubble and twisted iron," the crewman replied.

"Did they still want you to land?" Martin queried.

The crewman nodded. "Yes. They were very insistent. They said there were some valuables that they wanted to collect. But the skipper wouldn't have it as the place was all flooded as well. There was water for miles in every direction, still is. In fact you two are very lucky we came this way because we are on our way to rescue a family stuck on a roof top over near Rita Island. The skipper just thought a run down along Cape Bowling Green might find any more survivors from those trawlers," the crewman explained.

"Did the Barberinis have a gun?" Martin asked.

The crewman shook his head and looked puzzled. "No."

"You are lucky then or they might have made you land at gunpoint," Martin commented. "They were trying to kill us."

Carmen nodded. "They have been trying to kill us for four days!" she cried bitterly.

The crewman looked grim. "I know. Your friends told us yesterday. But they didn't mention the Barberinis, only the people on the trawlers. We just winched them up and then the body of their son. They said he was drowned when their trawler went down in the cyclone."

"He was," Martin confirmed. "We saw it sink." As he said this he was assailed by the images of the tiny vessel engulfed by gigantic waves and then of the ghostly image of the sailing ship in the driving rain. He shuddered and then felt angry. "So where did you land them?" he asked.

"At the Ayr Hospital," the crewman replied.

"Then we need to contact the police at once and have them arrested," Martin said.

"Arrested? Oh, I doubt if they will be going anywhere for a while. Every road for hundreds of kilometres is closed either by trees and fallen power poles or by flooding," the crewman explained.

Martin had a sudden image of Mud Crab Landing and through his mind flashed the notion that it was the crook's base.

The Barberinis want to go back there to collect their ill-gotten gains, he thought.

From that it was only a short step to him developing the burning desire to stop them.

I want them to pay for what they did, he thought. *I want to see justice done!*

A plan formed in his mind as though by magic.

Chapter 37

DETERMINATION

Carmen gestured towards the distant helicopter which was hovering low over the beach to the south of the lighthouse.

"What are they doing?" she asked.

The crewman looked. "Picking up a body we saw on the beach yesterday. I checked it out but he was dead."

"That will be Tyler," Martin said. "He tried to shoot us. That is his rifle." He pointed to the rifle leaning against the instrument panel.

The crewman hadn't seen it before but now he looked at it and then gave them both a hard and wary look. "Did he?" he replied. "You'd better tell this tale to the police."

Martin shook his head. "No. You get the police to arrest the Barberinis. They are the ones with questions to answer," he said.

The crewman nodded towards the helicopter which was now buzzing back towards them. "You can tell them. We will have you aboard in a few minutes."

Martin shook his head. "No. We are alright. Go and rescue those people on the roof," he said.

"I can't leave you adrift out in the sea," The crewman replied, plainly worried and annoyed.

"And you shouldn't leave a boat adrift to become a marine hazard," Martin retorted. He could see that Carmen was looking at him with astonishment, but he didn't care. He was now determined. "Just give us some water and a two lifejackets and we will reach shore safely. We are navy cadets. We are trained to use small boats and at sea survival. We will be alright."

"I can't do that!" the crewman cried.

"What if the boat's engine was working?"

"Maybe. But where would you go?"

"Cungulla?" Martin suggested, pointing west.

The crewman shook his head and laughed. "No point in going there. The entire place has been washed away. Most of the buildings are totally wrecked. A couple have been washed clean off their foundations. All that is left are concrete slabs and heaps of rubbish and fallen trees. If it hadn't been evacuated early there would have been a lot of dead people there. There's no-one there to help you and the road out is blocked by flood waters," he said.

When Martin heard that he suddenly realized that the disaster was much bigger and more widespread than he thought. But it also gave him more mental ammunition. "So your helicopter is needed more urgently there than wasting time ferrying us when we have a perfectly good boat," he said.

"What if something goes wrong?" the crewman queried. But Martin could see he was wavering and his radio was crackling asking what the delay was. He said, "We will be alright. Just get the motor going and we will get ourselves to Townsville."

"How will you navigate?" the crewman asked, still doubtful but obviously wavering.

Martin snorted. "I told you! We are navy cadets. We can navigate by the sun and the stars. Besides, we are locals and we know where we are. There's Cape Cleveland. Townsville is just on the other side of that. We can just follow the coast along and if anything goes wrong then go ashore."

The crewman hesitated, then shook his head. "No. I can't allow that. You don't have the right safety gear for a voyage on the open sea in a small boat. Do you have no radio?"

Martin shook his head. "No," he admitted.

"What about flares? And an EPIRB?" the crewman asked.

Again Martin shook his head. The crewman shook his head and said, "I would be guilty of negligence if I allowed you to stay in this boat. The boat will just have to take its chances. It should drift ashore somewhere over near Cungulla anyway. You can collect it later."

Martin was about to blurt out that the boat wasn't theirs when it occurred to him that maybe he and Carmen could be charged with theft. At that he glanced at her and she met his eyes and gave a faint nod.

"OK," he conceded.

The crewman called on the radio for the helicopter to return and then he briefed them on the procedure for being winched up. Until then it had not really occurred to Martin that he might have to be taken aboard the helicopter and when he considered it he was astonished at how anxious he felt. *It must be safe,* he tried to reassure himself.

The helicopter came to a hover and the safety harness was lowered. The crewman grabbed it and buckled it on while Martin hunched to shield himself from the spray and rotor downwash. Once he was ready the crewman offered the safety belt to Carmen. She nodded and slid it on then reached out for the rifle but the crewman shook his head.

"Leave that. Just go up," he shouted.

"But we can't leave a loaded gun in an abandoned boat," Carmen protested. "Some kids might find it."

The crewman nodded. "OK. I'll bring it. Now get in."

A few seconds later Carmen and the crewman were winched up. Martin sat there, neck tilted uncomfortably back and heart hammering with what he reluctantly admitted was fear.

You will be quite safe, he told himself over and over.

Squinting against the blast of air he watched Carmen and the crewman vanish into the centre compartment of the red and white helicopter. A minute later the crewman re-appeared and was lowered down. As he got closer Martin found he was gulping and swallowing as he tried to master the rapidly growing apprehension.

But then the crewman was there and gesturing to him to slip the safety harness over his head and shoulders. Martin wanted to say no and was now terrified of undergoing the rescue but all he could make himself do was pretend he wasn't scared and allow his quivering limbs to be guided into the harness.

The crewman then reached over and picked up the rifle by the barrel. Martin shook his head. "Careful! It is loaded," he shouted.

The crewman nodded and looked sheepish and then slung the weapon over his shoulder. He then reached forward and took a firm hold of Martin who was almost gibbering with fear by then.

And then pressure came on around his shoulders and suddenly the boat was below his dangling feet! Martin saw it getting smaller and smaller and he gulped and convulsively tightened his grip on the harness. Then he glanced up to see how much further he had to go.

Oh, I hope this wire rope doesn't break! he thought as he eyed the thin steel cable.

But there was the helicopter just above him and a moment later the landing skids passed his eyes and he saw the open doorway and another crewman reaching out. He tried to help but that didn't really. The second crewman spun him to face outwards and he was dragged backwards into the compartment and lowered to the floor.

Martin shuddered with relief and then tried to grin at Carmen's smiling face.

Safe, he thought, *well, as long as we don't crash!* He had never been in a helicopter before and was still scared.

Strong hands moved him to a seat and the harness was removed and he was buckled in beside Carmen. But then he found himself staring at the large plastic shape strapped across the floor of the compartment in front of him.

Oh no! Tyler's body! he thought.

The fear of being near a dead person sent his hair standing on end and his heart hammering again. To avoid seeing it he looked out through the open starboard door. That gave him a good view of Cape Bowling Green and the lighthouse.

The crewman unslung the rifle and slid it in under the seat and then took his own seat. He plugged in an intercom connection and spoke to the pilot. Martin felt the engine note change and then the helicopter tilted and his heart went into his mouth.

But it was just the machine changing attitude to go from a hover to forward flight and a moment later it settled on an even keel and Martin saw that they were racing low across the sea. Shallow water and sandbars flashed quickly underneath, dropping steadily away as the machine slowly climbed.

We are going south, Martin thought.

Bowling Green Bay was on the starboard side and the long line of Cape Bowling Green to port. He got a brief glimpse of the wrecked trawler in the mangroves before it slid from view. Then they were over more sand banks and winding channels. Ahead he could see the southern shore of the bay.

Then he looked out to starboard and when he realized what he was looking at he sucked in his breath and gasped.

"Carmen, look at the Haughton River," he cried.

Carmen did and so did the crewmen. Ten kilometres away a vast spread of water was reflecting the sun's rays. The glinting covered such a large area of what should have been dry land that Martin could only gape in astonishment. He knew it was flooding from the Haughton River because he could see where it flowed into the bay in a mighty brown swirl and the small sugar mill town of Giru was visible standing like an island in a vast brown lake. The buildings and chimneys of the huge sugar mill were lit up by the sun and that made recognition easy.

The crewman shouted at them, "It is the biggest flood they have ever had in the Haughton. It is five kilometres wide and every farm and house for miles is flooded."

"Anyone drowned?" Carmen asked.

The crewman shook his head. "Nah. Giru is used to floods. Besides most of the residents evacuated before the cyclone arrived in case the storm surge got that far inland," he said.

Martin leaned over and looked out and was astonished to see sunlight glinting off water in hundreds of places in from the coast.

And this is low tide, he thought, noting how much of the bay was now exposed sand or mudflats.

At that moment the intercom crackled and the crewmen both listened and then the one who had stayed in the helicopter said, "OK Chief. But we will be seriously overloaded. Can we drop this lot off somewhere first?"

Martin didn't hear what the pilot said but he could guess. He waited till the crewman replied, "Roger, over," before tapping him on the knee. "What is it?" he asked.

The crewman leaned across and shouted, "A Coastwatch aircraft have just located five people in the water out near Wheeler Reef. They are a family from New Zealand and their yacht was sunk in the cyclone. They are all in the water with lifejackets and must have been there for many hours. And there is a big shark circling them. We need to get there fast to rescue them but to make room we have to drop you off first."

"That's OK," Martin shouted back. "Just dump us at the first farm you come to. You can come back later and get us."

Carmen nodded agreement. "We are alright. But those people might have been in the water since yesterday so they will be in a pretty bad way," she said.

The crewman nodded. "OK, I'll tell the Chief you are happy with that." He began talking on the intercom.

As he did Martin glanced down and saw that they were rapidly approaching the coastline. His mind told him that they were still flying south but that the people who needed to be rescued were out to the east. Then he realized that the channel they were flying over led into the mangroves to where the settlement of Mud Crab Landing was.

Or used to be! Martin thought, noting that he could not make out any buildings but could see the vehicle track winding in across the now exposed mudflat.

His mind raced and he stared to check whether there were any vehicles or people visible. None were and a plan formed in his mind in an instant. Pointing down he shouted, "Drop us here."

The crewman glanced down and then shook his head. "There's no-one there."

"We don't need anyone," Martin shouted back. "We know where we are. That is Mud Crab Landing. We will be alright. Just give us a bottle of water and come back and get us later."

"But.."

But Martin's determination had crystallized. "Look, you need to fly east and fast. Every minute you fly south to find us a farm is wasted. There are farms just out along that road. If we have to we will walk to one of them. Now land us here, and the body."

The crewman glanced down again and Martin looked as well. They were passing over a wide belt of devastated mangroves which had been broken off by the storm surge and then piled in a gigantic windrow that extended for miles in both directions. Inland of that was a belt of surviving mangroves but Martin could see that they had been shredded of most of their leaves and that many trees were broken off or had lost branches.

Then the actual settlement appeared below and he saw that the report was correct; there wasn't a single building remaining intact. The big sheds were gone and so were all of the old huts and houses. Even the Barberinis' new concrete block house was a pile of rubble. The whole place was just a wasteland of smashed off trees and pieces of rusty corrugated iron.

By then the crewman was talking fast to the pilot and then he looked up at him. "You kids sure you don't mind?"

Carmen answered. "No. It is only for a couple of hours. We've been here before. We know where we are. Don't worry about us. Now put us down and get going, quickly."

The crewman nodded and again spoke to the pilot. A moment later, just as the still sodden mudflats flashed underneath, the helicopter tilted to port and then swung round in a tight circle. Martin was nearly sick and experienced some rapid heartbeats but he was secretly elated.

The Barberinis wanted to come here so there loot must be here, he thought.

Looking out to port he saw they were circling over the mangroves to the east of the ruined settlement. Mud Crab Creek was clearly visible and so were the clearings and clumps of ruins but he again looked to check that there was no sign of any people or vehicles.

If there are I will veto the plan, he thought.

Looking down he saw that the place had been washed clean and almost every tree uprooted or snapped off and there were piles of rubbish and debris tangled around the remaining posts and trees.

As the helicopter came lower and settled to land on the grass to the west of the ruins of the Barberinis' house the crewman said, "Are you sure?"

Martin nodded and to his relief Carmen did too. The crewman bit his lip and then nodded. "Alright then. And thanks. This cyclone has been the biggest disaster to hit North Queensland in a generation and we really need every seat in the machine at this moment."

The helicopter settled and their seat belts were undone. Martin found that his muscles had seized up and it took a few moments to get them moving again. The first crewman climbed down to help him out. Groaning with the pain he climbed down and stood beside the helicopter, very conscious of the rotor slashing the air apparently just above his head.

Carmen climbed out next and then leaned back in and grabbed the butt of the rifle. The other crewman moved to stop her but she shouted, "In case of crocodiles," and pulled the weapon clear.

The first crewman nodded. He handed Martin a plastic bottle of water and then pointed forward.

"Go that way so the pilot can see you."

Martin nodded and did so. As he hurried forward at an instinctive crouch he glanced back to check that Carmen was following and saw that she was. He also caught a glimpse of the crewmen sliding Tyler's body out. They lowered it into the grass.

By then Martin was 50 paces from the helicopter and he turned to face it. Carmen joined him and he saw the crewmen clamber back aboard. A few seconds later the helicopter lifted off and set off eastwards. As it swung around Martin and Carmen waved to it and arms waved back.

As the noise died away Martin grinned at Carmen and said, "That's better! Safe on dry land!"

Carmen moved to stand beside him. "It is! But why didn't you let them take us a bit further? We are stuck here until they return unless you feel like a good walk." she said.

"It saves them time," Martin answered. "I'd hate to hear that those people had died or been eaten by a shark just because we didn't want to walk a few kilometres."

As he said this he heard another helicopter and looked westwards to where the noise was coming from. In the distance he saw a large double rotor helicopter flying above where he thought Giru was.

Army Chinook, he thought. Obviously a major rescue effort was now underway.

Carmen then pointed to where the vehicle track was just visible on the mudflats. "Are we staying here or walking?" she asked.

Martin swallowed and knew that a moment of decision had arrived. "Walking," he answered. Then he pointed to ruins. "But I want to check out this place first."

Carmen looked shocked. "Why? It's just a mess," she replied, looking around her as she did.

Martin looked around as well. "I reckon the Barberinis have their loot stashed here, probably in their house. If we can find it then they won't have any getaway money."

"And what if they arrive? Do you plan to arrest them?" Carmen asked. She looked both anxious and angry.

Martin shook his head. "No. I don't want to risk anyone getting hurt. But we can hide and then later report their movements and that will help."

Carmen looked worried and shook her head. "I think it is a crazy idea. We are safe. Let's just go home."

"So you won't help me?"

"I didn't say that," Carmen hissed.

Martin looked at her and experienced a surge of fierce determination. "Well, I am going to look around. You can hide and keep watch," he said.

Again Carmen shook her head. Then she sighed. "Alright. But we don't want to stay long or the tide will come in and cover that road again. When does the tide turn?"

"Low water is in about an hour," Martin replied.

"Some lunch would be nice," Carmen said in a wry tone.

Martin laughed and could only agree. He felt so hungry and weak he was light-headed. Then he glanced at the rifle and said, "Might be a good idea to check that rifle and clean it."

Carmen looked at it and then bit her lip. "I'm not going to shoot anyone, except in self-defence. I couldn't."

"I'm not asking you to. I will use the rifle if you like."

Carmen shook her head. "No. I am the senior rank. I will carry it."

With that she clicked open the bolt. But as she tried to pull it back there were grating sounds and Martin saw that it had both sand and rust on it. Carmen gently brushed, blew and wiped as she eased the bolt to the rear. She extracted the bullet and slipped it into her pocket then looked down the barrel.

"Just as well I didn't try to fire this," she commented. "It is half full of sand. It might have blown up in my face."

Martin shuddered as he thought about that. But he nodded and concentrated studying the area while Carmen carefully stripped the weapon. She laid all seven bullets out on a handkerchief and then carefully cleaned and wiped the pieces clean and dry.

As she did Martin studied the ruins. The entire sandy rise and adjoining mangroves were just a scarred wasteland of shattered stumps. The scene reminded Martin of pictures of World War 1 battlefields.

"What a mess!" he croaked.

The whole scene was one of devastation. Many trees were stripped bare of leaves or had broken branches and quite a few trees had been snapped off and lay in a tangle. Martin noted that the mangroves had fared better than the melaleucas and eucalypts, most of which were splintered. The stand of trees where he and Letitia had reached cover beyond the last house was just a massive tangle of broken stumps and rubbish. A white object stuck out of the pile. Pieces of corrugated iron and other rubbish were wrapped around many of the trees and posts. To his astonishment he noted that the steel power poles were all bent right over and that most of the posts which marked the roadway across the mudflats were broken or missing. The mudflats were dotted with hundreds of logs and other debris

Once again he suffered nightmarish flashbacks to the storm surge pounding the lighthouse and he shuddered. "I wonder how far inland the storm surge went?" he commented.

Then sand flies and mosquitoes arrived. Carmen discovered them first, slapping at her bare arm. "Bloody mozzies!" she cried. Then she shook her head. "Where do mozzies go during cyclones?" she asked.

Martin slapped at a mosquito that had settled on his cheek and then shook his head. "God knows!"

Carmen walked to a pool and sluiced water down the rifle barrel, then held it up to study it. Satisfied she reassembled the rifle and reloaded it.

Clicking on the safety catch she said, "OK, ready."

"Good. Let's have a look around," Martin answered.

Ahead of them was a pile of concrete blocks and rubbish showing where the Barberinis' house had once stood. A few sections of wall were still identifiable but most of the blocks were scattered in a wide fan shape for hundreds of metres to the south across where the big shed and boat had been. Of them there was no sign. Beyond the pile of rubble the creek was just visible. The water was almost right up to the top of the bank and was muddy and full of debris. The floodwaters were obviously starting to drain out with the outgoing tide.

Martin shielded his eyes against the glare and then wiped perspiration from his forehead. Squinting and blinking he stared at the scene, trying to work out what he was looking at. "Where are the wharf and the sheds?" he wondered.

Then his gaze detected a couple of stumps sticking out of the water and he sucked in his breath.

That was the wharf! he told himself. He pointed them out to Carmen and she gasped.

"The storm surge has completely demolished it!" she said, as she shook her head in amazement.

"And all the buildings. There should be some old fishermen's huts just along here on our left," Martin answered.

Carmen pointed to the pile of rubble. "That is the most likely place to look," Carmen said.

Martin nodded. "Yes," he agreed as they began walking towards it.

Chapter 38

TRUST!

As he and Carmen picked their way carefully across the debris strewn grass Martin stared out to where the vehicle track vanished into the distant line of trees. "We need to keep watch in case the crooks come back," he said. As he said this Martin felt his stomach churn as fear swirled in it. For a few moments he had the impulse to just run and hide but then he gritted his teeth with determination.

I am going to do this, he thought. *It will only take a few minutes.*

But he didn't want Carmen placed at more risk. As they skirted an uprooted and splintered cottonwood tree that lay in the middle of the grassy flat he turned to her. "You can stay here and watch the track, ready for a quick getaway if anyone comes," he said.

Carmen stopped and looked out across the mudflats. "Which way will we run if someone comes?" she asked.

Martin looked around and then shrugged. "Has to be back towards the sea, into those mangroves. That way we can keep the ruins between us and any vehicle coming towards us," he answered. That wasn't very appealing but he thought they could safely make an escape.

It also got him thinking about which way they would walk out if the helicopter did not return.

Just walking along the track will put us at risk if the crooks do come, he thought. *We will have no cover.* That got him eyeing the tangle of broken trees and debris that now lined the banks of the creek. *Maybe we had better follow the edge of that? It will at least give us some cover.*

Carmen did not hide in the branches of the downed tree but continued to walk with him, stopping twice to stare into the distance. Martin did as well, now fearful lest the Barberinis appear. He noted that the distant line of trees was mostly hidden by a heat shimmer and that the closer sand rises which the track traversed had been almost scoured clean of any trees or bushes by the waves.

The storm surge must have reached those trees near the railway, he decided.

They came to the ruins of the Barberinis' house and carefully climbed the twisted remains of the pipe and chicken wire fence and then picked their way between and over the rubble to the concrete slab the house had been built on. Two short sections of concrete block wall still stood but only two courses high. Twisted steel reinforcing rods stuck up out of them and out of the slab, testament to the fearsome force of the storm surge.

On the far side of the house, near where the front door had been was a concrete structure almost buried in rubble and bits wall. Corrugated iron, splintered structural timbers, branches and trunks of trees and smashed household items were all tangled together around it.

"This looks promising," Martin said as he clambered carefully over the rubble and rubbish to get to it.

Carmen followed and a minute later they stood on the jagged blocks and stared at the corner of a steel door peeking out from under the wreckage. Martin noted that the door appeared to be set in the front of a small room made entirely of concrete.

"A storm shelter?" he suggested.

Carmen nodded, then frowned. "I hope.. I hope there isn't someone in it," she whispered.

Martin stared at the steel door in horror and his mind filled with fearsome images of drowning while trapped in such a room. "I hope so too!" he cried, wiping perspiration off his face. He unscrewed the water bottle and had a drink then passed it to Carmen.

She drank and passed it back then said, "Well, if there is a hiding place for loot it has to be in this strong room."

"Yes," agreed Martin, but he now had very little desire to try to find out. "But we will have to shift all these bricks," he replied, half hoping Carmen would say it wasn't worth the effort.

But she just wiped perspiration off her face and slapped at a mosquito before saying: "Blocks. They are concrete blocks."

She then leaned the rifle against a short section of wall and moved forward to the edge of the pile nearest to the door.

Martin bit his lip and quelled his apprehensive nausea before moving to join her. "You keep watch while I shift some of this stuff," he said.

Carmen nodded and moved to where she could see over the pile and out along the vehicle track. Martin bent and gripped a concrete block and as his hands felt the roughness of it he almost stopped there and then. But then he shrugged and took a firm hold and lifted the block and tossed it aside. It was heavier than he had expected and the effort told.

This might be harder than we thought, he decided.

Knowing that he was both physically and mentally exhausted as well as weak from hunger he stopped to think about what he was doing.

Then the vibration of an engine caught his ears and he jerked upright and stared out at the mudflats. But it wasn't a vehicle. It was a helicopter, a Chinook with a slung load, and it was flying southwards across the mudflats about a kilometre away. The big olive drab painted machine vanished over the trees lining Mud Crab Creek.

"Going to Ayr maybe?" he suggested.

"Probably," Carmen agreed.

Martin again bent to his task and tossed a few more blocks aside. Then he dragged a big sheet of rusty corrugated iron away. "This didn't come off this house," he commented.

"Maybe off those old fishermen's huts?" Carmen suggested.

Martin nodded and moved to toss more rubble aside. Several splintered beams and a couple of tree branches were added to the growing pile. After a few more minutes of hard work Martin stopped and wiped his face before having another drink. Then he resumed his task.

After another ten minutes he encountered a section of wall that was still intact, held together by mortar and reinforcing rods. As he started to drag this away from the pile he found he couldn't.

Carmen moved down to help. Together, after much straining and puffing, they managed to move the blocks a few metres away, enough to clear a corner of the bottom of the door.

Martin now saw that the entire concrete room had been broken clear of its foundations. Only some stretched and twisted steel reinforcing rods held it to the slab. The whole place stank and was wet but Martin felt sure there was no body in the room.

We would be able to smell it if there was, he reasoned.

But the idea made him feel ill and he had to stop for a minute to ease his heaving stomach and to get his shaking muscles under control. Then they resumed dragging and tossing rubble and rubbish aside. They worked for another twenty minutes in the blazing sun until they had cleared most of the doorway.

Then Martin saw that there were two combination locks set in the steel door. "Oh bugger!" he swore. "We aren't going to get that open."

As he said this the tremor of an approaching helicopter grew to a roaring clatter. By its sound Martin could tell it was another army Chinook and he straightened up and wiped sweat from his eyes to watch it fly by a few hundred metres away. It also vanished in the direction of Ayr.

As the sound died away he bent to study the combination locks. Then he stiffened as another engine noise came to his ears.

"What's that?" he gasped.

He and Carmen both looked at each other in alarm then scrambled up to peer over the top of the pile of rubble. As he did Martin felt a strong sense of reliving a nightmare. To his horror he saw it was a vehicle. It was a 4-wheel drive vehicle, a mud-caked brown Landcruiser with steel wire cages on the back and hung with junk, and it was heading directly towards them across the mudflats. Already it was only a hundred metres away and close to the sand rise.

"Quick! Hide!" he gasped as the fear pulsed in him.

It came with such force he felt like he was going to have a seizure. Impelled by near panic he turned and began scrambling back across the rubble.

Carmen did likewise, managing to stay a few steps ahead of him. On the way she scooped up the rifle and then went bounding away over the broken blocks and old iron.

"Keep the ruin between us and them," Martin cried as he hurried after her.

And then disaster! Martin felt his boot slip from under him as a piece of rubble he had jumped onto moved. Down he crashed, very hard. His head struck more blocks and darkness swam into his consciousness. He was so stunned that for a few seconds he could not even move but he was aware that he was hurting. The blocks and iron had bruised and cut into his legs and body and his left arm felt numb at the top and was tingling with sharp pain at the bottom.

"Get up! Get up! Run!" his terrified mind screamed, or he did.

Ignoring the pain of scraping and scratching himself on the rubble he heaved himself up and tried to stand. But as he did he found his legs would not function properly and that his knees felt like they were made of rubber. Shaken and dizzy he staggered and then fell again, sideways this time, adding more bumps and bruises to his already battered body and limbs.

Through eyes misted by fear and perspiration he noted Carmen bound over a remaining section of wall and go dashing away, obviously unaware that he had fallen. She ran towards where the leaves of an uprooted mangrove lay in the grass 25 metres away.

"Run! Get up!" Martin told himself.

Images of the Barberinis and of being shot at sent pulses of pure fear through him and gave him the energy to act. Again ignoring the pain he scrambled to his feet and went staggering across the rubble.

His ears were buzzing but they were still working well enough for him to detect the sound of the approaching vehicle. A hasty glance back to check whether he was shielded by the ruins gave him a brief glimpse of it and he instantly realized that he had no chance of getting further away. The vehicle was moving too fast and was now only 50 metres from the ruins.

In his haste and desperation Martin slipped, stumbled and then tripped again. The pain of banging his left knee on a broken block was so intense that he let out an involuntary cry of agony. With tears of pain blinding him he clawed himself to his hands and knees and then a glimpse of the vehicle passing the highest part of the pile sent him diving behind the nearest pile of rubble and rubbish.

That hurt as well and he lay there smarting all over and terrified. Driven by desperation he tried to get himself into some sort of hiding place. But the vehicle was right there! It had driven past the side of the house and was screeching to a stop at what had been the front gate.

Have they seen us? Martin thought, his heart hammering in his mouth.

Quivering and smarting with pain he edged in against the low pile of rubble, keeping it between him and the now stationary vehicle. To his added horror, he heard the vehicle's motor stop and then doors open and slam. People had obviously climbed out, but who? Martin found he just had to know.

We will look silly if they are just some SES people or something, he thought.

Next to him was a tangle of splintered structural beams and panelling and a jagged skyline of broken brocks. They offered a possible covered peephole so he cautiously dragged himself up to it while at the same time trying to master his rasping breathing.

His first glance confirmed his worst fears: it was the Barberinis! Both still wore the clothes they had been wearing the previous day, him an old pair of baggy shorts and a short sleeved shirt and her the shapeless cotton dress, pink with purple and white flowers on it. To Martin's intense relief neither appeared to be armed.

A second look helped calm Martin slightly. The pair were standing looking at the ruins and had obviously not seen him or Carmen.

But if they walk around to look they will see me for sure, Martin thought. There was no cover behind him and he broke into a trembling sweat at the thought.

If they find me Carmen will have to use the rifle, he thought. That got him glancing to his left. *Where is Carmen?* he worried.

He could see no sign of her but hoped she was in among the foliage of the uprooted tree. Anxiety and apprehension clutched at his throat and he found himself shaking so badly he could barely control his muscles.

Calm down! he told himself. *Get ready for the fight or flight.*

With his life in the balance Martin glanced down to find a weapon. All that was within reach was a jagged lump of concrete a bit bigger than a cricket ball and he did not dare move to reach a jagged piece of timber a bit further away.

This will have to do, he decided grimly.

Reaching over he clenched the lump firmly in his shaking right hand. Then he moved back to watch.

Mr Barberini and Ma Baker both stood and stared at the ruins of their house. Both their faces registered shock and disbelief. Ma in particular was obviously distressed.

"Our house!" she wailed. "It's destroyed!"

Mr Barberini grunted and then began picking his way over the wreckage and rubble. Martin tensed but then saw that the man was doing what he had expected. He was making for the strongroom. When Barberini got there he stood with hands on hips and stared at the scene.

Martin trembled. *I hope he doesn't notice that we have been shifting stuff,* he thought anxiously.

To moisten his suddenly dry throat he swallowed. Then a stab of genuine anxiety sent darts of fear through him.

The water bottle! I left it there, he thought.

For several seconds Martin was so scared that he could only gulp in air and shake. But then he realized that Barberini had not noticed anything amiss. Instead the man bent and tossed a few pieces of rubble away from the doorway and then grunted and turned back to the vehicle.

As he made his way back to the tray of the truck Ma Baker moved slowly forward, bending and picking up little items and staring around her in dismay and horror. Martin watched her picking her way across the rubble towards him and he felt his muscles tense again.

If she comes over here she will find me, he thought. And he did not expect any mercy!

Mr Barberini dug in the back of the vehicle and lifted out a crowbar and a sledge hammer. After wiping sweat from his face he hefted them up and began making his way back across the rubble towards the door. As he did, he called loudly, "Come on Ma, never mind all that. Help me with this door."

Ma stopped and shook her head. "Gone! All ruined!" she wailed. "All my clothes, all my paintings, and my good Wedgewood china!"

"Stop yer bleeting ya silly bitch and help me get this door open. You can always buy more of that stuff," Barberini called back.

Ma Baker shouted at him: "It wasn't stuff! It was my good china!"

"As I said, you can just buy more. There's enough cash in here to do that. We can replace what we lost," Barberini retorted.

"It won't replace my son! It won't bring Tony back!" Ma screamed, her obvious anguish sending stabs of distress through Martin.

"He was my son too!" Barberini yelled at her. He threw the tools down and then stood there with his fists clenching and unclenching. "And I didn't kill him. It was the cyclone and those bloody kids. And if I ever get my hands on them they will wish they'd never been born!"

At that Martin quivered with fear and felt his stomach churn. *Oh bloody hell!* he thought, tensing ready to run.

Ma muttered something and then began to cry. Barberini shook his head and turned to pick up the crowbar. He began levering rubble aside.

"Sorry luv. Now give us a hand eh?" he said.

Still muttering to herself Ma Baker turned and picked her way over the rubble to join him, much to Martin's relief. The pair then set to work clearing the doorway. With the right tools and 2 strong people they made short work of the rubble and wreckage and soon had a space cleared. Despite his flabby appearance Barberini was obviously a strong man as he used the sledge hammer to good effect, smashing up sections of rubble into smaller chunks that could be thrown aside. From where he lay Martin could not actually see the door but he could work out what they were trying to achieve.

After about ten minutes of hard work, during which Martin lay on the rubble being grilled by the blazing sun, they had it done. Barberini then tossed the crowbar aside and bent to look at the combination locks.

"OK luv, you put your numbers in," he said.

Ma moved over to stand beside him. Mumbling to herself she crouched and squinted at the combination lock and then set to work moving the dials. From time to time she glanced up at Barberini who stood beside her on her left. Then she muttered and straightened up.

"OK, yours now," she said.

That was a revelation to Martin. Then it dawned on him.

Two locks! They don't trust each other this pair, he thought.

Barberini nodded and then knelt to work on the lock. As his fingers twirled the combination dials his lips worked soundlessly and he frowned with concentration. Then Martin stared in astonishment as Ma, who was standing with her back to him, reached behind herself and dragged the back of her dress up with her left hand, exposing her ugly fat legs and huge knickers.

What the? Martin wondered, both repelled and astonished by the sight.

But then Ma reached behind her with her right hand and pulled a dagger from the back of her knickers. Martin saw the long thin blade glitter in the sunlight as she held it out of Barberini's view.

What is she going to do with that? Martin wondered, hoping that the awful suspicions crowding his brain weren't true.

Ma dropped the back of her dress and then stood still until Barberini looked up and said, "OK luv, that's it. We can open the door."

Barberini bent forward and pulled at the door handle. At that Ma's right hand swept up. The sun glittered again on the flashing blade and she stabbed downwards with all her might. Martin was so shocked by the speed and the horror of what he was seeing that all he could do was stare open-mouthed.

But Barberini obviously saw the movement out of the corner of his eye and was just quick enough to lift an arm to block the savage downward thrust. Her right forearm slammed into his left forearm, the blade being held only a few centimetres from the man's throat. Then he swept the blade aside and punched her in the stomach, ignoring the cut that resulted in his wrist.

"You sneaky bitch!" Barberini shouted. "You fat slut!"

With the speed of a striking snake he again lashed out at her, punching her in the face. Ma tried to slash at him again but he just knocked her hand aside and then punched her again, this time sending her crashing onto the rubble. The dagger went flying and the woman lay there bleeding and moaning.

Then, to Martin's horror, Barberini grabbed the sledge hammer and swung it high above his head.

Oh my God! He's going to smash her head in, he thought.

Chapter 39

MARTIN

Martin stared, his mouth agape with horror.

"No!" he croaked as Barberini swung the sledge hammer down as hard as he could.

But he missed! Just in time Ma jerked herself aside, the hammer smashing down and giving her only a glancing blow to the side of her head. Stone chips and grit flew. Ma flopped onto her back, scrabbling on the loose rubble and obviously stunned.

Barberini swore and hefted the sledge hammer for another blow. As he swung it above his head Martin rose to a crouch. He felt impelled to act.

I can't just let her be murdered, he thought.

It was plain that Ma's head would be pounded to a pulp if one of those pile-driver blows connected. Without conscious thought, Martin acted. In his hand was the jagged lump of concrete block; and as Barberini swung the sledge hammer up for another blow, Martin hurled it. He did it instinctively without aiming. Amidst the jumble of racing thoughts crowding his brain was the idea that he might at least divert the man's attention long enough for the woman to get up.

Now he will know I am here, he told himself, even as his eyes followed the flying lump.

And it hit Barberini!

The lump struck him on the temple and he just threw the sledge hammer into the air and collapsed like a bag of potatoes onto the rubble.

Martin stared, unable to believe what he saw. *Now I will have to run,* he thought.

He half turned, the decision to run towards Carmen already made. *She will use the rifle to save me,* he told himself.

But then he hesitated. Barberini made no move to get up. A sudden dreadful doubt flashed into Martin's mind. *Oh my God! Have I killed him?* he wondered.

He had heard of people being struck dead by a sharp blow to the side of their temple. Heart in mouth he stared at the man. To add to his growing sense of apprehension he saw that Barberini wasn't moving.

But Ma was. She twitched and then groaned but her eyes only opened briefly before rolling up into her head. Again, Martin hesitated.

Should I try to make them prisoner? he thought.

But he was afraid of going close and then being grabbed. He knew that would be a fight to the death and the notion made his stomach churn.

Oh! I have to know! he thought, anguish now flooding him. Gnawing at his bottom lip he took several steps toward Barberini. Still the man did not move.

Oh, I have killed him! Martin thought, guilt swamping his feelings of success.

Then Carmen called from behind him. "Martin, is he knocked out?"

Martin swallowed and felt ill. "I... I don't know. I might have killed him," he croaked. He took several more steps closer and stopped only ten paces from the man. Barberini lay on his side on the rubble and was not showing any sign of movement.

But then Martin saw a tiny lift of the man's chest and his own relaxed as relief flooded through him. "He's knocked out," he called.

"Quick! Tie him up before he comes to," Carmen replied. She came running forward, rifle at the ready.

Martin was still scared of going near the man but he nodded and quickly moved to the back of the vehicle. Now that the decision was made he acted swiftly. There were plenty of dirty old ropes on the vehicle in the cages and tray and he quickly selected two and then scrambled over the rubble to where Barberini lay. By then Carmen was standing to one side, able to cover both the man and the woman.

Martin glanced at Ma and saw that she was still stunned, her face pale and her breathing heavy. Ready to jump back if Barberini moved Martin then edged forward and quickly slipped a clove hitch over the man's left wrist. In a trice he had the right arm pulled back behind the man. He then half rolled Barberini onto his face on the rough rubble, wincing as he did as he knew it must be painful. In less than a minute he had Barberini's wrists securely tied with clove hitches and round turns behind his back. The rope was then led down and lashed around his ankles which were bound together.

"Now the woman," Carmen ordered.

Martin was reluctant to touch her and wasn't sure if it was a good idea if she had a serious head wound.

"She might vomit and drown herself in it," he said as he retuned with another rope.

"Roll her on her side into the Recovery Position," Carmen replied.

She looked very hard and unsympathetic and Martin shook his head in wonder. He had never seen Carmen so determined or serious.

Gingerly Martin took hold of Ma's left arm and tied the rope to her wrist. Then he rolled her onto her side. Grunting with the effort, for Ma was heavier than he thought, he then rolled her onto her front until he could get her other arm clear. Her hands were then tied behind her back. After pulling her back onto her side he lashed the ankles together.

Dusting his hands as he stood up Martin turned to Carmen. "What now?" he asked.

"We wait for the helicopter," Carmen replied calmly. "Let's see if there is any water or food in the vehicle."

Martin followed her over to the vehicle and they quickly found both food and water. Carmen leant the rifle against the vehicle and then unwrapped a sandwich and examined it.

"Corned beef and pickles again. They don't go for much variety this mob," she said disgustedly. But she still took a big bite out of it and began to chew.

Martin also took a sandwich and began to eat, his stomach instantly reacting to tell him how hungry he was. Carmen moved to sit in what little shade the vehicle cast and where she could see the Barberinis. Martin joined her, slumping thankfully onto the hot sand. As he ate, he gestured to the vehicle.

"We could drive this to town," he suggested.

"Can you drive?" Carmen asked.

"I thought you might be able to," Martin replied. He had an idea of how to do it but had never driven a vehicle.

Carmen shook her head. "I'm only fifteen. I can't get my learner's for another year yet," she replied.

"What if the helicopter doesn't come?" Martin asked.

"It will. Or someone else. They know we are here and they won't leave two kids stranded. Relax Martin. And if we have to we will try driving," Carmen said.

So Martin relaxed and they drank a bottle of water each and then ate the remaining four sandwiches. "Cheese and gherkin this one," Martin noted, his spirits reviving.

"You can have it," Carmen said.

Martin swallowed the last of the food and then looked at the Barberinis. Both still lay on the rubble out in the blazing sun. A little niggle of concern caused Martin to sit up. "Should we move them into the shade? They might get sun stroke or heat exhaustion," he said.

Carmen made a face. "I suppose so," she agreed. "But what shade?"

Martin's eyes now moved to the concrete room. He saw that the steel door was now ajar. "That room?" he suggested.

"OK. We had better check what is in there first," Carmen agreed.

That fired Martin's imagination. "Good idea," he said.

He levered himself to his feet, groaning as his sore and stiff muscles protested. Hobbling in pain he limped across past the Barberinis to the door. Carmen followed, rifle in hand.

Without waiting for her Martin grabbed the steel handle and hauled the door wide. It screeched and protested but slowly swung open. Cautiously Martin moved closer to peer in, his body quivering and ready to spring back.

It was quite a small room, about 2 metres by 2 metres. The walls were blank concrete with some shelves fixed to it. Two sodden mattresses stood against one wall and a steel gun safe and boxes of tools and electrical gadgets along another. The back wall had shelves and on these were several steel strong boxes. After checking for snakes and spiders Martin moved inside, Carmen crowding in behind him.

There were three steel strong boxes, all with handles at each end and securely fastened with large padlocks. They looked like tool boxes but Martin was sure they weren't. For a moment he fingered one of the padlocks and then he said, "Let's get these outside and then see if there are any keys."

The first and largest box was easy to lift and they placed it on the cleared space outside the door. The smallest box only needed one person to pick up and Carmen took it out. But when Martin tried to pick up a box about 30 centimetres by 20 centimetres he was astonished by its weight.

"Holy mackerel Car! Give us a hand with this one," he called.

Carmen was also amazed and wondered aloud what was in it as they struggled to carry it out through the door into the blinding sunshine. Martin had an idea and hoped it was true. He then moved to where Barberini lay and gingerly felt in the man's pockets. His groping fingers found what he wanted immediately, a bunch of keys.

As he tried to tug these clear of Barberini's pocket the man groaned. Martin flinched and let go. He found himself staring into the man's blood-shot but puzzled eyes at close range.

Barberini shook his head and looked around. "What? What the devil?" he cried.

He looked hard at Ma and then blinked at both of them. As comprehension came to him the look in his eyes changed to anger and then to hate.

"You little bastards! What the bloody hell! How did you get here?" he shouted.

He began to strain at his bonds and Martin stepped back in case the rope wasn't strong enough. But it was and Barberini strained in vain, mouthing crude obscenities as he did.

Carmen was not amused. "Stop your filth, you low pig!" she snapped.

That really got the man screaming. He shouted and swore and made vile threats and struggled to get free until he was almost foaming at the mouth. Sweat poured out of him and Carmen wrinkled her nose.

"You smell like a pig too," she said disdainfully.

"Why you little bitch! I'll..."

Carmen sneered. "You'll what? If you aren't careful we will let Ma go and leave you to her tender mercies," she retorted. "Now stop you gutter language and we might move you into the shade and give you a drink."

Barberini shook his head and blinked as sweat ran into his eyes. "Drink. Yes, water."

"Water?" Carmen replied coolly. "What do you say?"

Barberini glowered at her so Carmen repeated her comment, speaking as she would have to a small child.

"Please," Barberini at last muttered.

"That's better," Carmen said. "Give him a drink please Martin." She kept the rifle aimed at him from well out of reach.

Martin now noticed his half full waterbottle still lying on the concrete. He moved to pick it up and Barberini's eyes followed the movement. As Martin picked the bottle up Barberini swore again.

"You! You littler buggers were trying to get into our strong room!" he cried angrily.

"We were," Carmen agreed. "And we have. Martin, get his keys and then give him a drink."

At that Barberini burst into a torrent of abuse and obscenities again. Carmen just shook her head and kept the rifle aimed at him.

"Let's move Ma into the shade first then," she said.

That silenced Barberini and he was left to glower at them as they picked Ma up, not without considerable difficulty, and lugged her into the room. She was laid on one of the mattresses. This was sopping but Carmen just shrugged.

"It will help keep her cool," she said.

Martin studied the unconscious woman. "Shouldn't we try to get help?" he queried. "She might be seriously injured."

Carmen shrugged. "You can go if you like," she replied offhandedly.

The pair returned to Barberini and Martin moved around to the man's side and again reached in to get the keys. Barberini snarled but Martin just held the drink bottle in front of his face and he shut up and licked his lips. Once he had the keys Martin had a drink himself, then handed the bottle to Carmen. She drained all but a cupful and then handed it back. Careful not to get where he could be kicked or head-butted Martin held the bottle to Barberini's lips and allowed him to drain it.

Martin and Carmen then dragged the man into the strong room and dumped him beside Ma. "They can share each other's company," Carmen said.

As he walked back out of the cool shade in the room into the blazing tropical sun Martin wiped perspiration from his face and said, "Should we sit in there as well?"

Carmen shook her head. "No. We can sit in the vehicle or in its shade. Now, let's see what is in the boxes."

The keys worked and they opened the largest box first. As the lid was lifted, Martin whistled in amazement. It was almost full of bank notes, mostly hundred dollar bills. They were in bundles bound by rubber bands and they were swimming in water.

"They might be ruined?" Martin said as he lifted a bundle out.

Carmen shook her head. "No. Australian bank notes are plastic. Water won't bother them," she said.

Martin nodded and tried to calculate how much there was in the box. "Thousands," he commented. Then he revised it and said, "Hundreds of thousands."

Carmen agreed. They left the money and moved to the middle-sized box. As Carmen bent to open it Martin gestured to the small one.

"Shouldn't we open the smallest one first?"

"Eh? Why?" Carmen queried.

Martin grinned as good humour welled up in him. "That's how Goldilocks did it, first the one that was too big, then the one that was too small and then the one that was just right," he said.

Carmen laughed but kept on twisting the key in the padlock on the middle sized box. The padlock snapped open and she pulled it clear and lifted the lid. Once again Martin was astonished. The box was full of gold ingots. "Holy Moses! There must be hundreds of thousands of dollars' worth here," he cried.

"Possibly millions," Carmen added, "Considering the price of gold these days."

The contents of the smallest box also made them whistle and stare. It had several velvet-lined jewellery boxes in it and the diamonds and rubies that glittered and sparkled in their gold and silver settings put Martin in a state of awe for a few minutes. Very carefully he lifted out a diamond encrusted necklace and held it across his hand.

"This is really beautiful!" he gasped.

"Ma's jewels I suppose," Carmen said. "Pity she is too ugly to wear anything so magnificent."

"Car! You're being a bit harsh," Martin protested.

"No I'm not! The vicious, selfish bitch tortured us and then tried to have us drowned," she snapped back.

Martin shook his head and muttered agreement but then retuned to studying the jewels. They were a fabulous collection: rings, brooches, earrings and necklaces and he was seized by a sudden intense desire to have them. The meaning of the word 'covet' became crystal clear to him as he gently stoked and fingered a diamond brooch with almost loving urgency.

Then he shuddered and felt ashamed of his thoughts. Carefully he placed the jewels back in their box and then he firmly closed the lid.

There isn't much more to the tale. The pair sat in the shade of the vehicle until the helicopter returned about four hours later. This time when it landed Martin and Carmen met it but had to signal the crewman to join them. He just wanted them to get aboard but changed his mind when they told him about the Barberinis.

So the engine was switched off and the pilot, doctor and co-pilot all got out and came to look. When they were shown the trussed-up Barberinis the helicopter crew were astonished and the doctor angry. But they were even more amazed when shown the money, gold and jewels.

There was a delay of half an hour during which the Barberinis were transported on stretchers to the helicopter. Martin and Carmen helped, even though Martin was now utterly exhausted. The boxes of loot were carried over by the crew and then Martin and Carmen we told to get in.

It was all Martin could do to climb aboard and he slumped down into the seat feeling very battered and utterly exhausted. The crewman buckled him in.

As he did Martin said, "Do our parents know we are safe?"

The crewman nodded. "Yes. We radioed a report. They should be at the hospital to meet you. Here." He handed Martin a bottle of water which he drank greedily. By then Carmen was aboard and also strapped in. The crewmen climbed aboard and the engine began to whine.

As the rotors began to turn Martin turned to Carmen and grinned. "Safe!" he said.

A minute later they were in the air and flying low over the flooded mudflats. As the helicopter climbed Martin looked out to starboard and noted the long line of Cape Bowling Green.

There's the lighthouse, he thought, the fearful memories again flooding in.

They zoomed over the mangroves and twisting creeks and again he shuddered as he thought about crocodiles and violent death. Then they were out over the sea and he looked down at the sand bars and twisting channels of Bowling Green Bay.

"I don't think I will go fishing for a while," he said.

Carmen smiled. "Or at least not here."

The helicopter flew on at a thousand feet at 300 knots and was soon over the devastated township of Cungulla. As the helicopter flew on over the land and past the Mt Elliott Range Martin looked out to port and saw that the entire mountainside was also a scene of destruction. Millions of trees had been stripped of their leaves and thousands uprooted or snapped off. Bare rock and earth showed through except in pockets where the force of the wind had been broken.

The destruction extended all the way to Townsville. "Worse than Cyclone Althea in 1971," the crewman said. "They reckon it was the biggest and worst cyclone to ever hit the North Queensland coast."

"What category was it?" Martin asked.

"Five," the crewman answered. "Half the buildings in the city have been destroyed or damaged."

Thinking of his home on the banks of Ross River Martin asked, "Did the storm surge do much damage?"

The crewman shook his head. "Not in Townsville. It was only about a metre here but to the south of Cape Cleveland they reckon it was three or four metres."

"It was!" Martin replied with feeling, images of those massive waves bursting around the lighthouse sending tremors through him.

The city had certainly been hard hit. From the air they could see the damaged houses and fallen trees and the litter everywhere. Martin noted that the trees on Mt Stuart were also stripped bare or felled and that the slopes were littered with thousands of twinkling things. Only as he got closer did he realize they were pieces of steel or aluminium roofing, shredded off by the storm like a child tearing silver paper from a chocolate.

The helicopter came down at the hospital to a large welcoming group of medics, parents, news media and police. Only when he was safe in his mother's embrace did Martin ask about Letitia.

"She is in hospital suffering from exposure," his mother replied.

Huh! Indecent exposure more like! Martin thought, but managed not to say.

"What about the house?" he asked.

"Bit of damage. We lost some of the roof and had a window broken. Your models and books are all fine," his mother replied.

"And there is a tree down across the back fence," his father added.

With that he was whisked away on a stretcher by the medics. After 2 hours of checks and treatment he was handed back to his parent's care and they drove home. Letitia came with them and so did Carmen.

Andrew was waiting for them. It was then that Martin learned that the city had lost electrical power three days earlier and only a few essential services were getting power from emergency generators.

"They say it will be a week or more before power is restored. And there is almost no food," Martin's father explained. "All the roads are still cut by flooding or fallen trees. So they are evacuating people."

That explained all the air movements that Martin could not help noticing. The sky was abuzz with the vibrating clatter of army and navy helicopters. RAAF transport aircraft were flying in and out and civilian airliners were landing in a constant stream.

"Are you going back to Cairns?" Martin asked Andrew.

Andrew shook his head. "No, to Brisbane or Rockhampton. Cairns has been pretty badly knocked about too. It was big storm. It took out most of North Queensland in one hit," he said.

So Carmen and Andrew were flown out that the next day. Martin and Carmen were allowed to stay and it was not until the following April school holidays that the friends again met. By then the whole story had come out. To his horror Martin learnt that the Barberinis had murdered the owner of the second trawler and replaced the crew with their own gang, Long John Silver and Co. They had then carried out an illegal fishing operation. Because of the strict zoning regulations in Queensland coastal waters and along the Great Barrier Reef all trawlers are fitted with a transponder whose location is constantly monitored by the Fisheries Department. By taking the transponder off the stolen trawler and placing it in a small launch it could be sent to an area where fishing was allowed while the actual trawler was busy scooping up a catch in 'closed' zones.

Most of the fish were high value reef fish that bought a very high price on the Asian market. They were flown out on normal commercial flights and it had been a very lucrative operation for several years. The Barberinis had amassed a fortune of about $10 million dollars, the gold and jewels alone came to over $3 million, while they had pretended to be poor struggling fishermen sticking to their quota and to the regulations.

"So they were real pirates," Martin commented.

"Yes," Andrew agreed.

"What happened to Long John Silver?" Martin asked.

Andrew grimaced. "The doctors couldn't save his leg. They cut it off just above the knee. So he will look like a real pirate now, what with his black eye patch and his wooden leg."

"He is a real pirate. We should send him a parrot for Christmas," Martin added. To which they all chuckled.

Both the Barberinis were sent to prison. The only survivor from the 2 trawlers was Long John Silver—and he mysteriously vanished from the hospital.

"I wonder where he is?" Carmen said when told this.

"Off at sea being a pirate of course," Andrew answered.

Martin laughed, then shivered.

I hope I never run into him again! he thought.

Enjoy more C.R. Cummings stories

The Air Cadets

The Navy Cadets

The Army Cadets

www.ingramcontent.com/pod-product-compliance
Lightning Source LLC
Chambersburg PA
CBHW030812260626
47169CB00001B/287